The Name of Seven

By Peter Ashby

*Dedicated to the memory of my father,
who instilled in me his love of books and reading.*

Contents

Part One: The Awakening

1. North-West England: February

2. Whitehall, London: February

3. City of Drakonet: Kiklayda

4. North-West England: February

5. North-West England: February

Part Two: Transition

1. North-West England: Transition

2. North Atlantic: February

3. Southern Europe: May

4. Hyaquat

5. Hyaquat

6. Granada, Spain: June

7. Hyaquat

8. Granada: July

9. Albayzín, Granada: July

10. Albayzín, Granada: July

11. Night Time: Albayzín, Granada

12. Albayzín, Granada

Part Three: The Name of Seven

1. The Wasteland

2. Volk

3. The Wasteland

4. The Realm of The Seven

5. Transition

6. Beyond

# Part One: The Awakening

1. North West England: February

When the impact of the car threw her across the road, Sara Parkinson had little time to wonder what had happened before she lost consciousness. The high street angled away from her, fading in a red haze of shock and sickening pain as the passers-by dropped their shopping bags and ran to help.

It was the car. It was *the same green car* that had been following her for the last three days. Now it had screamed to a halt across the dimming road, and a figure leaped from the driver's seat and was sprinting towards her. She felt a cold hand cradling her cheek, saw the haggard face of a man with a silver ring through his left eyebrow, and heard a voice: *I'm sorry, I'm so sorry, but this had to happen...*

After that, Sara did not remember anything for a long time. She briefly came round in the ambulance, where she was swamped by a wave of nausea. The paramedics held her as she vomited burning acid, and then she mercifully passed out again.

Sara dreamed. To begin with, all she knew were icy lights spinning around her in a dark sky, as though she was free-falling through space. They were replaced by shadowy images of things moving through a monotonous void, like giants striding through fog.

Then she heard a sound in the remote distance, and she was running away from it without understanding why. It was a dull resounding beat like the thumping of a heart, repeating over and over again in a sequence of seven, and it was coming for her. She tried to run faster but the sound was growing louder - seven long slow beats, immeasurable and unstoppable.

She ran on through the grey limbo, twisting and turning in all directions but wherever she went, the same shape was always in front of her. It was an angular block of obscurity, like a monolith, and as it expanded so did the sound: seven ominous black beats, like the thudding of an alien heart.

The monolith rose ever higher until it was enormous beyond imagining. Sara fought to escape from it but she had no sense of limbs or body, and she was as helpless as if she had no physical existence. The dark edifice was rocketing into infinity, above and to either side. She tried to scream but she had no breath and no lungs, and still the seven thundering beats came from the blackness as the vast wall began to plummet on to her and sweep her out of existence.

Sara kicked and swore as she lurched into consciousness. A nurse on the other side of the room dropped the clipboard she had been looking at and was by the bedside in a moment, gripping her wrists and pushing her flailing arms hard into the mattress, but there was kindness and concern in her voice.

'Hey now, it's okay, pet. Just calm yourself down. Everything's going to be all right.'

The steady kindness in the nurse's voice managed to penetrate the receding terror of the dream.

'There was a wall. It was crushing me.' Sara gulped huge breaths, and sagged weakly against the nurse's chest. The woman held her and soon, her trembling subsided and instead of the black nightmare, there was brilliant artificial light, bare cream-coloured walls and a door that was half open on to a busy hospital ward.

As she became fully awake and began to process these details, the sickness and pain flooded back. The nurse eased her back into bed, propping a couple of pillows behind her and whipping a cardboard tray from the top drawer of the bedside cabinet. She held it to Sara's mouth while she spat blood and spittle, then wiped the residue from the young woman's mouth with a tissue.

'I'm bleeding,' wheezed Sara. 'What's wrong with me?'

'Don't worry, pet. You bit the inside of your cheek when you had the accident. Apart from that, you've got some concussion and a few bruises - no broken bones but we're keeping you in overnight for observation, just in case. You'll be canny sore for a day or two.'

'What accident?' Sara lay back on the pillows, exhausted and drenched with cold sweat, and tried to focus on the nurse's face. It was round and as red as her curly hair, and she had brilliant blue eyes - the face of a woman in her fifties, and a smile that Sara felt was genuine and not simply the requirement of her trade.

'Don't you remember anything? A car hit you, pet. In the high street.'

'Where? Am I in-?'

'You're in the Regional General, pet. They had to bring you over here. There's a bed shortage, you see.'

'An accident?' Sara tried to concentrate, and remembered something. *A green car.*

'I was - somebody was following me.' She caught the nurse's eye, then looked at her name badge, seeking the comfort of an identity. The nurse was called Audrey McCann.

'I know, pet,' said Audrey. Her smile had gone. 'You kept shouting about it in the ambulance. The Ward Sister's called the police.'

Sara was quiet. The police were coming? She didn't want this. Things like this did not happen to her, not in her kind of existence. All she wanted was to drive the shadows of the nightmare from her mind.

'Can I have some water?' Audrey poured her a glassful and held it for her while she drank.

'Thanks... Audrey.' Audrey smiled.

'I've got to go now. You know what it's like. Saturday night and we're run off our feet. I'll check in on you later, though. Don't worry, pet. You're going to be a hundred per cent in no time.'

Only minutes later, or so it seemed, Sara was startled out of a troubled half-sleep by the murmur of male voices outside the door.

'She's just through here,' said one. 'She's quite a looker. I wouldn't say no to - oh!'

The door opened. 'Thanks, doctor - I can see Miss Parkinson is awake.' The other voice sounded vaguely disapproving. The young constable who walked in was tall, dark haired and appeared to be exhausted but after he had pulled up a chair and sat down, he gave her a sympathetic smile

'Are you okay to answer a few questions? I'll try not to keep you long - you must be feeling terrible.'

They went through the formalities, and he jotted her biographical details down. Sara wondered how many times he'd had to take note of similar information, and if this time was really going to be any different from the rest.

'Sara - can I call you Sara?' She nodded. 'You said in the ambulance that you thought the car that hit you had been following you for some time? Is that right?'

'I can't remember what I said. I think so... No, I'm positive. It was the same car that I've been seeing for days.' Hearing herself say it out loud for the first time, she felt a sudden jolt of shock.

'Don't suppose you can give me the make or the registration, anything like that?'

'I'm sorry.'

'What about the driver? What did he look like?'

Sara turned her mouth down and shook her head.

'I think he had a pierced eyebrow, but that's about it. There's nothing else. But there were witnesses, weren't there? Didn't they... you know...' Sara could hear the lack of conviction in her own voice.

The policeman blew out wearily through his lips. 'That's just it,' he said, rapping the ballpoint on his notebook. 'Everyone we've spoken to says he scarpered pretty sharpish and he and the car just seemed to vanish in the rain.' He gave her a long look through narrowed eyes, and then he shrugged.

She could picture the car, parked on the corner opposite her flat and half concealed by a wheelie bin and the rain-streaked trunk of a cherry tree. Then again, in the supermarket car park, as she was running to catch the bus. That time she'd slowed down and turned round but the driver had suddenly put his foot on the accelerator and was speeding out of the entrance before she'd been able to get a good look at him. The third and last time before the accident, she'd seen the vehicle cruising slowly after her on the dark side of the street as she walked home last night from a local wine bar. That had been the worst, the most unnerving. That was when she'd started to be afraid.

She told the constable everything she could, but she knew that her words lacked conviction, even to herself. He said that she should contact him if she remembered anything more, but without something more concrete to go on there was little they could do except to wait and see if the mystery hit-and-run driver re-offended.

'This is stupid,' she breathed, settling back against the pillows after he'd left. *I'm fine. I just want to get home and stop wasting everyone's time.*

But as Sara Parkinson fell asleep, everything began to change.

It was near the end of a long hard shift, and Audrey McCann was bone tired. She longed for a breath of fresh air and to get away from the smells and sounds of the ward, however much a part of her life they were. Jim would already be waiting for her, standing in the rain with an umbrella. They'd be home in ten minutes, and she'd give the dogs and the cat a fuss before letting them out in the back garden, then they'd settle down with a bottle of wine, some fish and chips and a trashy film from the video rental store. Tomorrow, they'd drive over to see Becky and the kids...

But she'd promised to look in on that young lady one more time. There was something forlorn about Sara Parkinson that touched Audrey in her soft centre, as it still did, even now after all these years. She'd been sworn at by drunks today - water off an old duck's back - ranted at by irate and impatient doctors down the phone - she'd borne that stoically, as always - but she still had a minute to look in on Sara Parkinson. What little information they had gleaned suggested that her mother lived in Paris, but they'd had no direct contact since Miss Parkinson was a child. The father had remarried and his whereabouts were unknown, and there was an ex-boyfriend named Carl who hadn't answered the phone. A hit-and-run accident was always bad news, and took time to come to terms with. There was always that nagging doubt, after all, as to whether or not it had been intentional.

Audrey collected her bag from the cloakroom, said goodnight to the graveyard shift, and headed down the corridor. Miss Parkinson's door was three-quarters closed, just as the young policeman had left it, and she pushed it open cautiously, not wishing to disturb Sara if she was asleep.

In all her thirty-two years of nursing, Audrey McCann had experienced almost everything that her difficult profession could throw at her. She had sat with dying patients and counted their final breaths, the last human contact that they knew before they moved on into the unknown. She'd given both wonderful and devastating news to more joyful and despairing souls than she could ever hope to recall, consoled mothers on the loss of their children, and once she'd helped a new life into the world in the foyer of the old hospital. Audrey was pragmatic, stoical, sceptical about anything that she had not seen with her own eyes, and at the end of the day she believed fervently in human dignity and the goodness that surely resided in everybody, however deeply hidden it sometimes was.

Afterwards, Audrey doubted her own sanity before wondering just how low her blood sugar levels had dropped to play such tricks on her. Tiredness and hunger could have strange effects on people and in the surreal and frenetic environment of a hospital the customers were not the only ones to experience hallucinations. She saw the empty bed and decided that the young woman must be in the toilet, even though no tell tale strip of light shone beneath the closed door. Perhaps she was in trouble? Audrey walked in and as she did, the air rippled like quicksilver and a figure coalesced on top of the bed. It was Sara, sprawling on the bedclothes in a tracksuit bottom and T-shirt, her bare feet damp as if with rain, and there was an elusive fragrance of violets and woody spices that lingered momentarily in the room.

Within moments of her arrival, Sara knew exactly where she had come to. It was a shallow valley, only a mile or so from the coast. A country lane meandered down one side and crossed over a little stream at the bottom via a small humpbacked bridge, then ambled between tall hedges and past an old stone farmhouse. In the middle distance, there was a glimpse of the sea where the valley sloped down to a sandy bay, while inland the purple profile of the mountains rose over a rolling landscape of fields and copses.

She had come here more than a dozen times with Carl. They had usually parked the car on the wide verge just short of the farm before walking the public footpath down the valley to the beach. There, they would run barefoot on the sand and throw seaweed at each other or sit on the rocks and share a can of beer, and twice they'd come here at night and made love under the moonlight in a summer meadow of silver grass and sleeping poppies.

But it was not the same place. It was profoundly and magically transformed.

Sara was in the middle of the lane, just a few yards from the bridge. Immediately, she was immersed in a myriad sensations but it was the smell of the place that was first to overwhelm her senses, because her nostrils were filled with a subtle and shifting blend of floral and spicy aromas, mint and violets and cloves - *only they weren't*. They were unlike anything she'd ever experienced before, somehow piercingly fresh and alive as though it was the first time that she had ever truly been able to smell anything.

The setting sun had left a trail of jade and violet shimmers on the sea, and the dimming sky was so rich and velvety that Sara almost felt she could reach out and run her fingers through its satiny substance. Already, even so close to sundown, a multitude of emerald and sapphire stars were glimmering in sinuous, unknown constellations and a fingernail sliver of moon was hanging low in the sky above the opalescent mists in the high reaches of the valley.

As for the countryside, everything - the fields, the hedges, even the road - was alive with a subtle luminous aura of interplaying colours. Especially vibrant was the stream, which trilled and babbled over a bed of flattened pebbles under a swirling liquid rainbow aurora.

Where am I? 'It's called Endymion.' She said the words out loud without realizing what she had done and as soon as she did so, it was as though a brilliant torch beam of understanding had touched her in the twilight. *This is Endymion. There is no pollution here, nor global warming nor violence. There's no place or* need *for them. How utterly remarkable. This world had chosen not to have such things!*

In something akin to a state of bewitchment, Sara began walking slowly up the lane. She had nothing on her feet, not even a pair of socks, but the road was warm and yielded slightly underfoot. When she looked down she saw that it was covered with thousands of tiny, iridescent units like a mosaic, every one threaded through with a hairs breadth netting of light. The road was alive!

Ahead of her, the fading sunset cherished the farmhouse and its outbuildings with a brief embrace of tawny light. It was covered with creepers and looked like a rustic thatched cottage from an idealised postcard, with deeply recessed windows and a strangely organic appearance that reminded her of the buildings by Gaudí that she had once seen on a visit to Barcelona. A dim, orange-gold lamp shone in one of the lower windows.

In the hedgerows, little creatures were moving, tiny luminous animals like furry glow-worms that uncurled from beneath leaves and looked at her with curious blinking eyes as she walked by. The hedges were a riot of strange bushes and herbs with ferny leaves, blue entwining climbers with pendulous fruit that pulsed in unison as they changed colour, and snowy flowers like small water lilies that opened and bent towards her as she approached.

Where the lane wound to the right, a gate opened into a sloping meadow. Sara crossed the road and approached cautiously, because she could see movement. A flock of animals was moving through the knee-high grass in the direction of a wooden trough and towards the figure that was emptying something into it from what looked like a rough hessian sack. The animals had a slight resemblance to sheep, with dense woolly coats and a sheen that matched the smoky, satin grass through which they moved. They were high in the forequarters and had only one iridescent eye, and long feathered antennae that flicked back and forth as they gathered round the trough and buried their curved, anteater noses in the fragrant mixture of meal and vegetable trimmings.

They don't eat them. They only use their milk and wool.

The figure straightened up and Sara rapidly shrank back among the hedge plants, which helpfully moved aside then swished back again to conceal her. She'd never seen such a beautiful man in her life. He was tall and sturdy, with an unruly mop of black hair and a deeply suntanned face, and he was dressed in trousers that looked like faded jeans and a pale brown shirt with the sleeves rolled up above his elbows. There was some quality about him that Sara couldn't entirely define, except that he felt *right*, as though he was exactly where and when he was born to be.

The young farmer hummed tunelessly as he rolled the empty feed sack up and hung it over his shoulder, then he stood and watched the contentedly feeding animals with his hands thrust in his pockets. Sara was so absorbed in studying every aspect of him that she only noticed the car when it was already crossing the bridge. She crouched down and found herself at eye level with a family of the glow-worm creatures that crawled from under a frond and gently reached out with their soft tendrils to explore her face.

The car drew up outside the gate with an unobtrusively feline purr. It had a picturesque, art nouveau look about it and was all flowing curves and an intricate medley of patterning around the doors and wheel arches. The tyres were made of exactly the same material as the road and its headlamps emitted silvery beams of light.

Bioluminescence. Again, Sara had no idea about where her insight was coming from, simply that she knew. *There's no exhaust, either. It's completely self-sustaining.*

The man who got out was shorter than the farmer, with fair hair and features and - she could see through the leaves as he walked to the gate and called to his friend - bright green-gold eyes. The two men laughed and chatted over the field gate only a yard from where Sara was hiding. She could tell that they were speaking in English but it was with an accent that she did not recognize, and in such a relaxed tone that she could not follow the thread of their conversation.

After five minutes or thereabouts, the motorist slapped his friend on the shoulder, said his goodbyes and drove off. The car left a glowing trail on the road that slowly dimmed and vanished, and a blue night bird with rounded owl-like wings dipped in flight across the road. The man remained where he was, leaning on the top bar of the gate, the fingers of one hand idly twirling a blade of grass. He was so close that even in the dusk, Sara could see the dark stubble on his face, and his hazel eyes, and hear him breathing.

It was then that she made an embarrassing discovery, by way of her newfound intuition. The little furry glow-worm creatures were emotionally empathic and were able to mirror her feelings, because one of them opened its tiny expressive mouth and sighed luxuriously. Sara froze as the man turned towards her hiding place in surprise, then parted the vegetation with his broad hands and looked down at her, wide mouthed with astonishment.

'Wow...' He put out a hand to help her up, keeping hold of her once she was standing. She did not move to pull away. Evidently, neither of them was inclined to let go.

'Where did you come from?'

'It's a dream,' whispered Sara. 'It's not real. It's just a dream.'

He had not taken his eyes from her for a moment. 'Well, maybe it is. For me, at least, it's a lovely one. So you're the girl of my dreams.' His voice and the corners of his mouth lifted. 'You're beautiful!'

Sara opened her mouth but she was unable to connect her thoughts with her voice. The warmth of his hand and his baffled expression of surprise mingled with pleasure, the heat rising in response inside her...

oh and *oh*, but she could really, truly lose herself in a man like this, if only he existed. She stepped out of the hedge bottom, needing to be closer to him and to believe that he was more than a wishful invention of her traumatised mind.

Without warning, she knew that something profound and alarming had altered. An odd sensation was snatching at her from the darkness with invisible, urgent fingers. He saw her stricken expression and quickly plucked something from the bushes, thrusting it into her hand.

'You're not leaving me already, are you? ' He pressed her fingers tight. 'Don't lose this. It´s special.'

'I have to!' she said desperately, the invisible pull escalating into a desperate imperative. Somewhere in the night, an unseen breach was opening, and she had to run to it or be lost, maybe forever.

'I'm sorry! I have no choice.' She pulled free, the absence of his touch igniting like a burn on her skin, and then she ran, her bare feet leaving a dewy trail through the meadow grasses.

'Dream girl!' he shouted after her - then Sara was back and floundering on the bed in her hospital room, while an astonished Nurse McCann stood open-mouthed and staring in the doorway as if petrified.

Sara flew bolt upright as if electricity was coursing through her body. 'Audrey!' The nurse was gone, spinning on a penny and rushing off down the corridor. 'Please wait!'

It could only have been a dream, an incredibly rich and profoundly wonderful dream of the kind you never want to wake up from. That was all it was, but why had Audrey taken off as if the flames of hell were crackling at her heels? And why were her feet, and the lower half of her tracksuit legs, wringing wet?

Slowly, she swung her legs off the bed and walked into the toilet and shower cubicle. She looked at her face in the mirror, slowly registering the shocked expression that was goggling back at her. Every last vestige of pain had left her body; even the bruises on her arms and forehead had vanished. Then, she unwound her tightly clenched fingers and stared at the opalescent water lily blossom that was burgeoning into life and smoothing out its crumpled petals in the palm of her hand.

2. Whitehall, London: February

There are layers, and then there are layers, the Colonel mused as he strode purposefully down the corridor, his shoes clicking on the parquet floor.

Take this venerable edifice, for example. Ostensibly, it was a government departmental building which experienced a heavy diurnal traffic of civil servants and ministers but unknown to all the permanent staff, it was also a cover for certain covert MI-6 operations.

Then again, the people who came and went at night via secret doors and conducted their business in rooms behind false walls were themselves completely unaware of the level known as Basement C and the "listening post" that it housed.

Not only this, but Basement C's nameless operatives did not have so much as an inkling that their subversive activities were funded by the organization to which the Colonel belonged, their sole purpose being to create an elaborate smoke screen between what could be officially denied and what lay so far beyond the cognition of the security services that it made the very notion of "official secrets" seem like a kindergarten game in comparison.

The Colonel's various doubles within the department enabled him to come and go with impunity. As for these lookalikes, he had chosen them personally, offering them immunity from prosecution in exchange for their unquestioning loyalty. They had far too much to lose and would never expose the marginal half-truths they were party to. It was an immaculately choreographed performance that, in its various guises, had functioned smoothly for a very long time.

He came to a door near the end of the corridor and walked into his office. The secretary was a taciturn man in his late forties and he had been hand-picked for the role by the Colonel's associates. He was as dependable as he was impassive and the Colonel neither asked nor cared about his unknown past. He did not even know his name.

The man nodded briefly and checked the screen in front of him. 'You're clear.'

A voice-activated panel in the wall slid back and the Colonel entered a gleaming tubular steel lift, sufficient to contain one person and compact enough to run down through the granite superstructure of the Edwardian building, deep into the ground below. From this point on, nothing officially existed. The original construction team had all met with unfortunate accidents and the maintenance system was cybernetic and infallible.

As he descended, the Colonel reviewed everything he had learned about the developing situation in the north. It was an interesting twist of events, unexpected but not entirely unplanned-for. That the target was now active was beyond doubt. The nurse had responded well to questioning and she and the husband would have no recollection of the three missing hours in their lives, plucked from them out of the shadows during a rain-soaked walk home. As for the so-called accident, it had clearly been staged and this was not such good news as it meant that the opposition were aware of the Shiners' plans and would be taking extreme measures to protect the target.

The Colonel pursed his lips. The Shiners were not going to be at all pleased about that. He mentally corrected himself - the *Mawdrik*, as they liked to call themselves. They were fastidious and irritable and at times, working with them was like picking one's way through an endless minefield of bizarre protocol and - on their part - deliberate misunderstandings. Despite his decades of experience with the Mawdrik, their mercurial and impulsive behaviour could test the patience of a saint, let alone a stoical soldier.

It would have been better for the priest to liaise with them and smooth their colossal egos with his silken diplomacy and suave Latin tongue, but for unknown reasons, the Shiners had chosen the Colonel this time, such was their unpredictability. There had always been three, a soldier, a priest and a financier, and history recorded the names and infamy of some of them, though never their true identity or purpose.

Thanks to the Shiners, they had at their disposal resources of such magnitude that if they chose to, they could make or break the major economies of the world or manipulate the outcome of wars. If they had to sell their souls to the proverbial devil in return, it was a price worth paying as far as the Colonel was concerned. Why the Mawdrik had propagated and nurtured this strange relationship was of little interest to him, but he understood enough to know that they were driven by a hunger for acquisition that humanity had been able to fuel down all the long ages of its scientific and cultural evolution.

None of what the Colonel knew or didn't know, however, was of the least interest to the Mawdrik. The world - and its mundane affairs - continued spinning blindly on its way, unaware of the greater events that shaped its seemingly haphazard progress. And foremost among these events at the moment was the culminating matter of Sara Parkinson.

Privately, the Colonel believed that elimination was the preferable course. Once the Shiners got their hands on her, he was sure that they would no longer be quite so interested in collaborating with his organization on what had, up until now, been mutually beneficial enterprises. If she was taken alive and fell into the hands of the Shiners, she was worse than dead in any case. They would take her apart right down to the last screaming fibre in pursuit of her secret, and then they would torment whatever remained of her out of pure rage if they did not find what they were looking for. Not that the Colonel had any qualms about that: he was no stranger to the endlessly creative ways of dying that had been devised by humanity and the Shiners, among others.

Rather, he preferred to keep this box of delights securely sealed for a little while longer, until they were in a stronger position to compete with the Mawdrik on a more level playing field. Every delay increased the likelihood that Sara Parkinson might be spirited away by the Jellyfish or one of their interfering allies. The sanctimonious Jellies with their high and mighty morality offended something within the Colonel at a very fundamental level, for what in the world was the point of being all but indestructible if you crippled yourselves with a tree-hugging creed of non-violence?

Regardless of his views, the Colonel was certain that the Shiners would demand that she be taken alive. If her subsequent piecemeal destruction put the entire universe in an unholy turmoil, on their heads be it.

The lift went on its noiseless way. In spite of his preference for terminal action against the target, the Colonel had to admit that he was curious about the other worlds that Miss Parkinson must have visited. Since the Shiners first warned of her theoretical existence, he had speculated as to what might lie out there in the ether: resources to be exploited, ideas that could be adapted and improved upon, advanced weapons systems and the like. And, what if her talent could be isolated, or even used on other people in the form of an inoculation?

Perhaps, collaboration with the Shiners in a meticulous study of this ability might yet work in their favour. The Mawdrik were not scientifically minded and regardless of their impressive power, they had a tendency to use a sledgehammer to break the proverbial nut, precious contents and all. The Colonel, on the other hand, had access to the finest research facilities in the world, and was acquainted with scientists to whom scruples was a dirty word. And if it came about, it would not be the first time that the Mawdrik had reluctantly asked for the superior technical assistance of humanity.

The lift stopped and the door slid open to reveal a stark corridor with dull black walls and minimal lighting. At the end, a rectangular black void awaited him. It was all that was needed here, a location deep and secure enough for encounters to take place without the remotest risk of being interrupted.

It was the part of the job he least appreciated. Even now, after so much time spent with the Mawdrik, there was something fundamentally distasteful about entering their presence. It was as if they corroded the very air of whatever space they were inhabiting, and breathing in their astringent aura was not something that a lesser man could endure for long. Nonetheless, the Colonel did not hesitate in directing his purposeful steps along the soulless corridor and into the room beyond.

It was a perfect cube. Each side was around ten feet in length and it was unlit by artificial means so that the corners were in complete darkness. It was bare except for a black leather swivel chair in the centre of the floor. At the moment, this was turned away from the entrance, but it was bordered by a halo of frigid white light that radiated from its, as yet, unseen occupant.

The Colonel gave a stiff military salute and awaited his interlocutor's pleasure.

'Ah, yes… Colonel. You will have heard the news, we suppose?' The voice, in contrast to the austere and chilling surroundings, was strangely warm and laced with a volcanic intensity, if completely devoid of any convincing emotional nuance.

'Sir.' The Colonel had not yet relaxed his military stance. The voice laughed, again without any trace of feeling.

'At ease, soldier. Oh, you human creatures and your quaint and comical ways. Tell us, Colonel, how soon can we expect our trophy?'

'There are five units in the area, and we have implemented a three-kilometre quarantine perimeter around the hospital. As yet, I have received no indication that any enemy operatives have penetrated the exclusion zone.'

'Tut, tut,' said the voice. 'We have no *enemies*, Colonel. There are simply those who choose not to work with us because they know no better. We only have to show them the error of their ways. After all, we share the same universe and we should find ways in which we can all cohabit.'

The Colonel said nothing, preferring to hold his tongue against the sarcasm oozing from the unearthly voice. He found such games tedious, but he knew from experience that silence was the most prudent response.

'It is done, then. She will soon be in our hands. Won't she, Colonel?'

'Sir, we cannot fail. Short of… well, short of nothing.' *That* was rash.

'Do we detect a note of hesitancy?' The voice was abruptly cold and austere. 'You will not fail. We will have our key. You do not want to entertain the consequences if you disappoint us.'

The chair revolved slowly. In it sat a being of similar size and configuration to a tall, slim human male. It was dressed in an expensive tailored suit of dark fabric and sat with one hand across its lap, and the other lightly clasping the arm of the chair. Its hands and head seemed to be made of glass and were filled with white incandescence, but its eyes were as black and empty as doom.

3. City of Drakonet: Kiklayda

Kiklayda's Pink Sun was bathing the coastal suburbs of Drakonet with a warm and rosy afternoon light, and a delicate feathering of cool green cirrus clouds drifted inland to speckle the lilac sky as the international holiday drew to a close. The late spring weather had been superb for the three long and two shorter days of fun and frivolity. Now, after a brief night, the dawn of the next Blue Sun day would herald the start of a monumental clear-up, then everything would return to normality for the next five years - or for however long the regional councils were able to resist the demand for another planetary fiesta.

By all accounts, it had been a roaring success. Off-planet visitors had travelled from many light years around to enjoy the rich diversity of cultural events. The Kiladl and the Voul had chartered a number of luxury liners in order to attend and it was even rumoured that several Volk had watched some of the most important spectacles from their mysterious Ships, stationed high in the stratosphere. In the Kiklaydan arts capital of Drakonet, the theatre season had culminated with the hilarious new comedy by Kiklayda's favourite contemporary playwright, the wittily effervescent Tak Rajit, and the critics were suggesting that it might run for months.

Notwithstanding this and other highlight events, the excitement had been marred by one extremely high profile absence. The gossip sheets were still buzzing with it, even though the scandal had lost ground recently to the economic crisis and the news that a peculiar new sentient species had been discovered in the next quadrant. The fact remained that the absence of Kiklayda's greatest living composer had cast long shadows over the Drakonet Festival of Contemporary Music, and worried questions were being asked throughout the artistic community as to when or even if he would return from his self-imposed exile.

Immersed in a profound depression, Maestro Karmel Tragawlty languished on a couch in his luxury city apartment. He had turned the intercom off several days previously, sick to his spines with the endless stream of well wishers and reporters who would not accept the assurances of his press officer that he had gone away on an extended vacation to an exclusive celebrity health resort in the Mountains of Mool.

Karmel was not only depressed; he was more than a little drunk. Downing that third carafe of wine last night had not been a terribly good idea, especially when he threw the empty shatter-proof vessel at the wall and it bounced back and hit him on the forehead. The lurid green scar was going to take an age to fade, but once the initial pain had diminished, Karmel stopped caring.

He tossed and fidgeted uncomfortably on the couch, screwing his sore eyes up and squinting at the patio windows. The view from Karmel's apartment was one of the finest in the city, looking out as it did over the leafy suburbs and elegant avenues lined with towering fire pines, to the best greensand beach in the Province of Drakonet. A group of bifurcated airfins glided past, languidly flapping their seven wings as they sifted plankton from the air with their enormous pouched jaws, and somewhere below in the boulevard, the excited chatter of voices suggested that yet another one of those dreadful celebrity-spotting tours was doing the rounds of the millionaire district.

'Hmph! They won't be taking any more compromising pictures of *me* through the curtains,' he grumbled, waving a hand over the extendible console. It read his thoughts immediately and the expensive sea silk curtains swished to, while the lights dimmed to suit the late hour, his mood and his horribly pounding cranium.

All through the long day, Karmel had struggled unsuccessfully to get the last movement of his acclaimed Eighth Symphony out of his head. It was the piece he'd written especially for *her*, the soaring crescendo of ecstasy that she had ignited within him, made music. She... Zerafma, the passion and the bane of his life, a bright morning star and a bottomless pit of woe. Why had it been his destiny to fall so deeply and madly head-over-heels in love with such a beautiful, fantastic and terminally impossible woman?

He groaned and rubbed his inflamed eyes, remembering it all in spite of his black mood, and returning as he had so often to pick at the open wound of his agony and shame. It had started out so perfectly. He was the brilliant young composer; she, the world's most feted classical soprano. They walked out together, the glamorous and fabulously wealthy couple a star attraction at every film premiere and exhibition opening, and their every movement and whereabouts filling the celebrity gossip columns. Then, less than a year into the relationship with talk of marriage in the air, things had begun to sour.

In accordance with the time-honoured Kiklaydan tradition, two of Karmel's parents had been sexual people while the third was a natural neuter, who had served not only as his birth parent but also as the donor of the vital Kiklaydan racial memory to the unborn foetus. Regardless of his radical and dramatic composing style and liberal politics, Karmel was in many other aspects, a traditionalist. Zerafma, however, had a very different outlook on life.

She was one of those modern women who had taken to the controversial theories of the rabble rousing feminist writer, Stakana Madditch, and - Karmel was shocked to find out - was a paid up member of the aggravating old harridans Second Way Party. For days and nights they had argued about it, Karmel unable to break with the revered tradition of a hundred millennia, and Zerafma equally adamant in her belief in the male-female only marriage and the conviction that their children should be able to think freely without the burden of an obligatory racial archive to fog up their minds. Worst of all was her shocking insistence that they didn't need to deposit their combined seed into what she blasphemously referred to as a "surrogate".

The split was acrimonious, and very public. Zerafma had stormed out of the first performance of the Eighth Symphony and within a week, she had fled Drakonet to join the Second Way colony that had recently and illegally been established on an abandoned orbiting research station.

That had been half a year ago and since that terrible night, Karmel's life had continued to unravel. He'd finished none of his pending commissions, and he'd taken to drinking harmful alien alcohol in large amounts. After several long drunken binges and embarrassing confrontations with prying reporters, his press agent had respectfully but firmly advised him to retire from public life until he could sort himself out.

Karmel ordered the home management system to bring him another carafe of wine, which it refused, and after cursing it colourfully but pointlessly, he fell asleep. He was woken a few hours later, by the curtains opening as Blue Day broke, and by a nagging, buzzing sound from the global intercom screen which had somehow contrived to reactivate itself.

'Oh dear, dear, dear…' The thin and pitying voice was that of Exebius Clunn, the Maestro's publicity manager as well as one of his oldest friends. 'If the National Academy could see you now, not to mention the great Doggish Tragawlty, Gods bless his soul.' Exebius's long blue face and violet eyes radiated open disapproval, albeit in a one-dimensional fashion.

'I thought I'd deactivated that damned thing,' growled Karmel. 'Go away and leave me alone! And leave my late and venerated father out of it.'

'I'm afraid you no longer have the luxury of self-indulgence or self-destruction.' Exebius's voice hardened.

'What?' Karmel staggered erect and shook a fist at the screen. 'I'm buggered if I'm going to play games with you. Just let me alone...' He tottered a little and then added, with rather less acerbity, 'What do you want, anyway?'

Exebius did not reply immediately. Instead, he was regarding Karmel with a closed expression but his crystalline epidermis was losing its lustre and he was unable to conceal his trepidation.

'Well? What is it?'

'You need to pack for a journey... It's going to be very *long* journey, Karmel.'

It took Karmel a few moments for the implication of this brief statement to dawn on him, and when it did everything else was completely forgotten.

'My gods,' he said, eventually. 'So it's true. I had the strangest dream the other night, an intuition dream, I think... Is it the -?'

'Stop there, right now!' said Exebius. 'And order your home management to convert to a Code Five security link.'

Karmel anxiously complied and waited until the smooth opaque shutters had sealed every window and door, and a static crackle assured him that the domestic force field was fully activated.

'We can't be too careful,' hissed a flustered Exebius.

'It's the human woman, isn't it?' asked Karmel, once his friend's natural sparkle had returned.

'It is. Her name is Sara Parkinson.'

Karmel felt icy needles of dissonance crawling along his dorsal spine. 'Go on.'

'There have been problems. The guardians had to precipitate matters,' said Exebius. 'One of them staged an accident in order to break through her latency. Of course, the Volk were not very happy about resorting to such violent tactics but they had no choice. It worked.'

Exebius exhaled noisily. 'It worked too well. There is evidence that that she has already experienced the potential of her abilities. We'd hoped to unite you before that happened.'

'But she came back, yes?'

'She did, fortunately... this time. The next time, she might not be so lucky. That's why she urgently needs your moderating influence.'

'But I don't understand. Why did they decide to break her latency?'

Exebius seemed to be weighing his words carefully. 'She is in serious danger. The Mawdrik know about her.'

'Five Gods!' Karmel was horrified. 'Then she's as good as lost already.'

Mawdrik. The very word made his heart flutter and his throat constrict. Each planet, each race had its own distinct languages and dialects, but in every tongue that he could think of, *Mawdrik* was synonymous with one universally understood concept.

Fear.

'Don't be too hasty,' said Exebius. 'Gods willing, we still have a chance to intervene. Sara Parkinson is about to find out that she has some rather unusual friends.'

The link crackled and the image of Exebius wavered.

'There's no more time for talk, Karmel. You have half an hour at the most. Your contacts will be waiting for you. And one last thing... I don't think we'll see each other again. Gods give you speed.' The screen vanished.

He had half an hour, that was all. Thirty minutes, in which to turn his back on everything he had ever known, thirty minutes to *become as if he'd never existed*. Karmel looked helplessly at the musical scores heaped on tables and shelves, then at the storage threads of recorded works glistening on racks in a tank of preserving fluid. It was a priceless musical archive that had been collected from a hundred different races, some of them purchased for huge amounts of money, some hundreds or thousands of years old.

He did what he needed to do in order to cleanse his system of the harmful alcohol, then he went to the bedroom, changed into fresh clothes and put the very few things he would need into the pouches of a storage belt. After this, he went to the kitchen and took a small canister from the cleaning cupboard. Then he went back to the lounge, unscrewed the lid and placed the small metal container in the centre of the floor.

Karmel threw his key on to the couch and walked swiftly from the apartment. He would never need it again. Within ten minutes, a toxic cloud of corrosive vapour would destroy everything in the luxurious suite of rooms, down to the very last fingerprint.

He did not look back. Ahead of him lay a future that he had both desired and feared for as long as he had known what it meant to be sentient.

4. North-West England

Sleep was clearly going to be impossible for Sara. Since her incredible experience, she had relived every last detail, her thoughts racing fervently as they bombarded her with increasingly outlandish theories as to what had happened. All the time, the pearly white flower lay on the bedside cabinet, pulsating gently. She had examined it from all angles, trying to work out if it could possibly be artificial. Its double corona of petals was so membranous that she soon ruled that possibility out but, whatever its nature, it had survived crushing without sustaining the slightest damage.

Not only that, but something was going on outside her room, the sound of which made her very reluctant to go and investigate. There had been rumours of scuffling and raised voices, followed by a long and uneasy silence at odds with the character of a busy city-centre hospital on a Saturday night.

So long did the quiet last that when she did eventually hear something, she warily moved as close as she dared to the door in order to listen. Outside, somebody was talking on a mobile phone.

'Yes… yes, sir… she matches the description we've been given: late twenties, five foot ten, brown eyes, dark brown hair, attractive… I will, sir, as soon as they arrive… we can keep this under wraps until then…'

Sara didn't want to hear more. She crept back to the bed and sat down on the edge, her mind seething. Maybe they weren't referring to her, but if this was true, the coincidence in the description was unnerving.

Another anomalous happening was the rustling she'd heard from the waste paper bin next to the sink in the shower room. When she investigated she found nothing except the faint damp print of what appeared to be a child's foot. The implications of this were too much to process, and she relegated them to the bottom of an increasing list of worries.

By this time, Sara was fully dressed and determined to discharge herself at the earliest opportunity, locate a taxi and return home. There, she would have time to think over everything that had happened and then she'd decide what to do.

She thought about the flower. Should she take it to a museum, or go to the police? It might be contaminated, or maybe it was poisonous. But some intuition told her no, and that this unworldly bloom was not for anyone else's eyes. It apparently could not be damaged, so she folded the petals carefully in on themselves, wrapped it in a tissue and put it in the canvas shoulder bag she'd been carrying when the car hit her, along with her mobile phone and credit cards.

The door was still partially open, as it had been all day. Sara moved the bedside chair so that she would see anyone who came in before they saw her. As it was, tiredness started to prevail and, against her will, her eyelids drooped and her head rolled sideways against the cheap plastic upholstery of the hospital chair.

She was asleep for less than a minute. There was somebody else in the room.

'Who are you?' Sara flung herself out of the chair and backed away from the person who had sidled through the door.

'I'm sorry.'

'I didn't ask for apologies. I said *who are you?*'

'I'm sorry,' he repeated. He was dressed in a hooded grey sweatshirt, striped tracksuit bottoms and a pair of shabby old trainers. The hood partially concealed his face but Sara was able to make out the thin profile of a man in his early twenties, and the silver ring through his left eyebrow.

Then she knew. '*You!* Keep away from me.' Sara took hold of a box of wet wipes that somebody had left on the windowsill and brandished it in front of her. It was all she could find by way of a weapon.

'It was the only way!' the man said desperately. 'I didn't want to harm a hair on your head. Please - you have to believe me.'

'You tried to kill me!'

'No! I waited for days, looking for the right moment. I was so scared that I'd injured you.'

'You stopped... you spoke to me. *Why?*'

'I had to see that you were okay. I had to see your face properly, if only that once. You're Sara Parkinson.'

Sara was quiet. Slowly, she lowered the wet wipes but she did not move from her defensive corner.

'Listen, we don't have much time.' The rising tremble of anxiety in his tone was unsettling her. He looked ill and unkempt but there was something else, too. He was terrified. 'Maybe I can't convince you but - but, I know what happened to you. You've been to another world. You brought something back with you.'

'How-?'

'There's no time!' His wide grey eyes were staring and beads of sweat had broken out on his forehead. 'You have to get out of here now. They're after you. Do you understand? They will catch you, or worse. That must not happen - that can't happen!'

'How am I going to get out if these people are after me?' she said, panic constricting her voice into a squeak.

'Listen to me carefully,' he went on. 'There's a bag in the cubicle next to the toilet. Whatever you do, don't let it out of your sight but do not look inside. Have you got that? You'll know when the time's right.'

'But -?'

'When you get out, go to the fourth taxi. The fourth! There's a dream catcher hanging from the rear-view mirror. Just get in and go.'

With that, he was gone. There was no time to ask for his name, no time to ask what he was running from, and she was not about to risk looking outside until she had checked his outlandish claim.

Sure enough, there was a large green bag next to the toilet, a durable plastic weave bag of the kind that supermarkets sometimes gave away. Whatever it contained, it was bulky and lumpish and as she picked it up, she caught sight of what looked like a bundle of muddy clothing. It was going to be a burden but the handles were long enough so that she could hang it over her shoulder.

With this done, Sara took a deep breath and went to the door. The thought of leaving the room terrified her, but she could not stay there any longer. She had only the word of a stranger and the vivid memory of an experience so unlikely that on its own, without the evidence she had brought back with her, she would have disregarded it as the effects of concussion.

Sara would look back on this moment in the weeks to come and realize that it was then, as she took the first step outside the room and began to walk cautiously down the corridor, that everything began to alter irrevocably, and then that she had left her former self behind forever. How she managed to walk down the corridor, past the nursing station, down the stairs and through the foyer without attracting the slightest hint of attention, was a mystery to her. There had been three uniformed police talking to the staff at the night desk, then she had passed another four on her way out of the building but it was as though she was invisible, for all the attention her flight had attracted.

She pulled the collar of her fleece up and walked quickly through the driving rain towards the taxi rank. The bag pulled on her shoulder and she was convinced that the contents were shifting around of their own accord, but she hugged it into her side and quickened her pace.

One… two… there it was, the fourth taxi, a white Skoda with a small dream catcher hanging from the mirror in the centre of the windscreen. She could not see the driver, but as she approached it, the back door opened and she climbed in without a moment's hesitation.

It was a disquieting journey back to the west. The driver did not utter a single word and whenever Sara attempted to catch sight of her enigmatic chauffeur in the mirror, it seemed that her vision was momentarily fogged and all that she gained was a brief impression of a face descending into shadow as it turned away from her.

Meanwhile, the rain lashed noisily against the windscreen and the wipers pounded away at full speed. Lightning flickered from time to time in the distance and the lights of oncoming vehicles dazzled her briefly and sprayed the taxi with showers from the accumulating puddles. There seemed to be an inordinately large number of military trucks and Land Rovers on the road, and for half an hour they were caught behind a bulky wagon covered with dark green tarpaulins before it indicated and turned left.

Shortly after, the driver also slowed and turned on to a meandering lane that wound between skeletal hedges and past grey stone farm buildings huddled beneath the rough flanks of the hills. Sara was perplexed, until she realized that they were following a minor route that would also get her back home.

The mysterious driver clearly knew exactly where they were going, for they were travelling down muddy single track lanes and across a maze of obscure junctions and turnings that she only knew because of the country drives and pub visits she'd been on with Carl, a local lad to the core. Sara admired the driver's percipience but she remained silent and continued to hold the green bag tightly against her chest.

After an indeterminable period of time in which the ceaseless rain and the glowing dashboard lights had long since merged into a trancelike continuum, Sara was brought back to the here and now as the car turned into her own street and pulled up to the kerb outside her flat. The unknown driver merely indicated the door with a tilt of his covered head, and Sara got out. Weary and numb, she walked to the front door and was already turning the key in the lock before she thought to look back.

Odd. There was no trace of the car, and she had not heard it drive off, nor had she been aware of the swish of tyres in the water. Just now, however, she was too tired to care. She needed sleep, and the lure of a soft duvet was urging her up the stairs. Once inside, she groped for the bedroom door in the dark and dropped the bag on the floor, barely aware of the peculiar sound it emitted as it hit the ground. Within minutes of stripping her clothes off and sprawling crosswise under the duvet, Sara was fast asleep.

And then, without the slightest warning, she was excruciatingly awake. The transition was as painless and instantaneous as it had been the first time but she knew immediately that she had not returned to Endymion.

Gul. This world is called Gul. Naked and shivering, she was in exactly the same place as before, and at the same time of day. Sara knew what to do immediately. She needed evidence. Crouching down, she picked up a handful of coarse gritty soil and wrapped her fist tightly around it.

As she straightened up, she had her first intimations that this was a very different place from the enchanted fields and star-spangled heavens she had encountered during her first magical excursion. Her awareness unravelled slowly, probing reluctantly into a tainted twilight that, she realised, was little different from the sluggish daylight it was replacing. The air was chilly and carried an unpleasant rumour of putrefaction. She moved her toes in the loose soil and as her eyes grew accustomed to the fading daylight, she saw that it was some kind of dirty white gravel that consisted of small sharp fragments of something that was not stone. The stream was at her back but there was no bridge to span it and instead of water, the darkly meandering gash contained a slow and glutinous flow of black slime with the incessant shimmer and buzz of insects along the banks.

There was no lane and no farmhouse. Instead, the loose grey shale rose in a series of undulations like shallow dunes, strewn with tangles of rusting metallic waste. There was a high wire fence that sagged between concrete posts, and some kind of bulky industrial installation that spewed oily smoke from three enormous tapering chimneys.

Sara began to pick her way up the slope and among the sharp debris, acutely conscious that she was completely naked and keeping to the shadows wherever she could. How could it be the same in every geographical aspect and every conformation of the landscape, but so ominously different? Then she turned towards the mountains, but there were none. In their place rose an immense city of dark rectangles, dimly illuminated with thousands of pinpoints of dull red light.

A knot of dread twisted in her stomach. She recalled how she had been able to sense the essential quality of Endymion, and she now extended this supernatural awareness across the barren landscape towards the city of towers, the tops of which bristled with antennae and revolving dishes, or were hidden in a filthy pall of noxious pollution.

They've destroyed their world and almost everything that lives in it. All the forests have gone and the sea is dead. There are no birds, no other animals, only swarming carrion flies and bacteria.

She saw what lived inside the towers. They were bloated and riddled with the diseases of extreme obesity but they lived in jewel-encrusted opulence - human monsters hardly capable of movement without assistance, who spent their lives gorging in orgiastic feasts, served by dim-witted clones.

They've enslaved their own species! They've bred people into living machines. Now they clean and build, and wash and dress the corpulent bodies of their masters. They are bred to entertain them… and to meet every other conceivable need.

A jarring cacophony of noise pulled her attention back to the factory. She could see that it was just the first in a line of similar buildings that marched down to the sea, each of them belching out the same sluggish fumes and each linked to a rail track that diverged from a main line that ran up the valley. The black beach was lined with tall buildings, cranes and other heavy machinery, while the sea was lit by a residual red glow from the sun. It was dead calm and greasy with slicks and trails of floating garbage, and a huge pipeline jutted far out over the water on buttresses and spewed out pulsating gouts of black fluid.

An enormous rusting engine was grinding to a noisy halt in front of the nearest building. It was pulling wagons loaded with crates and through the bars of each one of them she could see dozens of pale objects, tightly packed together. Similar cargoes were pulling up outside the immense metal doors of every other factory down the line, then mechanical claws rolled forwards and began unloading the crates and piling them on to a conveyer belt, supervised by a swarm of brutish figures who seemed to be dressed in rubber suits.

Sara felt the bile rising in her throat and an unfolding insight that she fought to deny. She did not want to know any more. She wanted to run from this place with every last grain of strength that she possessed, back through the door to her own world, but she couldn't. Forced on by the awful conviction that she had to witness and remember, she climbed over a breach in the fence and approached the building.

Now the clamour of a siren was rising into the coming night like a discordant cry of despair and the metal doors were laboriously sliding open on poorly lubricated runners. The crates began to roll inside, stacked three-deep on the juddering conveyor. Sara hid behind a mound of foul-smelling debris and watched as they disappeared into a yawning interior of long shadows and quivering ruddy light. A formless murmur was coming from the crates and she could see movement inside them that became increasingly frenzied as whatever was inside fought to get out. White limbs thrashed and flailed through the gaps, while the thickset men in the rubber suits ran backwards and forwards, beating at the sides with metal bars.

The last one disappeared inside and the doors began to heave shut. Sara dared not move from her hiding place and for long minutes there was no sound except for the whistling of a thin wind through the detritus. Then the terrible noises began, so piercing and horrific that not even the thick doors were able to contain them.

Appalled, Sara clutched her hands over her ears and crushed her head between her knees but she could still hear the noises until, after hours, or so it seemed, they mercifully died away and the lament of the dead wind was shattered again by a metallic shudder as the doors began to open.

She got to her feet, trembling with cold and fear, and stumbled towards the doors, aching to deny the terrible truth that lay inside. She stopped in front of the vast entrance and saw pulleys and aerial tracks that ran into the depths of a space bigger than a football stadium. Dark wetness glistened in pools on the floor, and troughs of gleaming offal swung away on chains into a tangle of steaming and throbbing machinery.

And at the back of the enormous slaughterhouse were rank upon rank of hooks, ascending in tiers to the ceiling, and from them swung hundreds of gutted and bloody carcasses.

In that moment, she knew everything. *They breed them in their millions, all across this hellish world of Gul. They rear their own species in crates, like battery hens, and then they slaughter them and eat them. There is no other food here... nothing. Then they process what's left and feed the remains to the next harvest.*

Then somebody saw her. One of the monstrous slaughter men appeared and roared incoherently. Sara ran, her mouth screaming out soundlessly in rage and horror and as she skidded and lurched in the direction of the fence, she heard the splashing of boots in the gory pools.

Open, for God's sake, open! Where was it? There had to be a door! She made it to the fence and fell across the tangled wires, gashing her leg on the metal barbs, but she dragged herself up and staggered on down the slope towards the stream. She slipped again on the bank, scattering a cloud of carrion flies and almost pitching into the crawling rivulet of rotting waste and writhing maggots. She was trapped; they had almost caught her. She could hear their rasping breath as she screamed and felt their wet hands clutching at her thrashing legs...

Sara was still screaming when she returned. She threw herself off the bed and on to the floor where she curled up and put her fist in her mouth in an attempt to stifle the sobs that racked her body. Then she remembered what she had in her hand and gagging with revulsion, she ran to the window, threw it open and hurled the fragments of bone as far as she could into the pouring rain.

5. North-West England

A grey and windy daybreak found Sara curled up on a couch and watching rivulets of rain as they trickled down the windowpanes. An empty wine bottle and a tumbler sat on the coffee table and the air was misty with the smoke of incense sticks.

She had not slept. She'd showered five times during the night, scrubbing her skin desperately as if, by doing so, she could rid herself of the nightmare, but she could not erase the terrible images nor the stench that would not leave her nostrils, however many joss sticks she burned.

Huddled beneath a crochet blanket in the silent flat, she had tried and failed to make sense of all the impossibilities of the last eighteen hours - impossible, that is, if it were not for the evidence she had brought back from Endymion and the other place, the place whose name she longed to forget.

So, what now? She had been the victim of a deliberate hit-and-run accident. She had been visited by the perpetrator who, through some unknown means, knew about her extra-worldly excursions, and she had managed to escape from close surveillance right under the nose of the police. Did she wait at home to see what came her way, or did she go looking for answers? And, if so, how and where should she begin?

Another enigma was the green bag that she had been told to bring from the hospital. It had sat next to her on the couch all night and the touch of it had been the first thing to quell the screaming horrors. Why, she could not say, nor why she had no desire to look inside, but when she decided to walk to the minimarket two streets away she picked it up and hung it on her shoulder without a moment's thought.

Sara was ravenously hungry and, regardless of what the day held in store for her, she had to buy food. There was very little within date in the fridge and she did not have the inclination to open tins or slice vegetables, but she had not eaten for the best part of a day, and the craving for a bacon sandwich was becoming almost unbearable.

The force of the wind and lashing rain struck her as soon as she left the house. She passed Mrs Carrington from two doors down, but the old woman, normally so friendly, appeared not to have seen her. There were a surprising number of telecommunications service vehicles parked across the road and men in yellow waterproofs were at work overhead among the cables. The storm had obviously caused a lot of damage and some of the overhead lines were down. But, then, she saw two police cars parked on the corner and another at the far end of the road. Why would they be here in such force to oversee what were, after all, routine repairs?

Hugging the waterproof jacket tighter, Sara quickened her pace. She had chosen it on purpose because it was new and she had never been seen in it before. All the same, her trepidation was growing and she wondered if leaving the house had been such a good idea.

She reached the market without incident and pushed a coin into the slot of a trolley, then she put the green bag on the child seat. Sliced bread, butter, milk, bacon, maybe some chocolate biscuits and definitely more wine. She'd buy a box rather than a bottle. Perhaps some fresh pasta with Gorgonzola and cream for lunch…

Sara was so wrapped up in her food cravings that she did not look where she was going and ran straight into the man as he suddenly appeared round the end of the dairy produce aisle. He put his hands out to fend off the trolley and had started to apologise to her before cutting himself short. Before he had a chance to pull his raincoat around his lanky frame, Sara noticed the epaulettes of a military jacket.

She scarcely had time to react. The man looked startled and turned away, scanning rapidly to both sides as though he had suddenly lost sight of her. In the same moment, she heard an oddly nasal voice coming from inside the green bag. 'Keep going,' it said. 'Turn left, then walk down the next aisle to the till.'

The bundle of grimy clothing inside the bag shifted and a small greyish brown face with glittering black eyes glowered at her. 'And get some decent tea bags on your way.'

Sara checked out her few purchases in a daze. The bored check-out girl did not look at her as she wearily demanded payment, and the man had not reappeared by the time she exited the shop.

'What's going on?'

'Don't say another word,' said the voice. 'Go straight home and do not talk to anybody. I'm very angry with you, Sara Parkinson. You almost blew our cover by coming here.'

Balking at the reprimand and the incongruity of discovering a bad-tempered midget among her shopping, Sara nevertheless did exactly as he said. As she approached the house she saw that, while the vans and police cars were still there, every private car in the street had disappeared.

'Don't stop,' the voice repeated. 'Get inside, then we'll talk.'

Once in the flat, Sara put the bag on the floor and stepped back in astonishment as the midget crawled out and got to his feet.

'Shh,' he said before she had the chance to say anything. 'I need to check that we're alone.' He pattered to the window and stood on his toes to look outside, and then he went into the bathroom, then the kitchen. Sara heard cupboard doors banging, pans rattling and the flap of his bare feet on the linoleum, then he returned and stood in front of her, looking up with hands on hips and a frown on his bizarre face.

'Not that you were going to ask,' he said ill-humouredly, 'but the name's Terk.'

He was about three and a half feet in height and was dressed in a strange collection of clothing that was clearly intended for a toddler of around the same size - a dark blue anorak with a fur lined hood and a yellow teddy bear embroidered on the right hand pocket, and a pair of muddy pink trousers. When he pushed the hood back, she saw that he was completely bald, with leathery skin and lumpy lopsided features that made him look as if his tongue was permanently thrust into his left cheek. While his bare feet looked ordinary enough, his outsized hands resembled the four-fingered, clasping feet of a chameleon.

After what she had recently experienced, Sara was too exhausted to be shocked by his appearance, nor did she doubt the evidence before her eyes. Rather, she was at a loss as to how she should start a conversation with such an unlikely guest.

Terk seemed to be aware of this. 'I really would like a cup of tea,' he said pointedly, glancing towards the kitchen. 'I haven't had a decent brew in years.'

'Okay,' Sara broke her silence. 'And then you tell me what in the world is going on. Right?'

'I'll do my best,' said Terk, pulling himself on to the sofa and crossing his stubby legs while Sara made a pot of tea. He spent five minutes with his nose in the mug that Sara brought him, inhaling and slurping and clearly enjoying every last fragrant drop.

'Could have done with being a bit stronger.' He scowled at Sara. 'But - blimey, I'd forgotten how good this stuff is. You don't get it where I live. It's too dark for the bushes, you see.' He chuckled and gave Sara a sly glance, clearly expecting her to understand the implied joke.

When she didn't respond, he sighed and put the mug on the coffee table. 'You don't know anything, do you?'

'No.'

'Well…' Terk drummed his chameleon fingers on his knee for a few moments. 'To start with, I'm the one who helped you get out of the hospital last night without being seen. Yes?'

'If you say so. I have no idea how it happened.'

Terk shook his head. 'Take my word. No, that isn't enough, is it? I have this ability, you see. I can make myself unseen when I want to, and if I make an effort I can do the same for people and things around me. Do you get that?'

'You mean, you can become invisible?'

'You might call it invisibility, but it isn't that simple. There's more to it than not being *seen*. You have to make it so they don't *want* to find you. It's second nature for me and my people, so much so that it's almost impossible to describe how it works because it would be beyond your understanding. Or to turn things round, it's a bit like me and reality television. Now, what under the world is all *that* about?'

Sara found that she was smiling for the first time in days, and the release was invigorating.

'Go on.'

'You don't need me to tell you that you're being hunted.'

Sara pressed her lips together. 'It's true, then. None of this is my imagination. I thought I was going crazy.' And here she was, talking to a bald dwarf she'd found in a shopping bag…

It was uncanny, but Sara had the distinct impression that Terk knew exactly what she was thinking.

'What you won't know yet is precisely who is hunting you. There's something out there that knows you have travelled to another universe and they are very interested to find out how you did it.'

'It's happened more than once,' she said.

'Ah,' said Terk darkly. 'Last night was not the first time, was it? But it was the worst. Do you want to tell-?'

'No!' Sara took a deep breath and released it slowly. 'Not yet, at any rate. You were here, weren't you? If you saw me then you must have some idea. The first time it happened was incredible. It was like... I don't know... a vision of the way things should be, or would have been if we hadn't messed it up so badly.'

She relaxed a little more. 'In any case, you don't seem to be that surprised. Look, I want to know why these people are after me. Who are they?'

'They call themselves the Mawdrik.'

'The *what*?' She couldn't restrain a smile. 'Are you serious?'

'The Mawdrik,' he repeated without a hint of humour.

'It sounds like something out of a fantasy movie.'

'That probably suits their egos just fine,' said Terk caustically, 'but I promise you, there's nothing fantastic about these creatures. They are quite real.

'Mawdrik is only their current name. You'd recognize some of the others they have used. Individually they refer to themselves as lumen, a word they took from your science of physics, but it once had another use. In Latin, it means "light".'

'So where do they come from?'

'Come from?' Terk scowled. 'They don't come from anywhere. They have always been here, and you have always known about them even if you've denied their existence. That has been their intention, after all - to keep you all in ignorance. There's an expression you people use... "to treat you like mushrooms". Yes?'

'I know the one.' Sara smiled again. 'Okay, so these Mawdrik are following me? Why me?'

'They aren't simply following you.' Terk's tone darkened again. 'Mark my words carefully. They are powerful and ruthless beings. They are not phantoms or pretend creatures from fairy tales. They are driven by desire, for knowledge and control. There's worse. They can take you apart with their eyes alone and then keep your living essence alive but in torment, and they will stop at nothing within their power to find what they want. Do you understand me?'

He waited until he was certain that she did. 'It's as I said. They have always been here. They are as much a part of this world as you and me.'

Sara watched the rain beating at the window, then she turned back to her unlikely visitor. 'You said we've always know about them? How can that be true?'

'Because one of their greatest achievements has been to fool people into believing they are creatures of light and goodness. *They* are the angels and elves and guardian spirits that you humans like to imagine.'

Angels and elves... it made sense, of a kind. The desire of humanity for supernatural intervention was a powerful one, and such longings were older than history. When she had been very young, her mother had enthralled her with colourful folk tales about spirit beings, some of whom were helpful, others malevolent and capricious. Those tales had left an abiding impression on her.

'There is more,' Terk went on. 'It's also served the Mawdrik to distort the true nature of certain others, to give them a bad reputation that's been impossible to shake off. People like me, for example.'

'Do you mind me asking, what are you, exactly?'

'What do *you* think I am? What do you see when you look at me? A goblin, a gnome, some kind of a demon?'

Sara lifted her shoulders and let them fall again. She had no idea what to say.

'Yes, the Mawdrik have been supremely successful with their slander campaign and they've been at it for a very long time.'

Terk eased himself off the sofa and pattered into the kitchen. 'Any more tea in the pot?'

Once his mug was full again, he resumed his extraordinary history and Sara listened without interrupting, increasingly fascinated and disturbed.

'They've worked their deceit in other ways, too. They've masqueraded as divine messengers and they've planted visions in people's minds. You're a clever girl. I'm sure you can imagine how it goes - a handful of clever words here and there among the gullible, staging a miracle once in a while... They've watched men killing each other by the thousands in the name of one creed or another and they've stood back and laughed and then laughed some more.'

He gulped the last of his tea down. 'Now do you begin to see how dangerous they are?'

'But why?' she said, breaking her silence. 'I mean, you say they're interested in power. So are most politicians - that's nothing new. Why do they want me in particular?'

'It's because you, alone out of everybody, might be able to lead them to what they are looking for. They aren't interested in where you have already been. It's where you might go in the future, given the right incentive. They will either bend you to their will or if they can't do that, they'll extract the secret of your ability from you by other means.' His face fell into shadow. 'One way or the other.'

'What ability? I've absolutely no idea what happened to me!' Sara protested. 'I don't know how it happened. I didn't ask for it to happen and I can't control it. I don't want any of this!'

'Do you think they care about that? You can't just make things go away by pretending they don't exist. All they are concerned with is their own self-betterment. That is the Mawdrik for you. What they don't yet know is that there are bigger and darker things than themselves out there.'

'And what do you mean by "out there"?'

'You will find out soon enough,' he said.

'Okay. You don't want to tell me.'

'There is no time.' Terk went to the window and examined the street in both directions. 'We'd hoped for more, but when we heard that the Mawdrik had found you, we had to act without delay.'

The accident. 'You knew I was being followed, didn't you?' she said, a hint of reproach in her voice. 'That man in the car?'

Terk studied his toes.

'What is it?'

When he looked up and glowered at her it seemed that a kind of darkness had fallen over the room. 'You still don't believe, do you? Listen to me carefully, Sara Parkinson. You *will* learn to be afraid. One of us has already died to protect you and there will be more.'

'He's... he's *dead*?' Sara did not need him to tell her how he knew. She joined him at the window, saying nothing, but with the terrified face of the driver stamped like an accusation in her mind. So, the fear she'd sensed in him had been justified.

'You were there in the car with him, weren't you? That's why nobody could give a description to the police.' Terk nodded briefly and continued his vigil.

The street was still empty of private cars, and the rain had thinned to a misty drizzle that reduced visibility significantly, such that at first she could not see what was happening at the end of the road. Then, as her eyes focused, Sara could see that a strong barrier had been constructed across the junction, and that men in army uniform were standing guard. She also saw that every manhole and drain cover in the road had been lifted.

Terk chuckled softly. 'That's very clever. Very clever indeed.'

'What is?'

'Well, they tried to stop us making contact with you in the hospital. They put guards on every way out of the city. They even had a couple of helicopters in the air, but the one place they didn't think of looking was underground. Seems like the penny has dropped.'

'Is that where you come from?' she asked. 'Underground?'

'Course. Why do you think I haven't had a decent cup of tea for twenty-seven years? I don't make it up this way very often; only when I'm needed.' He spread his large hands, reversing one opposing set of fingers so that they were parallel. They ended in thick nails and now resembled the front paws of a mole. 'What did you think these were for?'

'And there are more of your people?'

Terk gave her a withering glance. 'I'm not the last of my kind, if that's what you're thinking. I've got a wife and three kids back home.'

'Sorry.' Terk accepted her apology with a terse nod. 'Do we stay here?'

'No,' he said firmly. 'We leave this afternoon. You have to get far away from here. The Mawdrik will show themselves before long.'

'And where are we going?'

Terk said nothing. He was still watching the rain-obscured activity in the street.

'Terk?' He turned slowly to look at her. 'Where?'

'A long way. Or rather, I'm taking you to meet someone who can set you on the right path. Understand this - what is happening is much bigger than any one of us.'

'And that is all you're going to tell me?'

'It's the way it has always been - that way, if any one of us falls into the wrong hands we can't reveal too much. What I *do* know is enough to for me to know how important *you* are.'

'I'm not coming back, am I?'

'I don't think so, no. Not to this life here, at any rate.' The flower from Endymion was lying on the table. Terk picked it up and cupped it in his strange hands and as he examined it, the petals flexed and glowed ever more brightly.

'Don't leave this behind, whatever you do. I have a feeling that it's going to be important.'

Sara nodded emphatically, for she had no intention of leaving it. 'It's my only link to Endymion. Without it I'd still be doubting my sanity.'

'Keep it with you at all times.' He was leafing through the wad of postcards on the mantelpiece above the gas fire. Sara never threw them out as she had planned to mount them all in a large frame she'd bought, but it had become just one of her many unfinished projects.

He selected one and put the rest back. 'Take this with you too.' She looked at it briefly, a sunny view of towers and battlements with a range of snow topped mountains in the background that she'd unexpectedly received from a brief acquaintance she'd met once in a bar. They had exchanged addresses, and that was all.

Sara was about to ask why she needed it when Terk cut her off.

'I'm going to have a look at the local news,' he announced, picking up the TV control. 'You should start packing.'

But how do I prepare for the unknown? She left him flicking through television channels and went into the bedroom. Opening the wardrobe, she stood in front of it indecisively, wondering just what she should take.

'A pair of strong shoes and a waterproof jacket would be a good idea,' Terk called over the sound of the regional news programme. 'A few summer items as well. Oh, and be careful to put everything in plastic bags and tie the tops.'

Sara puzzled over his timely advice, but nevertheless carried on searching for thick socks and T-shirts. She found her walking boots under a heap of sweaters and put them on one side. She had not used any of her hiking gear since the split with Carl.

I wonder if I should tell him something? Despite their official separation six months earlier, they had seen each other on several occasions since and had talked about getting back together, albeit in a half-hearted manner.

'Don't bother doing that,' said Terk. 'You can do much better than him.'

'I beg your pardon?' Sara dropped the day sack she'd been packing and strode into the sitting room, where Terk was sitting on the floor in front of the television. 'You read my thoughts! How did you do that?'

'Oh. I'm sorry.' He looked over his shoulder and made a comical face of contrition. 'I forgot to tell you. My people are also mind readers. Sometimes I detect thoughts without intending to – it's awfully rude, I know, but never mind about that just now. Come and have a look at this!'

He was watching the end of the regional headlines. A reporter was standing in the local high street, battling in the strong wind to keep hold of his umbrella and a microphone.

'- and all residents of South Bay Road and West View have been evacuated for the foreseeable future. The controversial decision of the local authority to call in the Army to oversee this operation has been justified on terms of the severity of the gas leak and the added danger of the extensive nineteenth-century mine shafts that, experts say, are located directly beneath the affected zone and could lead to widespread subsidence and devastation in the event of an explosion. This is Joshua Sykes reporting for the - '

'Utter rubbish!' said Terk, stabbing the off button with a blunt digit. 'I know this ground like the back of my hand. There aren't any mine workings within half a mile of here and that gas main is as sound as the day they laid it.'

'But how are we going to get out of here if the whole area is cordoned off?'

'I'm thinking about that. As you know, there are ways and means of reducing our visibility but if the Mawdrik are out there in person, it will complicate issues. I need to call in some assistance.'

He rummaged in the pocket of his child's anorak and extracted an ancient mobile phone, then talked rapidly for some minutes in a guttural language that was completely unintelligible to Sara.

'And now?' she said after he'd finished.

'And now, we watch and wait. Make sure you're ready to leave quickly. And some lunch might be a good idea.'

'Um... what do you eat?'

'Anything that you do. What about a bacon sandwich?'

The hours crawled by, time dragging as though impeded by the unremittingly oppressive drizzle. Terk sat by the window, munching his sandwich and staring fixedly into the grey and once she was certain that she had packed everything she needed, Sara came and joined him.

She wanted to ask so many questions, about his people and how he lived, and how many other races shared the world with them. She wanted to know how it was possible for people to go about their lives with no knowledge of what lay just beyond their perception. But instead she sat by him, peering into the endless drizzle and letting its fall drag her eyes down to the wet tarmac and her thoughts back to the nightmares of Gul.

Then Terk stirred and leaned forward, breaking through Sara's grim recollections. She gave him a questioning look, and he said, 'They're coming. Watch.'

Something was moving just inside one of the open manholes. A thin grey arm emerged, and then another, then a head appeared and a slender figure climbed out and got to its feet. It was about the same size as Terk but it was almost skeletal in build and with a strange texture to its skin as though it were covered with patches of mosses and lichens. Sara could make out little else through the rain but as it looked around with quick furtive glances she saw that it had large, reflective eyes like those of a cat.

Whatever it was, it did not wait around for long. As it loped away into the lee of a hedge, others were already emerging from all along the road until twenty or thirty of them had gathered. Some had hunched or bulbous torsos, others had four arms or grossly exaggerated noses like the beaks of herons. Many were so densely covered by mossy pelage that they looked like mobile pieces of forest floor.

Sara was spellbound. As she continued watching, other figures began to emerge from gardens and alleyways, dressed in dark coats with hoods that did not reveal much about their appearance, although there were both men and women.

'Who *are* they?'

'Wait, and you'll see.'

Sara did not have long to wait. As they moved off along the road, a man at the front suddenly threw off his coat and, almost faster than she could see, underwent an incredible transformation. In a second he'd thrown himself forwards and down and had become something very different - a large brown bear that turned his massive shaggy head and grunted to his companions as if in encouragement. They too were tossing aside their clothes and changing; first, a lanky grey wolf, then a bristling wild boar with enormous tusks, and a sleek tawny puma and others whose metamorphosis was hidden by the rain.

'It doesn't always happen that quickly,' Terk explained. 'Some of them take hours or days to transform. They're werepeople. Lovely folk but terribly misunderstood, thanks to the Mawdrik. The others are sprites. They're a forest race and they're very sensitive to noise and pollution so you can imagine that there aren't many of them left in Britain. Most of them headed into Europe and Russia around the time of your industrial revolution.'

'They look so fragile. What can they do?'

'Don't let appearances deceive you.'

He put a hand on Sara's arm. 'It's time to go. If the Mawdrik are here in person, even sprites and werepeople won't be able to hold them back for long.'

They left by the back door. The rear entrance opened to a narrow yard, paved with cracked stones and filled with weeds. A sagging gate that had not been repaired in twenty years gave onto a narrow lane and beyond this were the grey backs of houses in the next street.

Terk made a right turn and hurried down the lane. He moved surprisingly quickly but Sara had no trouble in keeping up with him. The overlooking windows were empty and black in a neighbourhood that was usually vibrant and busy but, more so, there was a sterile astringency in the atmosphere as if everything living had been leached out of the air.

Things are never going to be the same here. Something profound is changing. Something disturbing.

'Ah, good,' said Terk. 'Ivanov is here.'

A car was pulling up and had blocked the end of the lane, and Sara's heart lurched unpleasantly, until she saw that it was the same car that had rescued her from the hospital. The car with the dream catcher.

The silent taxi driver.

'Don't bother trying to talk to him,' cautioned Terk. 'He won't understand. He's Russian.'

'Russian?'

'Yes. He's a Vodyanoi.'

Sara had no idea what a Vodyanoi was, but she climbed into the back seat as soon as the door swung open. Terk swiftly clambered in beside her and the car sped away.

They drove through the abandoned outskirts of the town and were soon deep into the undulating hinterland that lay between the coast and the mountains. Either the driver knew the terrain well or he possessed an uncanny sense of direction, because he was negotiating every twist and junction of the narrow country lanes with speed and confidence, just as he had the previous night. They were heading southeast towards the looming cloud-capped bulk of the hills, between leafless hedges and an undulating patchwork of fields that were saturated to capacity after days of continual rain and were leaking their excess water onto the road.

The Vodyanoi seemed to relish driving through the flooded dips and dells and he ploughed through them without reducing speed, throwing up great fountains of muddy water that splashed down noisily over the car. In summer, this rolling pastoral landscape was an idyll of lush pastures and wild flowers, alive with butterflies and birdsong, but a long wet winter had stolen away all remnants of colour and joy from it.

Terk was sitting on the edge of the seat. The only visible part of him was the round tip of his blunt nose protruding from the fur-trimmed hood of his anorak.

Without warning, he said, 'There is a question you need to ask.'

'How did you -? Oh, of course,' said Sara. His ability to read minds was disconcerting. 'If it's these Mawdrik that are hunting me, why are the police and the army involved?'

'Because some of your kind made a deal with them a very long time ago. There are people who will go to the ends of the earth in their quest for power and knowledge.'

'Who are these people?'

'There are three of them, and they are always men. It has been this way for over a thousand years, and they're always powerful individuals who have enormous resources at their disposal. The poor fools. They don't realise how the Mawdrik have used them. And now...' he sighed.

'What about now?'

'Everything changes, Sara Parkinson. Everything. If we succeed today, the alliance will be broken.'

'You make it sound as though it's a bad thing!'

'You don't understand the implications. You will, I promise you.'

Sara had no time to puzzle over his cryptic words because at that moment they were both flung violently forward. The Vodyanoi had slammed on the brakes and the car skewed to a halt near the bottom of a tiny flooded valley where the road forded a stream. This had risen frighteningly and had transformed into a swirling torrent the colour of milky coffee. On the opposite bank, through the drizzle, they could see a cluster of military vehicles and a dozen soldiers lined up at the edge of the rushing water, their weapons trained on the stationary taxi.

The Vodyanoi did not move. Sara caught her breath, trying to focus on their driver but as before, he seemed to slide out of her vision as if he was made of liquid.

'Get out of the car. Now!' One of the soldiers was holding a loud speaker.

None of them moved, but the Vodyanoi seemed to have increased in size, and there was a damp smell of mud and pondweed in the car that Sara hadn't noticed before. Her heart was thumping in her chest as she automatically searched for Terk's hand. He squeezed hers tightly in response.

'I said, now! You can't go any further. If you try to reverse, we'll shoot.'

Terk started to laugh. 'They have no idea. He's a Vodyanoi! Hold on to the back of the seat tightly, Sara.'

No sooner had she braced herself than the car accelerated and plunged straight into the heart of the torrent. A sheet of muddy water leaped into the air, but instead of crashing down again it surged away from the taxi and rose into a churning brown wall between them and the military blockade.

As the car lurched and bumped over the rocky streambed, the water toppled and crashed down on the gunmen, pummelling their vehicles with such force that one of them slid into the stream and was dragged away by the power of the flood. As the soldiers scattered, the Vodyanoi slammed down on the accelerator and they sped away in a flurry of mud.

'That was very close,' said Terk. Then they heard the crack of rifles and the whine of bullets and when she looked back, Sara could see that the men were already jumping into the remaining vehicles. 'I should have been able to hide us. That means only one thing. The Mawdrik are already here.'

'But what does that mean for us?' demanded Sara, her voice juddering as the car thudded over a tiny humped bridge and swung left at a forked junction, on to a narrower lane that headed into the maw of a broad, u-shaped valley.

'It means that we *must* get to the lake,' he said, 'before they do, or they will block your escape.'

Sara knew exactly where they were, and the conformation of the road ahead. They were speeding into the mouth of the valley between narrow strips of rough pastureland and bare copses, and the sweeping heathery flanks of the mountains. For a few miles, the road widened between tall black hedges as it ran parallel to the racing stream, through farmland demarcated by dry stone walls. They sped through a small hamlet then past a clutter of byres and a squat grey farmhouse and as they did so, Sara shouted and pointed because a dozen soldiers were running for the vehicles that were pulled up in the yard.

Ivanov did not hesitate. They plunged on through flooded dips and despite her adrenalin-charged fear, Sara marvelled at the way the Vodyanoi controlled the taxi and managed to prevent it slewing into the wall. Shortly further on, the road forked with one route rising steeply over a dramatic mountain pass, and the other looping around the rough hillside on the left of the lake in a series of tight hairpin bends. Just before this, close to the near end of the lake, they would arrive at a parking area with a stile in the wall, and a track that crossed the sodden fields to the shore.

Sara felt that they were approaching their destination although, to what purpose, she could not begin to guess. However, they could hear the sounds of pursuit and looking back, she could see a convoy of vehicles bouncing after them, disappearing at times between hedges and into dips but each time they reappeared it was obvious that their pursuers were gaining on them.

Even more worrying was the noise from the sky. Sara wound the window down to listen. A flurry of rain soaked her face and then she heard it, more clearly this time - the intermittent hacking of helicopter blades.

They had reached another relatively straight section of road, and Ivanov was able to put a little distance between them and their pursuers.

'Listen,' said Terk. 'This is not going well, but our Vodyanoi friend still has a few tricks up his sleeve.'

'Just tell me what I can do!'

'When we reach the car park, we have to run. You must run faster than you ever have before. There is a promontory on the other side of the lake and once you get there, you have to call her name. She *will* come, I promise you.'

'Whose name?'

'Valu. The female is called Valu. Her mates are Urrin and Waa. I wish there'd been more time to explain. Valu... don't forget.'

'But what about you? Will you be okay?'

Terk's bulbous features wrinkled into a smile. 'Don't worry about me. I've taken care of myself for a very long time. You must reach Valu. She knows what to do.'

Valu. Valu. Sara was chanting the name silently, like a mantra. Suddenly, the Vodyanoi made a strange noise, a low gurgling rumble that emanated from deep inside his chest, then Terk pressed his hands and nose to the window and uttered a sharp cry of dismay.

Sara did not know how it was possible for the Vodyanoi to drive at such breakneck speed, but the thing that pursued them had no difficulty in keeping level. It was running parallel to them through the fields at a distance of several hundred yards, a tall thin bipedal creature so vivid and stark that it looked as if it was made of ice and lightning. It sprinted effortlessly through walls and hedges as though they had no substance, repeatedly turning its head towards them, and even at this distance, Sara could see that its eyes were blacker than the night.

She screamed in agony. For an instant, it was as if the creature's eyes had torn into her mind and stabbed at her consciousness with the cold precision of a surgical blade. Terk dragged her back from the window.

'Do not look at it!'

Now they could see a grey huddle of farm buildings among a cluster of leafless sycamore trees. Just beyond was the muddy turn off into the car park. Ivanov made one last effort and pushed the car to its limits and Sara fervently prayed that they could outpace the nightmare creature for long enough to gain an advantage, but what kind of advantage was possible over such a horror, she couldn't imagine. The creature had violated her very core, simply by looking at her.

'As soon as we're out, run!' barked Terk. 'Your life depends on it. No looking back.'

They skidded to a halt in a shower of gravel. The door flew open and they slipped and tumbled into the biting wind and drizzle. As they ran for the stile, the Vodyanoi flowed from the driver's seat and drew himself up to his full height. Sara had the briefest impression of a hulking form, shaggy with lustrous black hair, with a face completely hidden in a massive tangle of mossy beard except for luminous deep-set eyes that were the colour of the moon.

She had no time to indulge her amazement, but as they vaulted across the stile and fled down the slippery path, she felt the earth shuddering under her feet and heard the strangest noises coming from the soil as if the water was being sucked out of the sodden ground.

They ran, Terk's rough and leathery feet giving him a sure footing on the slick wet grass but Sara fell twice and was soon splashed with mud. The path angled across the field towards another stile, beyond which was a dense stand of pine and birch woodland.

'What's happening?' shouted Sara as they stumbled under the cover of the trees. When they looked back, they could see droplets and splashes rising vertically from the ground as though the rainfall had reversed itself, then they began to stream towards the bulky shadow of the Vodyanoi who was lumbering into view over a rise in the pasture to confront the lumen which had been gaining on Sara and Terk but had suddenly turned its attention to him.

'It's Ivanov. He can manipulate water. He'll make a water spout and use it to hold back the Mawdrik.'

'*Mawdrik?* I thought you said a single one was called a lumen?'

'There are always more than one. Come on - we're not staying to watch.'

The trees were sodden and dripping and the smell of dead wet bracken and leaf mould filled the moist air. Even though the woodland gave Sara a brief sense of protection they did not stop running nor did they slow down to catch their breath for a single moment. They could hear shouting, then the echo of gunshots and the crack and rip of branches overhead as bullets seared through the woodland canopy.

The path was steep and flooded, and in places the rain had eroded it into a little gulley of slippery clay, treacherous with exposed roots and sharp rocks. For all his short legs, Terk bounded over every obstacle with ease but Sara could not match his pace. He had to wait for her by the lakeside, but as soon as she had caught up he set off again, across a narrow shingle beach and past an old stone boathouse before rejoining the path which skirted a wide inlet then continued along the shore beneath a looming grey hillside. Sara was panting and with each breath, stabbing pains exploded in her lungs and when she looked back, she could see dark movement among the trees and was overcome with a cold flush of despair.

'I - I can't - '

'You can. You are brave and strong. Now run, again!'

Sara lurched on after him, her ragged breaths searing like fire in her throat, but as they rounded the cove and the track started to ascend across the scree above the ruffled waters of the lake, her strength began to give out once more. The pain in her chest was agonising and she toppled against a rock, barely managing to support herself as she struggled to fill her lungs. Terk spun round and ran back to her but as he reached her side, an army helicopter emerged from the swirling mist, banking steeply before heading straight for them over the water, searchlights probing to and fro across the hillside above them and dipping lower on every sweep.

They would be spotted within seconds, and there was nowhere on this bleak hillside to hide. Sara held on to Terk's hand and he squeezed tight as the beam swept over them and back, holding steady as the aircraft began to descend. It was so close that they could see the hardened faces of the men braced in the open doorway, guns trained on them.

'It's over...' whispered Sara. Then her eyes widened and she shouted out in amazement.

'Look!'

'Banshees,' said Terk, 'and not a moment too soon.'

Three shapes plummeted from the clouds, furling their silver wings as they arrowed towards the open hatch in the fuselage like stooping falcons. For a few long moments, the machine held steady, then it spun around and jerked upwards as though it had been struck by an invisible giant. It slewed to one side and began to fall, listing terribly, its rotors whining with strain. Now it was on its side, sliding out of the sky, the blades shattering on the hillside before it impacted with a reverberating thump and exploded in a fireball of red heat and oily black smoke.

Terk dug his blunt fingers into Sara's palm and dipped his head. 'They were my friends,' he whispered, and then he was pushing at her with all his strength.

'Go on! I will do what I can.'

There was no time to say goodbye. A surge of adrenalin and the brief halt were giving her enough strength to carry on for a little while longer. She looked back only once, to see the diminutive figure dressed in the toddler's anorak standing in the rain and watching her, and the long line of soldiers approaching at a run over the drenched moorland.

Five minutes more. That was all she needed. Five minutes and she would be at the promontory. The bitter wind was tossing white foam against the rocky headland and she could even make out the bent dark tussocks of rushes and tawny remnants of bracken along its length. Behind her, a remote thrumming noise penetrated the rush of wind and water, faint at first but growing louder every moment.

More gunshots came, shattering rocks off to the side. She realized that they were not shooting at her, but were trying to terrify her into giving herself up. She *had* to carry on. Somehow, she made it to the narrow peninsula, jarring her feet against boulders and twisting her ankles in crevices as she scrambled on to the top of it. Now she could see the entire length of the lake, and besides the billowing smoke and flames from the burning helicopter there were five motor dinghies, bouncing and slapping over the waves as they rapidly bore down on her.

She reached the drop off where the last few rocks gave way to the pummelling waves. Teetering on the edge in the strong wind, she dragged air into her lungs and shrieked out across the water; 'Valuuuuu! Valuuuu!!'

There was nothing except the rapid chop-chop of the waves slapping against the shore, the growing din of the motor boats and the noise of a second helicopter that was fast approaching from the opposite end of the lake.

'Valu! Please!'

The lake erupted, and three enormous figures rose from the surging water immediately in front of her. They had the colour and lustre of polished jade and they were strangely proportioned with elongated bodies and narrow waists. Their legs were impressively muscular, and their long arms reached down to their knees.

Their heads appeared to be disproportionately long, and they had rolling swathes of olive green hair that hung down in dripping coils. All three were naked. The males had scant hair on their chins and the woman, who was a little taller than her mates, had long flat breasts and broader hips. Her ears were small and pointed and were flattened against the side of her skull, and her nose was knife-sharp and angled downwards. Glittering canine teeth in her lower jaw were visible between her narrow lips.

It was her eyes that astonished Sara most of all, for they were vivid golden yellow with vertical narrow black pupils, and they were angled at an extraordinary degree. She was at least ten feet tall and in spite of her powerful and forbidding appearance, she was savagely beautiful.

They're ogres!

'Sa´parkiso´.'

Valu's voice was rolling and sonorous, echoing like the sounds of whales or the call of wolves.

'Valu?'

'Sa'parkiso'.' Valu spoke more softly this time, bending down from her great height and flexing at her waist so that she could look Sara directly in the eyes. Sara felt her cool breath on her face, and smelled water and peat moss. 'Come.'

'Where?'

'Under.' Sara's fear was instant and obvious because Valu reached out with her long, three-fingered hands, which she placed on the young woman's shoulders.

'Don' be afrai', Sa'parkiso'.' As soon as she had said this, Valu lifted Sara from the rocks, turned and strode rapidly into deep water. Then, without any warning whatsoever, she clapped her hand firmly over Sara's mouth and nose and slid beneath the cold grey surface of the lake.

A plume of black smoke from the shattered helicopter continued to boil into the sky. The second helicopter circled three times over the promontory where they had last seen the woman, then it abandoned the hunt and veered away towards the wreckage of its companion. Armed men and German shepherd dogs continued to quarter the hillside, but there was nothing more to find.

But as the first of the three motor dinghies approached the promontory, the gleaming figure sitting inside raised its hand and the pilot cut the motor. The lumen cast its head back and forth, as though trying to detect a scent, but failed to predict the explosion of water from below that tossed the boat in the air and sent the creature and the three marines accompanying it, plunging into the bitterly cold lake.

Urrin and Waa ignored the men, leaving them to flounder and haul themselves to shore, or to drown according to whatever their fate should be. The lumen of the Mawdrik, they seized by its arms and dragged it deep under water, swimming powerfully with undulations of their flexible bodies and webbed feet. The creature twisted and struggled in their grip but it was powerless to break free, and its captors were entirely within their element.

There, at the bottom of the lake, Urrin and Waa tore the lumen to pieces with swift ferocity, ripping apart its glassy luminous flesh, twisting its head off and pulling at its torso until it burst and the glowing contents spurted out and coagulated in syrupy loops and ribbons in the silt. This done, they turned and vanished into the cold darkness where the lake bottom plunged away to unknown and mysterious depths.

Meanwhile, on the gravel beach at the far end of the lake, the Mawdrik had arrived in greater numbers. There were ten of them, standing without movement at the edge of the water like a row of gypsum statues, the cold wavelets lapping at their feet as they stared into the distance. At their backs a man waited impassively, his face set like stone, his eyes devoid of expression.

The Colonel knew exactly what was about to happen. As he himself was no stranger to the taking of life, so his turn had come in the grim and inevitable cycle. Kill and kill and kill, that was the way of the universe; not the mystical pacifist nonsense of the Jellies and their worthless belief in the intrinsic value of life. The advantage was won by might alone. And if the Mawdrik were to carry this fight on at the expense of those who had failed them... so be it. It would be victory to the powerful, as it was meant to be.

One of them turned, looking past the Colonel but scorching him with its bottomless black stare, nevertheless. Seen close to, in daylight, it looked almost delicate but the fragile glassy appearance of its translucent skin and the faint swirl and pulse of the luminous contents were an illusion.

'You disappoint us, Colonel. No matter. We will continue this hunt elsewhere and without your services. I would like to say that it has been pleasant working with you, but...'

It looked straight at him.

A short time later, the lakeside had been abandoned and what remained of the Colonel had already drifted to the weedy bottom of the shallow bay, to be nibbled by small fish and crustaceans. In the deeper water off the tip of the promontory, other remains were twitching and stirring. Pieces of glittering skin and fibre began to writhe and curl, questing through the swirling weeds and looping through the ooze like phosphorescent worms as they searched for other fragments. The viscous contents of the lumen also sent out questing rivulets that branched in all directions to locate its larger parts, flowing into the base of the head and pulling this towards the reforming torso and limbs.

Within a matter of minutes, the process was complete. The creature lay in the silt for a moment, then it sat up and got to its feet. It started to walk without haste towards the shore, not needing to breathe and impervious to the extreme cold of the lake bottom.

Soon it had ascended from the muddy deeps and was into clearer water with a stony substrate. It emerged, walked to the shore where three others of its kind were waiting, and there it looked itself over, delicately flicking a fragment of waterweed from its chest.

'That was a distasteful experience,' it said. 'More so because she has eluded us.'

'That surely is of no concern at present,' said another. 'I am confident that you will find her and she will give us what we require.'

'In the meantime,' said a third, 'is it not time to awaken the grass men? They have slept for long enough and I crave their presence.'

'We concur,' said the first. 'You will attend to it.'

'Then I am pleased,' said the last to speak, 'for it has finally begun.'

Without further hesitation, the Mawdrik rose vertically into the sky as one, turning northwards before soaring effortlessly into the clouds. The lake and the mountains were empty again, left to the hissing of wind in the heather and the unremitting slap of wavelets on the barren shore. A single raven floated overhead, riding the wind on its powerful wings. It soared over the water to the place where Sara and Valu had disappeared, where it circled and croaked harshly before speeding away towards the high crags.

It might have been heralding the coming of stranger and darker times.

Part Two: Transition

1. North-West England: Transition

She was suffocating. The frigid water had paralyzed her so completely that she could not even attempt to struggle. Valu's hand was clamped as hard as iron over her mouth, and the other arm was folded tightly around her, inextricably securing her against the massive chest.

Sara was dimly aware of the powerful thrusts of Valu's torso as she swam almost vertically downwards, but the icy cold was penetrating her mind as well as her body and she knew that she was going to lose consciousness very soon.

Then, incredibly, they were arrowing upwards and she felt the rush of fresh air as they burst through the surface. Valu released her and she rolled on to her side, overcome by a wave of agony, her knees clenched up against her chest as she gasped and retched. It took her some while to pump oxygen into her depleted system but when the cramps that were wracking her body finally subsided, she managed to drag herself into a sitting position.

She was soaking and numb, but there was a suggestion of warmth in the air that was beginning to seep into her traumatised flesh. As her sight adjusted to the dim surroundings, she saw that she was in the centre of a large oval chamber with rough walls of rock. The light was emanating from glistening pale sheets and streaks that covered the walls, and Sara imagined that they were some kind of subterranean phosphorescent fungus.

Valu was squatting a short distance away by the edge of a pool of black water. Sara could see little of the ogress, apart from the wild mane of hair that hung almost to the floor, and the vivid yellow eyes that were fixed on her.

'Sa' pakinso'. Good?'

'Y-yes. Thank you, Valu.'

Valu stood up. 'Go now. You res' soon.'

Sara got to her feet, her legs shaking from the cold, but the ambient warmth was gradually restoring her senses and equilibrium. Opposite the pool through which they had entered the cave, a passage mouth opened into a regular, smooth walled tunnel. Valu led the way, walking with a rolling gait and making absolutely no sound despite her size and her enormous webbed feet. The passage was barely illuminated by the luminous fungus but Sara could see that it had been constructed with precision because the walls, ceiling, and floor were completely regular in height and width and the space was more than adequate to accommodate Valu.

The floor was mirror smooth and descended straight as a die, at an angle of a little over twenty degrees from the horizontal. It was not comfortable walking and after ten minutes or so, Sara's ankles were throbbing painfully.

Wherever they were going, it was deep. Sara's watch was not waterproof and it had not survived the icy immersion, so she unfastened it from her cold-swollen wrist and threw it away. However, she guessed that by the time Valu stopped, they had been walking at a steady pace for at least thirty minutes.

Valu looked back at Sara for the first time since they had left the cave. She was pointing ahead, to where the passage narrowed and began to curve gently to the left.

'Go.'

Sara was profoundly afraid. It was not because she doubted Valu's integrity, or the inevitability of what she was doing. *It's because when I go on alone, I know that everything is going to change forever.*

'What is this place, Valu?'

'The way.'

'To where?'

Valu did not answer. Instead, she slowly came to her and bent down, her incredibly flexible body once again bringing her face to face with Sara. Then, Valu kissed her on the cheek with her cold lips.

'Luck, Sa´parkinso´. Now go.'

With this, she straightened up and retreated along the tunnel for a dozen paces before turning to watch, silent and still. Sara began to move, the cool sensation of Valu's lips remaining on her skin. The passage began curving to the left, and Sara looked back while she still could. She could feel tears welling in her eyes but she could see Valu watching her. And as she looked, Sara could just make out the ghost of a smile on the dramatic and beautiful face of the ogress.

I can't give in. Not yet. She walked on. The passage was growing narrow, the ceiling started to drop and the way was twisting tighter like the coils of a snail shell.

It's like the universe. The notion came to her from nowhere. *It curves in on itself. To the left.*

It was true. In a way that transcended her understanding, the passage seemed to be imploding and taking her outside of the normal scheme of things, and Sara had the strangest notion that she was about to meet herself coming in the opposite direction. The glowing fungus had been replaced by an ambient lambency that had neither source nor direction and Sara began to feel mildly euphoric. Her earlier anxieties were gone and instead, her thoughts began to slow down. Then they were separating and drifting away into an odd but pleasant irrelevance.

She walked on. Her feet were dancing on air, and she was moving through light. The walls of the passage were losing their integrity, and Sara began to understand that nothing really mattered in this place. Just as her thoughts had done, all sense of time and place were falling away from her and Sara decided that she may as well simply lie down and close her eyes and stop thinking altogether for a while. It was so very peaceful here…

Sara drifted, not knowing if she was awake or asleep. When she decided to open her eyes, she saw stars. There were thousands of them, brighter and closer than she had ever seen them before. She rolled to one side. There were stars there too. She turned right over, apparently suspended in a tissue of substance infinitely fine but utterly resilient. There were stars there, as well. She was suspended in the cosmos, far from everywhere, and it was the most wonderful sensation that she had ever known.

She closed her eyes again, and memories from the distant past began returning to her. There were unexpected recollections of her parents, things she had chosen not to think about for years. Her mother was in Paris living with her lover, she knew that much, but now there was no anger or resentment that she had abandoned Sara as a little girl and given her up to the confused indifference of her father. Sara hoped that she had found true happiness for the first time in her troubled life.

Strange, but she could remember her mother's stories about the desert, and fairies, and magical worlds. Her father... she did not know, but for the first time in longer than she could remember, she actually cared. Sara hoped that he was happy, or at peace. Her anger towards him did not matter now. Sara sent him tranquillity and forgiveness, and moved on.

She thought about Terk. She did not know if he was alive or not but she sent her thanks out into the ether. And to Valu, as well. And for the man who had given his life in order to set her on this unknown path. After this, she went to sleep and did not think or dream about anything.

When Sara woke again, it was into clarity and instant awareness. She was lying on her back, looking up at the stars as before but now, she had a better understanding of where she might be. As she stood up and looked about her, the dawning implications of where that was were truly staggering.

She was entirely surrounded by star-filled space. It was above and below her, on all sides, everywhere. The circular floor on which she stood was translucent and yielded slightly to the touch when she bent down and probed her finger into it. It was maybe thirty yards across and as she walked to the edge, awestruck by what she was seeing, she realized that she was inside a transparent sphere. As she approached it, she could see her reflection staring incredulously back.

She put out her hand. The globe had a similar texture to that of the floor. It gave slightly yet was hard at the same time and warm to the touch: something, her new insight told her, that existed in a state between matter and energy. As she traced the patterns of the stars with her eyes, Sara became aware that it was in fact, a globe within a globe, and that the outer layer was faintly and transiently opalescent. Not only this, but in the space between were floating dozens of tiny glassy spheres, no bigger than her thumbnail.

Not knowing what else to do, she walked back to the centre and sat down. She could make no sense of how it was possible to be here, or how it had happened.

They first made their presence known with a momentary distortion of the starry heavens. Sara was immediately alert. As she watched, the stars appeared to change colour at two points directly overhead, but as she concentrated she realized that they were in fact inside the outer globe. More and more lights winked on, outlining two vaguely circular forms and tracing complex webbed patterns. Slowly, they revealed the shapes of two enormous discs, with expanded rippling margins like the wings of a manta ray.

Then, they began to turn in unison and as they completely reversed their position, Sara was bathed in their fire. They were enormous, each at least twenty feet across, and they had an intricate and fascinating structure like that of an exotic passion flower. Beneath the constantly rippling mantle were twelve oval structures like petals, above a corona of shimmering filaments and at the centre there was a convex structure like an umbrella with five spokes, each of which ended in a horned appendage.

They were alive with movement. Geometric and purely organic shapes in all imaginable colours flowed across every part of them, continually melting into each other, combining and reforming, as if the creatures were experimenting with the fundamental nature of light and structure.

One of them drifted closer and stopped just short of the inner globe where it flushed all over with a radiant display of green and gold. Something was happening at the apex of one of the horned structures, which was sinking in upon itself. Then it expanded and stretched to create an oval orifice resembling a mouth.

Then, it spoke. 'Hello, Sara.'

Sara was far too surprised to reply. They were incredible enough already, without this.

'Let me introduce myself. I am Amini Atrobar Volk, and this is my companion, Rishtini Craxo Volk. We are here to answer a few of your questions, and to introduce you to somebody.'

'What is this thing? Did you make it?'

'Yes, we did' said Amini. 'It is a meeting place for people from all places, a place of rest where they can enjoy each other's company and discuss whatever is on their minds. It is also a place of transit, as you will see. Are you comfortable, Sara?'

Sara nodded. She had never felt more relaxed in her life.

'I'm glad.' A purple ripple coursed along the margin of Amini's mantle, and Sara had the curious but vivid impression that it was smiling.

'How is the North of England these days?'

Sara was astonished. 'Uh - wet, and cold. It's February.'

'We visited the region once,' said Amini, 'in November, when it was very different. But that is not a story for now.'

Sara did not know how to respond. 'Forgive my impoliteness,' continued Amini. 'You have the disadvantage of knowing far less about us than we do about you. I hope I can redress this imbalance.'

'So do I!' said Sara. 'This is all so impossible.'

'I know, that is how everything must seem. So much has happened to you in a short time. We were not prepared for the speed of events but now that, as you might say, "the ball is in motion", we must make amends as best we can.

'Let me start by telling you about ourselves. We are Volk. We travel and sing, we learn and take delight in what the galaxies have to teach us. As you can see, our ancestry is rather different to your own. Also, we offer help to others when it is asked for, and sometimes we make it known that help is available when it is not requested.'

As it spoke, it revolved slowly, the colours surging and shifting and a new mouth continually reforming at the point closest to Sara.

'You're - what? Aliens? Angels? Extraterrestrials?'

Now Amini was laughing out loud, but not unkindly. 'It is true that our world is not yours. But in the cosmos there is more that unites us than separates us, more shared traits than not.'

'What about ogres and goblins, or whatever they call themselves? Where do they fit in?'

'On many worlds, including your own, evolution has progressed along more than one path, and these paths have converged many times. You will meet others who can tell you more about this. It is enough to say for the moment that the same life force runs through all of us and this is what draws us all together. So perhaps the true aliens are those of any race who choose to separate themselves in order to pursue a course exclusive to themselves.'

'The Mawdrik.'

'Ah, the Mawdrik,' said Amini. 'They might be considered a good example of what we are speaking of.' The Volk revolved a quarter turn, and reformed its mouth in another of the horned appendages.

'What are they?' asked Sara, her confidence and curiosity growing.

'The Mawdrik, as you have experienced them, are beings that have evolved on many different worlds although they have a common ancestry and they are linked by a common nature and purpose.'

'But are they even alive? I mean, the way I understand life? Like us? And what do you mean by their purpose?'

'They are alive, but the balance between matter and energy that created the Mawdrik differs from that of many other types of life including that of your own planet Earth. This is why they are not prone to the same infirmities and ageing processes as the plants and animals of your home world, Sara. Although they can eat and reproduce and they are not completely indestructible, their energy primarily sustains them. As for their purpose, it is to become greater than they are. They are not content with themselves.'

'Is that why are they so dangerous, because they want what they haven't got?' *Like my soul...* 'I hate the word "evil", it's so open to misuse, but when one of them looked at me, I felt as if it was taking me apart from inside. It just felt so *wrong*.'

'Evil is indeed a very subjective word, as you have rightly pointed out,' agreed Amini. 'To give you an example, when we first became aware of your world we were astonished and delighted by the human capacity for love and creativity and the appreciation of beauty. At the same time, we were horrified as never before by the capacity of those same humans to deny one another the most fundamental freedoms that are revered among all sentient beings – the right to think and believe what one will as long as it does not compromise the freedoms of others, the right to love whom one wishes, the right to be free of domination and fear. These were difficult issues for us, and we debated long and hard before we finally decided to establish contact with your world. We had only experienced this kind of doubt once before during all our long history of exploration.'

'It sounds as though the Mawdrik and humans have something in common.'

'The Mawdrik are rather different. To use another of your popular sayings, they march to a different drumbeat. I feel some reluctance in saying this to you, Sara, but on your world the Mawdrik regard you in a similar way to that in which your species views and treats many other creatures. They use you not because they are vastly superior in intellect, nor because you lack the capacity for physical and mental sensation and are therefore inferior beings in their opinion. They use you simply because they can, because they possess raw power, and raw power in the hands of those who impose no restrictions on its use is always a problematical issue.'

It was Rishtini who spoke next. 'But, Sara, you are very different to them. You have been able to manifest an ability that they seek for themselves, because it might lead them to what they are looking for.'

'And what's that? What do they want?'

Rishtini did not reply.

'Sara, we do not know,' said Amini.

Sara was astonished. If these Volk - these *superbeings* - did not know...?

'But in that case, why is all of this happening. It doesn't make sense!' She got up and walked to the far side of the globe, staring into the star-filled vastness as she tried to create some form of order out of what she was hearing.

'Then tell me,' she said when she returned to face the Volk, 'if you don't know why the Mawdrik are after me then why am I here? What am I supposed to do?'

'I must qualify what I said,' Amini responded tranquilly. 'When I say that we do not know the nature and essence of what the Mawdrik are seeking, we speak the truth. We cannot say otherwise. What we do know is that they are searching for a function that they believe will give them a great advantage over manifest life as a whole, and will thus give them the means to exalt their status and multiply their power considerably.

'In this belief, they are mistaken. The Mawdrik have forgotten that they are part of something greater than themselves. But that which they seek does exist, and as I have said already, they believe that you are the key to finding it. If it is found, however, it has the potential to unleash such chaos and opposition that even what is unknowable will be irrevocably altered. For the first time in our history, we are afraid. It is because you have woken up, Sara. That is why we are afraid. '

Sara could think of no words to respond to Amini´s disturbing premonition. Instead, she walked the perimeter of the globe, trying to formulate the other questions that were growing in her mind.

When she returned to stand before the Volk, she voiced her greatest concern.

'This ability that I have. Am I really the only one?'

'There is one other,' said Amini, 'but we are unaware of his motivations and the Mawdrik will not approach him. Whether he will make his position clear or not remains to be seen. He is currently an ambiguity.'

'But this place,' she persisted, indicating the globe, 'can't you use it to get to other worlds? I got here from Earth, didn't I?'

'It is true that there are doorways that make it possible to travel instantly through space,' said Rishtini. 'Many of these pathways converge here, where we constructed this globe. Your ability is very different. You have travelled to other dimensions that are parallel to and yet separate from this universe.'

'But as for being on your own,' continued Amini, 'that is not entirely the case. You have come here to meet somebody. He too possesses a unique ability. We and many others believe that together, you may be able to gain insight into that which is approaching.'

'He? Who?'

'His name is Karmel. Maestro Karmel Tragawlty. He is one of the most gifted composers it has been our privilege to meet.'

Karmel. It sounded like a mountain, not a musician. *Why do I have to meet a composer?* Sara was beginning to feel more bemused than ever. Amini hung above her, its filamentous corona radiating pulses and rings of calming turquoise and Sara became aware of a sense of reintegration, as though all the thoughts and experiences of the last days were beginning to unify and in so doing, were offering her an altered perspective and a new strength to face, at the very least, the challenges of the immediate future.

She also felt pangs of guilt for her impulsive reaction to Amini's admission that it did not know the precise nature of whatever it was that the Mawdrik were seeking.

'Amini,' she began tentatively, 'can you tell me anything about this Karmel?' She moved closer to the Volk, gaining in confidence. 'Is he like me? Is he human or something else?'

'He is Kiklaydan,' said Amini. 'In many ways, including in their superficial physiognomy and their emotional sensibilities, the Kiklayda are similar to your species, although their evolutionary history is very different. The bipedal design is a recurrent theme that has manifested itself many times throughout this and other galaxies.'

Sara thought she understood. However, she was rather more certain that Amini was smiling as it continued to speak. 'In other words, the Kiklayda are impulsive, reserved, creative, inhibited, uncertain, passionate, hopeful and despairing. Very much like humans.'

'There are other similarities,' said Rishtini. 'Humanity and the Kiklayda are the only species to have evolved a predominantly theistic and exclusive belief structure. All others, including ourselves, ascribe to a universalist and all-inclusive philosophy.'

Its rippling mantle changed colour, darkening as it took on dusky shades of purple and olive green.

'Yours are also the only peoples with a recent history of warfare. It is possible that the greater the need is to believe in something outside oneself, the greater the need to assert one's own idea of what that might be. Hence, the greater the predisposition towards conflict in order to assert one's differences rather than rejoicing in that which binds everyone together. We have often debated this matter.'

Sara wondered about this seemingly damning assessment of her species but detected no suggestion of superiority in the words of the Volk, nor any hint that she was being patronized - simply a calm and benevolent interest and a willingness to share their knowledge with her.

'Do they look different to us?'

'To a certain extent,' said Amini. 'The Kiklayda have a partially crystalline structure, and they are able to alter the colour of their epidermis according to certain physiological and emotional requirements. They also possess a unique ability to attune themselves with various cosmic functions, but we feel it is only respectful to let Karmel explain this to you himself, in his own time and in his own way. We believe that this will be critical to your evolving relationship.'

'Is he here now?'

'We brought him with us.'

'And... how much does he know? I mean, about me? About this task, whatever it is?'

'Karmel has known since childhood that his destiny would lie beyond Kiklayda. His unique abilities are partially responsible for his unsurpassed brilliance as a musician. He knows your name and where you come from. The Kiklayda have been aware of Earth for many years and Karmel has had the opportunity to study your languages and culture, and in particular, your music.'

'I wish I'd known about myself,' she said. 'Maybe I could have been ready.'

'Perhaps you did know,' said Amini softly. 'Sometimes, it is not easy to interpret the signs that life puts in our way.'

Sara shook her head slowly, but not in denial. 'There's so much. Just so much! We knew nothing about what was out here.' *And Terk, Valu, the Mawdrik.* Even her own world had become a mystery to her.

Amini radiated calm. 'In some ways, Karmel is similar. Although his people's knowledge of what lies beyond their own world is rather greater than yours, I must tell you a little more about him. He doubts himself. He lacks faith in his ability, and circumstances have left him wounded inside. It is our hope that, with your help, he can discover a purpose and a way to heal.'

'Okay. Okay.' Sara lifted her shoulders, sighed. 'I don't really understand. Or rather, I don't understand at *all*. But what's going to happen now? We're not staying here, are we?'

'Karmel has already chosen a place where you can be safe for a while, and where you can seek direction.'

Saying this, Amini and Rishtini began to lift away from the inner globe. 'It is time. We cannot stay, although we would like to speak with you for longer. One more thing … the Ship would very much like to meet you. Is this acceptable?'

'I've no idea. I suppose so.' In fact, she did not have a clue what Amini was talking about. How could a *ship* meet her?

The Volk were beginning to fade. 'Goodbye for now, Sara,' said Amini. 'It is not our intention to abandon you to an unknown fate, but we cannot involve ourselves in what you must do next. This is something beyond our present understanding.'

With that, they were gone, but in their place a strange object was descending against the starry backdrop. It looked like a giant golden starfish with three limbs, the tips of which were coiled tightly. It was revolving slowly and as it approached the globe, one limb unwound, penetrating the outer and inner globes and extending itself towards her.

As it did so, it fluidly transformed into a shining likeness of a human arm. The hand was outstretched, the palm open, and Sara knew that it was perfectly safe to reach out and take hold of it. It was warm and soft, with a faint pulse at the wrist, just as it would have if it had been constructed of real human tissue. It tightened, then let go and retracted, reforming into the heavily textured golden surface of the ship.

Where it retreated, a thin pencil of light was inscribing itself from the floor to a point some way above her head. It began to widen until a bright rectangle had opened up. Through it, a figure was advancing, a slender and urbane figure dressed in an elegant pale suit.

He stepped into the globe, and the doorway sealed itself behind him. Sara looked at him curiously; he looked at her with his head awkwardly tilted to one side, the fingers of one hand poised on his chest and his narrow hairless brows drawn uncertainly together.

She moved closer on an impulse with one hand extended to touch his arm but he suddenly shrunk back.

'Don't, please. We - I prefer not to be touched.'

'Sorry,' said Sara, stepping back hastily. Instead, she studied him. He was a whole head taller than her, and very slender. As the Volk had said, he was more or less humanoid although his waist was almost as narrow as his long neck and he appeared to have an excessive number of fingers.

His face was narrow, small-nosed and small-eared, and his rounded cranium was completely bald, with two slight ridges running front to back from just above his shallow brows. His mouth was wide and looked as though it could be expressive, although at present it was set in a narrow, tense line. He had oval eyes of a luminous and misty shade of violet, with no pupils.

However, it was the colour and texture of his skin that Sara initially found most surprising. It was a pale greenish blue and it sparkled whenever he moved, as if covered with a million tiny diamonds.

Sara did not easily give in to embarrassment, but his awkward silence was making her feel uncomfortable.

'No, no,' he said, stooping slightly as if trying to avoid an invisible slap. 'It's me who should be sorry. The Kiklayda are not a tactile people. It's my fault. I should have told you. My fault. You're Sara, I suppose?'

While it was clearly not the product of human vocal chords and had an oddly metallic quality, Karmel's speech was clear and cultured, his English perfect in almost every respect.

'Yes, for my sins.' Sara kept her distance, not certain of exactly how close might be construed as inappropriate. 'And you are Karmel?'

'That's me - for my sins.' He smiled and his skin tone began shifting towards the blue end of the spectrum. 'I'm sorry - again. You don't have to keep so far away from me. It's just...'

'Don't worry,' said Sara. 'I have a lot to learn.'

'And so do I,' admitted Karmel. He walked to the centre of the globe, his gait elegant and light-footed. He was dressed in a simple but exquisitely cut suit of pale material that would not have looked out of place on a Milan catwalk. Other than this, he wore what looked like a money belt around his waist and nothing else, no adornments or jewellery of any kind. *But then*, thought Sara, *if your skin is made of diamonds, you don't really need to wear jewels.*

'Listen,' he said, turning to face her, a little of the green returning to his complexion. 'I'd love to stay here and chat for a while, but the Volk are going to open another doorway for us and it's best we leave all the awkward questions until later.'

'Where are we going?'

Karmel grimaced. 'Somewhere where nobody recognizes me, thank the gods. Are you ready? It should be opening just about - now!'

Another hair's breadth of light was rising from the floor but this time, when it opened, it revealed something that to Sara was rather familiar. It was a narrow passage that curved to the left.

'I've been here before,' she said, easing her backpack so that it rested more comfortably. Karmel looked at her askance. When he frowned, it etched a single vertical crease on his forehead.

'Here? Before? I don't understand.'

'I mean somewhere like this tunnel. It's how I got here.'

Karmel shrugged. 'Come on, then,' he said, and led the way inside with Sara close behind and trying not to speculate as to what or where their unknown destination might be.

2. North Atlantic: February

The dark ocean was restless. As far as any eye could see, shuddering angles of water heaved and peaked and broke apart, shedding plumes of dull white foam under a heavy and oppressive sky. Only on the far western horizon did a band of yellow storm light alleviate the troubled seascape, and even this was fading rapidly.

The wind was force eight and rising. All of the shipping in the area had long since moved south, out of the way of the vast depression that was scouring the empty quarters that lay south west of Iceland. No seabirds remained, no fulmars or petrels riding the gale in hardy defiance of the elements. It seemed that life had all but abandoned the northern ocean to the final ravages of winter.

Almost. But then, those who had gathered here did not conform to the conventional laws and limitations of life and were seemingly unaffected by the elements. The Mawdrik had come here in their hundreds from across the world to this remote place and were gathered in a wide circle high above the angry sea. Neither the force of the gale nor the churning waves made the least impression on them. They faced inwards, unmoving and unaffected as their lengthy debate ran on from one hour to the next.

A male was talking. Although his tone was relaxed, his voice easily penetrated the endless thunder of the waves and raging wind and could easily be heard by the other lumen.

'And so we come to this. Although recent events might be regarded as an irritation, they will be to our advantage. We will continue the hunt beyond this world, and we will utilize the many tools at our disposal. She has gone, and we have dispensed with the human trinity as planned.'

'The three have been removed?' another questioned from the far side of the circle. 'I have come from Nunavut. News, as you know, is hard come by there.'

'And I, from Aotearoa,' said another.

'And I, from Ussuriland,' said a third. 'Tell us when this was accomplished.'

'Our brethren in Rome dealt with Cardinal Benaducci three days ago,' said the first to speak. 'At our request, they ensured that in his madness he spoke of visions of angels and demons and was heard to do so.'

'And the banker?'

'David Feinbaum was tracked to his villa in France, where he met with an unfortunate accident. This suits our purposes well. The escape of Sara Parkinson has released us from the last of our tiresome obligations. The termination of the priest and the financier have caused much gratifying unrest due to the public attention they commanded.'

'What of the soldier?'

'We attended to him personally.' The lumen permitted a hint of smugness to enter his voice.

'And Orla?' said another lumen, a female.

'We do not concern ourselves with Orla,' responded the first. 'While it is true that he has been seen in various locations, his purpose remains concealed from us.'

'Yet since the castigation,' the female persisted, 'we have continued to dismiss his purpose as merely "unknown". This is not because he poses no threat to our machinations, but rather due to our current inability to intimidate him.'

The first lumen considered her words carefully before responding in the same calm and unhurried manner. 'As we have already said, we need not trouble ourselves with Orla. He is one. You are legion.'

Another female spoke. 'And what of developments elsewhere? I have come from Washington and I am pleased to report that there has been considerable disruption along the Eastern American Seaboard. It has proved sufficient to shake the established socio-political institutions of the region and promote a certain disintegration in public order.'

The first lumen received this information impassively, along with the similar reports of other lumen from around the world, but when he continued it was with more than a suggestion of satisfaction in his icy voice.

'Since we withdrew our control, the grass men have started to feed in many locations, primarily in northern Europe, eastern Asia and as our comrade has informed us, throughout the New World. As their hunger grows, so will the utility of their particular appetites be of increasing benefit to us.'

Another male spoke. 'I and many others have grown tired of this world in recent ages. We have waited patiently and, some might say, unnecessarily, to begin our rightful ascent.'

'Not unnecessarily,' said the female who had come from Washington. 'We have learned more from these human creatures than from any others. That is why we have tolerated them for so long.'

'No,' said the male flatly. 'We have not learned from them, we have merely adapted some of their excesses to our own ends.'

The first did not reply. It seemed at first that he was preparing to take issue with this but soon the rest of the Mawdrik noticed that he had adopted an unusually attentive stance. Soon, all of them were equally alert as to the cause.

It was a measured vibration, travelling through the air and the sea from a great distance. There were seven slow pulses, then a pause before the cycle was repeated. As one, the Mawdrik turned towards the source like a radar dish homing in on an unidentified aircraft. None of them spoke, but all remained transfixed on the trajectory of the unknown pulse.

As it drew closer, the heaving seas began to dance and tremble in synchrony with the low frequency beat. Some of the Mawdrik began to rise from the circle as if to investigate the phenomenon, but the first one quickly spoke to restrain them.

'Stay, brethren. We will wait and allow this intrusion to manifest. It is unlikely that it will merit our attention.'

The pulse grew in magnitude until it filled the sea and the sky and seemed to displace both with its enormous presence. Still the Mawdrik remained motionless. In the western sky, a shadow was reaching over the curve of the sea against an acid yellow sunset. It looked like a massive shred of dark fabric that slowly twisted and turned in the air as it flowed eastwards towards them.

They held their place, even though the power of the elements had ceded to the force of the pulse and the sea was now leaping in spouts and sheets of spume. They were the Mawdrik and they gave way to nothing. They had watched the evolution of life on this world, moulding and channelling the history of mankind for thousands of years, directing the movements of the famous and infamous as though they were marionettes. When it suited their needs or merely satisfied their foibles, the Mawdrik had sown fear and awe, spreading confusion and doubt whenever it appeared that mankind was breaking free of the shackles that had been forged for it. They held the answer to a thousand unresolved mysteries, infamous crimes, miraculous manifestations and terrifying apparitions. They were the *Mawdrik*. What did they have to fear?

The shadow was closing on them. Now it drew in on itself and formed into an opaque brown ribbon of huge proportions that undulated as it swept towards the parliament of the Mawdrik. It was then that as one, they perceived a novel and disquieting possibility and, as one, directed their bottomless gaze on the object, tearing apart the molecules of the atmosphere to assault and disrupt the advancing presence.

Their offensive met with nothingness. The combined force of their searing vision vanished into the brown void and ceased to be.

Then, the outrage of their situation struck the Mawdrik like a mortifying blow of humiliation. The shape was not even on a direct trajectory with their circle. It would merely pass by them, with one part of the presence sweeping through a third part of their congregation. This was not possible. That they might not be its primary objective ... they were the *Mawdrik*!

It was upon them. It was miles wide, an impenetrable unknown that all of their extreme perception was unable to penetrate or comprehend. One vast curving plane moved through their circle, and then it had passed, speeding eastwards and twisting into a looping, dwindling plume as the seven-pulsed beat receded. A third of their number had completely vanished.

The remaining Mawdrik did not move, but a vague ripple of reaction passed from one end to the other of their broken circle. This was unknown, and what was unknowable to the Mawdrik, was consternation.

'Peace, my brethren,' said the first, sensing and responding to the shared angst. 'Our comrades will reform, as we ourselves have recently done.'

They waited. The pulse diminished, then disappeared completely as the storm reasserted itself and all light on the western horizon was extinguished as the clouds drew in. One hour, and then another. In the dead of night the moon broke through and made shattered silver patterns on the raging ocean.

The Mawdrik remained there all night as the northern Atlantic Ocean expended its fury and subsided into a troubled slumber but still the lost lumen did not return. Eventually, at first light, the first broke the silence of their vigil.

'This is troubling, although we hesitate to use such language that is not befitting of us. We will think on this.'

'And what now?' asked the female who had spoken about Orla. 'What is our course?'

'We continue as before,' replied the first. 'The grass men are hungry, are they not? Then let them feed.'

3. Southern Europe: May

The boy walked down a dry white track to the sea. Squat pines leaned away from the wind, their dark crowns whispering against the fierce blue sky and making shadow pools where the ants scurried and lizards lay among shreds of curled bark. He was sun made, browner than the branches or the hanging dead fronds of the rattling palms. Crack, crack, crack - the fronds tapped endlessly on the trunks in the hot breeze. His hair was the dry pale gold of the tufts and ridges of grass that grew along the dust banks on each side of the path. He wore faded shorts and a T-shirt with the sleeves ripped off, adults' sun glasses with mirrored lenses that he'd picked up from somewhere in the dust, and worn-out trainers that kicked lazily at the parched ground.

He came to a ruined building with fallen-down walls and crumbling white plaster and the dark-blue empty sea beyond. There was a low, spiny pomegranate tree on one side with flaming orange flowers, and, in the angle of the walls, a place where the wind brought the small dry things it didn't want anymore, and twisted red metal creaking on a frame of old wood.

The boy stopped. He looked into the corner, mouth hanging slack and swinging his hand against his hip, back and forth.

'Grass man.'

The grass man is fifteen feet tall, and comes out of the sand and the dust. He has no face and no arms. It looks like he is made of the pale dry grass that the wind carries away, if you can see him. He comes out of the sand and takes people down with him, and then the sun eats them.

In the trailing bougainvillea overhead, a mantis waited for moths. The crickets were roaring tonight, and Alfonso smoothed back his greasy black hair, scratched his bristly jowls and picked up a bottle of red wine. He poured, and curved fractions of light danced around the glass. The woman nodded in thanks and continued eating the meal laid before her on the chipped Formica table. There were other people at the tavern, eating and talking in subdued voices. Others were just sitting, listless in the stifling night air.

The woman was called Macklin. She was a stranger to this place, a foreigner. Macklin stretched her elegant calves under the table and pushed the plate of tapas away, the olives, artichoke hearts and fried rice balls. Alfonso shook his head and took the half-eaten food away.

'More wine,' he said, tilting the bottle over her glass. He knew she was half drunk already, but most of them there tonight were already far gone in their cups. It was like every night these days. There was little else to be done except to get drunk and wait.

'I'm sorry,' she said. 'The food is good. I don't want to waste it.'

'It won't be wasted,' he said in a voice made of gravel and rough tobacco. 'We eat, we drink. All night long.'

Macklin considered this, then downed the glass and asked for more. She could go nowhere now, this visitor. She had come to the end of the track, the end of her journey, and now she may as well wait in the night with the others and get drunk until the sun came up.

'Ah, damn it,' said Marco, leaning over the veranda and letting his ash fall into the thorns and the scattering of old beer bottles. 'Since they came, there is no more good living. We have to drink and smoke the cheap rubbish now.'

'Everyone loses, Marco,' muttered another in the faceless shadows of the candlelight. 'Everyone.'

There was a faint noise, like stray dogs scavenging in the maquis. A slight figure came into the muted light, unnatural in the fogged strangeness of the tavern. It was the boy, in his torn shirt and sunglasses. People stared at him, then turned away. Nobody spoke.

He walked to the bar and took some figs and dry bread, and ate quietly. Then, he went to Marco and held out his skinny brown arm, as if to give something to the man. The crickets roared louder in the dark and everybody turned away again. Except Marco. Marco, with his black eyes staring back at the boy like empty sockets as though the life had already gone out of them.

He held out his palm, rough and furrowed with the burn of ropes and nets. Into that palm that had endured for so long, the boy dropped something. It was a small silver coin with a hole in the middle. The boy stood and waited, shuffling his feet a little on the scuffed floorboards and looking who knew where behind his expensive tourists' sunglasses.

Marco nodded slightly and the boy turned away, walking off into the bushes and into the night. And Marco already looked like the mere husk of a man, and did not lift his head again.

When the grass man calls, you must go to him. To the dry desolate places where he lives. If you don't, it will be worse for you, for he will come in the heat of the day, when the sun is at its highest. He will come through your window and find you where you lie sweating and sleepless. Only he will not be quick, and you will not be the only one.

In the early morning, Macklin walked along the shore to the place where the railway terminated, the track just running off beneath the sand because nobody could be bothered to finish the work. A train would never run here now. She slipped her heels off and flexed her toes in the sand, thinking of how she was like the railway, all run out and with nothing ahead of her. She must be indoors before the sun rose but, for a time, with a half hour before the fullness of day and the thing it inevitably brought, it was almost good to see colour in the world again and feel a breeze that was close to being fresh.

The boy sat astride a pine bough that dipped like a saddle over the path, waiting as the first white rays slashed through the thorny scrub and made grasping shadows of each writhing bush. Another long shadow moved over the ground towards him and the boy turned swiftly, birdlike on his branch, and watched from behind his glasses as Marco approached. The man walked like an entranced thing, or as though his flesh had been replaced by fibres of wood, a man marionette moving through thick oil. If he saw anything at all, he did not notice the boy on his branch, but the boy saw and knew that in his knotted hand Marco still carried the small silver coin with a hole in the centre.

Give it a little while. Wait until the heat is searing and the crickets' dirge has been replaced by cicadas, and the ants are winding in black strings across the path. Wait until the sound of the breakers comes like a pressure on dead lungs, muffled by the dunes and their grass fringe.

Then he dropped to the ground, landing with a hollow thud on the path. The trainers had almost come apart, but soon he would walk again to the empty town along the coast where there were plenty of shoes to be had, just lying there for him to choose. Maybe tomorrow.

He was in no hurry. There was time to throw small brown stones lazily into the mirage that rippled across the path, and try to stamp on the quick little lizards that were always too fast for him. He saw the walls and white plaster of the old house through the scrub. There were other things drowning in the thorns – cars angled into the dusty soil as though half-driven into the ground. One had its indicator light winking orange and futile against the sun's intransigence. Nearby, the sprawled corpse of a goat slowly imploded with a roaring fervour of maggots.

The boy was oblivious to the stench. He stepped through a gap in the ruined walls and seemed to belong there, a thing of dust and sun himself, as desolate and devoid as the abandoned landscape and the monstrous task laid on him by the Mawdrik. He squatted and drew a decreasing left-handed spiral in the dust with his finger, revolving inwards until he could go no further. And at the centre appeared a small shiny thing, emerging suddenly from beneath the earth. It was a silver coin and he picked it up, put it in his pocket and went away to sleep until the night called him again.

The grass man has the day, but there is no sanctuary in the night. He always comes and he cannot be denied. The harvest grows thinner, but he will not stop until the crops are reaped and stowed.

Among the detritus left by the Army when they fled, Macklin had found a stash of batteries. Almost all of them were dead, but a handful had some vestigial power within them still and that night, Alfonso was tinkering with his old radio in the hope that somewhere, something remained.

He turned the tuning dial, again and again, to its limits and back but could find nothing except the hiss and crackle of a blank world. Then something; a brief snatch of a voice talking rapidly and earnestly. It was gone within moments, but Macklin and the others thought that it sounded like Norwegian. Scandinavia had been among the first places to go, along with most of the United Kingdom, parts of the States, China and Japan. Now they had come south. There had been rumours that southern France, the Middle East and the Iberian peninsula were still free but nothing could be confirmed, since they had finally lost contact with the capital three days ago.

'Then it's true, we are alone,' said Alfonso unnecessarily. They all knew this already but it was often on their lips. They knew that, one by one, the lights were going out and that very soon now, it would be dark everywhere and only the cruel sun would remain.

That noise again, like night scavengers, and everybody stopped drinking and fell silent. It was the same ritual, only there were fewer each night to enact it. It was the boy, come at his appointed hour, walking up the wooden steps into the tavern with his head on one side to avoid the trailing vine stems, and clenching something in his right hand. Now would come a time of limbo, an eternity of personal horror before the choice was made.

'No!' roared Alfonso like a raging bear. The boy waited impassively. 'Not tonight. You go. You tell it - tell him - that we want them back.'

Nobody moved. The breath caught in the back of Macklin's throat and was close to a sob. Alfonso stood, hunched and grizzled with his fists raised and his jowls trembling. The boy waited as though he had seen and heard nothing, then he raised his hand and removed his sunglasses. And before he turned and walked back into the night, they all saw that the boy had no eyes.

There was a cruel and lonely wind blowing in from the sea, shearing white spray from the crests of the breakers. The golden arc of the beach stretched away under the boy's sightless gaze and a shimmer of heat haze flawed the empty blue of the cloudless sky, making whirling wraiths of distortion across the sand.

When the boy spoke, his voice was dry and featureless, like the ghost of something lifeless and desiccated.

'They want them back.' The words blew away on the hot wind. Palm leaves rattled incessantly against the trunks and twisted hanging metal ground and moaned on and on without pause. Nothing changed.

Then there was alteration, a movement above the strand of tossed weed and driftwood, like another, higher tide line stretching far along the beach and into oblivion. At first it was a vague motion in the sand like the massed writhing of worms. Then the beach heaved and roiled and white things began to emerge part-by-part, turning over, sinking and re-emerging, some angled, some curved like bowls of ivory. There were spines, ribcages, mandibles, all dislocated from one another. Stark as snow against the dull gold of the beach, it was a flotsam ridge of countless thousands of human bones, brought up from below to bake and creak in the hot wind.

The grass men are everywhere, in every town and village. Orla comes first, silently watching in his shattered agony, and then the Mawdrik, to find the one they require. Here and in the north and across the sea, they are everywhere. At night they sleep, and in each place a single child seeks out those who remain and does the choosing. Just one child as empty as the bones that the grass men leave behind.

Beware the sun.

4. Hyaquat

Sara and Karmel walked through the opening. Immediately, it closed behind them, cutting them off from the starscape. It was exactly as it had been on the first occasion, a tunnel curving to the left in ever decreasing coils, only this time she did not experience quite the same curious feeling of distorted consciousness as she had on her way from the lake bottom.

They emerged into the middle of a tangle of untended hibiscus and bougainvillea where shafts of greenish light angled through the foliage. There were other plants that were rather less familiar to Sara: ferny saplings with polished silver trunks, leafless climbers with furry stems and bowl-shaped flowers the size of teacups, and flabby translucent rosettes of succulent foliage pressed to the soil.

As soon as they were out in the open, the shining doorway vanished and Karmel gestured for her to stop. She almost bumped into him.

'One thing you need to remember before we book in,' he cautioned. 'Try not to gawp at anything. Try to look as though you've been here before. It's been a while since the last approved migration from Earth and that's been plenty of time for the novelty to wear off.'

'Book in?' Sara said, uncomprehending.

'Yes, of course,' responded Karmel. 'Where did you think we were going to stay? We have hotel reservations.'

They emerged from the shrubbery and onto an immaculate lawn of curly pink grass. They were at the bottom of a large sloping garden of winding paths, fountains and subtropical flowerbeds. Several Kiklayda were strolling along the paths, each one of them as tall and elegant as Karmel and dressed in similarly elegant clothing. A solitary individual was sitting on a bench with his legs crossed, reading from what appeared to be a newspaper, printed on material as fine as a spider's web, which gently wafted in the air before him.

The garden sloped up to a broad patio and an enormous, gleaming white building that sparkled like the skin of the Kiklayda. It was shaped rather like a traditional jelly mould, encrusted with tiers of semi-circular balconies and with four elaborate towers like Chinese pagodas at its apex. The sky above was a delicate shade of lime green, speckled with trails of small fluffy clouds.

'Where are we?'

'Welcome to the Hyaquat Regency, as human guests like to call it.' Karmel spoke in a clipped manner. He was wearing a tight smile and appeared to be nervous.

'That's not what I meant,' said Sara, half under her breath.

'I know,' said Karmel shortly. 'We're on a world called Hyaquat. To be exact, we're in its capital city, Yazoon. Let's check in and while I make a few calls you can read the tourist brochures.' He walked off across the rose-coloured lawn that crunched underfoot and emitted a spicy aroma reminiscent of nutmeg.

'Oh.' He stopped and Sara almost ran into him again. 'I'm sorry. This is your first new planet, isn't it?'

'Ahh … yes.' Sara looked at him quizzically, smoothing strands of hair from her damp forehead where they had attached themselves in the muggy warmth. 'Until a couple of hours ago, I had no idea that extraterrestrial life even existed. It's not something I've spent much of my life wondering about.'

'I forgot,' said Karmel. He looked so contrite that Sara suppressed the irritation she had been starting to feel towards him. 'Things haven't been good for me recently. My personal life, that kind of trivial nonsense … I get preoccupied… And now this. I promise I will thaw out a little once we have settled in; then later we'll go and eat and maybe we can both start to get our heads around what's going on.'

I do hope so! thought Sara. There were questions and more questions brimming in her experientially overloaded head and she was feeling almost effervescent, caught as she was between euphoria and incomprehension. *I'm on another planet! Another planet!*

They entered the grand foyer of the hotel. The enormous concourse before them had a polished floor of golden tiles and rose a hundred yards to a vaulted ceiling of domed skylights patterned with violet and turquoise glass, through which Sara could see the fantastic pagodas soaring into the sky. There were Kiklayda everywhere, gliding elegantly by or standing around and passing the time of day in their mysterious language.

There were also people, human people! Sara was amazed to see a number of predominantly middle aged and elderly couples, some by themselves, others with the Kiklayda and chatting to them in English. Most were dressed as if for a Mediterranean beach holiday, in brightly coloured tops, shorts and sandals and wearing baseball caps or sunshades.

Karmel and Sara approached an enormous service counter. It encircled the base of a pillar that rose in the centre of the floor and branched off in multiple ramifications, like a strangely geometric tree. The Kiklayda behind the desk rose from his swivel chair and made a fluid gesture with his elongated hands from his forehead to his chest. Karmel did likewise.

They spoke for some moments in Kiklaydan, then a pinpoint of light rose from behind the desk and twirled three times in the air before vanishing into Karmel's forehead.

'What the heck was *that*?' asked Sara.

'The key to our rooms, of course,' replied Karmel offhandedly.

'And he was the receptionist, I guess?'

Karmel made a noise in the back of his throat that sounded very much like a tut. 'Yes, *she* was the receptionist. Now, mind yourself. The lift's here.'

Sara barely had time to jump aside as one of the slender branches of the pillar swept down towards them. It bifurcated into two flattened paddles, one of which wrapped around Karmel's waist where he was standing calmly. The other groped about for a moment before it located Sara, then the two of them were lifted swiftly into the air and deposited on a high walkway before their feet had grown accustomed to the sensation of being off the ground.

The lift had let them down them directly outside their rooms. Another limb emerged from the curving wall above the arched doorway, scanned Karmel's forehead and vanished back into the fabric of the wall without trace as the featureless door faded into translucence, and they walked inside.

Karmel stepped back, allowing Sara a few moments to enjoy the splendour of their lodgings. If this was typical Kiklayda design, then the

Kiklayda clearly did not like straight lines, for only the floor was flat, if at a slight angle. Everything else was a medley of curves and arches, from the furniture that flowed out of the flooring as an integral part of the room, to the walls with their indents and alcoves that radiated soft light, and were lined with silky cushions. Sara guessed that they were in part of the jelly mould because the ceiling was transparent and domed like the hotel foyer. Several short passages led off to what presumably were the sleeping areas, and directly opposite the entrance, mullioned glass doors stood wide, opening on to a balcony and letting in a flood of bright green-gold sunlight.

'This is incredible,' she said when she regained her voice.

Karmel beamed. It was the happiest, the most relaxed that she had seen him. 'I do like these rooms. I'd hoped they were free. Go and enjoy the view while I perform my ablutions, then you'll find some interesting reading material on the table over there. And don't fall over the edge,' he called over his shoulder as he disappeared down one of the corridors.

She stepped outside. The balcony faced what she believed to be south, over a fabulous city whose broad avenues sloped towards a wide, half circle bay with a beach of pink sand and a turquoise ocean.

The hotel was located in the upper district of Yazoon and had one of the best views in the city. Most of the buildings were constructed in the same extravagant style. The roads fanned out from a point not far below the Hyaquat Regency, and the main avenue ran shorewards from a plaza in front of the hotel gardens. It was wider than a motorway and lined with the most enormous trees that Sara had ever seen. They must have been taller than giant redwoods and they resembled colossal pine trees or cedars of Lebanon, but the upper surface of each tier of branches was aflame with a scarlet mist.

She could see many people, both Kiklaydan and human, strolling along the wide sidewalks or turning off to visit what appeared to be open-air cafes and shops. There was little traffic on the road, but she did see a number of extraordinary and elegant carriages pass by. These seemed to consist of a fragile glassy framework without wheels, which glided along drawn by odd things like spiralling luminescent globes with spines that bent slightly where they touched the surface of the road.

Towards the beach, the avenues widened into airy esplanades bordered by lush parks, before giving on to a beachside promenade lined with tall fan palms and busy with people. The beach itself was thronged with recliners and parasols, and the unhurried surf broke in wavelets on the sand. In the middle distance, a spine of towering islands angled away into the distance like a row of colossal shark's teeth, their western faces reflecting the light of the pale green sun in a lime-tinted sky streaked with rows of almost spherical white clouds.

It's a holiday resort, she realised. *A holiday resort on another planet...*

It must have been twenty minutes or more before she was able to draw herself away from the phenomenal view. She was ravenously hungry, and realized with surprise that she had not eaten since she'd shared that bacon sandwich with Terk.

Thank goodness! On the table, somebody - presumably room service - had put several transparent bowls of what she hoped were not some kind of alien pot-pourri. Sara threw herself onto the deep, shallow couch that was presumably designed for Kiklaydan proportions, but as she settled herself into its luscious folds, it moulded itself exactly to her dimensions and requirements.

Fortunately, the bowls did contain savoury snacks rather than air freshener, and Sara continued eating avidly as she picked up a large brochure written in English, and began to read.

The Kiklayda had discovered Hyaquat many centuries previously, but it was not until a hundred and fifty years ago that the present colony was established. This coincided with a period of political and social instability on the Kiklaydan home world that led to the decline of many age-old customs in favour of new and frequently radical ideas. A group of traditionalists, eager to preserve what they could of the old and elegant ways, requested permission to establish a colony on Hyaquat. In the interest of social harmony, this permission was duly granted, with the proviso that the colonists should have no further contact whatsoever with home world. In other words, they were entirely on their own.

Despite early expectations, the Hyaquat colony thrived, thanks in part to the generous quota of scientists and engineers among the migrants. Hyaquat was a large planet, approximately three times the size of Earth, although nearly nine tenths of the surface was covered with ocean. Except at the poles, planetary mean temperatures were stable year round with a maximum summer high of thirty-five degrees centigrade and winter lows holding well above freezing.

The Kiklayda, ever economical and respectful in matters of land use, chose to occupy only a small corner of the biggest continent where they established several elegant cities. These became centres of art, culture and easy living while the rest of the planet was rigorously protected as a pristine reserve for the unique indigenous biodiversity.

Traditionally a space-faring people, it was not long before the Hyaquat colony forged economic and cultural links with a number of other races and, after several decades of mutually beneficial exchange, some of these were allowed to establish their own small colonies on Hyaquat. Thus it was that the Kiklayda became neighbours to the stoical and somewhat unimaginative Voul, the last surviving population of the almost extinct Kiladl and even the extremophile Dzzt, who found a perfect place to settle along the margins of one of Hyaquat's lava lakes.

Contact with humanity came about almost accidentally. The University of Hyaquat's Programme for Extraterrestrial Studies intercepted a sustained output of remarkable signals that, when deciphered and reassembled, proved to be an eclectic selection of radio and television broadcasts dating as far back as Earth's Second World War. Discreet contact was made possible through the benign intervention of the mysterious Volk, who already had dealings with Earth, and after another decade of covert relationships, several thousand humans were invited to migrate to Hyaquat. More than any other race, the humans interacted and integrated with the Kiklayda so successfully that many chose to live in Kiklaydan districts and to participate actively in local cultural activities, including theatre and musical concerts to which they contributed their own rich legacy.

Half an hour's reading and several empty bowls of food later, Sara had finished the first part of "An Introduction To Hyaquat", which - so a brief glance at the back cover informed her - was also available in Japanese, Spanish, German, French, Hindi and Portuguese.

She heard movement in what she guessed was the bathroom, then a sound as though a thousand tiny shards of glass had simultaneously fallen to the ground followed by another noise like a quick burst of compressed air. Shortly after this, Karmel emerged barefoot and wearing a diaphanous bathing robe. His skin shimmered with vigour and the light it reflected danced around him like a halo. He seemed to be in altogether better spirits.

'We're self-cleaning', he explained, 'It's our skin. The crystals. We can shed them at will, although it takes a little concentration, and that's why we need such a mineral-rich diet.'

Sara had half risen from her comfortable place, but Karmel waved his hand and said, 'Please, don't get - '

Mud. Freezing, bitter mud. Sara was lodged in thick, cloying mud up to her shoulders. She could not move her arms, or turn her body. Even the scream in her throat was compressed to nothing by the cold and the compacting force of…

Mud. Billions upon billions of cubic kilometres of mud. *This entire world is nothing but mud. Dead, cold mud.* She managed to twist her neck, looking frantically up and around but there was nothing else to see, only a sky that was the same colour as the mud, and the featureless desert of mud stretching away on all sides, endlessly.

Sara was back, dropping onto her knees under the weight of the mess that clung to her, and Karmel rushed to her but stopped short at the very last moment. From her feet to her shoulders, she was covered in a dripping layer of grey ooze that dripped in huge globules on to the floor.

'It's happened again,' she gasped, frantically scraping at the revolting coat of slime and choking on the sickening metallic smell it gave off.

Karmel was staring at her but it was with an expression of fascination rather than disgust. While he studied her, Sara became aware of a flutter of activity behind her. The couch was transforming itself into an instant clean-up service and had extended multiple pseudopodia that were mopping the floor and tickled her skin as they sponged and sucked the worst of the mess from her clothes and body.

Karmel was smiling curiously. 'Now, I'm starting to understand.' He moved closer and looked into Sara's eyes, frowning with concentration as if he was performing an ophthalmic examination. Close to, he smelled of cinnamon and the depths of his own eyes were awash with vortices of luminescence.

'When I met you, I had my doubts. I don't think I entirely believed that it could *really* be you. But now… Everything has changed.'

'Tell me about it,' Sara retorted, without any attempt at restraint. She threw her arms open, looking at her mud-stained sleeves. 'So I didn't live up to your expectations? Well that's just fine with me. Because I didn't *ask* to! I didn't want any part of this! I just want to go home and be *nobody*!'

She picked a cushion up and threw it as hard as she could against the nearest wall.

'Go on,' she raged, 'spout me some more of your cosmic nonsense and see if I care? People have *died* for me and I have absolutely no idea why. You tell me why. *You tell me!*'

Sara stomped away to the balcony and took a deep breath. This not only diffused her anger but also dampened her lightning fury, and after a moment she slowly turned round.

Karmel had not moved, but his skin had turned ivory pale and he looked aghast. His lower lip was trembling. This was more human and more touching than Sara had been prepared for.

'I'm sorry,' she said contritely. She remained where she was, wanting to reassure him but fully aware that she did not know how to. 'I shouldn't have lost my temper.'

His face was angled away from her, but she could see its angles, the soft shadows around his brows and the vertical line of intense worry etched on his high forehead.

'We are so alike, Sara Parkinson,' he said, so quietly that she could barely hear him. 'We're both lost in this flow of destiny. I don't want to be here either. I am terrified. Can't you see? I have no choice.'

He glanced at her sharply and in that quick look, she felt all his pain and resentment coalesce, and then it departed.

'It's forgotten,' he said briskly. 'Although I would like to hear about your experience when you're ready. Let's go and eat. We could have dinner in the hotel but you'll see more of the city if we go out.'

Sara went to her room to shower and change. The bedroom was a perfect hemisphere and was completely empty but as soon as she entered, furniture began to emerge from the floor; an enormous bed with satiny sheets and duvet, a bedside cabinet and a dressing table, complete with a vase full of exotic orchid-like blooms. As a final surprise, the mattress convulsed and regurgitated a white blouse, a pair of jeans, underwear and slip-on shoes, all of which were exactly the right size for her.

The walk to the beach was a joy and a revelation. Hyaquat's green sun went down with a plummeting abruptness, but enough light remained for Sara to appreciate the magnificence of Yazoon's Grand Avenue. From the sidewalk she could look back and see just how magnificent the Hyaquat Regency really was, especially now that it was illuminated by slowly shifting spotlights that picked out its glistening dome and spires against the deep green twilight.

The Avenue itself was alive with pedestrians and carriages and lined with elegant lamp posts whose muted pink lights were winking on, one by one. Most of the people were Kiklaydan and it soon became obvious that many of them knew Karmel well, because they had to stop and greet passers-by on at least seventeen occasions before they arrived at their destination. It seemed that the urbane Kiklayda were an impeccably polite race and time and again, they greeted her with the same hand and head gesture that she had first seen in the hotel.

As Karmel chatted with his acquaintances in Kiklaydan she turned and watched the traffic or stared up at the trees and breathed in the scented dusk. The trees were almost beyond belief. As they approached the first of them, Sara noticed that the trunk was in fact hollow and constructed of a fine web of smooth shining fibres that intermeshed so insubstantially that she was amazed that they had the capacity to keep such a large structure erect.

'They aren't really trees at all,' explained Karmel, seeing her staring up into their lofty crowns. 'They aren't even plants or animals as you would understand them.'

He gestured at one of the lower branches and when she looked closer, Sara noticed that it branched in a regular manner, similar to that of some types of coral. What appeared at a distance to be clusters of brilliant red flowers, were in fact dense upright brushes of waxy fingers that emitted a continual faint hissing noise.

'They're filter feeders,' said Karmel as they continued on their way. 'The red structures extract microbes and other nutrients from the air.'

'If they're not trees, how do you grow them?'

'You don't,' said Karmel. 'You have to persuade them to appear where you want them to. It's quite a skill - very well paid, too, seeing as how fire pines are so much in demand. Fortunately they like to make straight lines. Sometimes if they feel neglected, they retreat underground and sulk and that makes such an awful mess of the pavements.'

They had reached the promenade. It was lined on both sides with tall Washingtonia palms from Earth, and on the beach side, beneath the trees, were shops and restaurants. Some were single storey Kiklaydan structures built from the ubiquitous white icing sugar material, others were more like typical Mediterranean beach restaurants, right down to the seaward terraces that were covered with awnings or trained vines.

'What are you in the mood for?' asked Karmel solicitously. 'Italian? Chinese? Or would you prefer Mexican or Spanish? I'm afraid we can't do Kiklaydan. I can eat almost anything but your digestion couldn't cope with our cuisine. Too much silica and cyanide.'

'*Cyanide?*' Sara looked horrified. Karmel's eyes narrowed and he gave her a withering look.

'It's one of our most important nutrients. Well, what's it to be?'

Sara was not keen on pasta and she found most Chinese food too bland and slimy. 'Spanish, I guess.'

'That's a very good choice. My favourite fish restaurant on Hyaquat happens to be not far from here.'

El Pescaíto was a simply-constructed but comfortable restaurant with a candle-lit dining room adorned with a miscellany of lobster pots, fishing nets and other maritime paraphernalia hanging from the sea green walls. It had an open plan kitchen from which emanated a medley of enticing aromas, and the dining-room opened on to a terrace shaded by grapevines and other climbing plants. The tide was well up, and a gentle scurf of waves swished over the sand, making brief sparkles of phosphorescence and catching the light of Hyaquat's two green moons, currently half full and riding high in the western skies.

Several Kiklayda were already enjoying their dinner, and as the swarthily handsome waiter brought the starters, they bid Sara and Karmel a cheerful '¡Que aproveche!'

'What are these?' asked Sara, picking up one of the crispy fried pancakes and turning it round in her fingers.

'Tortillitas de Camarón. They're made with chickpea flour and sweet little shrimps, grown here on Hyaquat. Aren't they delicious?'

At last, they were able to sit and relax. Karmel was friendly with the proprietor, whose name was Juan Diego, and much to Sara's surprise, he chatted to him in fluent Castellano when he brought them a bottle of finest Albariño in an ice bucket. As he poured, Karmel appeared to hesitate before putting a hand over his glass. Looking apologetic, he helped himself instead to water from the jug on the table.

They talked about the incident earlier that afternoon, when Sara had been so unceremoniously transported to the lifeless mud world.

'It must have been an alternative Hyaquat,' she protested in the face of Karmel's doubts. 'I know the geography was very different. Okay, to be honest, there wasn't *any* geography. There was just mud. When it happened before, on Earth, I went to a place I knew. Both times. It was somewhere I used to go with Karl, near the beach. Only, it wasn't. It was nothing like it.'

Sara put her tortilla down and took a sip of wine, turning the glass around in her fingers as she remembered.

'I'd rather not talk about the second time. But the first time… oh, Karmel, it was absolutely amazing. I guess it was my world as it should be. So beautiful and peaceful. There was no pollution, no violence. Do you understand what that would mean for us, to live in a world like that?'

'I believe so,' he said thoughtfully. 'The history of my world has many parallels with that of Earth, although we have dispensed with our erstwhile passion for warfare, thank the gods. You're aware of my interest in your people already. Sometimes, I feel that your kind and mine are far too close for comfort. We laugh about the same things, we express our likes and dislikes in a similar way, sometimes to the worst extremes of personal despair.'

He paused for a moment.

'And we cry. We cry. Never mind. We must try and discover why we have been singled out by the universe to journey down such a different path.'

Sara drew the bottle of Albariño from the ice bucket and refilled her glass. 'You still haven't told me what you can do.'

'Oh, *that*. I suppose it is time I told you all about it.' There was a note of reluctance in his voice.

Just then, the waiter arrived with their main course. He was dark and handsome and he smiled appreciatively at Sara as he put the enormous dish before them.

Karmel served the oven-baked Gallo Pedro, which lay steaming on a bed of potatoes and green peppers in olive oil and came with a basket of crusty bread and a fresh green salad. The appearance of the fish coincided with the arrival of another party of diners. Sara had not paid much attention to the table nearest the terrace when they arrived, and she hadn't thought to question the absence of chairs or the objects resembling butcher's hooks that hung from the ceiling above it. The diners, though, were another matter entirely.

There were five of them and they looked like nothing so much as giant hunchbacked crabs made out of stainless steel. They each had twenty legs, a row of five red eyes, two bunches of writhing tentacles where Sara thought their mouths should be, and rows of hooks and flanges running from their small flat heads along the ridge of their segmented backs.

Sara dropped her fork on the floor and stared at them in wonder and bewilderment. For their size and unlikely appearance they were surprisingly agile, tiptoeing on the ends of their pointed limbs with rapid, mincing steps. They arranged themselves around the table and hoisted their silvery bodies up so that they were hanging from the ceiling by their shining metallic hooks. Each of them deftly picked up a menu with their agile tendrils and began to flick through the pages, grunting and clattering among themselves.

'Sara,' Karmel hissed at her, 'it's rude to stare.'

'What are they?' she said, ignoring his disapproval.

'It's the Morrisons,' he said. 'A nice family. You'd get on well with them.'

'The *Morrisons*?'

'Yes. They're Kiladl. It's fashionable among the Kiladl to adopt human names.' He raised his voice. 'Hello, Cynthia.'

Mrs Morrison made a belching sound in reply, and waved one of her tentacle clusters at Karmel.

'But why the hooks?'

'That's easily answered,' said Karmel. 'The Kiladl evolved as cave dwellers. They slept by hanging from the ceiling to avoid predators, and I suppose that old habits die hard. They're not the brightest stars in the sky, though. About two hundred years ago, they decided to do a little restructuring on their planet but the force of the nuclear detonations sent it plummeting into one of their suns. The only survivors were the Embassy staff on Voul and Kiklayda.'

As Karmel related the sorry tale of how the few remaining Kiladl were translocated to Hyaquat with the help of the Volk, the Morrisons' paella arrived and they gleefully helped themselves straight from the dish while guzzling iced sangria through straws from tall glasses that were adorned with paper umbrellas.

Karmel rolled his eyes. 'If the Kiladl were holidaying on earth, they'd be avid consumers of what I believe you refer to as the cheap package deal.'

El Pescaíto was getting busy, and the restaurant was filled with the hum and chatter of several human and non-human languages. Sara had finished her third glass of wine and had finally managed to take the edge off her ravenous hunger.

'You were saying, before the Morrisons arrived?'

'None of this is easy to explain,' said Karmel, lowering his voice in spite of the background chatter. 'The Kiklayda are a somewhat reserved people in many aspects, if not in others. What I am going to tell you is deeply personal and sacred to our species and we don't share the knowledge lightly, even though I have tried to prepare myself for this moment. Also, you are not Kiklaydan so it will lose many of the nuances associated - '

'Just tell me please, Karmel.'

He raised his eyes and hands to heaven. 'All right. You asked. We resonate.'

'You... resonate?'

'Yes, we - hmm...' Karmel sighed. 'We resonate. You know that we are, in part, crystalline. It's not only our skins. Our skeletal structure, our cerebrum, even our gonads contain complex crystalline silicates, carbonates and a few other compounds that you would not be familiar with. We evolved in a mineral-rich environment and rather than excreting these substances, our distant ancestors developed a metabolism that is able to synthesise things that you mammals never could. Do you follow me? If this is too much for you, you have only to - '

'I have been rescued by ogres and I've teleported to parallel universes in the last few days,' Sara said with an ironic smile. 'I think I can cope with this.'

Karmel ignored the humour in her words. Now that he had begun, he seemed eager to continue without interruption.

'Most life on Kiklayda is sensitive to a wide spectrum of emissions, light and energy waves and the like. It's part of our shared legacy. Some species use tiny sub-cellular structures for long distance communication, or to detect prey in muddy rivers or in the dark.

'With my kind, however, these abilities have become largely obsolete. It's rather like your poor eyesight and sense of smell. They have become of secondary importance, in favour of your bigger brains.'

'Or like the appendix,' Sara mused, unaware of whether or not Karmel knew what an appendix was.

'You could say that. Oh, it's true that most Kiklayda can detect powerful emotions over a reasonable distance and some highly trained personnel have been able to enhance their abilities to search for missing people, even to look for rare minerals. Even if our former senses are impaired, we still retain an awareness of the resonating cosmos. Everything is permeated by vibration, you see. It's all around us, if only we can attune ourselves to it, and the absolute limit of human scientific awareness is only the bare frontier of the unseen universe.'

'That all makes sense to me,' said Sara. 'We'd be arrogant if we thought we knew it all.' Recent events had, after all, completely overturned her preconceived ideas and torn open the door that had been firmly closed on her horizons. 'You're different, though.'

'Yes, I'm different. I'm very different,' he said in a matter-of-fact way. 'Do not ask me why, because I might as well ask you how you are able to visit other worlds.'

'Just tell me, Karmel,' she interjected, fearing that he was attempting to stall again. 'If we are both so special, I don't think it is going to come as such an enormous surprise to me, is it?'

She wanted to reach across the table and touch his arm but she knew this was not possible. Instead, she smiled and relaxed back in her chair, inviting him to continue.

'I am aware. I sense things, not just the emotions of other Kiklayda. I can feel places and events, far away.'

'How far?'

'On the other side of the galaxy. I can detect the resonance of other species and other worlds. I can feel their pulse from thousands of light years away... and sometimes it's terrifying beyond your darkest nightmares...'

He was talking quickly, and eventually he had to stop to take breath. Sara did not utter a word. The comfortable ambience of the restaurant, the good food, even their bizarre dining neighbours, were slipping into the background, and her every sense was attuned to what Karmel was saying.

'You know I write ditties?'

'I know that you are the most famous living composer in the galaxy, if that's what you mean.'

Karmel blushed purple. 'Well... if you like, yes. I write music. It's not nearly that simple though. I use my abilities to write music that does more than stir emotions and conjure up images. My music can inspire a collective empathy in races from a hundred planets. I can access the darkest yearnings of the Voul. I can make the Dzzt laugh - and the Dzzt never knew *how* to laugh before they heard my music. Can you explain that?'

'I wouldn't even try to,' she said. 'Go on.'

'There's more. I can synchronise my personal resonance with worlds I have never seen, if I have sufficient native raw material to use. It doesn't have to be an object. Even a sound will do.'

Karmel took a deep breath before continuing. 'You can travel to other dimensions but you can't yet control your ability. I can penetrate the heart of another world by choice, but not physically. Now, tell me if you believe it is mere chance that has brought us together?'

The Morrisons were enjoying their dessert, snipping pieces of melon and kiwi fruit into segments with the retractable pincers they usually kept hidden among their tentacles. The waiter was sitting on a stool at the bar, strumming on a guitar and favouring Sara with glances, but she was oblivious to his attention.

The implications of Karmel's revelations had not struck her with a revelatory thunderclap, but rather had blossomed with a sharp and pure clarity like a sunrise on a clear morning. Their abilities were similar, that was beyond question. The possibilities that lay within them scarcely needed stating. Maybe Karmel could find a way to focus her ability so that she could go where and when she wanted and, perhaps, by combining forces, the resulting synergy would enable them to travel together.

But there were so many variables at play here. Until now, two of the places she had been to were obvious parallels of her own world. The third had presumably been an alternative Hyaquat. Would she also be able to go to places that existed within their current reality?

Then again, Amini Atrobar had spoken about "another", whose motives were unknown even to the mighty Volk. If somebody else shared this ability, were the Mawdrik also pursuing him?

Karmel made a delicate sound in his throat. 'Do you want these?'

He was indicating the substantial bones of the John Dory. Roused from her thoughts, Sara looked at the remains of the meal with disgust.

'I presume not.' He picked up the spine with his eight-fingered hand and crunched it with relish. He had not appeared so profoundly alien to her as he did now. A tremble of apprehension made her look away, out to sea, where the bizarre sight of the two green moons of Hyaquat slipping below the horizon did nothing to quench her unease.

Karmel wiped his fingers and mouth on a serviette and took a gulp from his glass of water.

'Sorry,' he said. 'The bones are a dietary requirement.' Somehow, regardless of his elongated neck, pointed face, diamond studded skin and swirling violet eyes, Sara found his words and these simple actions reassuring.

'We are both frightened, Sara. I certainly am, more than you could imagine. You see me as something strange and exotic. Believe me when I tell you that is far from how I see myself.'

'Can you show me this ability?'

'Tomorrow,' he said. 'We will go somewhere quiet, where we are not likely to be disturbed. I have an uneasy feeling about Hyaquat. I hope not, but maybe *that* will be your first proof.'

'Do we have to leave?' She'd hoped to have more time and space to adjust.

'Sooner rather than later, I'm afraid. The problem we have is that I've absolutely no idea where we are going, let alone how to get there.'

5. Hyaquat

Hyaquat's green sun rose early the next morning, but as the planetary day was a little under thirty Earth hours long, Sara woke feeling wonderfully rested and relaxed. The bed had responded to her slightest movements, continually altering itself to provide exactly the right kind of support and comfort.

She woke only once during the night, nudged into consciousness by an indistinct dream about forbidding lifeless landscapes and broken planets that soon faded from memory. There was noise and movement coming from the lounge and it took her a while to realize that it was Karmel, walking up and down and muttering to himself in Kiklaydan. Troubled by the sound, Sara lay still and tense for some time, but the bed sent tendrils of warmth to massage her body and she was unable to resist the slide back into sleep.

Once Sara had showered and dressed, Karmel suggested that they take breakfast at a café near the beach before catching a cable car to the alpine meadows in the high mountains inland from Yazoon.

'We can walk and talk, or we can just find somewhere nice to sit and admire the view if you prefer. Maybe the fresh air and scenery will inspire us. Also, I'd like you to listen to something.' He sounded cheerful and breezy, but Sara had already noticed the dull purple patches under his eyes and the slight tic that was making his nose twitch. They were clearly the results of an unsettled night.

The café was situated on a boardwalk that ran parallel to the promenade, not far from the El Pescaíto restaurant where they had eaten the night before. There was a fine view of the sparkling ocean, and the sheer-sided islands that marched over the horizon scintillated in the morning sunshine.

Once they had chosen a table, Karmel pointed out the three Voul who were taking a morning dip a few hundred yards from the beach. They bore a close resemblance to the Volk and they were drifting languidly in the air just above the waves, undulating their vast circular mantles and dipping trunk-like appendages into the water to spray themselves in the manner of elephants. Unlike the Volk, however, they were coloured a uniform and dingy brown.

'They are the dullest company,' said Karmel. 'All they ever talk about is work. Work and their infernally complicated banking system. Do you know, they even have cybernetic implants in their brains so they can keep up to date with their stock market? Dull doesn't begin to describe them.'

Sara watched the Voul performing their ablutions, but her mind was drifting to other matters. 'Tell me what you know about the Mawdrik. Are we safe from them here?'

Karmel linked his impressive rows of fingers and leaned his chin on them. 'Nowhere is entirely safe from them. Plus, now that you have slipped from their clutches they will be furious. They'll be scouring the galaxy for you. Probably, for *us*. I tried to leave no signs when I left Kiklayda but the Mawdrik, well…'

'Why here?' asked Sara. 'Why did you choose Hyaquat if it's not safe?'

Karmel did not reply immediately. 'You ask a lot of questions, Miss Parkinson.'

'I'm sorry,' she said. 'I've always been like this, since I was a child. Sometimes I don't know when to stop.'

'Don't apologise,' Karmel said hastily. 'It wasn't a criticism. In any case, how else are we going to find solutions to our dilemma if we don't ask questions?'

'Well then, tell me - why Hyaquat?'

'Because this is one of the few places within fifty light years in every direction where nobody really knows who I am. Here I am Karmel Tragawlty, manufacturer of the finest quality formal wear, a single wealthy businessman with a liking for beach holidays and that's all.'

'I guess that answers one of my questions,' she said. 'But I need to know how much of a threat the Mawdrik are to us. Have you ever seen them?'

Karmel turned a pale shade of greyish green. 'No, I haven't, but I'm terrified of them nonetheless. Luckily, they find us distasteful for some reason. They've never been present on our home world though that isn't to say they don't have the power to affect us.'

'What do you mean, affect you?'

Karmel was by now a sickly greyish cream. His twitch had become more pronounced. 'There are worse things waiting out there than physical destruction, Sara.'

Sara was not daunted. She needed to know more, even if it was detrimental to Karmel's Kiklaydan sensitivities.

'And the Volk? Are the Volk in danger?'

Fortunately, mention of the Volk seemed to have a restorative effect on both his mood and his colour. 'Not from the Mawdrik. That is their overriding fault - their supreme arrogance. They think they're completely invulnerable, but they aren't. The major threat from them is that when they are thwarted they hit out like spoiled children with too much power. I worry about what they might be doing on Earth.'

He leaned closer. 'I'll tell you a story I heard from a friend in the diplomatic service on Kiklayda. It was something that happened perhaps two or three thousand years ago; he wasn't entirely sure of the facts as the records were highly classified and some of the details had been altered. Apparently, the Mawdrik were once so incensed by the invulnerability of the Volk that they declared war on them. It was a thousand Mawdrik against only *three* Volk. For one whole year the Mawdrik focused all their combined hatred on the Volk, but they just floated there in deep space, chatting and philosophizing as if they were entirely unaware of the horde that was trying to take them apart. Since then, the Mawdrik have steered clear of the Volk - as I said, humiliation doesn't rest easily with them.'

The door of the café opened and a middle-aged human couple walked in. As soon as they saw Karmel, they both smiled broadly and the woman waved to them.

Karmel got up. 'Sara, I'd like you to meet a couple of old friends, Eileen and Ted Howkins.'

The Howkins were perhaps in their late fifties. Eileen was of comfortable proportions, her skin had seen too much sun, and her faded perm was falling out. Ted was portly, with white hair and beard and, Sara would soon discover, he usually let his wife do most of the talking.

Eileen had the brightest, bluest eyes and they twinkled in her brown face as she took hold of Sara's hand and patted it.

'It's so lovely to meet you! Karmel's told us *all* about you but he didn't tell us how pretty you are.' Sara glanced at Karmel, who was shaking his head discreetly in denial.

She drew breath to reply but the opportunity was already lost.

'Let's send the men off to get some coffees. They go back years, Karmel and my Ted. They'll have a lot of catching up to do.'

As Karmel and Ted Howkins went off to order, Sara tried again.

'So...' She was not entirely sure what to say, and Eileen once again leapt into the breach.

'Oh yes, dear, we've been here - um, let me think - ten years now. Delightful, isn't it? Where are we from? Bournemouth, originally. Yes, my parents were contacted by the Volk back in the thirties as part of their time tr - ah, I shouldn't really say anything about that, should I? But my dear old mum let me into the secret, so I knew about the other races when I was a child and of course we had the *souvenirs*... we always had to be careful when our friends came to play, just in case they saw something they shouldn't. Then when Hyaquat started accepting immigrants from Earth, we were near the top of the list ... all that palaver with the paperwork ... faking our disappearances and the rest, I'm sure you know the kind of thing. And here we are, happy as Larry! And what about you, dear?'

'I'm ...'

'Of course you are. How are you finding the weather? Oh look, it's the Morrisons! Morning, Cynthia, Bill.'

The family of crablike Kiladl were scuttling up the beach from where they had been making sandcastles. Bill Morrison's segmented back was covered with sand, the result of his offspring's attempts to bury him.

The waitress brought coffee and croissants, and Eileen slipped off her flip-flops and stretched her legs under the table. She was wearing baggy purple harem pants and a sleeveless top with a floral motif.

'I know who he is.'

Sara froze. Eileen Howkins was looking out to sea, smiling innocuously and watching the Voul who were currently engaged in an odd ritual that consisted of linking their tentacles, pulsating rhythmically and revolving slowly like an outlandish merry-go-round.

'Oh, come now, did you really think that the great Karmel Tragawlty could remain incognito?' Her tone remained light, and now she turned to look at Sara. She was still smiling but her eyes were hard and bright.

'Don't worry, dear.' She leaned over the table and squeezed Sara's cold hand. 'If there are any sides at all in this affair, we're on yours.'

'I don't understand.'

'I wouldn't expect you to. That's what I said to your little friend Terk the last time I saw him.'

'You know about *that*? But how?'

Eileen continued smiling vacantly, looking every part the innocent holidaymaker breakfasting on the beach. 'Not everybody back home is completely ignorant. This retired ex-pat image suits us well… it is true, in part, but it's also a good cover. Somebody has to keep an eye on things, especially now.'

She sipped her coffee. 'I know it's been hard for you, being thrown into this mêlée without warning, but sometimes things don't work out quite as we would like them to.'

She glanced at Karmel and Ted who were still chatting at the counter. Karmel was eating a large Danish pastry.

'Just a few words before they come back. You need to leave Hyaquat.'

'Yes, we already know that,' said Sara in a low voice. 'How soon?'

'You have maybe a day at the most, so you and Karmel need to get busy. We'll be leaving ourselves. We're needed back home, by all accounts.'

'A *day?* I thought we had longer-'

'Be quiet and listen. Listen hard, because your life depends on it and the lives of many others besides. Orla has been seen on Hyaquat.'

'Look, I don't know who or what Orla is. I've never heard that name before and I wish you would say something that makes sense.'

Eileen looked nervous, then she reached down and scratched her ankle. *She's trying to look as though nothing is wrong* realized Sara. *Hyaquat isn't safe.*

'Wherever Orla appears, things start happening. Frightening things. There's something moving in the furthest corners of the universe and he knows what it is.'

'Is it the Mawdrik?'

'No, this is something different. We've always had the Mawdrik. All the same, *they* must not find what they are looking for. You *have* to - '

Karmel and Ted were on their way back with their coffees and a plate piled high with chocolate filled croissants. The disturbing conversation was over and Sara had to mask her unease behind a bland smile and a string of pleasant and appropriate responses to the general chitchat that ensued for the next half hour. Fortunately, Karmel had a talent for making charming conversation that lacked content, an ability that was undoubtedly assisted by the non-human inscrutability of his eyes. Several times, she tried to catch his eye and saw nothing but swirling inner light and the blandest of attentive smiles, but she was starting to wonder if he knew something of her disquieting talk with Eileen.

Half an hour later, they parted from the Howkins with a promise to meet again for breakfast the following morning. Rather than catch a taxi, Karmel decided that they should walk to Upper Yazoon, where the cable car station was located. They headed in an unhurried fashion through elegant residential suburbs of wide avenues lined with fire pines that contained an eclectic medley of traditional Kiklaydan architecture, and a hotchpotch of human styles ranging from Arab to colonial American.

Above the multi-coloured sea of pagodas, spires and arches soared the almost shockingly white limestone mountains of the Hyaquat interior, rank upon rank of ascending ridges that marched with implacable determination into the green sky.

They reached what Karmel had referred to as the cable car terminal and boarded a translucent oval shuttle with a handful of humans and Kiklayda who were all dressed in very conventional hiking gear. For Sara it was a revelation - as well as a source of private amusement - to see the tall and slender Kiklayda with their glittering ultramarine skin, dressed in thick socks, walking boots and shorts and carrying hiking sticks and back packs.

The shuttle sped away silently along a single track that hung in the air like a thread of mercury, unsupported by any visible means that she could see. It curved steeply through the outlying mountains and Yazoon was soon far beneath them. Because the shuttle was transparent, Sara was able to look straight down between her feet into the billowing forests and to the coiling rivers in the valley floors, several thousand feet below.

Karmel sat in the chair behind her, pointing out sites of interest - the Japanese Buddhist monastery clinging to the side of a sheer cliff, the lenticular Kiklaydan soul house where mystics of his race communed with their five deities, the plumes of waterfalls that arched from cave mouths at such altitude that they were dispersed by the wind long before they ever reached the ground.

It was not easy to draw her eyes away from such marvels. Besides, Karmel appeared to be so relaxed that she was loath to intrude on his tranquillity. But do so, she must.

'Who is Orla?' He almost lunged at her, so quickly did he startle. His eyes darkened to a shadowy burgundy before suddenly brightening again, all in the space of a few brief moments.

'Oh, of course. Eileen.'

'That's right. But how did you know?'

'It is a charade that we play. I know that the Howkins are not simply innocent retired migrants from Bournemouth, and they know that I am not a rich clothing manufacturer with a liking for beach holidays on Hyaquat. We never talk about it openly. It´s far too risky. Though I wondered if she was going to say anything.'

'Orla?' Sara prompted him.

'What did she tell you?'

'Not much, and what she said didn't make sense. All she said was that Orla has been seen on Hyaquat.'

'I knew it,' he murmured.

'What do you mean?' The shuttle was beginning to slow down but Sara was no longer concerned with the scenery.

'Last night... I couldn't sleep. I sensed that some kind of wrongness had come to Hyaquat.'

'What did you feel?'

He looked at her, a shadow on his face that was at odds with the bright Hyaquat noon. 'Pain,' he said darkly. 'I felt pain.'

'What?'

'We'll talk about this later,' he muttered. 'We've arrived.'

The shuttle was gliding to a halt next to a rustic, wooden, Swiss mountain chalet, with sharply angled roofs and window boxes spilling over with bright flowers. To the rear, an enormous meadow of pink grass swept up to a deep rift between spine-tipped mountains. The meadow was punctuated by vast trees that resembled cypresses with weeping metallic blue branches, and the sky was even greener here and speckled with a perfect grid of evenly spaced clouds.

'It's like Heidi meets Alice in Wonderland!' she said as they disembarked.

Karmel laughed. 'Indeed.'

'How do you know these things?' she quipped. 'Karmel, you know *too much* about us!'

'Don't forget that the Kiklayda are great admirers of all things human. Also, our average life expectancy is twice that of yours. That gives us plenty of time to improve our minds.'

'That would account for your perfect English, I suppose?'

'Yes, it would. *And* my perfect Japanese, *and* Spanish, *and* Hindi...' added Karmel, with just a hint of smugness.

They were hiking away from the chalet across the vast meadow. The springy grass crunched underfoot, releasing its powerful cinnamon odour and bouncing into place again at their passing. The air was richly fragrant with the spicy aroma and the mingled perfume of a dozen strange flowers that coiled and gaped and snapped shut as they walked by. It was subtly warm, yet inexplicably refreshing at the same time, and Sara could not imagine how this could be possible.

Nevertheless, it was a steep climb away from the chalet and the thin mountain air did not make the task any easier. Halfway across the meadow, the ground levelled out a little and Karmel called a halt.

'This is as good a place as any.'

He inhaled deeply, enjoying the enervating mountain air, and then he opened one of the pockets in the small bag he always carried around his waist and rummaged around inside. Meanwhile, Sara took a look around. Above them, the edges of the meadow pulled in towards a perfectly V-shaped opening between the mountains, in which was framed a wedge of sky and a flotilla of small round clouds. Several stands of the blue firs stood off to each side and above them, vivid against the white rocks, strange creatures glided effortlessly in circles. They were fiercely scarlet and they appeared to consist of one single narrow wing, several metres across and curled up slightly at the tips, with no obvious body. They dipped and banked soundlessly, and every now and then one of them extended a sucker from its underside, attached itself to the rock face and rapidly folded itself up, origami style, into a small neat bundle.

To the west, over the almost-vanished roof of the chalet, the valley fell steeply away into forested deeps and chasms with, in the far distance, a shimmer of ocean.

Karmel was unfolding a diaphanous sheet of material that resembled fine colourless silk. It was as long as his arm span, and when he had finished opening it up, it stayed put in the air exactly as he'd placed it.

'What is it?'

'It's a banderil,' said Karmel. 'It plays music.' He was unrolling a ribbon of similar material, but much smaller.

'And what's that?'

'These are the headphones. Sit down and make yourself comfortable. I'm going for a short walk and while I'm gone I'd like you to listen to something.'

Sara made herself comfortable on the grass. A dozen scintillating creatures like six-winged beetles spiralled up from the herbage and danced around her before settling again. The air was heavy with the smell of spice, mingled with the woody sandalwood perfume of a gently pulsing bloom at her right elbow that resembled an old gramophone speaker made from blue leather.

Karmel had now taken out a wallet with multiple pockets and was coaxing fine glassy threads from it with his finger. His hand was on fire with cold flame and Sara could hear the faintest sound like the trembling of a tiny crystal chandelier in a wisp of air.

'This contains what little remains of my musical collection,' he explained. Now he was directing the four threads he'd removed, towards the banderil, and as each one separated and merged seamlessly into the fabric it flashed brightly and the banderil emitted a chiming yet oddly vocal sound.

'I had to destroy everything else when I left Kiklayda.'

He then directed the headphones towards Sara. She felt a brief, cool touch as both ends caressed her ears, then nothing.

'I want you to listen to three short pieces of music, then a longer work. The first three are a Kiladl sonata, a Voul choral work, and a Dzzt concerto. They are all masterpieces, the highest, purest expression of these races artistic achievements.'

'And what's the fourth one?'

Karmel looked at the ground. 'It's my Sixth Symphony.' He looked at Sara with darkening eyes. 'Be careful with it. Don't try to move, don't try to stand up. It's my most *human* work and it might… well, I think it will help you to understand me better.'

'What do I do with this thing?'

'Just touch the banderil once. It only needs to know your resonance.' He inclined his head, suddenly and strangely formal, and then he walked quickly away from her towards the high meadow and the mountain pass.

Sara stretched her legs out and slipped her shoes off. With the grass caressing her bare feet she looked at the banderil with trepidation before reaching out and touching it.

The Kiladl sonata was ghastly. Thankfully, she only had to endure the horrible racket for less than five minutes because it sounded like nothing so much as somebody repeatedly shaking a bucket filled with pebbles and mud.

What was all that about? By the time the hideous din came to an end with a final liquid squelch, Sara was hoping fervently that the Voul choral piece would be rather more conventionally melodious. Having watched the Voul taking their morning dip earlier that same day, however, she had her doubts.

She was right to be dubious. What ensued was ten minutes of agony. If the miasma of tortured screams and moans had been several octaves higher, they might have sounded rather like whale song, but instead they howled and creaked and groaned as if the performers were in extreme and perpetual suffering. The whole gut-wrenching performance was interspersed with metallic screeches that made Sara think of the wings of large aircraft being torn off very slowly.

Sara waited for the promised Dzzt masterpiece. When it came, her attention was wandering in search of relief, so that she almost missed it. She heard a quick buzz and crackle like the sound a large insect meeting its end in the grid of an electric fly killer, and that was all.

Was Karmel's own piece of work going to be similar or – heaven forbid – even worse? Sara dreaded having to lie to him and she was so preoccupied with this train of thought that to begin with, she did not realize what was happening.

How would she describe it afterwards? Was it merely a complexity of sound that was growing around her and within her, or was it something more? How could she explain the way in which it coursed through her and flooded her with a thrill of comprehension?

First, it came in words. *What am I, here alone and exposed, the past stripped away and the future irrelevant? I am Sara. I'm waking up for the first time. I stand alone. I'm beautiful exactly as I am. Every possibility is held within me, right here and now. I can reach out my hands and touch the universe.*

The music washed in like waves on a vast beach, crashing in silent elation around and over her in the moment of her rebirth. Now it was a fabulous sunrise that leaped up from the darkness of pre-existence to welcome Sara into being in an aurora of grand tones that spoke to her and welcomed her at the moment of her self-discovery. Without hesitation she rushed to welcome and affirm its invitation to know her true self.

Yes, oh yes! Come inside me, fill me, show me who I am. I'm awake. I am all and everywhere and joy and possibility. I am Sara!

Joy! The music leaped and cavorted with her and she let go of her last sense of limitation as she danced on starlight at the centre of a kaleidoscope vortex of rippling sounds that sprang away like living things and invited her to give chase.

She knew what she was looking for and when she saw it she plunged into the rushing channel of thundering blue sound that pierced the spiral, tobogganing away among triumphant crescendos that boomed and pounded like the fists of gods at play striking against each other. A blossoming roar of red – *lust!* – and as she gasped and caught her breath, the river carried her on, and then down and slower, slower...

... and on a slide into dusk. Sara was going deep, but she was losing momentum as if the ecstasy was leaving her like a long sigh of loss and defeat. There was *discord*, a something knotted and twisting against itself that wasn't right, away in the corner of her mind. There was sorrow and a dark slide towards a pulsing well of void that contained fear – of dying, of losing everything, of not existing. From it came a slow dull beat, and that something knotting and coiling and twisting against the fading harmony as if it were trying to warp the fundamental nature of being. Bereavement. Slowing now, coming to a stop in a place where even light could not move, on the brink of a bottomless trough of despair.

Please, no! I'm not ready for this. I cannot stay here. I am moving again, struggling against what seeks to engulf me. I'm free of it! I am carried on the wings of my destiny, onwards to something I cannot see, but it waits for all of us.

The music was racing once more, seemingly exuberant but pierced through with fear and a sharply piquant lure of danger. She was rushing at a thousand miles an hour, the sounds of possibility merging into flying arrows to keep pace with her in a frenetic race into the future.

Revelation. Knowledge. Understanding. A myriad concepts grasped at her, or burst in fire shocks as she hurtled through them and was briefly on fire with the thrill of almost *knowing*.

This could not go on! It was all coming together, every spiralling joy, every empty shadow, every burning revelation, they were all converging to form an impossible crescendo that was flinging her upwards towards the finale that waited for her and that could only be the final truth and the doorway to oblivion.

Sara never reached it. It was over. She was just as she had been, sitting on the grass. There were no high emotions, nor crying or any other outward evidence of how it had changed her, just a profound and silent inner astonishment regarding what it had revealed to her about Karmel's ability and, just as significantly, about herself.

He was returning. Apparently, he had timed his walk precisely to the length of the recordings. Sara watched him approach in silence before turning her gaze to the sky. He did not speak as he folded the banderil carefully and restored it to its pouch. When he had done so, he moved away and sat down in the grass.

'I only have one question,' she said without looking at him. 'Right at the end... you didn't finish the piece, did you? There was something that you couldn't or wouldn't include, wasn't there?'

'Yes,' he said. 'It's always the same. I see more than I should and I have no right to go there. That's for you and the others to discover when your time comes.'

'I have a confession to make,' he added after some moments. Sara turned slowly and looked at him.

'I lied about the first three pieces. I wrote them as well.'

'So that's what made the Dzzt laugh - and the Dzzt never laugh, right?'

He smiled. 'That's right.'

'And now we need to make sense of it all, and find a way to combine our abilities for who knows what purpose. I think I understand better now. What I can do is physical, spatial, whatever you want to call it. You are mind and soul. Together - there's no knowing what we might achieve. '

'That also seems to be right,' said Karmel, 'although in the same way that I had to see what you were capable of, so you needed to believe in me, too.'

His tone blunted. 'I'm sorry. I'm afraid that however much we understand already, we don't have much time left to put the pieces together. In fact, it's almost too late.'

'What do you mean?' His words sent a cold shock of premonition through her.

'First of all, you need to know about Orla. He has been appearing on many different worlds for several decades now, long enough for him to be known and feared across the galaxy.'

'What is he?'

'Nobody knows. He's a complete enigma. He appears to be enveloped in some kind of mantle of fractured light and space as though he's continually falling apart. What's more, it hurts to be near him. It doesn't seem to be a deliberate act on his part, rather some kind of unintended emanation.'

'And what does he do? Does he speak?'

'He does nothing. He vanishes as suddenly as he appears, and the only word he's ever been heard to say is what everyone assumes to be his name: Orla. It's what happens afterwards that is so disturbing.'

He drew breath. 'On the Kiklaydan colony of Tragathapna the entire population of three hundred people vanished without trace, shortly after Orla appeared to them. In what used to be Kiladl space there is a beautiful little planet called Etrin Boskadoo - it's a peaceful, pastoral world with colonists from many races. In fact, it's a little like Hyaquat but after Orla was seen there, some form of madness swept through several remote settlements. People reported seeing terrible things emerging from the ground and strange golden waves of luminosity that moved across the countryside. They said it was like a tsunami, a silent wave that leached the life from the land. People disappeared there too, although eventually the phenomena ceased. Do you see why I am afraid of what might happen here?'

Sara put her shoes back on and got to her feet.

'Orla,' she said quietly, then again, 'Orla. Who are you?'

She looked at Karmel. 'I don't know what your music did to me. It's as if I know myself better, or I've had to confront things I never wanted to face up to, and now I can move on. Does that make sense?'

'When I am composing, a part of me enters into the spirit of the piece,' he started. 'Whether that means a physical place, a theme, a racial conscience - it's different every time. So yes, that makes perfect sense. Every time I come into contact with some artefact or even a sound or scent with a powerful presence, it causes an empathic resonance within me that enables me to strengthen the link. It's like throwing a rope across a torrent; by creating that first connection, you can eventually build a bridge.'

'Wait a moment,' said Sara. 'You need something to work with, right? Any object will do?'

'If the resonance is powerful, even a scrap of paper is enough.'

Sara had already begun to rummage in her backpack. Everything that Terk had told her to bring was still there, wrapped in plastic supermarket bags. She found the postcard, crumpled and ragged from the lake water that had managed to seep through, but still more or less intact.

'Would this do?' Karmel took it carefully from her between his slender fingers and examined it. As he looked at the picture and read the printed text on the back, his skin began to sparkle.

'"Would this do" she asks me,' he said in a marvelling tone. 'Sara, a part of me is already there! This is splendid. I don't often manage to bridge the gap so quickly but this... this city is no ordinary place.'

'But we still have to find out how to do it,' she said. 'If it's even possible. I know, I shouldn't doubt. I *know* we can do it. Besides which, I'm sure that Terk made me bring this card for a reason.'

'Sara,' Karmel said, quietly but insistently.

The swift urgency in his tone was lost on her. 'Just think about it, Karmel! We could go anywhere. We could even find out how to go back to - to Endymion! I've got the flower. You'd love it there.'

'Sara,' he said, louder this time and now his warning broke into her exuberant flow of words. 'Look. Look out to sea.'

They were at such an altitude that on the far western horizon, they could see the curve of the planet. The day was calm and the evenly spaced, stationary clouds of Hyaquat dwindled into a uniform checkerboard pattern and then at last to a far and final brightness.

Except that, where the world curved away, there was a shadow, a patch of amorphous darkness at odds with the buoyant ambience and luminosity of Hyaquat. As she strained her eyes to focus on it, Sara had the strangest notion that it was not so much a physical presence as a mouth or an opening though into what, she did not care to know.

'What is it? A storm?'

'There are no storms on Hyaquat,' said Karmel. 'My eyes are much better than yours. It's moving towards us.'

'Can you… *feel* it?'

'There is nothing there to feel,' he replied. 'It is like an absence of everything. It should not be here. It shouldn't be anywhere.'

They looked at each other, Sara with a stricken expression and Karmel with inscrutably obscured eyes.

'Then it's true,' she said. 'We really don't have any time left.'

6. Granada, Spain: June

After a merciless day of peaking temperatures, dusk fell quickly over the exhausted city. The sun had decided to stop punishing the land for another day and its fierce stare was fading from the high bare flanks of the Sierra Nevada. In the western sky, a fine sliver of moon shared the sky with shrieking bands of swifts that coursed over the tiled rooftops and the square towers of churches.

Twilight brought little relief. A suffocating blanket of hot stillness was smothering the heart of Granada, and nowhere, from the plains of the Vega to Plaza Larga in the old Arab quarter of the Albayzín, was it possible to find even a moment of cool respite. For the thousands who had arrived in the city over the past weeks and had to sleep under the stars, it would be another night of discomfort. Every plaza and park was crowded with an uneasy shifting mass of people that grew daily as refugees from north and south passed through on their way to undecided destinations or swelled the encampments that were testing the resources and patience of the beleaguered authorities.

The murmur of activity was everywhere, but in one steep and narrow lane nobody was as yet looking for a corner in which to bed down for the night. Thus, there was no-one to notice the slight movement as the lip of a grimy manhole cover lifted away from the cobbles. Two grey chameleon-like hands gripped the edge of the iron disk and edged it aside, then Terk emerged from the ground and crouched next to the hole, silent and alert.

He was pale with the dust of travel, and the clothes he wore were so filthy with grime that it was almost impossible to tell what was cloth and what was skin. He listened for a minute before shifting the manhole cover back into place as noiselessly as he was able. It was true that he had a certain ability to mask his presence, but times and circumstances were making him particularly wary.

Nevertheless, he was attuned to the darkness and the nuances of its minute alterations. Small things moved in the gathering gloom and he was aware of all of them: a gecko, skittering diagonally across a white house wall, crickets churring repetitively in the weed-filled shell of a fallen-down building, the tintinnabulation of a fountain in the walled garden of a carmen.

Once he decided that the vicinity contained no immediate dangers, Terk moved off without lowering his guard but relieved in every part of his body and soul that his journey was almost over. Food, rest and the hospitality of old friends were waiting for him nearby.

Terk's strange and, at times, desperate journey had taken the better part of four weeks, mostly via familiar underground ways well known to his people. It had not gone smoothly. Since the troubles began, not only the surface world was in turmoil. Many of his people's traditional routes had vanished in rockslides or were flooded. In other places he'd come across ancient sealed tunnels that had opened up again and had given him such horrors that he immediately returned to the surface to avoid them.

His original plan was to head south through England and Wales, using underground paths when possible, or following ages-old ancient greenways and other surface trails that were still under the protection of friends. From the Pembrokeshire coast, he would descend through narrow passages to a subsea tunnel that would take him straight under the Bay of Biscay to make landfall in the north of Spain.

The first stage of his trek passed without incident. Keeping well clear of the coast, he made his secretive way through forgotten thickets and along hidden trails at the bottom of ancient hedges. He slept in badger setts and hollow trees and sustained himself on pignuts and wild carrot roots. Sometimes, he was aware of the watchers whose benevolence helped to weave an imperceptibility around him. Occasionally, he met up with others and was able to rest for an hour or two in congenial company and share the news.

In Cheshire, shortly before he was due to move west into Wales, he encountered a sister of Valu on the moonlit reedy shore of a tarn. From her, he gleaned some valuable but discouraging information. Wales was a devastated land, the towns largely deserted as people fled away from the sea and flocked into the lowlands of an erstwhile complacent and sleepy middle England.

The coasts and the uplands were now the domain of the grass men. Since their first shocking manifestation, a tide of disbelief had initially paralysed Britain before creating an upheaval of tectonic proportions in the human world. It had not only been the first wave of disappearances, nor even the horror of the altered children who had brought fear to many remote communities in the north of the country. It was also the immense unwillingness of people to challenge their assumptions about the nature of reality and fable. Terk had always been amused that, among humans, there were those who had the luxury of time to speculate about the existence or otherwise of spirits and monsters, yet were oblivious to the real nature of those with whom they shared their own world. Moreover, he was certain that most of them had no real desire to see their dreams made reality because to do so would be to confront the sheer inconvenience of what such revelations might signify. In other words, there was a great deal of security to be had in ignorance.

Terk and the ogress had sat on the soggy bank of the tarn among the bulrushes, sharing a leather flask of hard spirits, watching the shooting stars and reminiscing about times gone by. Terk was a mere seven hundred and fifty years old, but his drinking companion remembered a time before the Romans came, when men had been more attuned to the rhythms of a world unsullied by the relentless march of discovery and destruction.

They talked of the Volk, who were the oldest of them all. Their memories spanned an enormity of time and space that made the Earth and its small ways seem youthful. They could sense the flux and flow of cosmic cycles and they had foreseen the confluence of energy that heralded the onset of current events. Terk had met the Volk, long ago, and he knew from them that this cycle was like the immeasurably slow beating of the universal heart, or the ebb and flow of a tide that created and destroyed but was neither good nor bad. Only the humans and the Kiklayda saw these functions in such terms and attempted to create an ethos of blame and guilt where none existed.

All the same, even the Volk admitted that there were disquieting variables this time. The direct involvement of a human and a Kiklaydan had been unexpected, and the few centuries that they had been aware of Sara Parkinson's family line and what was growing within it were only the blinking of an eye to them. Both humanity and the Kiklayda were such raw and unformed species, both had great potential but were prone to violent contradictions and were wracked by a chronic fear of failure.

Following the advice of the ogress, Terk changed course and slipped through the heightened security at Dover then into the Channel Tunnel. In Brittany he met up with others of his kind and enjoyed several days of comfortable respite in homely subterranean surroundings. From them, he learned that the French and German Governments had collapsed and widespread riots in Paris and Berlin had caused almost a hundred fatalities as religious and political extremists clashed.

The coming of the grass men had fomented spiritual turmoil as well as material chaos. Some people saw their terrible depredations as a kind of judgment against a wicked world, while humanists pointed to the seeming randomness of their appearance and cited this as evidence against the involvement of a higher power. In the absence of any plausible response from the international scientific community and the disastrous consequences of the military intervention, no human authority was able to offer a believable explanation as to the nature of the terrible predatory force that had appeared from under the ground and was gaining in strength across the Northern Hemisphere as the summer advanced.

To compound the situation, the Mawdrik were beginning to show themselves openly, and some people were heralding them as divine messengers. As Terk sat by the hearths of the Breton elders and shared a hospitable sulphur pipe, they pondered on what it all might mean and to what extent the wrath and petulance of the Mawdrik at the loss of their quarry was going to impact on the older races of the world.

It was in Brittany that Terk had a stroke of luck, when a French banshee agreed to fly him south and across the Pyrenees. With cloud to conceal them and a high northerly wind at their backs, they made good speed and were descending over the foothills into Navarra when disaster struck.

The Mawdrik were waiting for them, and with the combined wrath of their gaze they succeeded in mortally wounding the banshee, for all her valiant attempts to evade them and counterattack with balls of corrosive fire. As she plunged a thousand feet to her death, Terk leaped from her back and was only saved when he plummeted through the decaying ceiling of a hayloft and landed in a mound of fodder. He burrowed swiftly and deep, into the ground under the old building, using his powerful hands and natural abilities to narrowly evade the searching Mawdrik.

From there on, the journey was much more difficult. He kept underground whenever possible, surfacing occasionally at night to hunt for food and try to find out what was happening. The vast interior of Spain seemed to be free of trouble, apart from the endless stream of refugees moving south by whatever means they were able to, be it on horseback, by overloaded wagon or on foot. Near Toledo he found a week-old English newspaper, and learned that the grass men were already in Italy and North Africa.

Finally, to Granada. By the time he emerged above ground in the Albayzín, he was exhausted beyond the experience of all his long years. There was just a little way to go now, although he would have to rely on his intuition to guide him the rest of the way. He kept to the dark places at the base of walls, avoiding the yellow lamps with their swirling halos of moths and midges, pausing in recesses where wispy kittens melted away through gaps in ancient doors, and beneath magenta fountains of bougainvillea that cascaded almost to street level.

Now a turn to the left, then a quick and furtive ascent up a set of shallow cobbled steps with the high pale walls and small forbidding windows of a closed convent ahead. Looking back, Terk saw the red walls and towers of the Alhambra palaces and the wooded slopes beneath them, plunging to the rank and murky trickle of water that was the River Darro. The Alhambra and the hill on which it stood were lit up with spotlights – all very different from the last time that Terk had been here, long before the advent of electric lighting in an age when even the colours of the land and the nature of the sky above were different. Then, he'd walked unseen through the fabulous halls and chambers of the Nazrid palaces in the small hours of the morning where, even in the last years of the sad king's rule, it was still adorned with brilliant fabrics and lit with a thousand lamps whose light shimmered on the intricacies of Moorish tiles and Arabic scripts, and the still warm air was heavy with the scent of myrtle and jasmine.

The air was thick with other odours now – the sickly stench of uncollected rubbish and the fetid unpleasantness of dog excrement. Terk's keen nostrils could detect the perspiring mass of people who packed the mirador nearby and he was thankful that he was heading away from the smell of overcrowding and tension.

He had arrived. The empty callejón was a neglected cul-de-sac of abandoned houses to the right, with shuttered windows or shards of dirty glass rimming empty black sockets like broken teeth. On the left was a single large house that might once have been elegant but was now in a similar state of disrepair. Some of the red roof tiles had slipped and lay broken on the cobbles and at one end of the building, an ancient store room was folding in on itself and was now little more than a tenuous framework of weathered grey beams and the vestiges of a sagging roof. The shutters had not been opened for so long that in the cracked lintel of one upper window, a small fig tree had taken root, and trailing toadflax grew through the rusting bars of the narrow balconies.

Terk pattered up the two steps of narrow red bricks and stopped in front of a wide double door of cracked wood. Above it was a round window of blue and green glass, protected by a metal grill, with an opaque white crescent moon in the centre.

He knocked twice and stepped back, knowing that many eyes would be watching him through the gaps between the shutters. For a long moment, the only presence in the night was the incessant shrilling of crickets, then one side of the door opened silently inwards. A young man looked out and grinned when he saw Terk. He was of authentic gypsy blood, dark and stocky with a mane of glossy black curls, a gold earring and a gold medallion around his neck.

'¿Qué pasa, primo?' Then, in English. 'Come in, quickly. She is waiting in the salon.'

Inside, it was another world. The floors and walls were covered with brilliantly coloured enamel tiles that formed intricate repeating designs of triangles and crescents. Recesses in the walls held flickering candles and the ceiling was spanned with connecting arches and panelled with stained wood.

Terk walked with his guide along a short corridor, through doors that swung silently inwards and gave into a large room with a huge empty fireplace, furnished with sumptuously embroidered Arab-style couches and dotted with tables inlaid with marquetry. Twenty or more people were gathered there, drinking glasses of sweet mint tea from silver teapots, talking quietly or reading books and newspapers, but as Terk and the young man entered everybody fell silent.

Some of them appeared not to be fully human. One corpulent man put down his tea and nodded gravely as they walked past. Half of his face was dark and ponderous, with a jowly, unshaven cheek and an impressive slope of shiny forehead. The other side was feline and predatory, lightly covered with a velvety softness of tawny fur, with a huge yellow eye and a small pointed ear laid flat against his skull. Two male banshees sat at one of the tables with a game of chess between them. They were lithe, muscular and as brown as polished mahogany, with large green eyes, fine sharp features and silvery wings sprouting from below their shoulder blades. From one corner, two statuesque Turkish Djinns watched them with pinprick eyes that glowed like red fireflies, entirely enveloped in white cotton robes and turbans that almost completely concealed their willowy bodies.

Terk knew them all. Some were friends, a few he remembered from the travels of his youth. The current safe house was a century old, but there had been a refuge in Granada for more than a thousand years. Terk had visited others in different countries and in times long past, each sanctuary having its own character and overseen by a different race but everybody who needed a secure place to hide, or simply somewhere to find a little relaxation and company in an often lonely and isolated existence, was welcome. Even humans had been sheltered from time to time - among them, accused witches condemned to burn in Scotland, and Cathars fleeing from torture and death in medieval France.

Whatever their past and present dealings with humanity, Terk was acutely aware that the significance of his arrival in Granada would not be universally welcomed by all who silently watched him as he approached the door on the far side of the room. In particular, he felt a palpable emanation of antipathy from the Djinn and, though he'd had benevolent dealings with their kind before, he was careful to avoid their smouldering stare.

His guide opened the door and stood aside to let Terk past. 'She is coming out of her transformation,' he whispered as if to prepare him, but Terk put a reassuring hand on the man's arm.

'Don't worry, Juan. I have seen it before.'

Inside, the atmosphere was refreshingly crisp thanks to the air-conditioning system. The room was smaller and had a more intimate and welcoming feel, and evidenced many concessions to more eclectic décor than the Moorish-themed lounge. Picasso and Dalí prints adorned the walls, and in one corner there was an enormous bookshelf, with a variegated devil's ivy plant cascading down one end and creeping along the bare brick floor. In the opposite corner, a set of half-open double doors gave way to a square courtyard edged with enormous terracotta pots containing aspidistras and ferns, and a pedestal fountain in the centre that tinkled and sparkled in the slanting quicksilver light of the half moon.

'Come on through, Terk,' said a deeply melodious and heavily accented voice. 'I'm nearly done.'

It was the voice of a very old friend, and Terk felt the aches and tiredness ebbing from his bones as he pattered across the room and pushed the door open.

María Angustias Rodríguez Acosta was relaxing in a swinging wicker garden chair, a jumble of books and magazines scattered around her feet. There was a small table with tea things and a carton of longlife milk, and a large waste paper bin on the ground close by. She was a substantially built person with an ample bosom, dark skin and a large nose, her long greying hair tied in a bun. At the moment she was dressed only in a simple cotton dress and just one sandal, on her right foot. This was because her left leg and arm were decidedly reptilian in aspect, with stretched fingers and toes and finely scaled skin as iridescently green as the wing cases of a tiger beetle. One of her eyes was black, the other yellow like a hawk's and the tip of a spiny tail dangled over the edge of the chair, twitching where it touched the floor.

'I'm sorry I can't get up yet,' she apologized. 'This won't take much longer.'

Terk went to the fountain and washed the dust from his face and hands, then slapped at his clothes to get rid of the worst of the dirt.

'I hope that's proper English tea.' Terk approached the table, sniffing dubiously at the steam wafting from the full cup that was waiting for him.

Angustias chortled, her deep husky laughter as big as she was. 'Would I dare to offer you anything else. Come, come. Pull up a chair.'

Terk did so and settled back into the cushions with a luxurious sigh, taking every sip of his tea with relish as though it were a magical elixir. Angustias continued her transformation, every now and then pulling a piece of shedding skin from her shrinking limbs and tossing it into the waste bin. She was a werewoman, a member of a diverse worldwide community of people who had the strange ability to change their forms under particular circumstances. Some were affected by increasing sunspot activity, while others were influenced by tectonic movement and certain atmospheric conditions. The archetypal "werewolf" was a surprisingly rare manifestation and many people in their altered state resembled nothing else that lived on the planet. One shy young man whom Terk knew had a particularly hard time, because when he became extremely nervous, his entire body lost its integrity and degenerated into an amoeboid and highly mobile slime - inconvenient when in polite company, but a useful aid nonetheless to gaining access into otherwise inaccessible or dangerous places.

Angustias took the form of a small but powerful green dragon, complete with very efficient wings and the ability to breathe flames. Her transformation was linked to her time of month, and she had wistfully hoped that, once she went through the change, she might be granted a reprieve from this particular aspect of her biology. It wasn't to be, however - not that changing into a dragon on a regular basis didn't have its advantages. In fact, her past exploits in the defence of her people had won her enormous respect as well as bestowing on her the rank of unofficial leader of the Granada safe house.

Finally, all was done except for her oddly coloured eyes. She screwed them up and rubbed at them hard, restoring them to their rather less dramatic appearance. 'Madre mía, it never gets any easier. But now we can talk.'

She folded her thick arms over her breasts. 'When we heard about Claudette ... I was afraid you hadn't made it either.'

'Are those her brothers out there?' He was referring to the two banshees.

'Yes, that's our François and Lionel, los pobres. They brought us the news. They said they searched for you for a whole day but there was no sign, nothing. Nada.'

'I had to go under.' Terk sighed. 'I´m sorry for their loss. She was bright and beautiful but the Mawdrik were too strong for her...'

'Ych!' Angustias pulled a face. 'They are everywhere, them and their creatures, these grass men that should never have been woken again. They should be sleeping in the darkness where they belong. Except here. There's sanctuary in the south for the moment, but for how long..?' Angustias shrugged. 'You tell me, my friend. You´ve seen what´s on its way.'

She poured herself some tea without milk and dropped a slice of lemon into the cup.

'But now, we have to think about other things, no?' She fixed him with her large dark eyes. 'Are you sure she will come? Is it certain that they know the way here?'

'I'm sure they do. Before I took her to Valu, I found the key in her flat and made sure she took it with her. She will remember it when the time comes.'

He sucked his teeth contemplatively. 'We already know what this Kiklaydan, Karmel, can do, and we know what Sara is capable of. All they need to do is find out how to put two and two together.'

'*All* they need to do. *Phff!*' Angustias flapped her arms. 'I wish I had your faith in this English woman, Terk. But I suppose we must be prepared for anything and for everything.'

Terk remembered her inclination towards scepticism from other times and merely smiled benevolently and lifted his bald, crinkled eyebrows, inviting her to continue.

'They could turn up anywhere. What if they land on top of the Cathedral or in the middle of a crowd? Granada is full of crowds these days.'

Terk scratched his lopsided chin with a blunt grey finger. 'I've noticed. We need to be watching out for them. It won't be easy, though. This is a big city.'

'On that count, I suppose you needn't worry. Our people are everywhere. We are doing what we can. Even the Djinn… the Djinn…' She faltered.

'Is there a problem with the Djinn?' Terk had only the most rudimentary understanding of these obscure and secretive desert dwellers. They kept their own council and made their own alliances, and it was unusual to see two of them here tonight.

'I'm not sure,' said Angustias, then she sighed enormously. 'Not everybody here is happy about the prospect of bringing a full human into our little family, even if it proves to be for a short time only. The Djinn are a case in hand. Recently they've isolated themselves even more from the affairs of this mad world. They have gone into the wildest parts of the eastern deserts and they are not keen to return. I know that they were among the first to sense what was coming and they blame the humans and their clandestine alliance with the Mawdrik.'

'But we need the Djinn.'

'Yes. We need the Djinn. They're among the few who can take down the Mawdrik, *and* they know how to destroy the grass men. They had dealings with them a long time ago. The problem for us is that they are so few.'

'So, we have to hope that we can retain their goodwill,' said Terk. 'How many Djinn are here?'

'Far too few. More are coming, but how many will answer our call, I don't know. What about Ivanov?'

'Ivanov didn't stay. He has gone back to his people in Baikal.'

'A pity,' said Angustias. 'The talents of a vodyanoi would have been useful. It's the *sequedad* here, the dry. It would have been too much for him. Still… I retain some of my draconic abilities once the cycle is over, and the Mawdrik don't like my fire. It reveals them for what they are. Hollow things with no soul.'

Angustias got up, walked to the fountain and passed her fingers through the dancing spout of sparkling water, before looking up into the sky with a contemplative expression. The bleached light of the waxing moon accentuated every wrinkle and blemish of her strong features. She was starting to look old, thought Terk. These difficult times were taking a toll on everyone.

'We know they are here,' she said, without taking her eyes from the moon. 'The Djinn can feel them. How long before they unleash their creatures… it's hard to say. We'll endure, as we always do, but the people… there are too many people here. They hope against hope that they are outrunning the trouble but they are wrong. Oh, but the feast will be terrible.'

'Is it only the Mawdrik? When I was with my people in Brittany I heard the strangest rumour that faerie have been seen in large numbers, moving south.'

'Ych!' Angustias grimaced. 'Bichos asquerosos! Revolting little creatures. They feed on carrion then poison you with their bite. They've always followed in the wake of the Mawdrik.'

Then she turned and looked at him tellingly. 'You know what's funny about this? The Mawdrik are afraid.'

'Tell me what you know,' he said. 'I don't think it will come as a big surprise.'

'Well, then.' She sat down by him once more. 'A few weeks ago we had word of an event of some kind in the north Atlantic. Something happened that put the Mawdrik into an unholy chaos. We heard that they were holding an enclave there to gloat over their successes but it didn't go according to plan.'

'I remember it,' said Terk. 'I was travelling and I felt the trauma in the earth,' said Terk. 'Others felt it too - changes in the air, disturbance in the water. Something came into this world that has no place here. What's more, it wasn't long before that, that *he* came.'

Angustias turned her attention to the stars again. 'An interesting choice of words, Terk. *It has no place here.* Do you mean only on this world, or everywhere?'

'I mean, no-*where* that we know of. If you ask me what I think, I reckon that a door has been opened into something that should have remained unknown. It's too easy to suspect the Mawdrik. That is what we have always done, but if they are truly afraid after what happened to them in the North, maybe I'm right. Why would they deliberately bring destruction on themselves, unless it was an accident?'

'Why, indeed.' Angustias settled her ample derriere back into the garden seat. 'Thanks to the Djinn, we know rather more about the Mawdrik than they'd have us know. Such as, they are similar in many ways to primarily physical forms of life but the balance of matter and energy within them makes them *seem* to be invulnerable to most ordinary threats. When the Djinn choose to talk about these things, they admit that there are similarities between themselves and the Mawdrik. You know the old human myths about the Djinn that say they are made of fire and smoke? In a way, they're not far wrong.'

Terk grunted contemptuously. Before his destiny had led him off along many an unexpected path, he had studied the scientific and mystical traditions of humanity and those of a number of other terrestrial and extra-terrestrial races.

'Isn't that the problem with humans? They think in pieces. When they hit on a new idea they rejoice because they believe they have found another part of the cosmic jigsaw puzzle.'

'And you think that everything they think they've discovered takes them further away from the truth?' She was smiling. It was a discussion they'd had more than once. 'You think that if they were to see something really beyond their understanding, like fat, grumpy old Angustias turning into a fat, grumpy old dragon, they wouldn't be able to cope with it?'

Terk's eyes sparkled. 'Yes, but now there is one exception. Sara Parkinson. What happened to her was enough to drive any ordinary person insane. There were things she didn't tell me about the second world she visited, but I read her thoughts. I saw the horrors she saw there.'

'Ah, Sara Parkinson,' mused Angustias. 'One part of me is looking forward to meeting her, at last. If she is even half the woman you say she is, it should be quite an experience. I'm scared too. Scared deep down in the coldest, loneliest part of my soul.'

'Because of what *he* said?'

'Yes, because of what *he* said. For as long as we have known of him he has scarcely spoken a single word. Now we have this. What are we meant to understand from it, Terk? That is why I am afraid of him, because he has finally broken his silence and it is to speak the name of this annoying English woman who apparently has the key to Pandora's box.'

Angustias laughed and slapped her ample thighs. 'Enough. You need to eat and sleep, and I need to sleep and then eat. Then tomorrow, we have to speak to the others and hope that we don't have a riot on our hands before the day is out. But there is just one more thing.' She directed a piercing glance at Terk, her dark eyes stabbing through the shadows, and when she spoke again all trace of humour had gone.

'Who *did* he appear to? You haven't told me.'

'Ah, you wily old she-dragon,' said Terk. His words were light, but there was no levity in his tone. 'As if you don't know already. It was me, of course.'

'Why you?' she mused.

'Because somehow he knows about my connection to her.'

He returned her look and added ominously, 'I tremble to think of what else he might be aware of.

7. Hyaquat

'We have to do something.'

Sara dragged her eyes away from the shadow. As far as she was able to tell, it had neither moved nor increased in size. The day was as calm and bright as ever and the clouds continued to hang in the green sky as though on a painted backdrop. Even so, she knew that something was already profoundly wrong with this world. It was not a sensation that she could define but it was there, in the ground, in the air; the murmur of something that pulsed and jarred in discord to the tranquillity of Hyaquat.

'Evidently,' said Karmel.

He had scarcely moved, and he was still holding the postcard. Every part of him that was visible had brightened to the palest of blues and his eyes were intensely and ominously purple. Sara felt a quick pang of alarm as, for an instant, she recalled the luminous creature with the bottomless eyes that had so nearly caught her during her flight to the lake.

'The dwarf gave this to you, yes?'

'If you mean Terk - '

'This city.' He cut across her protest, turning the card over and over again with a fluid movement of his many fingers. 'It has a powerful presence. It's like...' He struggled for words. 'The past and the future come together there. I don't know how else to explain what I feel, but we *have* to get there.'

He looked directly at her and Sara almost took a step backwards. The uncanny resemblance to the Mawdrik was unsettling.

'I'm going to suggest something,' he said. 'I don't want to do it. I'm *terrified* of doing it.'

'I know what you're going to say,' she said. 'We have to touch.' She did not know why, but the idea of coming into physical contact with Karmel frightened her too.

'I suppose that holding hands is the best way? Your kind appear to like doing that sort of thing.'

Karmel's brilliance was dimming a little and his usually smooth features were creasing with indecision. They were standing far enough apart that they would barely be able to touch each other's fingertips even at full stretch, but neither of them wanted to make the first move.

'I guess so,' she said. 'Well, here goes.'

She stretched out her hand, palm down as if unwilling to be the instigator of such an outrageous action. Karmel hesitated a little longer before extending his long arm, the hand open to the sky.

Their fingers touched. A fraction of a second later, or so it seemed, they were both staggering away from each other as if a bolt of lightning had touched them.

'Oh!' breathed Sara.

'Um - yes,' was all that Karmel could say. The smell of jasmine, red walls that radiated an unremitting heat, an acrid tang of decay, the murmur and uneasiness of crowds – those and a score of other impressions were firing like a strobe light in her mind.

That wasn't all. It was Karmel. She had seen inside him. For one tiny particle of time, like a speeding dart of energy, she'd seared through his alien neurones and known what it was like to *be* Kiklaydan, and then in the same instant she had forgotten all but a dim echo of him.

'Who is Zerafma?'

'And why are you so angry with your mother?' he countered instantly before flinching as though Sara had slapped him across the face.

'*No!* We mustn't go there. Not now.' His chest heaved and he exhaled mightily. 'I think that was a partial success.'

'We need to try again,' Sara responded. 'Quickly.' The urgency in her voice required little explanation.

'What's happening to the grass?'

The fragrant pink grass had lost its buoyant candyfloss appearance. Every blade seemed to be straining and quivering as if an invisible gale from the sea had flattened the entire meadow. Even more disturbing was the change in the sky, because the clouds were losing their static conformity and had begun to shed thin white slipstreams as if they were struggling to remain still in a rising wind.

Worse still, the shadow at the far edge of the ocean was growing. More than ever, it was beginning to resemble a huge, gaping maw. At the edge of its reach, the cloudscape was disintegrating into a radiating corona of vapour trails. It was as if the elements themselves were trying to outrun their fate.

I know that sound! I've heard it before. Sara could feel more than she could hear it - seven ominous beats like a pulse from beyond the edge of the universe, and it was coming up through the soles of her feet and making the branches of the giant trees shiver. The gliding scarlet creatures had started to wail in distress and some were simply crumpling in mid air and plummeting in fire and ruin to the ground.

'Again!' insisted Karmel. This time, he did not hesitate when he gripped her arm, and she took his other hand, crushing the ragged postcard between their palms. This time she could see the city in stunning detail, the white houses and tiled roofs and narrow lanes that crammed together on a baking hillside, the red towers on a forested promontory and the dim line of mountains in the hazy distance.

Once again they were flung apart, but when Sara regained her senses she knew that more than just a few seconds had elapsed. Now the sky was darkening to a sickly olive pall, and a rending, crashing tumult tore through the air as first one then another and then more of the mighty trees slowly toppled earthwards, their roots and branches groaning and shrieking as they splintered. The maw had consumed the western horizon and the chain of pointed islands was vanishing into it. They could hear the shouts and screams from the chalet station as people realized that something awful was happening, and tiny figures were running from the building and scattering across the meadow towards them.

'It isn't working!' she screamed above the thundering noise. 'Why isn't it happening?'

'We have to keep trying,' yelled Karmel. The ground had begun to undulate underfoot and as it trembled and buckled, his long thin legs gave way. Sara screamed as they were thrown apart by the convulsing earth, then they were hurled back together again so that they almost crashed into each other.

Think, damn it. Think! How did I do it before. How did we get here?

Then it came to her, an infinitely quiet but powerful little whisper in the choking fog of her confusion. *The universe curves in on itself, to the left. The universe is an ever-decreasing spiral and if you know how to follow the inward path, you can go anywhere!*

'Karmel! I've got it. I know what to do!'

The shuddering ground was jerking upwards and forcing them apart again. Karmel sprang to the rim of the tearing ground just as it lifted away from Sara, then he leaped down to join her on a tilting plane of soil and turf that was crumbling all around them.

'Tell me!'

'*Think* a spiral that curves inward to the left, like a snails shell! *Think* it, Karmel! Imagine it with every atom in your body!'

The ground was splitting in all directions and jagged black rifts coursed away from them as though the earth was shattering like a thing of glass. Karmel and Sara staggered as their precarious foothold began to sway and tilt. Everything above them was a dead brown inkiness, filled with whirling fragments of branches and clods of earth. The entire landscape began to subside, while from the chalet came a ripping tumult as the roof was torn away by the impact of a dislodged cable car that hurtled and twisted through the raging sky and straight towards them.

'Now!' cried Karmel, throwing himself at her. They clung tightly to each other, the overpowering thunder of seven roaring at them and as the world was torn apart, they *thought*.

8. Granada: July

They crashed down in a tangle of floundering limbs and landed painfully on top of a metal postcard stand. It toppled over, scattering its contents on to the street like confetti and throwing Sara to the ground with an agonizing bone-jarring jolt. Karmel's gangly limbs were against him and he tripped and fell backwards through the narrow doorway of a shop, disappearing through a garishly hued curtain of sequined tapestries and racks of cheap cotton pashminas.

Sara picked herself up, swearing without reserve from the pain of a cracked knee, and lifted her eyes to meet the shocked and hostile gaze of a dozen onlookers. Unfortunately, the narrow lane was filled with a seething and sweating crush of people and their unusual arrival had not passed entirely unnoticed. There were shouts and curses, and a dark man in a dirty white T-shirt bellowed something incomprehensible at her, which attracted the attention of others.

Almost unconsciously, she stepped backwards towards the shop entrance, painfully aware of the banging and crashing noises that were coming from inside. *Karmel!* He'd had no chance to disguise himself because they'd had no time to think about what they might be coming to. They would have to find a safe place to hide and some means of disguising the Kiklaydan musician but before anything else, Sara had to extricate herself from the sudden and unwanted attention.

The constricted lane was thronged with little shops, some of which appeared to have been abandoned or looted, and the roughly cobbled way ascended in a series of broad shallow steps and meandered out of sight. Just opposite her was some kind of exotic tea house with ornate Arab-style arches over the windows and a glimpse of cushioned alcoves and silver teapots on low tables and inquisitive faces that were peering out at her to add to her discomfort.

Above and below, the lane was heaving with people, all with the dusty and unkempt appearance of those who had come here unwillingly and unprepared. The ground was strewn with bits and shreds of rubbish, flyblown fragments of food and overturned boxes of stinking debris and through it all wandered a baffling conglomeration of humanity. There were Africans dressed in flowing djellabas and blond hikers with peeling red skins, tripping and stumbling as they shoved and collided against one another. Stringy dogs slunk among the shifting forest of legs, snatching scraps from the drifts of waste accumulated against the shuttered metal fronts of untenanted shops. Further up the lane were sagging shelters of plastic and old wooden planks, and next to one of them a cluster of veiled women crouched around a fire they had set in the cut-off rectangular base of an olive oil canister, roasting sweet potatoes skewered on sticks.

It looked like a refugee camp. With her body still trembling with the thrill and the terror of their narrow escape from Hyaquat, Sara thought quickly. She began to waft herself frantically with her hands, her rapid breathing lending weight to the charade.

'No English.' She stabbed her thumb at her chest and then gestured at the fierce blue sky and the high merciless sun. 'Is hot. I sick!'

As she warmed to her playacting she raised her voice and shouted angrily at the bemused crowd.

'Sick! No look at me. You all stupid people!' With this she turned dramatically and marched through the doorway. Her heart was pounding like a hammer but after she'd stopped and listened in the welcome darkness and heard no evidence that anyone had bothered to follow her, she slumped against the door frame, overcome with exhausted relief.

The tiny shop bore all the signs of having been ransacked. The till was broken and empty and crumpled clothing, smashed trinkets and cellophane packets of teas and spices were scattered on the floor.

After her eyes had adjusted to the darkness, she spotted Karmel who was cowering behind the tiny counter, hugging his gangly legs against his shockingly bare torso.

'Are you all right?'

'*All right?* They must *not* see me like this,' he spluttered. He was still wearing the simple, diaphanous Kiklaydan clothing of the kind that he had been wearing when Sara met him. During their escape, his flimsy jacket had ripped open and Sara could see the corrugations of his ventral spine and the inverted 'V' on his abdomen where it bifurcated to support the upper skeletal structure of his legs. His left arm glistened with an oozing silvery moistness.

'You're bleeding!'

He dismissed her concern with a perfunctory jerk of his head. 'It is nothing. We heal quickly. I am more concerned about my appearance. You have to find me something else to wear.'

'Then I'm going to have to go out there and look for something, aren't I?' she said, ignoring his terse manner.

Karmel pursed his lips. 'I imagine that we have no choice.' He began to rise, but when Sara unthinkingly reached out to help him, he flinched away from her.

'Thank you, but I can manage perfectly well by myself.'

Sara was mystified by his formality. Maybe he was affronted and embarrassed by the unwanted level of their recent physical contact. As he had reminded her on more than one occasion, the Kiklayda were, in terms of tactility, a very reserved species. Even though she knew this, she wondered if she would ever come close to understanding this non-human man. He was, by sudden and unpredictable turns, remarkably human then profoundly different and as he stood in the darkness of the shop with his peculiar skin shimmering and his violet eyes not quite meeting hers, she felt the same chill of strangeness that she had experienced not long ago in the restaurant on Hyaquat when she'd watched him eating fish bones.

Karmel appeared to be oblivious to her discomfort. 'You must be careful. Our being here is not an accident.'

'Do you know something?'

'Only what I have been able to sense during our translation here. Which is considerable. I know the history of this city. It stands at a crossroads in time. I feel its rhythm, its breath. I know that something is coming and that we must be ready for it. I also know that we will find friends and enemies here.'

Only now did he look straight at her, and his strange eyes without pupils were cold and unreadable. 'So, do try not to be too impetuously human. We can't afford the risk.'

'Okay, okay. I'll try not to be myself,' she retorted, rather more hastily than she intended. When she reached the door, she turned round.

'I'm sorry,' she said. 'I feel as though I'm walking in the dark.'

Karmel said nothing, and did nothing except to watch her steadily. Sara hadn't truly realized until this moment that he never blinked.

She stepped out into the angry sun and heat of a Granada afternoon and was quickly absorbed into the anonymity of the crowd. She was buffeted and crushed within moments, immersed in a confusing sea of pungent odours, a clash of unknown languages and a visual assault of garish colours, all of which seemed to be accentuated by the searing blue roof of sky that was firmly clamped down over the stifling street like an impervious lid.

Sensing that there would be an advantage in finding a viewpoint, Sara decided to head upwards. She spotted a pair of sunglasses lying in the rubbish and managed to dip quickly among the mill of legs to rescue them. Within minutes, she had put her concerns about Karmel elsewhere and her instinct to deal with the moment to the fore. She saw a newspaper kiosk ahead and acting on instinct, she meandered towards it, treading on feet and tripping on debris as she did so. A teenage boy with shaggy black hair and a partially healed scar on his chin was vending what appeared to be badly printed one-page news sheets. Sara had no money but she felt herself drawn to the stand and, trying not to meet the youth's hopeful gaze, she quickly scanned the headlines.

It was all in Spanish and she did not understand a word, except to decipher the date at the top left land. 16 de Julio. *The 16th of July*. That was impossible! She had only left England a few days ago, and then it had been February…

Sara had no time to mull over what it might mean. Just ahead, the throng of people was thinning out and she quickened her pace in an attempt to find a spot where she could breathe more freely. The constricting odour of unclean bodies and slimy maggoty waste was almost unbearable and brought back unwanted recollections of another place, but when she reached the top of the lane the way ahead opened into a large plaza and the atmosphere, although hot, was considerably less offensive.

There was something approaching a semblance of normality here. Even though the plaza was noisy and packed with people, the cafes around the perimeter were all open and the misting systems beneath the awnings discharged a continual stream of welcome cooling fog over the clients who sat in the shade with glasses of beer and summer wine.

Drawing her thirsty eyes away from the bars, Sara discovered an oval of welcome shade beneath the ferny branches of a pepper tree. Here, she took stock of her situation. After the balmy air of Hyaquat, the Andalucian heat was suffocating and her body was already drenched with sweat, the unsuitable alien clothing sticking to her skin and chafing annoyingly.

She had no plan, other than to find some kind of disguise for Karmel. After that, she did not know whether or not his percipience had defined a course for them that would enable him to leave his insecure hiding place. This city was entirely unknown to her but as she looked around, she gained an odd sense of familiarity – snippets of words, names, images of times and places that made little sense but gave her the strangest impression of having been here before.

Terk´s insistence that she take the postcard with her meant they were not here by accident. She felt uncomfortable at the notion of their movements having been controlled but, on the other hand, Terk had risked his life to save hers and might even have lost it in the process. She had to trust him and hope that somewhere in this sweltering and overcrowded city, answers were waiting for them. Not only this, but there was the terror of what had happened on Hyaquat to contend with and the certainty that it had been no coincidence.

In one corner of the plaza, there was a congregation of people wearing colourful djellabas and what Sara imagined to be Bedouin turbans. Clothes like that would be ideal for Karmel, but how was she going to get hold of them? She couldn't simply walk up to somebody and ask him to give away his clothes. Besides, the few words of Arabic that her mother had taught her as a child were all but forgotten. Perhaps there was a shop somewhere? But then again, there was the problem of money.

More certain was the unpleasant awareness that she was being followed, and that the prickling at the nape of her neck was not only due to the heat and perspiration. She tried to make herself as inconspicuous as possible by pressing herself against the rough red trunk of the pepper tree while she continued to scan the plaza, but she had no idea what she was looking for.

Moment by moment, she was increasingly certain that she was being scrutinized by something that nobody else was aware of. Then she caught a glimpse of something, a fragmented golden ripple above the blind multitude in the shadow of an alleyway that twisted and undulated like a wisp of silk captured by a breeze - strangely beautiful yet repulsive at the same time. It was something half there, half elsewhere but Sara knew with certainty that *it should not be there at all.*

It's the grass men. They're coming for me.

Who or what the grass men were, she did not know. Sara had no memory of either the name or the concept but she knew beyond hesitation that she had to move quickly. She had already spotted several likely routes out of the plaza and in the furthest corner from where she was trying to conceal herself under the pepper tree, a tiny alleyway between an old three-storey house and the steps of a church seemed to beckon her. She moved warily out of the leafy shadows and pushed the sunglasses back up her nose as she tried to think invisibility. Winding and sidling through the crowd with her eyes flitting in all directions, she reached the shade of the alleyway in less than a minute.

Nothing seemed to be overtly amiss, but Sara quickly knew that she had made a mistake. The lane was quiet - much too quiet, considering its proximity to the crammed plaza. Nothing moved except for the flitting of a few dusty sparrows and a slinking, leggy black cat that glared at her before disappearing through a gap in a door. She moved off, hoping that the claustrophobic lane might soon give into another plaza where she could hide among people and rethink her strategy. The narrow way was flanked by high whitewashed walls over which spilled cascades of snowy perfumed jasmine and magenta bougainvillea, while further back in the secluded carmens the fronds of palms and dark spires of cypresses stood against the fierce blue.

It was between the cypress trees that she caught her first sight of the towers and battlements of the Alhambra and the hazy profile of the Sierra Nevada mountains far beyond them. She immediately recognized it as the image from the postcard. How odd that a forgotten memento from a sometime friend should have been the means to bring her here from the far reaches of the galaxy. But Sara did not have time to stand and admire the view.

She turned onto another, narrower lane that slanted away to the left at an acute angle. It was completely empty like the one she had just left, the only sound being the almost painful shriek of a cicada, but above the jumble of walls and roofs not far away she could see another church tower, a low parapet wall and the movement of people.

Sara reached the far end, climbed a set of cobbled steps and turned right onto another lane. It was hot and heavy going and she had to stop every minute or so to wipe the stinging sweat out of her eyes. Ahead, where the alleyway angled sharply to the left and away from the church, a hint of pale gold mirage rippled over the cobbles like the movement of cascading water. Something did not strike true. Her breath caught in her throat. She looked back, and saw that the lower end of the lane was fogged by the same obscure presence, like fragments of straw chaff caught in a heat vortex.

She was drenched with a cold sweat of fear. From where she stood, she could see no way out of the lane, except to go forwards or back. Either way would lead her into the source of her dread. The walls were too high to climb and the few thick wooden doors she had passed looked as if they had not seen a key in decades. She crept into the recess of the nearest doorway, squeezing herself so tightly against the ancient wood that the iron studs holding it together dug into her back, praying that what she feared was nothing but her imagination.

I'm not HERE. You can't see me! Please God, don't let them see me.

But already, above the opposite wall, a misty golden swirling rose into view between the cypress trees and she knew that any attempt at concealment was meaningless.

The cicada chirred on, singing its incessant doom beneath the dangerous sun, then it stopped dead. During what followed, Sara had no time to draw breath as a hand closed firmly over her mouth and she was dragged back through the door that had suddenly opened at her back.

'Don't move,' a voice hissed. 'Don't speak.'

Paralyzed with surprise, she felt herself being supported by strong arms that hauled her into the shade of an enormous spreading fig tree. At the same time, a pair of immensely tall and thin entities shrouded in billowing white garments, swept by her with a sound like rushing wind and gusted out through the door.

The hand loosened and she reached for support against the tree trunk, then blinked away the sweat to get a first look at her rescuer. She had never seen him before. He was young and dark skinned, and he boasted a mane of black glossy curls and an open white shirt that showed off the gold medallion on a chain round his neck. But though she did not know the man, she instantly and joyfully recognized the small and lopsided character next to him, carrying a lumpy bundle of clothing in his short thickset arms.

It was Terk.

They reached the door of the safe house several hours later, while the walls of the Alhambra were still on fire with the glow of the setting sun. They had waited for thirty minutes in the overgrown garden, baking and perspiring even in the dense shade of the ancient fig tree, before Juan signalled the all clear and they were able to move out. Barely a dozen words passed between the three of them as her rescuers took her by an erratic path through the baffling labyrinth of the Albayzín and back to Karmel's hiding place. Sara soon guessed that Terk's bundle was clothing for Karmel and it did not take much deduction to realize that they had not only been expected, they had been actively sought out.

How? Well, that was clearly a question for later. For the moment, she knew that silence and obedience was the imperative. She was aware of the almost palpable danger hanging in the muggy air. Subtle it might be, but it was evident enough to cause dogs to bark suddenly and for no apparent reason then fall silent too quickly, and to make shutters and doors bang shut at their passing - as if whatever was at large in the lengthening shadows could be kept out by such tenuous means.

After another half hour of ducking and dodging through passageways, creeping through crowded bars and sliding through back doors and across courtyards and gardens, Sara came to realize two important things. The first, and least surprising, was that nobody else could see Terk, and that people were barely paying any attention to her and Juan. This masking ability she was already familiar with from their first encounter.

The second was that the white shrouded figures from the garden of the fig tree had returned and were moving parallel to them though at a distance. From time to time they appeared briefly in shadowy archways or slipped out of sight around corners like creatures made of night mist and moonbeams. There was a feeling of the vodyanoi taxi driver about them, in that whenever she tried to fix her eyes on their half-veiled faces, all she managed to gain was a fading impression of smoke and dull fire.

The Djinn. They reminded her of the fairy tales her mother used to tell her when she wasn't yet old enough to go to school or know what the pain of separation was like. But she remembered those early precious times with an almost photographic clarity, the fantastic stories of genies and flying horses, and the desert spirits that had the ability to fascinate and disturb at the same time. *The Djinn. They will always exist, at the edge of belief, out there in the wilderness where fantasies come alive. And maybe, just maybe, you might meet a Djinn yourself one day.* And Sara had cuddled ever more tightly into her mother's chest, throwing her arms around her waist and wishing that neither she nor her stories would ever go away.

When they reached the shop, Terk handed the roll of clothing to Sara and waited outside with Juan. As she entered the dark and cluttered room, it was to encounter a Karmel greatly changed from the one she had left because he rushed to her in a frenzy of agitation, babbling with relief and contrition.

'Oh, Sara! I'm so sorry! Can you forgive me? But where have you *been*? By the five gods, I've been worried half to *death*! I didn't mean - I mean, it's -'

'It's fine! *That's* what it is.' Sara spoke firmly and calmly. 'We are safe now. I've got clothing for you and we're with friends.'

'But I must say sorry - you have to accept my... my behaviour, it was... not appropriate...' Karmel was entangled in a confusion of guilt and formality and he did not seem to know how to extricate himself.

'You were scared,' said Sara, putting the clothes down on the counter. 'After what's happened to us, I'm hardly surprised. Karmel, you are my friend. Friends forgive each other.'

This had a curious effect on Karmel. His words faltered, and then he drew himself up awkwardly, with an uncertain smile flickering alive on his blue face.

'Friends? You mean - *us?* Well then, thank you, Sara Parkinson. I am glad to be *your* friend too.'

Sara turned her back on him as he changed into the clothes they'd brought, but he continued muttering the word *friend* as though he was experimenting with the novelty of it.

'What we had to do to get here,' he said, the words muffled by the djellaba that he was pulling over his head, 'the physical contact - it was stunning. I have never known such intimacy with another person until now. Don't get me wrong!' he added hastily. 'It's not that kind of... I mean, I'm not...'

'And I never knew that I had such an electrifying personality,' murmured Sara. Karmel's acute hearing caught her words and she heard him laugh hesitantly.

'Do not underestimate yourself, Sara Parkinson.' After the terrors and misunderstandings they had endured that day, Sara felt a rush of relief at his response.

'That is not what I meant,' he continued. 'We are a physically reserved people, or at least the traditionalists among us are, and I come from deeply traditional roots.'

'What are you trying to say? Don't you ever touch each other?'

'Very rarely,' he said, 'and then the contact is under intensely controlled and mutually respectful circumstances. For example, during surgery and certain important rituals.'

'But what about when you...' She was acutely conscious that her question might be considered disrespectful under the circumstances but her curiosity was more powerful than her prudence. 'What about reproduction?'

'Five Gods!' Karmel was aghast. 'Especially not then.'

'But how do you - '

'Our reproductive process is somewhat different to yours. Please, let's change the subject. It's making me feel a little queasy.'

When he had finished dressing, Karmel showed off the results to her.

'Will I pass?' The light blue djellaba covered him from neck to floor, and he had made a very plausible attempt to conceal all but his eyes with the white turban.

Sara smiled and nodded encouragingly. 'You look every bit the Bedouin tribesman. You'll pass.'

Outside, in the slanting light of late afternoon, introductions were made. Unable to use his hands for the traditional Kiklaydan greeting because of the long sleeves of the djellaba, Karmel simply bowed formally. Juan responded with a broad glittering smile and a 'Muy buenas', while Terk returned the bow and peered up into the veiled face of the lofty Kiklaydan.

'Maestro Tragawlty. It is truly an honour to meet you. I am a great admirer of your work, especially the Fifth Symphony.' Whatever Karmel thought about this unpredicted salutation, Sara couldn't tell because the wrappings concealed his expression but she imagined him to be surprised and hoped that he was feeling more than a little gratified.

'Time to go,' said Terk without further delay. 'We have probably already attracted some unwanted attention.'

They moved off along the bustling lane, this time heading downwards and then west via circuitous ways to slowly gain the high ground again. Sara was once again aware of the willowy robed figures that were flanking them. Juan led the way, with Karmel flowing along behind in his robes, then Sara, and Terk at the rear.

The little grey man quickened his pace and drew level with Sara.

'We can talk, at last,' he said in a low tone. 'There are things you need to know before we get there.'

'Get where, Terk? And how on earth did you get *here*?'

'All in due course. There'll be plenty of time for rest and chat when we get to safety.'

'At least, can you tell me where we're going?'

'That I can. It's a place of safety for those like me and for many others. I'm sure you have seen wonders since we parted company and I expect you won't be too surprised by what you see there.'

He took her by the hand, his chameleon grasp warm and soft to the touch as he hurried her along to catch up with the others.

'A word of warning, if I may. Be careful, Sara. Not everybody is going to welcome you with open arms. Our guardians in white, for example.'

'Who are they?'

'They are the Djinn.'

I knew it! 'What do they have against me?'

'You're human,' replied Terk.

'But so is Juan,' she said, confused.

'Not entirely, but he will tell you about that in his own time. In the case of the Djinn, they have had a long and sometimes difficult relationship with your kind. They are not happy about allowing you into what they consider to be an elite fellowship. Take care in your dealings with them, Sara.'

Though she was brimming with a welter of questions, Sara had no further opportunity to ask them because Juan and Karmel had quickened their pace again. They were walking together and she could hear them both talking in rapid Spanish. After a quick exchange, Karmel dropped behind.

'More Djinn are coming,' he said. After what Terk had just told her, this prospect did little to put Sara's mind at ease. 'It seems that a lumen has been detected in Sacromonte, and another close to the Hospital Real. Juan says that they have no knowledge of the whereabouts of the safe house but they mustn't be allowed to see the route we are taking.'

They were drawing close to the Mirador of San Nicolas, Granada's most famous viewpoint where, in less dangerous times, thousands of tourists flocked to marvel at the splendid view of the Alhambra palaces and fortresses with their mountainous backdrop. The odours of smoke and cooking drifted in the stifling air and as the little party skirted the Mirador and Sara looked over the ramshackle encampment of tepees and tents, she wondered what could have happened to the world during her preternaturally extended absence.

'It isn't far now,' said Terk as they re-entered the twisting, tangled labyrinth of the Albayzín. They arrived at the intersection of three lanes, where the way broadened into a triangular plaza. On one side was the domed brick roof of an ancient Arab water cistern, and a public drinking fountain with a spout of cool water that babbled into a round stone trough. Across the plaza a large pepper tree drooped its weeping branches almost to the ground. Opposite were a small shop and a bar, both closed.

Nothing moved here that Sara was aware of, but Juan lifted his hand to stop them. Instinctively, Karmel and Sara drew closer together.

'What's happening?' she whispered.

'I don't know,' said Karmel. 'I can feel something. Predatory. Malevolent.'

'Faerie,' said Terk. 'They have been tracking us. They've been under the power of the Mawdrik for a long time. Look, quickly! There, in the tree.'

Something was moving surreptitiously among the flaking red branches. At first, Sara thought it was a snake, but then she saw the entwining tail slip from view, then a twiggy limb and a webbed and clawed hand that parted the ferny leaves. She glimpsed a single luminous eye, and heard a rattle and a flutter like moths wings as the thing darted back into the dense foliage.

'Are they dangerous?'

'Not in themselves,' said Terk. He winced. 'Well, they have a painful bite and they could put your eye out with those claws. They feed on rubbish and carrion that they track down with an excellent sense of smell, and that makes them good trackers. What makes me uneasy is that this one has allowed itself to be seen. Maybe the Mawdrik think that they can intimidate us into making a mistake.'

He nodded. 'It′s time we left.'

Somehow, two Djinn had materialized nearby without Sara having noticed them. At such close proximity, her skin prickled with the harsh dry heat that emanated from beneath their spotless white robes and, knowing what she did about their antipathy towards her, she had no wish to get any closer to them.

Juan led the way out of the plaza, silently urging haste, but Sara could not resist looking back. The Djinn had separated and were facing away from them, then as if through some kind of silent communication they both spun towards the weeping tree. There was a noise like a rising wind, then a blast of heat and a stench of sulphur and desert dust. Flurries of rubbish whirled up from the ground and swept around the plaza in a mad dance, but at the centre the branches of the tree were perfectly motionless. There followed shrieks as first one, then a whole shower of writhing, burning shapes fell from the tree and the surrounding rooftops and twisted into black cinders on the ground.

With the trackers dealt with for the moment, they were able to reach the safe house within another five minutes.

Remember Terk's warning. Don't antagonize the Djinn. But as they waited and listened to the sound of approaching footsteps from inside, Sara was ever more certain about what she had to do.

The door was opened by a banshee. He was quite the most exquisite creature that Sara had ever seen, naked except for short trousers that came down to his knees, with taut and silky skin like burnished wood, long red-gold hair, large green eyes and a light but muscular physique that might have emerged from under the chisel of a master sculptor. Furthermore, he had wings that Sara thought were feathered until she realized that the furled silvery blades were more like some kind of flexible metal that had been beaten so thin as to be translucent.

'Bonjour, François,' said Terk. François looked from Terk, and then to Sara on whom he rested his mesmerising sea green eyes, an expression of wonder lighting up his sharply defined features.

'C'est elle? Rèelment c'est toi, Sara Parkinson. Je n'aurais jamais penser être vivre pour voir ce jour-ci.'

As they followed him through the ornate hall, François kept looking round at Sara with a smile on his sensual lips, but she was too preoccupied to pay much attention either to him or the exotic opulence of their surroundings. Karmel had unwound his turban to reveal his ridged cranium and a glittering skin that was flushed jade with nervousness and anticipation.

They came to a door.

'Un momentito,' said Juan, opening it wide and standing aside to let them pass. They were clearly expected. The room was filled with over a hundred whispering people, who fell quiet and drew off to the sides as soon as they entered. Sara recognized more banshees and the short, grey hooded figures of many of Terk's people in the flickering light of the dozens of lamps that covered the tiled walls. There was a short, voluptuous Caribbean woman dressed in red and yellow robes who watched her with an odd smile and frightening eyes like white fire, and an enormous, lanky grey wolf lying in front of the unlit fireplace that lifted his grizzled head and scrutinised them with a distant yellow glare.

Further back, over the sea of heads, two ogres loomed between the pillars. They were smaller than the mates of Valu whom she had briefly encountered at the lake, but still their heads almost touched the ceiling. Next to them stood a vast trollish bulk with twisted horns, a face that resembled that of a particularly ugly warthog, and a hairy hide as black as ink and, as Sara briefly caught its eye, she was certain that it winked at her.

All of them were stiller than the dead of night and Sara knew that, in spite of Karmel's striking appearance, nobody was looking at him. She, however, had no concern for either the intensity or the nature of the scrutiny because she had found what she was looking for. In a far corner, in the darkest, most shadowy reaches of the room, was a gathering of twenty or more Djinn, and though they were veiled up to what might serve as their eyes, she could feel their volcanic hostility searing into her.

'Stay here, Karmel,' she said. He looked at her in surprise but did nothing to prevent her as she walked to the centre of the room and turned to face the waiting people, but with her back to the Djinn.

'I'm Sara,' she began with a waver in her voice. 'Sara Parkinson.'

Nobody moved. Nobody spoke. She drew in a quick breath, then continued with more confidence.

'You've heard of me, I know. And I know that some of you are not happy about me coming here but I can't help that.'

The wolf rose to his feet and made a low sound in the barrel of his chest, and the troll shifted its weight from one tree-trunk leg to the other but apart from that, nobody else moved or spoke.

'A few days ago, something incredible happened to me. I suddenly found out that I could travel to other worlds. Some of them are fantastic, some of them are horrible... believe me, you wouldn't want to know what I have seen. At first I didn't want to accept it. I mean, what was I supposed to do? Who could I tell? Nobody in *my* world was going to believe me, were they?'

Only then did she turn to face the corner where the Djinn were gathered. 'Then other things started happening. I realized that this planet isn't the predictable human world that we think it is. There are monsters out there, as well as good people like you and me... there are the Mawdrik.'

This created more of a stir, and from the Djinn came a collective hiss as they drew themselves up, looking more forbidding than ever.

'Then I learned that we are not alone here, that there are other races in the universe. Everything I thought I knew was turned completely upside down.'

She took a few steps towards the Djinn. A few people shifted to make room for her. Now she was looking straight at the shrouded entities. They in turn faced her impassively, a wall of ivory pillars.

Her voice rose. 'What I want to say is, I didn't ask for this to happen, any of it, but sometimes destiny comes our way when we don't ask it to, let alone want it. I know that people have already died, trying to protect me and hunting for me. I hate the thought, but there you go. I'm involved in something so big, so terrifying...'

She had to stop and swallow back the constricting knot in her throat. As she collected her thoughts, she became aware of movement at her back, a shifting and gathering around her that she hoped and prayed was mute support. She was painfully conscious of Karmel's proximity and the stress emanating from him, but she could not, she *dared* not look at him. Everything depended on what she did now.

'There's more. All of you, and me, and Karmel, we are all part of this destiny. I can't help what or who I am but I know that I've come here to find out what I'm supposed to do, and nobody is going to stand in my way. Help me now, or leave me alone.' She stared at the Djinn, hard and unflinching.

Then the power started to leave her. 'I'll do what I have to do.' She was folding in on herself and she was tired beyond tolerance.

'I'm not asking for anything in return,' she said, in barely more than a whisper. 'That's all.'

It hadn't achieved anything. It had all been futile. She wanted nothing other than to crawl under a stone like an insect and disappear. But in the asphyxiating pause that followed, one of the Djinn drifted forward slowly, almost cautiously as if not to alarm her. He inclined his turbaned head to her blanched and perspiring face and when he spoke it was with a voice like the rushing of wind and sand.

'You have spoken well, and shamed us.' He looked up and swept his veiled gaze around the room.

'We will defend you to the end.'

9. Albayzín, Granada: July

Sara must have slept until mid-morning because when she eventually succeeded in prizing her leaden eyelids apart, a bright sunbeam lay crosswise over the light cotton sheet that covered her lower body. Birds were chirping noisily outside and as soon as she had focused she was able to take in the homely simplicity of the room: its roughly textured white walls and dark wooden ceiling, the red brick floor and the cool green leaves of a large fern on a wrought-iron stand in one corner.

François was sitting in a wicker chair, his legs tucked crossways under him, watching her with his chin resting lightly on meshed fingers. Sara wasn't at all surprised, because during the night she had woken twice and seen him there, like a statue of silver and ebony in the moonlight. She hadn't known why and was too tired to wonder about it, but his presence had made her feel safe and she had soon fallen asleep again.

Now, as she eased slowly into full consciousness, she watched him dreamily as he looked back at her with his large sea-green eyes that were fringed with long golden eyelashes.

François unlinked his fingers. 'You were dreaming,' he said, bringing even more sunlight into the room with his disarming smile. His accent was strong but his voice was light and smooth as honey.

'I don't remember,' she mumbled. 'Why did you stay with me?'

'I like watching you,' he said without hesitation, flashing his dazzling white teeth at her. 'You are beautiful. Also, my sister died helping your little friend to bring the news of your coming. I have a duty to honour her memory by watching over you.'

He jumped out of the chair and stretched, arching his back in the sunlight. His body shimmered like dark golden satin as he flexed.

'When you have eaten, Angustias would like to see you.' He indicated the tray of food on a table next to the bed.

'Do you know where Karmel -?' She was too late, because François had already sprung through the half-opened shutters. She heard the momentary beat of his wings, then the merry twitter of the momentarily disturbed sparrows.

Sara picked at the toast drizzled with honey and olive oil, hungry but too preoccupied to eat much, although she drank most of the jug of fresh orange juice. Who was Angustias? Perhaps he, or she, would answer some of her questions at last.

After she'd splashed cold water on her face and brushed her hair, Sara stepped into the corridor. It was empty, and she did not know which way to turn.

'I'm out here, Sara. Come and join me.'

Both the bedroom window and the short passage opened to a large square courtyard that was awash with morning sunshine. Squinting against the brightness, she saw a wooden gallery that stretched round the whole of the first floor beneath the sloping tiled eaves, enormous potted aspidistras, a tumbling fountain and a stately woman in a turquoise tracksuit, who was approaching her across the cobbles.

'Are *you* Angustias?'

'I can't deny it,' the woman replied heartily. 'Did you sleep? Have you eaten? This heat - it kills the appetite.'

'I'm fine, thank you. Okay, I'm not exactly fine but I think I'll cope.'

'Mmm.' Angustias took her by the arm and steered her into the cool, beneath the balcony. Here they walked slowly, keeping to the shade.

'You made quite an impression last night. I think the Djinn adore you already. That's a first. They have never heard anything quite like *that* before, I can tell you.'

'You were there?'

'Oh yes, watching and listening from the wings. I didn't want to bother you. You were asleep on your feet and you needed to rest.'

'Do you know where Karmel is?'

Angustias laughed. 'Sleeping like a Kiklaydan. I never knew they could snore like that. Dios mío!'

'You've met the Kiklayda before?'

'Many times. And the Volk, just once, and the Kiladl, the silly things. And you don't need to tell me because I can understand what you're going through. I was completely ignorant of such things until just after my thirteenth birthday. Can you imagine it? A naive young girl from the barrios of Granada who wakes up one morning and finds out that white was black and that the world had gone completely loco. But I'm… *cómo se dice en inglés*… going off along the branches, no? You have questions, lots of them. And don't worry because we have plenty of time.'

'And you're sure you can answer them?' Sara sounded dubious.

'Some of them, to the best of my ability.' They walked on. 'I hope that François didn't frighten you when you woke? He did insist on being your night guard. I think he's quite sweet on you.' She winked.

Sara felt the blood rushing to her cheeks. 'That's something I don't understand, for a start. He's a *banshee*, right? I thought they were a Celtic myth. Aren't they women who are supposed to scream?'

'Hah! You can blame the Irish for that nonsense. All it took was one little quarrel involving a funeral and the ownership of a bridge, and some foolish arrogant bard decides to make a name for himself and condemn a gentle people to be known forever more as "screaming banshees". Though I've always suspected that the Mawdrik had something to do with it, too.'

'Terk said something like that to me when we first met, back in England. About the Mawdrik and how they've managed to twist things.'

Angustias sighed. 'The Mawdrik and their lies. They've doomed so many innocent peoples to be hated and feared, or dismissed as legends; the Aswang, the Kelpies, many, many more… Not to mention all the ridiculous hoaxes - decaying mermaids washed up on beaches and the like. As if any of us would be stupid enough to leave our corpses lying around to be dissected. '

'Are you saying that mermaids really exist?'

'Tch!' Angustias rolled her eyes. I've never understood why they should all be maids. Mer*folk* exist, but I can assure you that not a single human being has ever seen one, either dead or alive. They're neither fish nor men, and they get very upset at any suggestion to the contrary.'

'Okay, so merfolk are real, and so are ogres and trolls. What about vampires?'

Angustias started to laugh. 'They are pure myth. Not even the Mawdrik would lower themselves to invent such nonsense. Vampires are purely the imaginings of ignorance and a primitive fear of the dark. The real terror comes with the rising sun.'

'The grass men.'

'Let's sit down before we talk about them,' said Angustias. They made themselves comfortable in the swinging garden chair and helped themselves from the pitcher of fresh iced lemonade that somebody had thoughtfully placed there for them. François, perhaps?

'Now the grass men, they are something quite different. They're mindless, soulless things made of raging hunger and they were uncontrollable before the Mawdrik discovered a horrible way of manipulating them.'

'What did they do?'

Angustias looked disgusted. 'They took the innocent and the vulnerable and made human go-betweens of them to choose those who are going to die. What we know is that the grass men are relicts that came into being during a very early period in the history of this world. The Djinn remember them from the last time they walked the Earth, before they went to sleep. They should never have stirred again. It is the Mawdrik who woke them up.'

'Why? Why would they do such a horrible thing?'

'Spite. Cosmic pettiness. Revenge.' She laid a plump hand on top of Sara's. 'It's all because of you.'

Sara didn't know how to respond to this. She sipped her glass of lemonade and watched the sparrows flocking down to pick at the crumbs that somebody had scattered around the fountain, knowing that she was not quite ready to hear why. Hadn't Angustias had said there was time? That was something she had not had much of during the last frantic days.

'Let me tell you something about the nature of things,' said Angustias. 'When life first came to this world it didn't just make itself known in the little creatures. You know, the bacteria and the other microscopic organisms. It also combined with the fundamental energy of the universe to make other kinds of entity, simple beings to begin with that had no solid form but were no less alive for all that.'

'You mean, like spirits?'

'I didn't say that,' said Angustias, 'but some people mistakenly think of them as spirits, or phantoms or whatever other *tonterías* pop into their minds. But we're getting ahead of ourselves.'

'I'm sorry,' said Sara. 'Please, don't stop.'

'Tsch! Don't be sorry. I'm telling you how things really came to be. It isn't going to be easy for you.' She hoisted her impressive bosom up and made herself more comfortable.

'So the ages went by and the fish came out of the water and so on and so forth, and while all of this was happening, the creatures of energy were altering too but they could do something quite special. You see, while the physical beings were mostly limited to sexual reproduction the others weren't bound by these processes and they could combine and change almost at will. From time to time, they were also able to join with the animals and plants to create yet other forms of life, and that's something that happened many times over and is still happening today. Do you understand? Are you following me?'

'Ye-es, I think so. So is that what made the other races, this mingling of different kinds of life?'

'Exactly. It's always happened. It's also why things that once seemed impossible to you are real, like invisibility and mind reading, and lots more besides. Magic is real, Sara. It just takes a different perspective to recognise it for what it is.'

'I think that in a way I've always believed,' said Sara wonderingly.

'Now, why doesn't that surprise me?' Angustias smiled, and continued.

'Some of us are blessed or cursed with more of the universal essence than others and that's why we are not bound by what people believe to be possible. It's also why ordinary humanity suspects our existence but cannot prove it. We have been around for a very long time and we've had plenty of time to learn how to use our different abilities to conceal our existence. There's another advantage too. When we die, it doesn't take long for our energy to go back into the ether and in the process it alters what's left to leave very little trace that we were ever here.'

'But you're as much flesh and blood as I am, surely!'

'Yes, I am,' said Angustias. 'I am as human as you are, but because of something that happened to my ancestors a very long time ago, I am something else besides. Maybe my great grandmother a hundred times removed fell in love with a creature that looked like a man but was something else. I don't know, but there are enough legends in the world about humans falling in love with sirens and angels to hint at what might have happened.'

'And the Mawdrik, too? Are they part of this?'

Angustias looked sombre and thoughtful. 'Even the Mawdrik, yes. Though they predate mankind, like the Djinn and a few others, and they are not just present on this world. They have only adopted the human form during the last six thousand years or so because it suits them at the moment. There is very little substance contained within the Mawdrik. That's why they have been able to alter their appearance so many times and masquerade as things they most certainly are not.'

'Whatever they think they are, they want me and it's because of me that everything is in such a mess,' Sara muttered, staring at the ground.

'You did nothing to cause this, Sara. The Mawdrik may be strong but they are emotionally crippled. They are so full of their self-importance that they hate the slightest notion of failure. They knew you were coming, just as we did. They were waiting for you, but when we managed to spirit you right out from under their glowing noses, they were enraged enough to go on a rampage that has so far caused the deaths of many thousands of people.'

'And it's all because they want something from me? Either that, or they want me to do something for them.'

Even the idea was shocking, that they might try to manipulate her.

'Have you any idea what they want?'

Angustias settled her substantial rump more comfortably in the chair. 'Only an inkling, but it is a beginning. I need to know how best to help you. If within your ability lies a key that the Mawdrik are seeking, we have to know both the key and the lock it is intended for. I think it's time you told me everything, right from the very beginning.'

And for the next two hours as the sun peaked and the cicadas reached their shrilling zenith, Sara related the events that had started on a rainy afternoon in northwest England with a hit and run accident. She told Angustias about the hospital, and her magical visit to Endymion, about the Vodyanoi and encountering Terk, and the horror of Gul, the lake and Valu's rescue and meeting the Volk. It was all so vivid in her memory that she hardly needed to stop and recall a single detail.

When she'd finished, Sara was exhausted. She had relived every emotion, each moment of terror and incredulity, right up to the destructive force that had come to Hyaquat and the discovery that she and Karmel made just in time to save their lives.

When she'd finished, Angustias sat for a while, twisting a strand of her greying hair between her thick fingers.

'Almost everything fits in with what I'd understood, all except one thing and that's what happened on this planet called Hyaquat. No, there's something else but I cannot quite put my finger on it.' She knotted her brows.

'I have it! There is a time that you have not accounted for.'

'But I've told you everything, literally everything! There's nothing else.'

'Yes, there is. After the car hit you. You woke up in the ambulance. What happened *before* you woke up? It was the accident that made your ability come alive. It's the way it is for some of us, in those first moments when we become aware of our true selves. We sense things. '

'I was asleep. Nothing happened. I don't remember…'

The dream! 'I had a dream,' she said excitedly. 'It didn't make any sense. There were shadows, and some kind of huge obelisk that was about to squash me.' *And the sound.* 'Seven.'

'What did you say?' Angustias was instantly alert.

'It was like a heartbeat, or a drum, or a giant machine. I've no idea what it was meant to be - I mean, I thought it was just a dream. There were seven beats then it stopped, but it repeated over and over again. And *it was the same on Hyaquat.*' She stared incredulously at Angustias.

Angustias surged to her feet. 'Come with me. I have something to show you.'

The house was a cool and welcome retreat after the midday heat. Angustias led Sara up some stairs, then along a corridor and ushered her into a substantial but comfortable chamber filled with the rich aroma of old leather.

It wasn't just the enormous hide armchairs that contributed to the smell. The room was a library, and its walls were lined from the tiled floor to the darkly panelled ceiling with solidly constructed wooden shelves. There was not a space among them, except for an alcove containing a desk and a computer. The shelves were packed with volumes big and small, ancient and modern, hardback, paperback, and leather-bound. One tier of shelves was full of stacked folios, another was fronted with glass doors and apparently had some form of environmental control because Sara noticed a white box with a flashing green light, mounted on the outside.

'That's where we keep the most precious items,' explained Angustias, 'the Medieval codices and the like. We have herbals, demonologies, all kinds of rare works that we have collected over the centuries. The bestiaries are particularly entertaining - you should have a look at them sometime. Ay, how those cloistered monks liked to fantasize about what we look like, when they didn´t really have a clue about what lay beyond the monastery walls. One of our most prized possessions was the Codex Granatensis, until the University got hold of it; but that´s another story.'

Angustias ran her hands along the bindings. Sara followed her, fascinated by some of the titles. She saw "Alternative Evolution", and "What Darwin Never Knew", alongside a comprehensive collection of battered Mills and Boon romances ('Those are mine', explained Angustias). One section appeared to be devoted to psychology, with titles such as "Werechildren - Surviving The Teens", and "A Study of Psychosis among Lithuanian Dryads". There were books about the Volk, the Kiladl, the Dzzt, and a large collection of scholarly tomes that treated with a panoply of human philosophies and religions from Animism and Atheism to Zen and Zoroaster.

'Amazing, are they?' said Angustias. 'We have an impressive collection. It's one of the best of any of the safe houses, though the Bogotá library is worth seeing. Come in any time you want. It never gets too hot in here.'

'How have you done all this?' marvelled Sara. 'If you all have to live in secrecy… I mean, the safe houses and all these books. Everything's so well organized.'

Angustias rested a hand on the shelves and gave Sara a patient smile with just a suggestion of weariness.

'Sara, we were doing this before your kind learned how to grow crops. Now, let's see…'

She found what she was looking for, and pulled out a large, brown hardback volume, then they crossed to a wide oak table that stood beneath the window and sat down.

The book had a plain binding with the title and the name of the author, in black Gothic script:

Complete Transcriptions

William L. Grace

'This,' said Angustias, 'is a limited edition. In fact, it is so limited that this was the only one ever produced, at the expense of the author. William Grace was a compatriot of yours, and a wereperson like myself. On the surface he was a Victorian gentleman explorer, a great student of the natural world and ancient history. Unfortunately, when he was only forty-three he came to a sad and very premature end in northern India.'

'Why? What happened to him?'

'Well, William Grace was a *lunar were*; that's to say, every month, around the full moon, he transformed into a tiger and, one afternoon in 1905, he was shot dead by George V who was on a hunting trip in the region. I believe that his skin is still preserved in Buckingham Palace. But let's not dwell on his death. As I've said, William was a keen student of ancient history, both human and otherwise. In his twenties, he travelled throughout northern Europe and the Scottish islands in search of the pre-human civilizations of the north. He had a great interest in comparative religion and his specialty was primitive belief systems, which is why he spent so much time among the Scandinavian ogres and the Hebridean kelpies.'

She opened the book. Each page was divided into three vertical columns of text. The first was a script of lines and crosses that made no sense whatsoever to Sara. In the middle, the language was also unknown to her. The column on the right hand, however, was English.

'This is a very old form of the Celtic runic script,' explained Angustias, indicating the left hand column. 'It predates anything known to human archaeologists. Here in the centre, this is Scots Gaelic. It was while he was searching through the archives of the kelpies that William found something that really caught his attention, something that was to become his life's work, in fact. He was on the trail of what he hoped might be some related Sanskrit texts when the King of England shot him.'

Sara merely nodded to show that she was paying attention as she continued to scan the mysterious lines. Even in English, it made no sense to her. She saw that the words 'convergence' and 'separation' were often repeated, and something about balance and numbered phases, but the style was dense and the sentences appeared to be unfinished in some places and nothing more than random words and numbers in others.

'What does it mean?'

'I only wish I knew,' sighed Angustias, 'but I'm sure that these words contain nuances and subtleties that could show us wonders and terrors. I've spent many hours poring over these pages, trying to find some meaning in them and, with few exceptions, I am only a little the wiser.'

'But what do you think it means? Surely you have your own ideas?'

'Of course I do. Ask anybody who knows me and they'll tell you that Maria Angustias Rodríguez Acosta has an opinion on everything.' She chuckled.

'I think it's a map. It is a map of time and space and the tempo of the universe - or at least, the way that the ancients saw these things. There are patterns within patterns, little glimpses that shed a tiny light on some cosmic principle or other but as soon as you've grasped it in your hand - *pff!* It's gone again.'

'So how can this book help me? Help us?'

'I'm coming to that. Don't forget that I said "with few exceptions". Most of this book contains transcriptions from many different documents. We believe that they were written in a particularly obscure code, even in their original form, that as yet we haven't been able to decipher except for the odd fragment. Sadly I have never learned how to read the runes. However…' She continued turning the pages.

'Here we are. This is the part that interests us. William Grace paid special attention to this document. He discovered it in the famous kelpie library under the standing stones of Callanish in Scotland. He believed that everything else he'd discovered up until that moment had been leading him to this one archive, and he spent more time studying it than any other. Look at it, Sara.'

Sara gasped. Each column was horizontally divided into seven parts.

'What William Grace found at Callanish was something he claimed to be evidence of ideas so old that they predate the end of the last Ice Age in the north of Europe. That's why I think he was in India, searching back through history for the origins of what he'd found in Scotland.'

'When you say 'old', just how old are we talking about? No, hang on a moment; I don't mean how old. I mean, was it human?'

'Originally, I don't think so,' said Angustias. 'Perhaps some elements might have made their way into some of the ancient beliefs, like Hinduism and Buddhism. Whatever. What we have here is something different. It seems to be an attempt to understand and describe the forces that make the universe tick. A kind of fundamental structure of things, if you like.'

'So how old is this text exactly?'

Angustias shrugged. 'At the very least, thirteen thousand years.'

'That *is* old!

'Here,' said Angustias, pushing the book across the table towards Sara. 'You read it.'

'I'm not sure if I-'

'It's not very long. Each of the seven parts has a name and a description, and each is little more than a list of words but it ends with something that links it to the next, all except the seventh which is different, as you'll see. I don't know how much sense William Grace made out of them. A few pages of his diary survive though they are not enough to know what he really believed he'd found, but I think that what he called the Seven Codex lies at the centre of this cosmic map and is what holds it all together.'

'Alright then.' Sara resigned herself to the werewoman's will, and began to read.

'The first is Ru. Ru is silence, emptiness, non-being, void, limbo, latency, but it is also "preparation".'

Ru. To Sara the very word sounded like a sigh of despair. In a flash she was taken back to Karmel's symphony and the dark pit of hopelessness the music had so nearly taken her to.

'The next is called Mah. Mah is first light. It is awakening, coming together, birth and rebirth. It is also "awareness".'

Sara was barely conscious of the world outside or the sound of the door opening and closing softly. All her attention was on the strange book in front of her.

'Three is named Lei. It is direction, evolution, progress, structure, creativity and possibility. It is also "ascent".'

'Number four. Hiree. Brilliance, culmination, ecstasy and completeness. He's made an annotation here… It says, "I always think that Hiree sounds rather like 'hooray". However, it is also "descent".

'Number five is called Dul. Dul is change, doubt and loss. It's also "destruction".

'Then we come to six. Horroth is conflict and disruption, disintegration, deceit and distortion, but it has another and very unusual attribute, as it's also "approaching wisdom".'

'Seven is waste, dereliction, fear and nightmare, shadow and doom, but it is also "knowledge" and stranger still, it's also "the unifier", although that isn't its name.'

That was all. Sara was confused. 'That can't be everything. What is the name of seven? Angustias?'

'There isn't one. Seven has no name.'

In the courtyard, several people were enjoying an afternoon stroll. Sara watched the black troll and an ogre walk by, deep in conversation. François was perched birdlike on the edge of the fountain, enveloped in a golden halo of sunlight reflected from the dancing water and, when he looked up and caught Sara's eye, he smiled.

'I know what the Mawdrik are looking for,' she said, penetrating the long silence that had come between her and the werewoman. 'It's obvious. They're trying to find the name of seven.'

'That's what I believe too.'

Angustias got up slowly and stiffly as though she was feeling the weight of her years. She went to the shelves, and slid the book into its place.

'Words are powerful. They can become weapons in the wrong hands. Obviously, they think that you can help them to find the seventh name. What I don't understand is how they could know about it in the first place. The Kelpies have guarded their secrets for thousands of years. Before William Grace was allowed to see the Seven Codex, it's not possible that anybody else could have gotten into their library.'

'Why not?'

Angustias laughed dryly. 'You haven't met the Kelpies.'

'Maybe there's another copy,' Sara wondered aloud. 'Or perhaps the Mawdrik have already tried to find the name.'

'There is another possibility,' said Angustias darkly. 'There's a chance that they have known about the name and where to find it for a long time, but they can't reach it by themselves. There is something I haven't told you, Sara. It's the reason why you are here.'

'I thought our coming here was an accident.'

'Oh, Sara,' said Angustias wearily, 'you already know that isn't true. Why do you think that Terk insisted you take the postcard? Why do you think that your friend sent you the postcard in the first place?'

'But that can't mean anything. I hardly knew her. I can't even remember her name - I think it began with an R.'

'Yes, it does. She is called Rachel, and you met her in a wine bar one evening last summer after you'd had an argument with Carl, your boyfriend, and she was very kind to you when you poured your heart out, and she bought you drinks then insisted that you exchange addresses. Is that right?'

'And then I tried to get in touch with her when Carl and I split up, but the phone number and address didn't exist. Then the postcard arrived.'

'Exactly,' said Angustias. 'And you never throw postcards away, do you? Rachel is a werewoman. She was staying with us until a few days ago.'

'So what you're trying to tell me,' said Sara uncomfortably, 'is that this is all some kind of plot. A set-up?'

'No, no, Sara. Ah... how do I say this? We knew that you would be safer here than almost anywhere else, that you'd be among powerful friends whom, I have to say, now include the Djinn.'

'I'm sorry,' said Sara. 'I didn't mean to sound ungrateful. This is all so hard to take in.'

'You only have to bear with me a little longer,' said Angustias. 'I am afraid there is more. You can show yourself now, Terk.'

Now she knew who'd opened the door earlier. Terk swung round on the swivel chair in the computer bay to face them.

'Being here doesn't only give you and Karmel a breathing space and a chance to recover. It's why Terk is here. It's the reason why François's sister, poor Claudette, was killed by the Mawdrik while she was helping Terk. Somebody is coming, somebody who you have to meet. '

'Who?'

'Orla.'

'That can't be right! No!' Not Orla, the herald of doom and destruction? The same Orla who had ushered in the horror that had almost killed them on Hyaquat?

'What do you really know about Orla, Sara?' She posed the question gently but her face was immobile, her dark eyes hard and unblinking.

'Well… nothing really, I suppose.'

'Listen and learn, then. It´s true that he has always appeared just before something dreadful has happened but he himself has not done a thing to harm anybody. From what I know, he seems to be incapable of doing anything except to say his name. Don't you think that he might be attempting to warn us about something rather than threaten us?'

'I'd never thought about that,' admitted Sara. 'It makes sense, but what I don't understand is why you think he's coming here.'

'Because this is where you are,' said Terk, breaking his silence, 'and because he has spoken again and this time - for the first time - it wasn't to say his own name. He spoke *your* name. He said "Sara".'

10. Albayzín, Granada: July

She had to find Karmel. At last, a significant piece of the puzzle had slipped into place, causing her mind to race with ideas. She had no doubt that the mysterious name of seven was far more than just a word and that the Mawdrik were searching for something that lay within its meaning. How it was connected with the terror they had survived on Hyaquat, she couldn't imagine. But Karmel had said something about it having no place *anywhere*. Maybe, in the light of what she had found out in the library, he might have some further insights.

She found him sitting in the shade of the courtyard and trying to read a newspaper that kept drooping over his face. François was next to him and as soon as he saw her, he rose and took her by the hand, making her sit in the shadiest place. Sara had the impression that if she'd allowed him to, he would have fluffed up the cushions for her. She realized, pleasurably, that his attention wasn't in the least embarrassing. He gave out such an air of spontaneity and self-will that Sara truly believed that he did not have an iota of guile within him. And his dazzling smile was mesmerizing… and he was very beautiful…

As François sauntered over to lean on the edge of the fountain from where he could watch her *('J'aime beaucoup te contempler parce'que tu es très belle'*, he'd said), Sara asked Karmel how he had slept, and what he'd been doing. He was sprawled unevenly in a chair with the newspaper half concealing his face and his legs tangled inelegantly in the folds of the djellaba.

' Where have you been?' His voice sounded rough, its metallic quality a tinny rasp.

'Are you alright, Karmel?'

Karmel flapped his arm at her clumsily as if trying to send her away, knocking the newspaper to the ground in the process.

''Course I am. Why shouldn't I be?'

'Karmel? What have you done?''

'Stop judging me!' he snapped. Sara took a pace back. What could possibly be wrong with him?

'I only had one. Just one little drink.'

He tried to cross his legs under the uncooperative garments and managed to tangle himself up yet more. Giving up on the idea, he slumped to one side and rested his head unsteadily on the curve of the wicker chair.

'It was the ogres. You know what they're like. Love their drink. I just had one glass, it´s the truth.'

'Stop apologizing to me, Karmel. I don't care if you have a drink problem.'

'Alien alcohol. Just alien alcohol. It intra - inter – oh, damn it, it messes with our metabolism.'

'I don't give a damn what it does to you.' Sara's patience had run out. He was not here for her and she needed him, focussed and sober.

Karmel floundered back in his chair and turned an unpleasant shade of puce, but Sara's outburst had made an impact and he clamped his mouth shut in a thin, tight line.

'Do what you have to do to sober up, then we need to talk.'

Karmel pouted like a fish out of water, then said thinly, 'The Kiklayda are able to cleanse themselves internally as well as superficially. One moment, please.'

Sara waited with scant patience as his colour returned, as did the very worst of his distance and formality.

'I beg your forgiveness, Miss Parkinson. I can assure you that you will not see this again. Now, how can I help you?' He was shrinking so far away from her that if he'd been able to, he would have disappeared through the back of the chair.

'Forget it, Karmel,' she snapped. 'We'll talk some other time, when you have decided which one of your many faces you want to wear.'

She strode away forcefully, trying to quell her rage and determined not to look back and give him the opportunity for an instant repentance. *Arrogant, fastidious idiot! He needs to know about the name of Seven, he has to be ready for anything, and all he can do is get drunk.*

François was immediately beside her, and she didn't hesitate in linking arms with him. She needed to forget about Hyaquat and the dark threads that were beginning to ravel together. It was all too much to process just now and she needed a distraction.

'Where are we going, François?'

He took her to the enormous kitchen where a happy bustle of activity suggested that a fiesta was in the making. Sara was soon requisitioned to chop vegetables and taste dishes among the most extraordinary team of cooks she'd ever seen. The troll, whose name was Janet, made the best Andalucian gazpacho she'd ever tasted, and François' younger brother Lionel, insisted that she try his ratatouille.

'They call it pisto here,' he said dismissively, 'but I am *French*.'

People came and went, boxes of bread, cheese and cured meats arrived and were unpacked and the happy cacophony of conversation drew Sara ever further from her troubles. And Francois was there, his warm breath on her neck as she sliced chorizo, his hand guiding hers in gentle rotations as she stirred oil into the almond milk soup.

'Be gentle with the ingredients,' he said. 'Do not beat them to death. Cooking is like making love.' And she did not need to see his face to know that he was smiling.

Later, he showed her the rest of the house, from the cool subterranean depths of the wine cellars and the passages and caves where the trolls and ogres had their lodgings, to the highest windows with the best views of the ancient and fabulous city.

'Let's go to my favourite place,' he said after he'd pointed out the Cathedral, the Hospital Real and the other imposing landmarks of Granada to her. They climbed a staircase and came out into an unfurnished square space, with a stone floor and a wooden ceiling and three white arches open to the air on each side. Even though heat of the day was at its zenith, somehow this crow's nest managed to catch the slightest breeze and channel it to create a cool fresh sanctuary from the heat.

'Angustias comes here sometimes,' said François. 'She calls it her - *ah, laisse-moi penser* - her room of infinite possibility. I'm not sure what that means but, here, I'm always happy.' He sat in one of the arches with the sunlight making a halo around his exquisite form and shimmering in his red-gold hair, while Sara went to each side of the tower in turn, looking down into the courtyard, or across the mass of tiled rooftops and gardens that was the Albayzín, to the mountains that seemed to guard the approaches to the city on every side.

One building in particular caught her attention. It was a little further up the hill and on the surface was no different from many of the elegant carmens in the neighbourhood. It had a walled garden with palm trees and cypresses, a swimming pool and a large terrace shaded with grape vines. There was a tower similar to the one they were in now, and on the top floor of the building a long gallery, open to the air, that ran around two sides of the building with one aspect facing south and the other, towards the Alhambra.

Why she was drawn to the gallery, she had no idea. In the afternoon sun, the shadows of its outer pillars made diagonal stripes across the inner wall. Nothing moved there, nor in the garden or on the terrace, but she spent a long time looking at the place, wondering what it would be like to be there alone. Again and again, she felt herself walking the bare wooden floor, always in the same direction from right to left, but never quite reaching the far end, over and over again.

She felt the radiant heat of François's body next to her, and the light touch of the hairs on his arm against her skin. Startled, she turned to find herself nose to nose with him, feeling the warm breath of his smile and transfixed by his brilliant sea green eyes. She was surprised to find that he was as tall as she was; he spent so much time sitting cross-legged, or resting on one knee, that he'd always seemed to be smaller. She was also aware, more than ever, of the beauty of his physique and his complete absence of self-consciousness. He leaned forward, almost delicately, and kissed her slowly, and then he leaped into flight through the nearest arch.

The kiss lingered deliciously, soft as silk but firm enough to send a thrill of passion through her. Sara ran to the arch and saw him arcing into the blue sky with the afternoon sun scintillating on his wings. He turned an ecstatic somersault and waved to her, then arrowed out of sight.

Bemused but delighted, Sara made her way back to the courtyard with a mind to search out Karmel and apologize for the awkward confrontation, but he wasn't there and nobody had seen him for some time. She wandered through the elegance of the common room, among the sculpted pillars with their intricate geometric patterns and through angled pools of colour from the stained glass windows, then out along the rainbow tiled passage, all the time enjoying the lingering sensation of François' lips on hers.

Now she was approaching the front entrance, walking through the oval of light cast on the floor by the round window with the crescent moon motif. Somebody was knocking on the door, three sharp loud taps, and without thinking Sara pulled back the heavy iron bolt, turned the bronze latch ring, and opened it.

A girl was standing there in the fierce light. She was maybe nine or ten years old, with ropes of dirty light brown hair to her skinny shoulders, and brown skin. She wore a stained sleeveless dress, and orange flip-flops and sunglasses that were too big. As Sara hesitated in her surprise, the girl extended her hand and opened it. Lying in her palm was a small silver coin with a hole in the middle.

Suddenly, as though they had materialised from thin air, two Djinn were in front of Sara and were blocking out the afternoon glare with their willowy robed forms. They took the girl by the hands and lead her inside, and she went with them passively as they swept away down the corridor and out of sight. More Djinn were gathering, and the thunder of running feet came from all directions.

Sara did not know where to turn. She suddenly found herself surrounded by a throng of looming ogres, all staring at her in consternation with their extraordinary yellow eyes, a band of Terk's little people, banshees whom she had never seen before, the lumbering troll and others, all muttering in consternation. Whatever invisible siren had alerted them was beyond her perception, but now she could see Angustias battling her way through the crowd, out of breath and with her broad hips swaying dramatically. Pushing her way through the people to Sara, she looked as pale as her dark skin would permit.

'Are you safe? Did she touch you?'

'Who was that girl, Angustias? Where have the Djinn taken her?'

'It is too late for her, Sara. *Did she touch you?*'

'N-no. But what are they doing with her?'

'They will help her go to sleep.'

'Sleep?' Sara was horrified. 'You mean-?'

'Come with me,' said Angustias. 'You need to see this for yourself. The rest of you, stay here and be watchful.'

With a coterie of Djinn behind them, Angustias and Sara quickly descended a flight of stairs to the basement of the safe house, and entered a cold, candle-lit room with white walls and a bare floor of beaten earth. Juan was standing by a trestle table in the centre of the room, on which lay the motionless body of the little girl.

Juan was agitated, his chest rising and falling rapidly and a bestial snorting noise coming from his nostrils. Sara could feel the raw fury raging from his black eyes.

'Tranquilo, Juan,' said Angustias. 'Not yet. Save your anger for when we need it most.'

They approached the table. Angustias bent down and removed the girl's sunglasses, and Sara saw with horror that she had no eyes. Where they should have been, there was nothing.

'This is how the Mawdrik work,' said Angustias icily. 'This is what they have done to the children. They have made them into mindless empty shells to do the bidding of the grass men.'

'Juan,' she said, 'make sure that she is decently buried tonight, with all due respect. Sara, come with me.'

They went not to the courtyard, but to Angustias' private rooms. She had a small bedroom, concealed by a beaded curtain, and a cosy lounge with double doors that opened onto a small balcony that was busy with a riot of trailing geraniums.

'Madre mía! This calls for something stronger than orange juice.' She made Sara sit down by the open balcony doors, while she poured two large glasses of rosy red *pacharán*. Several mouthfuls of the fruity liqueur helped to steady both their pounding hearts and their shattered nerves.

'The Virgin be thanked that she didn't touch you. If that had happened, the fight would have come sooner, while we are still not fully prepared.'

'What did the Djinn do to that girl, Angustias?'

'The Djinn have the power to take your breath away,' said Angustias sadly. 'It is not an ability they use lightly or indiscriminately. There really was nothing else we could have done for her. She was beyond hope the moment she fell into the clutches of the Mawdrik.'

She topped Sara's glass up from the square bottle.

'What happens now?' asked Sara.

Angustias hunched her broad shoulders, then let them fall heavily. 'Thankfully, the situation is not as desperate as it might have been, although I'm afraid that the Mawdrik now know where we are.'

'That girl?' said Sara. 'Do you think that the Mawdrik were able to communicate with her in some way before she - before the Djinn took her?'

'I fear so. Whether directly or through the grass men, I don't know. What troubles me is that the grass men are already here in Granada, but they have only shown themselves openly once when they tried to attack you. The Mawdrik are clearly planning something special for our city.'

Angustias shook her head emphatically as if to break this undesirable train of thought.

'The good news is that word of you has spread. More Djinn arrived this morning, more than I've ever seen before. There must be fifty here now, with another twenty or thirty waiting in the badlands of Guadix, and they can be with us in less than half an hour if needed. They'll mount a guard around this place that not even a hundred Mawdrik will be able to penetrate. The problem is that you can't stay here forever. Sooner or later, Orla will come.'

'We wait, then?'

'Yes, we wait, and tonight we party.' Angustias had a steely and determined look in her eyes. 'They can't break our resolve this easily. We are going to sing and dance and eat and out *there*, the Djinn will be watching and waiting. We will be ready for them. I think that this incident is yet more proof of their growing desperation and fear.'

'More proof? Are things not going well for the Mawdrik?'

Angustias flexed her shoulders again, and this time when she relaxed, it was if she was shrugging away some of her angst and tension.

'I don't want to say that we know what their plans are, but yes, we have reason to believe that they are feeling a little bit insecure. We've heard that their campaigns in North America are running into trouble. The Djinn are part of an alliance of similar peoples and we know that their kinsfolk haven't just held the grass men back. They are actually destroying them.'

She folded her arms over her bust. 'There's more. The Mawdrik like to hold conclaves in remote places so that they can enjoy a mutual gloat over their supposed superiority. Pah!' She spat flamboyantly.

'They usually choose somewhere uninhabited and spectacular that feeds into their colossal egos. Sometimes it's the crater of an active volcano, or the Antarctic ice cap, or at the bottom of the Marianas Trench. A month or two back, they decided to get together in the face of a storm front over the North Atlantic between Iceland and Greenland, but something went very wrong for them. Something that, come to think of it, sounds very much like the experience you had on Hyaquat.'

'I have gone over that in my head, so many times,' said Sara, helping herself from the pacharan bottle and topping up Angustias' glass. 'I know it was like the dream. I just didn't realize it at the time - we were so busy trying not to be killed. It was the pulse of Seven again. The name we don't know, the one they're trying to find. There's something loose out there. Something that shouldn't ever have been set free - unless it broke free of its own accord.'

'Once again, your perception astounds me,' said Angustias, admiringly. 'Terk told me how remarkable you are and now I can see it for myself.'

Sara barely heard her. 'What happened to the Mawdrik? Come to think of it, how did you find out what happened?'

'It was the Merfolk,' said Angustias. 'They're a true oceanic people, nothing at all like those stupid Hollywood wenches with their silly fish tails and bouncy breasts. They're barely on speaking terms even with us, but they do have relatively cordial relations with the Kelpies. It's a water affinity that they share, don't ask me to explain it. Whatever, they saw what happened and then they brought news of it to the kelpies on the islands of St Kilda, then the Scottish ogres passed it south, and so on and so forth.

'There were a hundred Mawdrik at that gathering, but after whatever happened to them was over, a third of them had ceased to exist. The Djinn are their equal and they can tear them apart, but the Mawdrik always renew themselves. To obliterate them entirely and irreversibly is something else. There are too few of us who can do *that*.'

'And whatever it is,' said Sara, 'it's as indifferent to the Mawdrik as it is to the rest of us. But in that case, why are the Mawdrik trying to find its source? The book - doesn't it say that one of the meanings of the name of seven is "knowledge"?'

Angustias simply raised an eyebrow and took another mouthful of pacharan. 'And you're saying it again, Sara, only this time in the light of what you now know. So I really don't think that you need *my* opinion to work the rest of it out.'

Then she looked out through the doors to the cascading geraniums and beyond, drawing a long breath in through her prominent nose as though she was testing the air.

'I thought so,' she said. 'The rain is coming.'

11. Night Time: Albayzín, Granada

Sundown and twilight. A waxing moon riding high in the sky and a flitter of bats about the courtyard, dipping and swerving as they gathered the gnats that danced in ephemeral clouds above the fountain. By half past ten, the courtyard was filled with people and a lively buzz of chatter, and a dozen folding tables with dishes heaped with food and stacked with bottles of wine were set against the walls.

Sara had asked around among the current female inhabitants of the safe house for suitable clothing and the results were a pair of pale lilac harem pants and a plain white cotton blouse. After soaking in the warm pool of the sanctuary's luxurious Arabic baths, she took a breath-takingly cold plunge then dried herself and splashed her skin with headily perfumed jasmine water.

She joined the party early, and found herself among a mixed group of ogres and werepeople, along with the troll Janet and her bearish partner, Paco, who had arrived that afternoon by way of the extensive tunnels that linked the safe house to many remote forest and mountain retreats throughout the southern parts of the Iberian peninsula. Once she had grown accustomed to Janet´s bass growl and her disconcerting habit of slapping you on the back so hard that you almost fell over, Sara discovered that the troll had a scandalously earthy sense of humour and that she was considered to be a great beauty among her people. The ogres, for their part, were smaller and darker skinned than their British counterparts, with sapphire eyes, and spoke not a word of English, but as soon as Sara mentioned the name of Valu to them, they made it known to her that they knew and loved the northern ogress as a cousin.

Another of the trolls was deftly carving slices from a cured ham, curling them off the bone and flipping them onto the plates of the diners who were helping themselves from a sumptuous selection of dishes. There were bowls of cod and orange salad with black olives, crunchy lettuce hearts drizzled with oil and fried garlic, and baskets of fresh bread from the famous bakeries of Alfacar. Lamb cutlets and sardines sizzled over the embers of a barbeque and in one corner a huge iron pan of fragrant rabbit paella bubbled over a fire. Another was filled with chunks of goat in garlic sauce, and for the larger guests there were whole legs of cold roast mutton, aromatic with wild rosemary from the sierras.

While, from time to time, Lionel would slip into the dark interior of the building with plastic buckets of raw fish and bloody meat. Doubtless, thought Sara, there were people here who not only chose to avoid the light, but who also preferred their sustenance uncooked.

Sara had never been a victim of shyness. In her teens she had partied every weekend until the early hours of Sunday morning, but sometimes she'd never felt more alone than when she was dancing away the cruel night, drunk and despairing under the mesmerizing lights of some quickly forgotten club, with the monotonous music devolving into a meaningless hopeless thunder.

But to be here, among these extraordinary people, *this* was a revelation of the highest degree. This was wonderfully and restoratively different, so much so that she wished that she could say that it remade her faith in the potential of humanity to party without prejudice, but she could not… because these diverse and extraordinary people were not human. Instead, they seemed to have discovered something greater, an ability to put aside differences far more profound than race or species and to come together and share good times without the least reserve. Trolls laughed and joked with ogres, banshees sat and put the world to rights with Terk´s gnomish kinsmen over a couple of bottles of rioja. Everybody, or so it seemed, wanted to spend time with Sara and she found herself jostled and chivvied from place to place like the valued guest of honour that - she was beginning to realize with delight - in all reality she was.

Dusk had long since deepened into night, but the courtyard was lit from ground to eaves with hanging lamps and candles. Juan sat by the fountain, playing the flamenco guitar intensely with his eyes shut and an ecstasy of concentration on his face, and by slow degrees Sara found herself drawn in among a group consisting, among others, of Terk, the trolls, a dark Spanish ogre and the unnerving Caribbean woman with the white eyes.

'I won't be staying on much longer,' Terk was saying as Paco´s huge, shovel-like hand reached over to top up the little man's wine glass. 'This heat doesn't do much for my skin. Give me a nice damp earthy tunnel and I'll call it paradise.'

'What about your family,' asked Sara. 'Are they safe?'

'They are safe but I sure do miss them. Don't worry about us, Sara. We will go on whatever happens here, up on the surface. So will the rest,' he indicated, sweeping his arm to include everybody in the courtyard. Three of his kinsmen had silently joined them and were listening intently to his words. They were all wearing the typical soft leather breeches and jackets of their kind, covered with elaborate swirling designs and looking like beings from the myths and mists of time.

'There's a storm coming, Sara.' His words made a strangely quiet and intimate place among them at the heart of the noise and merrymaking and Sara was immediately alert. 'It will be a real storm of rain and lightning, but it's going to be far more than that. A storm of the soul.'

'I know,' she said, watching the movement and hearing the babble of conversation, but suddenly apart from the rest and intimate within the circle of the few who were gathered around the table and were a party to Terk's unsettling prediction.

'I'm a Seer, darlin',' said the woman with the white eyes. 'One of the last true Seers. I know what's gonna happen and what's gone before, but I ain' ever met a case like you before. You like a close book, girl.'

'Can't you tell me anything?'

'Yeah, sure. You need to follow your heart always. But that ain' what you want to hear. Any low-down no-good fraud gonna tell you that.'

She leant forwards, and bored into Sara's eyes with her frightening white orbs. 'You gonna suffer, girl. You gonna hurt so bad you wish you were dead, but then you gonna find somethin' you never *dreeeam* you find again.'

She lapsed into a fit of chuckling and sat back in her chair. The ogre, who'd said nothing until now and had occupied himself in staring at the waxing moon with his fiercely blue eyes, now shifted and leant forward, looming massively over all of them.

'Si, es verdad. Llegará una tormenta y te irás. Puedo olerlo.'

And what did he say, beyond what is obvious? I know that "tormenta" means a storm. Do they have to remind me that these few snatched fragments of happiness can't last? Can I change the future even if I should come to know it? Is he predicting my fate as well?

Not long after this came the distraction that Sara had hoped for, and it was timely and welcome and managed to take her mind off the Seer's troubling forecast. It was François and he had changed his clothes, although the ephemeral toga-like affair that hung over his shoulder and encircled his waist, only covered him minimally and succeeded in accentuating his classical physique and reinforcing the allure that Sara was finding increasingly difficult to resist.

He chose to sit on the ground next to her, watching the activity and appearing not to observe her, though she could see the profile of his face angled towards her, and caught the occasional glint of his green eyes as he flashed her a quick look, and saw the half smile that lifted the corners of the mouth that had joined briefly and exquisitely with hers that afternoon.

Then, as if by some unspoken understanding the hubbub of conversation trailed off, and the people began to clear from the centre of the courtyard, leaving Juan and his guitar. The tempo of his playing picked up as Angustias walked out into the light, dressed simply in a black skirt and an embroidered fringed shawl around her shoulders. She began to dance, foot stamping, twisting and snapping her fingers and twirling the scarf as Juan plucked magic from the guitar strings. And as Angustias danced on and the audience of trolls and ogres and dwarves stamped and clapped and swayed, it felt completely natural and right that François should lay his head in Sara's lap, and that she should caress the elegant curve of his neck and run her fingers through his golden hair.

That night, Sara dreamed that she was walking slowly along the upper gallery of the house on the hill, the house she'd been so drawn to that afternoon just before François' kiss had stolen away every preoccupation from her mind. Every footstep she took pounded like a toll of thunder, until every eighth step, which was utterly silent, and, try as she might, she couldn't seem to get any closer to the sobbing figure that stood at the far end of the gallery with its back to her. Then it turned to face her with its hands over its eyes and when it took them away she saw that it was the empty eyeless girl that the Mawdrik had destroyed.

She floundered awake, beating away the thin cotton sheet then forcing herself to lie still while her heartbeat slowed to a more regular pace. Instinctively, she looked across the room and saw with relief that François was once again sitting in the wicker chair, watching over her, his body silver in the light of a moon that was only a day away from full.

Morning brought a change in the weather. While the heat if anything had intensified, the blue had leached from the sky and a heavy haze completely obscured the dramatic profile of the Sierra Nevada. After taking her breakfast in the kitchen, Sara went to the library and took William Grace's book from the shelves. She relocated the section that described the Seven and read through it over and over again, trying to fix every word in her memory and searching for some kind of pattern in the text that might help to open a door into some kind of new insight.

Again, she wondered why the name of Seven was unknown - or had it been lost or deliberately concealed? And if this was really what the Mawdrik were searching for, what use would a single word be to them without some existing insight into how to use it?

Her thoughts were drifting along these lines when Karmel found her.

'Hello, Sara. Can I join you?'

'Of course you can! Are you all right? Angustias said you were meditating. Is that why you didn't come to the fiesta?'

He inclined his head, then slid a chair out from under the table. He looked fresh and restored, and by the sheen of his skin, Sara guessed that he had just shed his crystalline epidermis.

'The Kiklayda can enter any one of a number of levels of consciousness at will, according to their need. Sometimes it´s to heal a physical or mental trauma. If we have to search our racial memory we can slow down our metabolic processes in order to focus more completely. It´s a form of suspended animation, a little like hibernation.'

'And that's what you were doing?'

'I wanted to see if there was anything stored away in my race conscience that might help us. You understand? Something left over from the past that could help us hone our ability.'

'I wish you'd heard what Angustias told me yesterday,' said Sara.

'I already know,' he responded. 'I saw her early this morning.'

'Did you? I haven't seen her today.'

'Nor will you for the next few days. I came out of trance just as she was coming to the caves. It is her time. That's where she likes to go for her transformation.'

He looked at the book.

'Is this it?'

'Take a look.' She turned it around for him to see. He read without comment, then leafed through the adjacent pages with his spindly fingers, scanning them rapidly with flickering violet eyes and a vertical frown line wrinkling his forehead.

'I can make nothing of this code,' he admitted. 'Maybe it´s not meant for us. I don't believe in prophecy, not since I lost my faith in the Five Gods, but I think that circumstances can sometimes draw together to shed light on a dark place and show the way ahead.'

He blanched an unpleasant shade of bone white, but recovered almost immediately.

'I was looking for you,' he said quickly. 'There is something I need to explain. It might answer some of your questions. You don't mind, do you?'

'What do you mean? Of course I don't mind. You can talk to me about anything – okay, not anything. You're Kiklaydan and I respect your limits.'

'But that's exactly the point,' said Karmel, leaning closer to her over the open book. 'I feel that since I met you, some of my "limits" as you call them are beginning to seem a little absurd.' The ensuing long sigh implied more than just physical exhaustion.

'Whatever. I am going to tell you about Zerafma.'

'Ah, right. I remember,' she said. 'That is the name I picked up when we touched, that first time on Hyaquat. What is Zerafma?'

'You should say, *who*. She is - she *was* my great love.' Karmel pushed the book aside and stared at the table, spreading his fingers wide and slowly rippling them up and down on the solid oak surface.

'We were very much in love but, now I can look back on it, it was an intense and dangerous affair that should never have been allowed to explode out of control.'

Sara likewise had leant forward across the table and was as close to Karmel as she felt they could both tolerate.

'How can you have a passionate relationship without physical contact? That's what I don't understand. Most humans are very tactile. At least, I am.'

He didn't reply, or at least not in a direct manner. 'My father was Doggish Tragawlty. He was Kiklayda's most eminent philosopher of the modern age. It was my father who wrote the definitive work on Kiklaydan-Human relationships but even though he broke the mould in this area of research he was deeply committed to preserving our traditional culture. After the Separation, I was brought up strictly according to the traditional norm.'

'Wait a moment. What do you mean by "The Separation"?'

'That's a considerable part of what I need to tell you,' said Karmel. 'Do you remember when you asked me about our reproductive processes?'

'Mm-hmm?'

'You see, the Kiklayda have two fertile genders that basically equate to your female and male types. I am considered to be male,' he added, flushing a vaguely embarrassed mauve before continuing. 'There are others. We call them the Nons. They are not exactly neuters, because they are able to carry children to term but they don't contribute any physical matter to their genesis. What they *do* do, is to give something just as important and that's to provide the Kiklaydan race-memory to the foetus. When a couple decide to have a child, the Non takes the male and female germ into itself. It's a deeply honourable task and the Nons prepare all their lives for this moment. Then, when the child is born, he is immediately removed and taken to a sanctuary in the mountains where he spends the first five years of his life in isolation and deep meditation.'

'Say what?' Sara wasn't sure that she had understood what Karmel had just said.

Karmel looked at her askance. 'The newborn. He is taken to an isolation cell. It´s essential for our children to develop their appreciation of self. Kiklaydan children are very independent from the moment of parturition.'

'I thought that's what you said. I hope you don't take this the wrong way but isn't that rather barbaric, to just abandon a newborn baby for five years?'

'It might appear so to you,' he responded calmly, 'but every Kiklaydan child is planned for meticulously and unlike your species we do not breed indiscriminately, nor do we kill our unborn children. As a result we have never overpopulated our home world and our quality of life and environment remain intact. Can you say the same about this planet?'

His expression softened. 'Sara, every Kiklaydan child is loved and cherished. Besides, we more than make up for those early years during our adolescence.'

'And that happened to you?'

'When I came out of Separation, my parents were there to greet me with the Kiklaydan equivalent of open arms and the festivities lasted for more than three weeks. It was a celebration of my uniqueness and in my case it was especially significant because during those first years I had discovered my musical ability, and the other… the one I kept secret.'

'And what about Zerafma? Why didn't it work out between you?'

'Because she was a modernist. She hated the idea of the Non partnership. She claimed that in our distant past we didn't have them and that we didn't need them. And she said that physical contact between married couples was a beautiful and honourable thing.'

He looked at her aghast, his mouth sagging open. 'Oh Sara, she was beautiful and brilliant but I rejected her. I couldn't hear what she was trying to say to me.'

'I wish I could help. I don't know what to do.'

'You are already doing more than enough! If you can be a friend to somebody like me, *that* is redemption. I will not disappoint you again.'

'Karmel, you haven't disappointed me. You have only ever been yourself.'

He lifted a trembling hand and it seemed that he was actually going to touch hers. Instead, he withdrew and quickly stood up.

'Thank you,' he said, then turned away quickly and walked from the library. Sara was not to see him again that day.

Sara's actions for the rest of the day were motivated by a mounting sense of premonition. She went to her room and made sure that everything was packed and ready, and that the flower from Endymion was still safe. Someone had left a change of clean clothes on her bed, practical clothes that would be good for travelling in, and she already had the lightweight waterproof that she had brought from home, rolled away at the bottom of her pack.

There were plenty of signs of preparation throughout the rest of the safe house too, comings and goings, low voices talking behind closed doors, and in the face of such activity Sara began to feel somewhat helpless and wished that Angustias was there to talk to. But Angustias was going through her transformation and Sara still had no idea about the nature of the werewoman's other self.

Neither had she seen anything of François, and his absence troubled her. None of the other banshees were to be seen either, but this gave her scant reassurance. That afternoon the haze lifted and broke, though the sky remained sultry. A stack of cumulonimbus was building in the west and as the searing screech of cicadas gave way to the softer trilling of crickets, there were a few distant cracks of thunder but, by the time it was fully night, the sky was clear and the full moon shone down once more into the courtyard.

Dinner was a strange event. It took place in the great kitchen, which had a set of double doors that opened onto a small terrace filled with lush foliage plants in raised beds and large terracotta pots. There was an enormous table and the ceiling was high enough to accommodate the height and breadth of even the largest diners.

The trolls were sitting at one end of the table on large sections of tree trunk. At the opposite end were two Spanish ogres, while Sara was halfway along between Terk and another of his people, a battered old warrior called Naga. The timber wolf that Sara had seen when they arrived, had now transformed into a tall, thin Norwegian with chilly blue eyes called Eric, who had a scarred face and a haunted look and did not speak once during the meal. None of the other werepeople present were currently in transformation, and among the twenty or so at the table, Sara noticed a number of strange faces.

Others had gathered in the kitchen who were not sharing the meal and preferred to keep to the darker parts of the cavernous and dimly lit room. Five Djinn bowed reverently to Sara when she walked in, then slipped back to join the others in the shadows. While the food was being served, Sara took the opportunity to look around and managed to spy odd figures in the dark. Among them was a sinuous figure that appeared to be a woman, but her glistening olive skin looked as though it was continually running with moisture and her arms and legs were covered with lank shining hair with the appearance of seaweed. Her face was strange and long with narrow dark eyes and a flattened nose and her mane of hair dangled to well below her waist.

She's a kelpie.

She remembered something that François' brother Lionel had told her yesterday about the Kelpies. There were some in Brittany, not far from his birthplace, and the reason that they were always wet was because, when they were on land, they secreted a salty fluid to keep their skins moist. Nevertheless, knowing the reason behind this strange behaviour did not make Sara feel any easier about the feral presence of the dripping kelpie woman, whose dark and unreadable eyes seemed to bore straight into her soul.

Others were even more peculiar: stick-like shapes that moved constantly in insectile motion, and others who had a peculiar fluidity about them that defied definition and were so unobtrusive that she soon gathered the impression that they did not want to be seen too clearly. Their eyes glimmered like little green lamps, and there was an aroma of mossy dampness in the room that, she was certain, emanated from them. Some of them reminded Sara of the wood sprites she had seen emerging from under the ground in the street the afternoon that she and Terk had escaped to the lake with the help of the Vodyanoi.

Whatever they were, it was clear that they had come to listen. The talk at the dinner table was subdued and it wasn't easy for Sara to hear what was being discussed among people with such strange accents.

'What's going on, Terk? I keep hearing stuff about "being ready" and "others" and "arrival", but that's all.'

'The news isn't good,' he said. 'We have a dozen banshees patrolling the sky and we've received news that the Mawdrik are reinforcing their numbers across the city.'

'Does that mean that we aren't safe here. If that's what you mean, I need to warn Karmel.'

'This house is safe, for the moment. It's seen bad times before, but -'

'*But*, I'm the problem,' she said. 'You don't need to say it.'

'Sara, don't misunderstand what is happening. You are both the problem and the solution. I know as well as you do that you will be leaving us soon. When you attempt to do so, that's when the Mawdrik will make their move. It won't happen until then and that gives us a little more time to prepare, but much depends on you, and that is where the problem lies because, until you know when the time is right, our hands are tied.'

'And at the moment I have absolutely no idea what I'm supposed to do,' she said flatly. 'Okay, here's a hypothetical scenario for you. What would happen if I left the house now and went for a walk?'

'Nothing,' said their eating companion, Naga. He looked much older than Terk and had pale skin, scars on his arms and a plethora of fine wrinkles around his mouth and eyes. 'They are waiting for a sign. The Mawdrik don't only want you, they want to know why you are here.'

'That makes sense,' she mused, 'even though I don't really know why I'm here yet except to meet somebody I am scared to meet. I'll ask another question. Why are there so many people here, if the Djinn are able to protect me?'

'They have come to do what they can to help,' said Terk, 'but that isn't all. The Mawdrik and their creatures have run amok for months, but now the chinks in their armour have started to show. They're allowing their blind fury to overwhelm their judgement.'

'I'd rather say, they've have been running riot for millennia,' said Naga. 'I have ample proof as evidence of their machinations.' He lifted his knotted and lacerated arms and turned them around for both to see.

'That's true,' admitted Terk, 'but you can't deny that we're entering a time of special change. It's been decided that here, in Granada, is where we will begin to draw a new frontier. We're planning to bloody the nose of the Mawdrik and, at the very least, remind them that they and the humans don't have this world entirely to themselves.'

'Yes… what about the people?' said Sara. 'I mean, the human people. Whatever happens, I'm still one of them.'

Naga grunted. 'Thanks to the Mawdrik and their use of the grass men, your comfortable little world is never going to be the same again,' he said grimly. 'Don't be too willing to defend *them*, either. You might be different from the rest, but mankind as a whole isn't blameless in this matter. They've let themselves be duped by the Mawdrik, time and time again. That's not made it easy for us.'

Terk lifted a hand. 'Calm down, Naga. This isn't the time or the place.'

After this, Naga became sullen and uncommunicative and the remainder of dinner passed amidst a vaguely uneasy clatter of utensils and short requests to pass something or other. Sara was relieved when the gathering started to disperse but although she was tired and all too conscious of the need to rest and prepare herself for whatever the following day might bring, she was not ready for bed. She lingered at the table, staring into the wavering flame of a candle after almost everybody else had left, and then she saw a movement in the courtyard. Motivated by curiosity, she stepped outside.

In the silver green night, among the arching fronds of potted palms and the enormous arrowhead leaves of colocasia plants, she saw a bench and on it was sitting François, resting his arms on one bent leg and watching her calmly as if he'd been waiting for her.

'Where have you been?'

'Là dessus, près de la lune,' he said. 'Flying.'

He patted the bench. 'Come. Sit with me.'

As soon as she sat down, François leant into her and rested his head on her shoulder.

'Why so quiet, ma cherie?'

'Oh, my François.' She let the words escape slowly as a sigh. 'It's all too much.'

'Pourquoi? Dis-moi.' When she looked at him blankly, he said 'Tell me.'

'I'm in too many different places at once and I can't keep up with myself. I have seen things that nobody should ever see and I don't know where this madness will take me next. And whatever's about to happen, I feel like I can't change anything. It'll just happen, good or bad. What am I supposed to do, François?'

'Things have their time and place,' he said. He ran his fingers down her cheek with a touch as soft as thistledown and she leaned close into him, feeling the security of his warm, firm body against her.

'Do not try to change them,' he added. 'Be here. Be alive. Here and now we have the moon. It is enough.'

But the moon was full and the storm was gathering, and Sara knew in her heart that soon, she would need much more than the comfort of friends.

12. Albayzín, Granada

The retreat of the storm front was only temporary. By mid-morning on the following day, clouds were once again gathering in the west. It was unpleasantly humid and the swifts that normally flew high were skimming over the jumbled red rooftops of the Albayzín, dusky heralds of the changing weather.

Sara knew that Karmel never removed the belt in which he stored his few possessions, even when he was asleep, but his state of readiness or otherwise wasn't what concerned her. She had not seen him since they had talked in the library and, in the eerily deserted building, there was nobody to ask about it.

She knew that the illusion of emptiness was exactly that - an illusion. All the same, it would have lessened her anxiety to see more tangible signs of life. However, as she climbed the stairs to the tower room, a Djinn materialized behind her. She hesitated on the stairs, wondering how to address him because even though she was certain that the Djinn had pledged their support to her, she'd only had direct dealings with them on the day she had arrived.

The Djinn bowed slightly and waited as she searched for words. She found that she was puzzling over what was hidden beneath his white robes because all that she could see through the narrow slit in his turban was a swirl of blue grey smoke that concealed a glowing core like smouldering embers.

'Excuse me. Do you know what's happening?'

The Djinn exhaled and she felt a gust of dry heat.

'We prepare to face the Mawdrik.'

He was silent again. Was that all? She needed more. As he faced her impassively, she knew what she needed to ask.

'If I need you, will you be here?'

He emitted the same scorching exhalation. 'We are always here. We watch you day and night. We never sleep.'

Unnerved and encouraged at the same time, she continued on up the stairs. She walked the perimeter of the upper room, studying the city from all angles and hoping for clues and hints of whatever was coming. Apart from the indistinct movement of crowds in every open space and the thin plumes of smoke that seemed to rise perpetually from the cooking fires of the refugees, the only signs of change were the clouds rolling slowly in from the south and west. They piled, tier upon tier, as they advanced over the plains of the Granada Vega, extinguishing the last slanting sunbeams and, every minute that passed, the dark that followed on behind the cloud front grew deeper and wider.

Sara turned her attention to the north, to the hillside called San Miguel Alto where the old city walls ascended to pine forests and a cluster of radio masts on the hilltop. Her eyes tracked down among the labyrinth of lanes, until they stopped at the carmen with the high walls and the open gallery.

Sara's breath caught in her throat. She felt as if her vision had suddenly been drawn into a narrow corridor and that her perception was being dragged through space to that one location. She didn't want to look, she tried to turn away but she couldn't. Nothing tangible had changed and across the neighbourhood not even the quick slinking of the ubiquitous stray cats intruded on the stillness, but Sara was beyond doubt as to what she had to do, and that time was short in which to act.

The Djinn was waiting for her at the bottom of the stairs.

'I need you now,' she said quickly. 'Are there more of you?'

By way of a reply, another five Djinn appeared instantly outside the door and as she set off through the building at a run they fell in beside and behind her, easily matching her pace with their effortless gliding motion. They exited through the main entrance. It was the first time that Sara had been outside the safe house since her arrival, and she did not know what lay further up the hill, but she did not hesitate. First right and then right again, she and her entourage came onto a narrow lane similar to that in which the grass men had so nearly succeeded in waylaying her.

She could see the high white walls of the carmen ahead and, inside, the soaring palm trees and cypresses of its hidden garden, half concealing the upper storey of the building and the mysterious gallery that was urgently calling to her.

The first clouds were almost overhead, their ragged outriders breaking into shreds and reforming, but all the time they advanced and drove the light further from the sky. Hot gusts of wind tossed pieces of rubbish and prematurely fallen leaves into the air and pulled at the robes of the Djinn, emphasizing their skeletal forms but, whatever their substance beneath the coverings, they seemed impervious to every external force.

They came to the entrance to the carmen. When she asked about it, Angustias had told her that it was the city home of a wealthy banking family who had left for their villa in Tenerife a month ago to escape the increasingly worrying situation in Granada. It was guarded by a high-tech security system that included closed-circuit television cameras mounted on the walls, alarms and automatic double doors made of reinforced steel.

Sara turned to the Djinn. 'Can you get in?'

One of them glided up to the doors and put his swaddled hands crosswise over the central part. She heard the whir and clicking of mechanisms inside, then the doors parted and silently opened inwards.

They passed through the gates and along a wide garden path that curved between aromatic bay trees and flowering oleander. Smaller paths ran off at right angles, among ponds with water lilies, beds of glossy-leaved bear's breeches and the blue and white globes of agapanthus. A set of shallow steps ran up to a terrace paved with red tiles and, to the right, under the gallery, an untended swimming pool was gathering dead leaves and the falling pink flowers of a bougainvillea vine that covered part of the wall.

Again, a Djinn came forward and effortlessly opened the door that led from the patio into the house. They passed through a colossal open-plan kitchen with stainless steel fittings and granite surfaces, then a lounge with a gleaming parquet floor, a suite of white leather couches and armchairs, and the largest television screen that she had even seen, and then up a cast iron spiral staircase. Open doors on the first floor offered glimpses into luxurious bedrooms and three vast bathrooms, each with a circular jacuzzi.

At the end of a wide corridor, two sets of double doors opened to the mirador, one of glass and the other panelled with mosquito screens. Both were open and, through them, Sara could see a wooded hillside and a cameo of the Alhambra palaces framed within one of the gallery's arches.

'Stay here, please,' she said to the Djinn. 'I have to do this alone.'

As she left the sanctuary of her Djinn bodyguard, Sara endured a moment of jolting vulnerability. The doorway ahead was like an eye, focusing all the scrutiny of a hostile world onto her, and the tiny windows and galleries of the adjacent Alhambra were a multitude of other eyes all bent hungrily on her as if she were a morsel of prey to be consumed.

She had to go on. She mustn't look back or she would have to ask her companions to come with her and she knew instinctively that whatever waited for her outside, it wanted her alone. She reached the doors, pulling them a little further inward to make room, and then she went outside.

Sara was at the southern end of the mirador. As she had seen from the safe house, it ran along the entire front and depth of the building, and each side was at least twenty metres in length. The floor was of old grey wood, bleached by long exposure to heat and sun, and the inner wall and pillars of the arches were stone, painted white.

The mirador was empty and devoid of any sense of presence or recent occupation, but Sara began to walk slowly towards the far end, counting her footsteps as they struck a dull rhythm on the dry planks. By now the sky was completely sunless, the foreground thrown into strange and detailed relief against a cloudscape so darkly grey and charged with electrical potential that she could almost taste its metallic quality.

She slowed down. What if she was mistaken, and this impulse was nothing more than a desperate need for something - for anything - to happen? Or maybe it was even worse. Could this be a cruel trick of the Mawdrik, to plant an impulse in her thoughts and isolate her from her friends so they could take her at will?

Then she grabbed at her head and winced as a stabbing pain pierced her cranium. It spread to her eyes and she clenched her teeth to stop herself crying out. As the first migraine wave subsided, she opened her eyes against the vertiginous discomfort and struggled to focus.

At the far end of the mirador, it was as if the jagged fragments of a shattered mirror were spinning in the air, dozens of whirling, gleaming shards whirling up from the floor and into a columnar vortex. At first, they outlined the most insubstantial of shapes, the barest suggestion of an irregular outline, but as more and more shards began to flicker into existence their dizzy spiralling began to describe the ghost of a figure.

The pain returned. Thorns burrowed under her skin, hammers pounded on her cranium but she forced herself to move closer, shielding her eyes against its painful light. From what she was able to see, the shape was barely human in outline and seemed to be constantly breaking apart and reforming itself. Where a face might have been, the light fragments spilled inwards in a whirlpool and, in its depth, she could see the dullest of eyes, dark and dislocated smudges like the eyes of something long dead.

'Orla?'

He moved his head, so excruciatingly slowly that she realized the slightest movement was an agony to him that was almost beyond endurance. But he was tilting his head down, degree by painful degree. When he raised his head again Sara tried to look directly into his face but she was swamped by a fresh wave of nausea and agony.

She dropped to her knees, gagging.

'Please! You're hurting me!'

Orla did nothing. He seemed incapable of movement, frozen into place by his own terrible suffering.

'Why are you here? Tell me! I can't stand this.'

Orla was moving again, battling to lift his head against the tempest of fragments that were trying to rip him apart.

'Follow,' he whispered in a tortured voice.

'*Where?*'

'Seven,' he said, and then disappeared.

She stared at the place where Orla had vanished. *Follow*, he'd said, and now she knew exactly where, and how. The she ran from the mirador as if the storm was hurling its fury at her heels, and the six Djinn swept after her, down the stairs, through the garden, and into the street and back towards the safe house and, she hoped against hope, to find Karmel.

They were too late. Near the bottom of the lane, the Djinn stopped. While four of them gathered around Sara, the remaining two lifted into the air and streaked away in diverging arcs, vanishing swiftly into the clouds. As they passed, the first boom and rumble of thunder reverberated from the hills to the city, followed by a flickering discharge of lightning.

'What is happening?' she demanded, her awe of the Djinn tempered by the urgency of the situation.

'Mawdrik. They have come.'

'Can we get back?'

'The way is closed.'

And so they waited there in the lane as the sky turned blacker and the first large drops of warm rain pelted on the ground, raising puffs of dust from the exhausted earth. Surrounded by the Djinn, Sara felt as if the oxygen was being leached from the air by their heat, which was fierce enough to make the air shimmer.

Then the first of the Mawdrik showed itself, strolling nonchalantly into view around a bend in the alleyway, a creature made of ice with black voids for eyes. Its outline trembled through the heat that radiated from the Djinn but its proximity was sufficient to fill Sara with cold terror and when she looked back up the lane, she saw another advancing without haste in the direction from which they had come only minutes before.

As the first continued moving towards them, it stalled and bent as though trapped against an invisible force and Sara realized that the power of the Djinn was too great for it. Her relief was short lived because, as the first shower passed, another lumen appeared on the roof of a house, then another soared down from the sky, and more, until Sara and the Djinn were enclosed in a circle that was twenty strong.

Then something happened that she could not have predicted. The ground began to shake and fissures appeared among the cobbles, and then the surface of the lane heaved and thrust up into a turmoil of earth and stones. A shape emerged from the ground, bowed at first so that all Sara could see was its curved back, then it rose massively and, as the billowing dust cleared, it revealed itself as an ogre wrapped in strips of steel armour and wearing a helmet of iron scales. In his left hand, he grasped a colossal scimitar that was probably as long as Sara was tall. A second burst of rubble from the ground behind them, and another rose mightily to his feet.

The Mawdrik gave no sign that they were in the least part disturbed, then one of them lifted away from the circle and rose high above its comrades, spiralling with its arms spread then coming to a halt with a hand extended towards Sara and the Djinn as though it was inviting her to join them.

'Sara Parkinson, aren´t you tired of this charade? Can't you see that your friends will never be able to protect you? We are Mawdrik. If you haven't yet realized that you cannot outrun us, you are among the most stupid of a very foolish race.'

'Go to hell,' she said. She had seen what the Mawdrik couldn't, for way above them with their robes billowing in the rising wind, a sweeping crescent of fifty or more Djinn was descending through the clouds. Not only this, but the ground had started to shudder again and from the holes made by the ogres came enormous black trolls, five of them, each with a sling and a sack of boulders slung over its shoulder. Close behind them was a band of small grey figures carrying what appeared to be crossbows and among them, she could see the grimy but familiar face of Terk.

He scuttled among the Djinn to get to Sara. 'You're not harmed,' he said with enormous relief. 'But we need to get to more open ground. These lanes are far too narrow.'

They began to move slowly, back up the lane, the first ogre striding towards the waiting lumen which held its ground and appeared completely unperturbed by the advancing band.

'Have you seen Karmel?' she said breathlessly.

'Karmel is in trouble,' he replied tersely. 'He's been trapped by the Mawdrik, not far from here. The Djinn are attempting to free him.'

'*How?*' Karmel had more sense than to wander off and walk straight into the hands of their worst enemies.

'Not now,' he said. The ogre was closing on the lumen and there was no sign that the creature was about to give way. Then with a swift heft of his scimitar, the ogre hurled all his strength at the thing, sheathing his blade in a moment, then walked on without a falter in his stride. The fragments of the lumen scattered in all directions like molten white lava, its gleaming head spinning through the air to smash against the wall close by, spraying globs of pearly fluid as it did so.

'Is it really dead?' asked Sara.

'Unfortunately not,' Terk replied grimly. 'You can't dispatch a lumen of the Mawdrik that easily. You'll see.'

They skirted the walls of the carmen, hurrying up steps and through alleyways that could scarcely accommodate the breadth of the trolls. More thunder muttered and growled and with it came something else, the rushing of more Djinn as they flew in from the north to hold back the phalanx of the Mawdrik. Sara's robed bodyguard rushed her forwards, up yet more steps, on the heels of the striding ogre and with the snorting breath of the trolls at their back. Then, they came out onto a semi-circular promenade with a low balustrade that ran around the perimeter of an area planted with ornamental trees and, to the rear, a white church and the gates of a convent.

Immediately, the Djinn spaced themselves around the perimeter of the walkway, joined by others who had been waiting for them among the trees. Sara walked to the parapet and stepped on to the rail, regardless that she was in full view of the gathering Mawdrik, but nobody moved to stop her. Curtains of rain were drifting across the city, first obscuring the domes of the San Geronimo convent, then the great Cathedral of Granada, until the entire lower city was hidden, but leaving a clear gulf over the hillside below them and an iron grey storm wall against which the Mawdrik were arrayed.

There must have been two hundred of them by now, ranked in three semi-circular ascending tiers and blazing almost as brightly as the arcs of lightning that were coming every thirty seconds or so. Facing them were the Djinn, taller and more impressive in their robes that flew like battle pennants in the wind, but they were far fewer. Sara could hear the sounds of more arrivals at her back but she didn't look round. All her attention was on the Mawdrik, all her thoughts on what they were going to do next to break the stalemate.

Terk climbed on to the rail next to her. His compact frame was covered with hardened leather armour, including a pointed hat with earflaps that at another time might have looked comical. Sara, however, was way beyond doubting his incredible valour. He sidled closer and raised a lumpy eyebrow at her.

'Weather's looking a bit dodgy, isn't it?'

Sara smiled down at him. 'It´s just like an English summer. Actually, I feel quite at home.'

'Um. You're not about to do something reckless again, are you? Like the other day, when you put the Djinn in their place?' He did not sound overtly alarmed at the prospect.

'Am I developing a reputation?' she said with a grim hint of amusement. 'Well, I'd better not disappoint anybody then, now had I?'

Sara cleared her throat and straightened up. 'You!' she shouted. Her voice carried through the wind and across the space, magnified by the buildings that made their gathering place into an amphitheatre.

'You Mawdrik. Are you listening to me or are you so obsessed with yourselves that you don't realize how dumb we think you are?'

She was playing a dangerous game. Of that, she was completely aware. Sara knew that her very existence provoked these creatures, and losing her once had spiked them into a fury that had cost the lives of thousands. Here and now, she would do anything she could to try to goad them further and divert them from more destruction, or expose the slightest flaw in their self-proclaimed supremacy. More so, she had to do something to draw their attention away from Karmel and his rescuers, wherever they were.

Nevertheless, there was no reaction from them. Although she knew that their eyes were fixed on her with every projected iota of hatred that they could muster, she was impervious to their fury, thanks to the implacable front that the Djinn had thrown up around them. She had to change tack. Time was running out.

This time she altered her tone. 'I know what you're looking for. You think you're so clever, don't you? "We´re the great Mawdrik. We're the masters of the world. We're the angels and guardian spirits that *aren´t*. We can play with the lives of millions and we can lie and cheat, because it´s our *right*." Well, I have news for you. You're pathetic. You've absolutely no idea just how much *I* know about *you* and just how sad and feeble I know you really are.'

At first, the Mawdrik made no response. Then one of them moved forwards from the centre of the first rank, as far as it was possible to do so in the face of the Djinn.

'Yes, that got your attention, didn't it?' She waited for effect before risking her bluff. 'I've met *him*, you know. He told me about you. You know, the truth. Not your self-loving lies.'

'Shut up, little girl.'

Sara laughed into his cold face. 'You don't like it, do you? Somebody ruffles your feathers and you go to pieces. You're not so powerful after all.'

'We will show you what power is,' said the lumen. He withdrew and as he did do, Sara could see others rising from among the buildings and speeding through the air towards them. This was exactly what she had hoped for. Maybe some of them had been assaulting the Djinn who were trying to liberate Karmel, and this would give them the space for manoeuvre they so desperately needed.

But now the Mawdrik were very angry and in such numbers that she had no idea of what they might be capable. Within moments she would find out. Those in the first tier flowed together into a tight core, then, as one, angled forwards to create a point of focus against the Djinn. Then, with a violent discharge of searing light they threw their combined power against the balustrade.

The shockwave of their rage struck the parapet, blasting a massive hole in the ground. Sara and Terk were blown off balance as the trees bent and boughs were torn off and hurled through the air. Even the ogres staggered back and had to fight to remain on their feet. Worst of all, one of the trolls was ablaze with leaping pale tongues of fire. As his comrades lumbered forward to help him, he roared and shook them off and with a final bullish bellow, plunged over the ruined parapet and crashed to his death on the hillside below.

Sara got to her feet. The robes of many Djinn were smouldering and falling apart in glowing shreds but their line had not moved. As she watched, she saw what the robes concealed as the Djinn revealed their true selves. They were like whirling serpents of smoke with fire at their centre, and they immediately sped towards the Mawdrik who, incredibly, were breaking their formation and were *fleeing*. But the Djinn were too fast for them. Each was pursuing a lumen and when they caught up with the scattering creatures of white light they wound tightly around them, throwing constricting coils about the struggling entity and squeezing. Then, as one, the Djinn raised their smoking heads and plunged them deep into the craniums of the Mawdrik.

The Mawdrik broke apart, exploding into a million falling droplets, like white molten metal in a foundry and raining down on the rooftops. The twisting serpents of smoke that were the Djinn remained, and as the rest of the Mawdrik fell back and regrouped with their second tier, the four remaining trolls lumbered up to the parapet, loaded boulders into their slings and began to hurl them at the enemy while they were preoccupied with the Djinn, breaking through their second rank and forcing them to retreat even further.

'Look!' said Terk. 'You'll see why the Mawdrik aren´t so easy to destroy.'

She returned to the parapet and stared down to where the hillside fell away for twenty yards or so in a jumble of prickly pears, agaves, old refrigerators and other household detritus that local people had dumped there. Everywhere the remnants of the Mawdrik had fallen, the fragments were flowing along the rough ground or across the corrugated red tiles of buildings, searching out the other pieces and forming into amoeboid masses whenever they flowed together. The Mawdrik were reforming themselves. Even so, the naked Djinn undulated through the air, dipping and plunging through the glistening half-formed creatures as they tried to reform themselves and blasting them apart again and again. But they were too few and the Mawdrik that had fallen into dense vegetation and among the clutter of disintegrating walls and roofs at the bottom of the slope were soon rising again, fully formed, to rejoin their kindred.

A flurry of rain swept across the treetops and came between Sara and the others clustered along the parapet, hiding the confrontation for a long moment. Terk spat and cursed and the trolls muttered and glanced at each other, slings at the ready but with nothing to aim at. The shower took an eternity to pass then, as the rain lifted, one of the ogres bellowed and plunged back among the trees, swinging his scimitar through the shattered branches.

The trees were seething with a tide of movement so dense that it was hard to tell the difference between the thrashing branches and the worm-like bodies of the faerie. They advanced in a wave of crackling and shimmering wings and luminous cyclops eyes like a devouring wildfire, their claws tearing through leaves and twigs, and then they plummeted in a shower of screeching chaos, tearing at the eyes and ears of the flailing ogres and trolls and forming into a speeding arrow of writhing bodies that twisted and plunged among the lumbering shapes as it headed straight towards Sara.

The impact threw her painfully back against the parapet and onto the ground, jarring every bone in her body and knocking the breath out of her lungs. Now the rain was falling heavily and, as the faerie hoard broke apart, it swept around and dived at her again through the downpour with a thousand tiny sharp mouths and claws ripping and snapping at her. She tore at them, feeling their little bones crunching in her fist and beneath her flailing heels, but more came, blotting out the sky in a mass of tiny seething bodies that swamped her like a boiling mass of ants.

Then she was wrenched upright and away by a strong arm that lifted her clean off the ground before setting her down again a dozen yards away and, as she struggled up, she saw François sweeping away from her and up into the lightning-wracked sky. The banshees had come, a dozen or more, and they were stooping through the faerie mass, slicing and hacking them into fragments with their bright daggers. Sara felt the trunk of a tree at her back and pulled herself upright, in time to see the drama that was unfolding. From the left, a knot of Djinn flowed into the plaza, and at their centre was a blue robed figure who was crying out her name. *Karmel!* Karmel was here!

Everywhere else was chaos. Kelpie women were crouched among the trees, their hair streaming with wetness as they fired off arrows into the sky at an impossible speed. A pack of wolves raced past her and one of them leaped into the air, dragging down a lumen into the centre of the ravening snapping pack. She saw the dark shapes of ogres and trolls battling against the bright shapes that repeatedly stooped on them from the clouds, and a phalanx of Terk´s people firing bolts from their crossbows that sizzled with blue fire as they struck the Mawdrik.

But she was alone, completely alone, and as she tried to find her feet they went from under her in a welter of water and wet leaves and she was on her back, staring up into the stark faces of the dozen Mawdrik that were descending over her, their arms outstretched to grab her and wrench her away into the heart of the storm.

She screamed and slipped and fell again. *It can't end like this!* Then a brightly golden form plunged down through the trees, all wings and beauty and fury, and threw itself into the circle of the Mawdrik, slashing at them with steel blades in both hands before they had time to react.

'No!' Sara shouted in terror. 'Not for me! You mustn't!' Two of the Mawdrik were clutching their throats and had fallen back among the trees but the others had come together again and this time they were prepared when the banshee dove at them. There was a searing flash like a burst of lightning, then a scream that ripped through Sara's heart, and the figure was falling, crying and broken and flailing among the branches to crash sickeningly upon the ground only a few yards away from her.

'NO!' she screamed. She dragged herself across the rain-drenched paving stones, across the circles of muddy red earth around the bases of the trees, desperately searching for his out-flung hand in the driving rain and the rushing ground water. She felt his cold fingers meshing with hers and she fumbled blindly upwards to find his shoulders. Her arms were around him, then she cradled the broken bloody head of François against her breasts, sobs racking her whole body as her dripping hair hung down like a veil over his face.

François coughed and gagged, and opened his brilliant green eyes, looking up into hers with a dawning expression of delight and astonishment.

'Is it really you, ma cherie?'

'Yes, yes, it's me. Don't go, my François. Please don't go! I can't stand it!' She drew him closer to her and felt the broken bones grinding in his body. He smiled weakly, and a brief gout of blood spurted from the corner of his mouth.

'At least...' She felt the gurgling in his chest as he struggled to breathe, then more blood came. 'At least I got to kiss you.' His eyes flashed wide one more time and a flicker of radiance lifted the corners of his perfect mouth, and then he died.

Sara screamed again, flailing her fists against the compacted earth then clutching madly at the ground, seizing anything that she could find and hurling fistfuls of leaves and torn bark at the Mawdrik.

'I HATE you. I HATE YOU!' She surged to her feet and tried to jump at them and grasp their heels as they slowed their ascent. There were females as well as males among them, and each icy face was a little different, each an individual mask of cold curiosity or supreme contempt.

'She hates us, she hates us,' they mocked. 'Poor sad Sara Parkinson. We must ease her pain, brethren.'

Their faces were downturned and as their black eyes paralysed her and began to leach the warmth from her body, they started to laugh.

'Silly little girl. You have never truly imagined what it means to suffer. Let us be as a revelation to you.'

It was only long afterwards that Sara was able to reconstruct the events of the next few minutes. As she fell back from the derision of the Mawdrik and reached out to hold François one last time, she saw Juan running headlong through the trees and, as he came, his torso and head extended and arched forwards and then his entire body rose up, instantly metamorphosing into a towering, glistening colossus of fury - a massive black bull with huge solid shoulders and red eyes and a head wider than a tabletop, with sweeping horns that slashed again and again as he reared and plunged through the Mawdrik and threw them aside as though they were nothing but dry sticks.

From the opposite side of the plaza came a rush of air and the beating of massive wings that churned the rain into vortices. The creature that roared through the trees was emerald green, with a writhing forked tail and sinuous body coated with an intricacy of scales and spines. The frills on either side of its head lifted and spread, and it opened wide its fanged jaws and spewed green fire at the Mawdrik, but it was no ordinary fire. This fire tore through them with such force and destruction that it blew them apart and what remained of them fell to the ground in a snowfall of dead grey ashes that would never rise again.

Angustias!

As the dragon banked and plunged again, and the Mawdrik were extinguished or scattered in outraged confusion, Karmel came running through the rain. He didn't hesitate to reach out his arm and drag Sara from the ground where she was clutching François' broken, rain-soaked corpse. She never, ever wanted to let go of him. He was joy and brightness and everything that the world was losing but the Mawdrik had taken the light from him and his big green eyes were still gazing up into the sky as if, even in death, he was looking for another moment of happiness with her.

In the end, Karmel had to force Sara from him and drag her across the plaza and away from the battle that continued to rage there. She was aware of the rising energy flowing between them as his fingers dug into her flesh and of the desperate explanation that Karmel was pouring out, but she barely understood what he was trying to say.

'It was Zerafma! I′m so sorry, Sara - Zerafma came to me and called me away but by the time I realized it was an evil trick of the Mawdrik, it was too late. How can I ever atone? It′s my fault! It′s all my fault.'

'Don't, please *don't*, Karmel!' She was torn between sobs and breathlessness. They had reached the far side of the plaza and were crouching against a wall with the rain pouring over them from the gutter above like a waterfall. Karmel had not let go of her and the energy was mounting between them, pulsing through her in waves that wracked her body like jolts of electricity.

'I know where we're going! We're going to find the name of Seven. It has to be now, before anybody else dies for me!'

'Show me! I′m ready. I'll go with you to my death, if that's what it takes.'

She told him and as they counted together and imagined the leftward spiral that would take them away from everything they'd known before, the rain poured down on the city and the battle that would change the world raged on.

Part Three: The Name of Seven

1. The Wasteland

When Sara came back to herself, she was lying face down on a cold, granular surface. Her face was crushed painfully against the ground and one leg was twisted awkwardly under her, with the other foot embedded in the rough substrate as though she had been repeatedly kicking at it. Her eyelids were gritty and glued together with dust and tears, and she had to prize them apart and blink away the residue. When she could see again, she was able to confirm what she'd begun to suspect - that she was on a surface of old compacted snow.

She lay still, listening. There was no sound except for the magnified rasp of her own breathing against the frozen ground, nor was there the least trace of a breeze. She couldn't even decide whether or not it was warm or cold because, apart from the cold bed on which she lay, the still air had an indefinable but eerily neutral quality about it.

Sara did not want to face whatever waited for her in this place, nor did she want to think about the nightmare she had just been through. It was too soon, too raw and bloody and horrible, but she couldn't simply lie on the snow wishing that everything could pass her by and allow her not to exist for a while.

She rolled onto her back and winced at the discomfort of the lumpy pack when it dug into her skin. The sky was uniformly pale and colourless, with the white disc of a sun almost directly overhead that was clearly far too large to be the sun of Earth. Even stranger was that she could stare directly at it without hurting her eyes and that she could feel no warmth from it whatsoever.

Shifting on to her side, she managed to ease her aching body onto all fours before standing up. Straight away she threw herself back on to the ground in terror and disbelief. For those few moments, she had been standing at an angle of some forty-five degrees, on a slope of the same gradient.

This had to be impossible. Perhaps she was suffering from concussion and it had affected her sense of balance. She quickly checked her head all over with probing fingers but could find no trace of pain or swelling. She had to try again.

This time, she got to her feet in cautious stages but as she straightened up, the astonishing truth was confirmed. Sara was standing without slipping or falling, between the vertical and the horizontal, on a bleak mountainside that was streaked with patches of snow. She took a step. Nothing happened. Then she tried to adopt what she believed to be the perpendicular and promptly fell over.

The fall was heavy, for the surface of the snow had hardened into a thick crust. After she'd got up, she tried to swallow down the nauseous sensation that she was about to fall from the slope and then she took stock of her surroundings, soon realizing that they were every part as disturbing as the influence they were exerting on her.

She was half way along the side - and close to the top - of a deep oval depression. It was, perhaps, a mile across and twice as long, and all along the rim it was crested by sharp crags that curved inwards, giving the effect that she was inside an enormous stadium carved out of rock. The entire perimeter was mottled with irregular patches of snow and on the far side of the bowl the charcoal grey slope was marked with vertical striations.

A perfectly oval lake occupied the bottom, far below. The water was dazzlingly sapphire and the surface was churned into peaking waves with foaming crests but they were completely motionless as if the water had been frozen in a fraction of time.

Sara began to practice walking in circles and then she risked jumping but even after she was certain that this was reality and not illusion, she could not accept the fundamental wrongness of what she was experiencing. She wondered how Karmel was managing.

Karmel! *Oh my God, where is he?* Sara cast around in all directions, her eyes confused by the stark contrast between rock and snow, and then she saw the mound of blue clothing several hundred yards away along the slope. She called his name but although her shouts were clear enough to her they seemed only to travel a short way, as if sound itself had no will to endure in this place.

He had pulled the djellaba so tightly around himself that it accentuated every angle of his body, which was curled into a tight ball.

'Karmel, it's me. Sara.'

He did not answer her, even when she approached and crouched down on the stony ground next to him. He was trembling, his rapid breathing interspersed with low whimpers. Karmel was terrified.

'Karmel, I don't know what's wrong but I am going to stay here with you. I won't leave you.'

She sat down.

'There is something I need to leave behind before we go on.' In this most unlikely of places, where everything screamed against reason and sense, the conviction of what she had to do was absolute.

'I'll just keep talking so you'll know I am here.'

It hardly mattered where she started. Karmel was suffering, and so was she. Now, she knew, was the time to release her pain and help him to come back from whatever shadow he was immersed in, so that they could move on together. She talked about her childhood, and the earliest times with her mother and father and her naive belief that all the world was the three of them and it was perfect, and then the first awareness of change when went away and the dimly aching space of his absence was filled with her mother's stories about other worlds and mysterious beings. Why? Why she had told Sara such compelling yet disturbing tales was something that had haunted her down the years? If she'd known something about what was to come, why hadn't she told her?

Instead, she had left her, early one morning and without explanation, in the care of her father, a troubled and distant man so deeply immersed in the warfare of his personal universe that he had no time for a little girl with a soaring imagination and a need to be loved. But the man who should have carried her forth into the world and helped her faltering wings to spread wide with burgeoning confidence, had only ever been a face disappearing into a book in response to her endless questions, and a back turning away from her desperate need to feel nurtured and secure.

Into adolescence and the anxiety and fear of her search for purpose and identity; a fractured belief in herself, but attempts to assert her identity that were met with a wall of grey confusion from her father and his new wife, and an implicit shunting aside of all her achievements with a *we knew you could do it*, and sometimes a *you could have done better*, and always the turning away and the face buried in the book that came to signify the ultimate symbol of rejection, so crushing because it was done without intent, and without wisdom.

There was the humdrum world of university and employment. Then came the terminal rupture with her father and the futile search for her mother whom she'd worshipped but who had by that single act of cruel abandonment, become the greatest betrayal of all. Paris and the Middle East, dirty bedsits and one-night stands, on and ever on and into a plunging spiral of mediocrity but always with the desperate hope that life might mean more than this. *Until.*

Until the accident. Until Terk and the Vodyanoi, until Valu and the Lake. The Volk. Hyaquat and François. Until dear, sweet dead François.

'I'm here, Karmel. I've made it back.' In this place that made no sense, Sara Parkinson had arrived, and in so doing she had come back to find herself and to realize that, after everything that had gone before, she was still intact and just maybe, she had the strength to carry on.

Karmel's trembling had subsided, and he was now silent. Sara, for her part, was utterly spent and with the tears drying on her face she was able to do nothing more except wait for him. When Karmel came back to her, it was quick. He sat up and pulled the clothing away from his face, looking around in puzzlement for a moment before fixing his eyes on Sara. He looked momentarily disconcerted and then he focused on her and lifted his eyebrows as if in mild but relieved surprise.

'I can't say that I understand what you experienced during your childhood,' he began to say, slowly as if he were measuring every word. 'No Kiklaydan child is ever abandoned by his parents. It's unthinkable. That's not to say that we don't suffer the pain of loneliness, but whatever you might think of our child-rearing practices each one of us is celebrated for what he is, and none of us are subject to the approval or otherwise of our elders.'

'You heard everything, didn't you?'

'Of course I did,' he said. 'Every last word of it. I want to thank you. It helped.'

He got up with an effort, apparently unsurprised by the peculiar gravity of the place. 'Ouch! I landed with a bump.'

He rubbed his side, and then he said something unexpected. 'Not that it was anything I didn't know already.

'What do you mean?'

'That first time we touched. What you forgot about me, I remembered about you. The difference this time was that you told me willingly.'

'Okay,' she said, attempting to hide her uneasiness at the prospect of whatever else Karmel might have gleaned about her.

'What is it about this place that scares you so much?'

'It terrifies me,' he said quickly. 'I do not know why because I can sense almost nothing because there's nothing here with which I can resonate. There are no traces of life, no magnetism or radioactivity in the rocks, no meteorological activity, no seismic movement. Either it's completely frozen in time, or it doesn't exist.'

Sara shivered. 'That's a possibility I don't even want to think about.'

He gazed at her calmly. In the most disconcerting way, the place seemed to suit him because the complete lack of movement in the air and the indefinable gravity made the folds of his robes lie perfectly, almost elegantly, against his lithe body.

'There are traces in our racial memory that hint about something like this but I'd always assumed that it was something to do with religion. I lost my faith years ago so I didn't pay it much attention.'

He sighed. 'When I was meditating in Granada I travelled deep, and I saw a shadow that passed by on the outer edge of my awareness but it didn't stay long enough for me to grasp its true meaning. I am afraid because this isn't a *where,* as you might understand it. We are nowhere, but nowhere exists in time and space. I lack the ability to interpret this conundrum.'

By now, Sara was well used to the florid way in which Karmel often expressed himself, and she was comfortable with the notion that being succinct wasn't always the best way to say what you meant.

'Is there anything else. Anything at all?'

He shook his head. 'I am sorry. I will keep searching my memories whenever I can but it will be far more difficult here.'

As they talked, the huge cold sun had descended until it was almost touching the rim of the caldera but instead of setting it started to rise again on a shallow trajectory that was completely unrelated to its previous course.

'Orla said, "follow".' Sara was staring at the lifeless sun. 'Well, here we are. That is all we have to go on. I can only think of one thing to do.'

'And that is?' asked Karmel.

'We start walking.' She picked up a flat stone that, although it fitted into her palm with room to spare, was so heavy that it cost her a great deal of effort to lift it. Then she threw it with all her strength, hoping that the impetus would carry it away far enough to fall into the lake but it skewed to a halt in mid air only a few yards away, and there it remained.

She approached the stone and tried to move it, but it was as fixed in nothingness as if it were mounted in crystal.

'We have no food,' Karmel said.

'Are you hungry?'

'Not in the least.'

'Me neither,' she agreed.

'Well, then. It's time we were on our way so we won't worry about it until we have to. I have a feeling that whatever direction we take, it won't make a lot of difference.'

'Let's go straight up,' said Sara. 'If it *is* up.'

Karmel shrugged, and they set out, walking side by side at a slow but steady pace. The mechanics of walking was not a problem, even when the slope angled steep enough to give them the sensation that they were walking on their backs. What affected them acutely was the absence of any reference to altitude and distance. Sometimes, when Sara looked back, the lake appeared to have moved closer when every last grain of reason within her said that it had to be further away, and there was always the eerie silence, scarcely broken by the unnaturally muffled sounds of their footsteps.

By slow degrees, they approached the toothed horizon. Neither of them had shared a word since they had set out, nor did they do so as they drew closer to the rim, but Sara was filled with a mounting sense of trepidation over what they might encounter on the other side.

When it happened, the transition into what lay beyond the caldera was instantaneous. To their surprise, they found that they were standing more or less vertically according to their idea of what vertical should mean. However, nothing could have prepared them for the utterly shocking and surreal landscape that now opened up in front of them.

2. Volk

It had been another very successful opera season and, as Akami-restrup Volk left the theatre that morning, it reflected contentedly on the triumphal completion of the entire Ring Cycle that had culminated to great acclaim the previous evening. This year's Wagner season had been such an enormous success largely due to the efforts of the sentient scenery, which had now gone off on a much-deserved holiday.

Wagner was enjoying a renaissance on Volk but next year, under the artistic direction of Akami-restrup, the company was scheduled to return to more familiar territory, with the Magic Flute planned for the opening night, followed by Beethoven's Fidelio and then a light-hearted summer season of Gilbert and Sullivan operettas. Earth works were eternally popular, and the current trend was to retranslate them back from Standard English, German or whatever the relevant original tongue, into Volk lightwords and to perform the two versions simultaneously.

Akami's ship was standing by in the stratosphere, waiting to carry it to the Hall of Quorum, but when it signalled its readiness, Akami politely declined. On such a beautiful autumnal morning, it preferred to float. As it drifted along at a leisurely speed, it inhaled the pleasantly fresh atmosphere that was hovering comfortably at a little below minus thirty Celsius. Pleasant weather for an early stroll, mused Akami, as it carried on its way through the billowing green and pink clouds and towards the disc-shaped building on the horizon.

The Volk planet was a gas giant with a small metallic core and a complex layered atmosphere, which, at its outer edge, was more than a hundred times the diameter of Earth. Its multi-coloured panoply of weather systems supported a fantastic diversity of ecosystems and associated creatures, including floating oar weed forests, giant airfish that endlessly patrolled the spiralling tempests of million year old storms, and teeming lakes of opalescent condensate suspended between laminate clouds.

The Volk themselves were the most ancient beings in the galaxy. Liberated by their refined biology and their fundamental nature from the constraints imposed on other races by the necessity to compete, they had no ethos of greed and were not constrained by the messiness of sexual reproduction: thus, they were able to devote themselves to metaphysical speculation, exploration of the universe and non-invasive research.

Because they filtered nutrients and minerals directly from the atmosphere, processing them internally to produce everything they needed from sustenance to building materials, they were completely free from intra-species conflict for resources, and the very notion of warfare was a distasteful curiosity to be studied and wondered at in other races.

At a very early stage during their galactic travels, the Volk encountered the Reem, a nomadic race who were almost as ancient as themselves. These enormous tri-symmetrical beings forged an intimate and lasting relationship with the Volk and because of the role they chose in the partnership, they began to call themselves the Ships. They were humorous, emotional, sensitive and sometimes impetuous, and despite their profound commitment to their Volk partners, they retained an independence of thought and action that the Volk respected and honoured and, at times, turned a blind eye to.

The Volk's political organization was simplicity itself. They were few in number and so attuned to one another that since time immemorial, the planetary council had consisted of the Quorum, from which no Volk was excluded. Decision-making was dignified and often surprisingly rapid; those who attended were already aware of the will of those they were in contact with and, in the absence of ego or partisanship, what needed to be done was done.

As it drifted along, Akami extended its sub dorsal vibrissae from time to time to snack on some interesting compound or other that it encountered in the clouds, and thought about the unusual messenger who had arrived on Volk earlier that same morning. They had been aware of his coming, and had followed his solitary progress - so atypical of his kind - until his proximity had started to upset the Ships. At their request he had been carefully intercepted by a single Volk and a single Ship, so as not to suggest a threat. Then, after he made his intention known to them, he continued on his solitary approach, unaided because a Ship would never agree to carry one of his kind.

Now he was here, waiting just outside the planetary gravitational field until the Quorum had gathered and were ready to see him. Akami remembered the last time that a member of another species had addressed the Quorum: a Kiladl, requesting help for the survivors of his species after the self-induced disaster that destroyed their planet. The Volk neither encouraged nor dissuaded visitors, and within the Hall of Quorum were incorporated luxurious suites of accommodation suited to the needs of over twenty races, but they were rarely occupied. This visitor, however, was different, and throughout the long history of the Volk, not once had one of his kind knowingly been made welcome.

Akami was approaching the Hall of Quorum. It was one of the largest buildings on the planet, a pale metallic green discus that was utterly featureless on the outside but quite beautiful in the way that its smooth walls mirrored the surrounding clouds. The Operatic Director glided up to the edge of the disc and passed straight through the outer wall and into the foyer.

Other Volk were waiting in the transparent circular gallery that ran around the entire outer edge of the Hall, and Akami was greeted by a welcoming flourish of colour. One of them approached, radiating a particularly effusive greeting that was flushed with admiration.

'Akami! That was a tremendous closing night. Well done!' It was Thisrop-babran, the venerable Archivist of the Hall of Quorum and one of its few permanent residents.

Akami flushed modestly. 'Don´t give me any credit, please. It was all down to a highly talented group of performers, not to mention a very appreciative audience.'

They drifted along the gallery together as they chatted.

'Where did you get to?' asked Thisrop.

'I went to a party with the scenery. And you?'

'There's a wonderful new restaurant in the Eye of Thirdstorm. Atriban took me to dinner. They do the most amazing volatiles and the view from the terrace is phenomenal. Have you heard about it?'

'I believe I have. I'll have to go when I get back from Voul. I won't be eating out *there*, of course.'

'Perish the thought,' Thisrop said. 'The Voul have many virtues but their cuisine isn't one of them.'

'And what do you think of this morning's reception?' solicited Akami.

'Ah, this puzzles me,' said Thisrop, sighing thoughtfully. 'Uncertainty isn't something we're accustomed to but I have to confess, it bothers me.'

Strong words indeed, thought Akami. 'What troubles me is why they should want to involve themselves with us at this late stage. We know their attitude towards the Volk. The entire galaxy knows how they feel about us.' They both smiled.

'Clearly, from what the envoy has already given away, they want to remind us that we can do nothing to stop them in their latest enterprise,' said Thisrop. 'Nothing directly, that's to say.'

'Of course, they know that we are there, "behind the scenes" if I can use such a metaphor.'

'You do love your metaphors, Akami. You've never held back on using them in the past.' They drifted on in companionable silence.

'To restate the facts,' said Akami, giving voice to its thoughts. 'We know what they are looking for, and we know that once before they came very close to finding it, but that the most unexpected turn of events denied them their prize.'

'And we know that, thanks to them, something was released that has the power to destroy but must never be destroyed itself. Also, that until it perceived a threat to itself, it did not itself become a threat.'

'Which brings us back to our visitor,' said Akami. 'I have a theory, and a question. I hesitate to pose the question because it is a little far-fetched, I have to admit.'

'I am all ears, to use one of yours,' said Thisrop.

'Very well, first the theory. Could it be that, if they feel threatened themselves, they have come to ask for our protection?'

'If I had eyebrows,' said Thisrop, 'I would raise them. And the question?'

'The question hardly needs asking. We know what they are looking for but what lies beyond it? What do they really want it for? Ah, we're going in.'

The Volk had begun drifting through the inner wall and the two friends followed suit. Inside, the Hall of Quorum was covered, floor and ceiling, with smooth round recesses, a thousand of them which if necessary could accommodate every single living Volk. This morning, upwards of five hundred were occupied.

Akami and Thisrop were among the last to settle into their places. As the chatter died down, one recess in the ceiling of the Hall began to extend, forming a gleaming tongue with a translucent bulbous end. Then, as the top of the protuberance parted, it left a platform on which was standing a shining white figure. It was a lumen of the Mawdrik.

Afterwards, as the Volk gathered in the foyer to discuss what had been said, or drifted outside to meet the golden ships that descended vertically through the clouds to collect them, Akami and Thisrop took stock of the proceedings.

'That was not unexpected,' said Akami.

'Insofar as the Mawdrik never ask, they merely tell - yes, that was predictable. They will do what they feel they have to, as always.'

'And we will not stop them,' said Akami. *If we did*, it mused privately, *we would no longer be Volk.*

'Their error is that they presume to know us,' said Thisrop. 'I mean, everything.' It showed its friend what it was thinking, mind to mind.

'Ah yes. That, of course, we can do nothing to prevent.'

They continued to float, side by side, as they watched the golden ships ascending in their dozens through the rainbow stratosphere of Volk.

3. The Wasteland

The land that plunged away from their feet and stretched into an indefinable distance was a place of bald mountains and truncated buttes, and grey plains split open by black fissures the size and depth of which could not be guessed. There was the same bleached sky as before, but here it was lit by the diffused radiance of two suns. One of them might have been the same bloated white disk as before but the other was a smaller crimson globe that seemed to be watching them like an unblinking and malevolent eye.

Everything else about this new world was beyond the bounds of surrealism. Far beneath them was another oval lake at the bottom of another precipitous caldera, but the water in this one had rushed to the far end as if the entire land had suddenly been tilted to the left. There, it was piled up into a monstrous wave of churning white confusion that arched over the containing walls like a mighty waterfall in reverse, and there it remained, utterly frozen and trapped inside a moment in time.

The sky held more than suns. At first, Sara thought that the huge reclining hemisphere that dominated almost a quarter of the heavens, was a waxing crescent moon, until she registered the oceans and continents, cloud formations and a fractured inner edge with a cloud of torn pieces suspended all around it as though it had suffered the impact of another similar body and like everything else in this impossible place, was condemned to remain forever in limbo. There were other broken worlds, some close, others mere misty outlines but all were paralyzed in varying stages of destruction or decomposition.

On the edge of sight, above the mountainous skyline, there was another similar horizon of torn peaks and, in the twilit space between them, shone a thousand cold stars.

Words were beyond them for a long time. The silence was complete and not a breath of wind blew against their skins, while the air was devoid of taste or smell.

'What did this?' whispered Sara. 'Is this where the planets comes to die?'

'It isn't a graveyard,' said Karmel. His voice was small and flat against the emptiness. 'Graveyards are for the dead. I can sense nothing here that was ever alive.'

'Can't you feel anything? Anything at all?'

'Nothing except a sensation, something I can't explain. Every time I try to locate it, it slips out of my reach. What's different is that it is coming to me in the shape of words. That very rarely happens.'

'What words?'

'"Source", and "Locus". What do you think that could mean?'

'I wonder if it's Orla? Maybe he is trying to guide us.'

'If you are right,' said Karmel, 'I don't know where he wants us to go. Direction doesn't seem to mean anything here.'

He turned and looked back, over the incline they had just ascended.

'Come and look. I think this proves my point.'

The lake had gone. Instead, the land stretched into another impossible distance, under a sky filled with broken planets and three small cold suns, to the all-encircling horizon that might have been a thousand miles away for all they were able to tell.

'All we can do is walk.'

'Do you think that the Mawdrik know where we are?'

'I don't see how they can do,' said Karmel. 'Unless… unless they have been here before.'

Neither wanted to pursue this disturbing line of speculation and Karmel was the first to move. He had only taken three paces before Sara shouted at him to stop. He had walked smoothly on a sloping trajectory into the air, and was gazing over at his shoulder at her in confusion from several yards above the ground.

'Come back and try again,' she suggested. Karmel did as she said but this time he had not gone far before he threw up his arms in defeat, because he was now waist-deep in the ground.

'Maybe now is the time to concentrate on that sensation of yours,' said Sara, 'or we won't be going anywhere.'

This time, Karmel advanced cautiously, feeling ahead with his toe before taking a step. Everything seemed fine and when he had gone a dozen paces, Sara began to follow without incident.

They skirted the near edge of the lake, keeping well away from the edge although they were close enough to be able to see straight through the frozen tsunami and to make out the dark scythe of one of the shattered planets through the motionless water. From here on, the way sloped down among ashen hills until it levelled out and expanded into a dreary plain riven with black ravines that stretched unchanging to the double horizon.

As they continued, the threatening gullies pulled in closer on each side. To Sara, it felt like walking along a ridge through a ploughed field of impossibly gigantic proportions. By degrees, the path narrowed as the clefts angled inwards and it seemed inevitable that before long they would be marooned at the tip of a spit of land. The thought of having to trek all the way back and start again filled Sara with heaviness and despair.

'What are we going to do?' Karmel, apparently, was feeling equally pessimistic.

'We carry on as far as we can,' she said grimly. 'Then...' She shrugged.

Within just a few minutes, they could go no further. The two clefts joined to create a plummeting chasm and the last few hundred yards of ground petered into a needle of brown rock that was far too narrow for them to risk walking on.

Not a word passed between them as they turned their backs on the futile void and sat down. Sara put her face in her hands and tried to hold back the hopelessness that was threatening her. Orla had said *follow*. That was all they had.

'It was stupid of me.'

Sara lowered her hands. Karmel had not moved, and she said nothing as he continued talking in a quiet voice that nevertheless, was closer to tears than she had yet heard from him.

'I should have known that they were going to try to weaken me, but they caught me off my guard. It was Zerafma, down to the last detail -

the way she wrinkles her nose, that little lift in her voice as if everything in life is a question. She was always asking questions, rather like you.'

His breath caught in his throat, then he continued. 'I had to follow her. Then when I realized what I'd done, when it showed itself for what it really was, they were already surrounding me. They were laughing at me, Sara. It was horrible. The odd thing is that they couldn't get near me. I've heard awful stories about Kiklayda being trapped by the Mawdrik for so long that they starved to death. You see, the Mawdrik can't touch us but they can kill us in other ways. But even if the Djinn hadn't come I think I could have gotten away from them. They were laughing at me, but they were *scared*. Can you explain that?'

'No, and I wouldn't try to either,' she said. 'We have both made mistakes. Maybe if I'd warned Francois not to get involved... We can't change what's happened. It's like he said; all we have is now.'

She glanced over her shoulder. 'Look!' The chasm had vanished. In its place the barren plains stretched on as before, unbroken by so much as a boulder or a crevice.

They rose stiffly to their feet and walked on for what seemed to be hours. Buttes and sharp spires dotted the land at a distance and gradually, the upper part of the horizon disappeared below the rim of the desert and the two suns crossed overhead, the red orb traversing the white giant before each began its descent on opposite sides of the sky.

Sara wanted to lie down and sleep, but something was keeping her from tiredness. It was the same with regards to the absence of hunger and thirst, but a nagging awareness was growing within her that before very long this false idea of well-being was going to exact a toll on her physical and mental capacities.

It was Karmel who was pushing on ahead. His tall blue turbaned shape against the grey desert and blandness of the sky made him look more like a dry land nomad than ever. He had not looked back at her in hours and it bothered Sara that his initial reaction of terror had been converted into a wordless determination to press on at the exclusion of anything else, including concern for her.

At last the landscape was changing. They were climbing a shallow rise that passed between truncated buttes which framed the visible upper half of a shattered planet, silver and blue from reflected light. The suns were setting in unison, and as their light faded large stars appeared that were so close and so dull that it was possible to see the flickering coronas made by their solar flares.

She was baffled by the magnitude of such chaos. This was something on a scale far too great to comprehend. What could possibly be responsible?

'Karmel, please. We have to stop.' He continued plodding up the slope as if he had not heard her.

'Karmel!' He looked back, his violet eyes luminescent on the gathering dark.

'We must stop. I´m not going any further until I've had a rest.'

'What?' He almost snapped out the word before his shoulders drooped. 'I´m sorry. I´m not thinking. Of course you should rest. I've been lagging behind, haven't I?'

Sara did not speak as she removed her backpack and dropped it on the ground before stretching herself out. During the long trek, she had occupied herself by trying to determine the composition of the ground but apart from the vague sensation of her feet touching it, it had little substance. Now, as she lay back with her belongings as a pillow, she stuck her fingers into the earth and rubbed it between her fingertips. First it felt like sand, then gravel, then greasy silt that numbed her touch. Then an unpleasant thought came to her. It was the handful of horror that she had brought back from Gul, its searing touch burned into her memory forever. She quickly withdrew her fingers and wiped them on her jeans until they felt clean.

Suddenly, she sat up and looked towards Karmel. He was sitting hunched up a short distance away from her where he was apparently contemplating his toes.

'What do you mean, you've been lagging behind?'

'You were so far ahead of me, I could hardly see you, ' he replied without looking round. 'I called but you didn't hear me.'

'But that's not right!' she exclaimed. 'You were way in front of me.'

Karmel turned slowly and quietly regarded her for a long time, the vertical frown line on his forehead etched in shadow.

'Then we must be more careful,' he said at last. 'Something is at work here. Maybe this place is trying to pull us apart. We can't afford to lose each other.'

He pulled the robe tighter around himself and looked away again, leaving Sara to lie back and stare bleakly at the frigid stars.

Eventually, she slipped into a half-sleep where she drifted between fragments of dreams and painful splinters of memory. She saw François' bloody face and staring green eyes in the rain and woke moaning, then slid back into a hazy jumble of barely understood images and, among their jostling one-dimensional senselessness, a thin white something that was stretching out like a hungry leach as it tried to reach her.

François returned to her again, his rain-drenched face smiling in death, and for a wild moment of hope she thought that maybe she could use her powers to travel back in time, to warn him and get him away to safety before the Mawdrik came. But in her sleep the crushing realization came to her that, in her universe and in her reality, it was not possible, that François was lost to her forever.

At the last she was a little girl once more, standing in the freezing drizzle outside the house after school, crying because her father had forgotten to pick her up again and she didn't have a key, but the figure approaching her from the shadows along the garden path wasn't her father. It was pale and hideous, a broken thing badly remade and yearning to destroy itself, and it reached out a malformed arm to grip her anorak as it whispered, 'Follow.'

She woke with no idea of how long she had slept, to hear Karmel calling her name.

'Quickly. Come and look.' As soon as she stood up, she realized that a change had come over the wasteland. It was just as barren and lifeless, but the buttes had unaccountably transformed into thin ivory spires and the ground seemed to be much steeper than she remembered it. The mountains were closer, too, and their highest pinnacles were bathed in the light of a rising sun.

Karmel was gesturing for her to join him from the top of the rise. As she reached him the first rays of a different, blue sun made long shadows from the spires and threw into contrast what now lay ahead of them. It was a shallow valley, several miles across and, at one time, a river with three parallel courses might have flowed through it, but now it was dry and long dead. On the far side the valley rose again in formless hills to another featureless skyline and a sky dominated by the broken worlds and their frozen debris. It was what lay halfway up the far slope, however, that immediately grabbed her attention.

It looked like a set of unequally proportioned arches rising out of the ground in ascending order with the largest one further away. From that distance, Sara could not make out much detail except that they were rounded in cross section, and had a rough, ribbed texture.

'Have you any idea what they are?' she asked Karmel.

'I´m not sure, but I think they might once have been alive. Let's go and have a look.'

They walked into the valley bottom and climbed down a steep bank into the first of the ancient river channels. It was filled with large, flattened boulders and as they picked their way among them, something caught Sara's eye.

'Look.' She pointed and Karmel bent down to investigate. It was the faint but recognisable outline of a long curved leaf, like that of an ancient fossilized fern or a cycad. They continued on their way, scrambling over banks and traversing more courses, but they didn't see any further signs of life, either recent or ancient. By the time they clambered out of the fifth channel, they knew with resignation that the wasteland was deceiving them yet again and it took them more than an hour of laborious walking across a dozen more before they finally saw the opposite bank.

From the riverbed they could see nothing of the mysterious arches that had disappeared into the folds of the land but as they struggled out of the final channel they both quickened their pace, eager to resolve the mystery.

Slowly, the arches began to emerge above the grey dunes. From their angle of approach they were almost head on and seemed to tower up a dozen yards or maybe more, icy blue and black in the low light of the early sun. Sara was the first to reach them, hauling herself gasping to the crest of the ridge where they stood. They stood at a regular distance from each other, in a straight and regimented line, but she saw straight away that they were not artificial. Each was divided into hundreds of segments, like a worm, and every segment was pitted with rows of holes, every one of which contained a stalked eye like that of a crab. Between the eyes were oval mouths edged with ranks of fine sharp teeth and bunches of petrified tentacles.

Sara touched the thing. It was cold, hard and completely unyielding, and she guessed that it had been dead for a very long time.

Karmel had passed her and was walking around and under the tallest of the arches, studying it from every angle.

'I think these are all part of the same creature,' he said eventually. 'Most of it must be underground. I've never seen nor heard of any animal like this.'

'Let's carry on,' urged Sara. 'We might find more.' *Or something else.*

They had not gone much further before the growing light revealed the next surprise. From a distance it looked to Sara like nothing so much as an odd collection of stainless steel cutlery embedded in the ground, but Karmel soon recognized it for what it was.

'It's a Kiladl.' The creature was lying on its back, with only a small part of its underside exposed but with its jointed limbs and tentacles stiffly erect. Karmel touched one of its rigid feet and Sara knew that he was trying to detect something from the frozen body, but he merely looked at her and shook his head.

As they ascended they came across more and more creatures, both familiar and outlandish, that were embedded at strange angles in the grey dunes. They walked around an enormous triangular leathery and feathered wing, like the fin of a manta ray, and saw the forequarters of a herd of impala leaping eternally from the ground. There were scarlet flights of the gliders from Hyaquat and a spiny monster with multiple, suckered limbs, a sinuous neck and a hatchet beak clamped tightly around its final prey, a giant winged eel. Every ridge they ascended, there were more: the massive tail flukes of a diving whale, the unrecognisable flanged and bifurcated torsos and appendages of nightmare creatures from unknown words, an entire petrified stand of giant redwood trees.

They began to see pieces of machinery, buildings and other artefacts tangled among the organic debris, the scythe shaped wings of a Kiklaydan aircraft, a red Ferrari, the worn statue of a Mayan god. They passed under the shattered dome of an alien palace, covered on the inside with the most exquisitely fine carving that Sara had ever seen, and out the other side where they walked along the wing of a 747. It was as they climbed down from its tip that they found it was no longer possible to walk on the ground. From now on, they would have to pick and scramble a precarious way over the chaos.

They stopped for a moment in the shade of the wing.

'I have changed my mind,' said Karmel. 'This *is* a graveyard. Though I've noticed something unusual.'

'What is it?'

'I have seen many pieces of Kiklaydan technology; ventilation systems, desalination equipment and the like. All of them are modern. Nothing I have seen is more than a hundred years old.'

As he said this, Sara thought about the creatures she'd seen. Although the mayan statue and the other carved artifacts were clearly ancient, there were no dinosaurs or mammoths among them. None of the animals from Earth were extinct. 'So, whatever is happening here hasn't been going on forever?'

Karmel did not answer. He lunged forward with a small, strangled cry and began to climb like a thing possessed over the tangle of metal, ripping his robes free whenever they snagged. Sara quickly followed, troubled by his alarming behaviour, and caught up with him as he was throwing debris aside to uncover what he had found.

It was a Kiklaydan child, a little girl of no more than seven or eight years. She was dressed in a plain green robe. Her feet were rooted in the ground and there was a look of bewilderment on her face, her violet eyes wide as if she'd been petrified in the very instant that she had seen her fate coming for her. She had her arms raised, hands on the verge of opening as though she had been trying to hold on to something when she was taken.

Karmel dropped to his knees in front of her. Sara could hear the rasp of breath in his throat and the tremor of his almost inaudible sobbing.

'Every one of them is precious,' he whispered. 'Every one.'

Sara waited and said nothing as Karmel unwound the turban, and took something from his forehead. She could not see what it was, but he reached forward and with his long fingers, he tenderly placed a tiny something that shone brightly on the child's head, then he made the flowing gesture of respect that Sara had seen before among the Kiklayda, before turning to her.

'It's a simple gesture of respect for the dead,' he said, composed once again. 'A living crystal from my body, so that she will take the song of the Five Gods with her into the afterlife.' A trickle of clear blood ran down his forehead and to the side of his sharp nose, and there was a small indentation in the skin of his cranium that was quickly sealing itself.

'If you need to stay…'

'Thank you,' he said, 'but we have to go on. I am sure that your moment is coming and I'll be there for you, as you are for me.'

He did not mention the incident again. Before they had travelled much further, the way became so difficult that any attempt at conversation was virtually impossible. Gravity was again playing games with their perception and every movement had become a struggle. It was as if the air had thickened into an invisible but resistant syrup. Breathing became harder, but even when the slope steepened dramatically, she had the feeling that, if she fell, the congealed atmosphere would hold her. To Sara, it felt as though they were climbing to the top of a colossal rubbish dump; or it would have been so if it were not for the complete absence of odour and the unnatural inertness of even the smallest fragments. Sometimes, when she dug her feet hard into the slope, small pieces of wire or fragments of strangely coloured metal or other unknown materials would fly into the air, only to stop dead like the stone she had thrown by the lake.

She spotted a familiar object among the rubbish and picked a laborious course through the debris to investigate. It was a stainless steel refrigerator, lying on its side at the top of a mound of unidentifiable flotsam. She tramped tediously up the slope and hauled the door open with difficulty. Inside, she discovered eggs, salad vegetables that looked fresh in every way except for having turned a lurid shade of purple, fruit juice, and a carton of milk paralysed in the act of tipping over and spouting a shower of white droplets. Sara touched one, and it dropped to the side of the fridge and bounced. In the door compartment, she discovered chocolate and two packs of cereal bars.

'I wonder if they're safe to eat?'

Karmel had opted to wait for her at the bottom of the mound. 'I don't see why not. Nothing here seems to have been affected, except everything that was alive when it was brought here.'

Sara didn't need any more encouragement to rip open the wrapper of one of the bars and take a bite. It had a peculiar, bland texture and no taste at all but as she chewed a hint of flavour slowly returned.

'It's cranberry and oat, and... wait a moment... honey.'

She threw one to Karmel, watching it spiralling in slow motion to his outstretched hands, then she took the rest and put them in the backpack with the unopened carton of orange juice. They had solved one problem, at least.

By now they had climbed so high that they were once again able to see the double horizon of mountains with, between them, an opening to a far and distant strip of star filled night. In the intervening space were scores of isolated plateaus and lakes, one of which had shed a river of displaced water that meandered into the sky.

The way ahead was different. Where the slope curled up to what should have been the skyline, there was no solid horizon. As far as they could see on either side, the monumental gradient vanished into a bank of pearly mist. Karmel spent a long time scrutinizing this interface and when he eventually turned to Sara he announced what he had seen.

'There are things moving up there.'

'Living things?' Immediately, she felt silly for asking the question. What else could they possibly be?

Karmel gave no sign that he'd even heard her. 'They look like ants picking through the leftovers. I don't think that they have seen us. I'm not even sure that they *can* see.'

'If there are creatures here, maybe they're intelligent enough to know something. If they can talk to us, I need to see them.' She started off up the incline without waiting for him to follow. This was new; this was a fresh possibility. They had wandered in this unknown place for too long and had come too far without answers; but now, if there existed the remotest chance of a revelation, she had to know.

Soon, the way had become so steep that she was scrambling on hands and feet, and she was digging for holds in a scree of soft matter that should not have remained stable at such an extreme angle. The mist was nearer and she could see what Karmel's excellent vision had been able to spot from far below. It was the silvery movement of hundreds of indistinct shapes on the slope, milling like scavenging cockroaches scuttling through a monumental pile of refuse.

Before long, she was close enough to make out the nature of the creatures and what she saw made her spirits drop. Her first impression of scavenging insects had not been far wrong, after all. There were hundreds of them, strung out along the slope, and as she came closer she began to see that every single one was different and looked almost as if it had been thrown randomly together from a nonsensical collection of unrelated parts. Most were less than two feet in length and many had flattened or bulbous torsos and multiple limbs but, within those sketchy parameters, possibility had run riot. There were triangular hairy bodies and star-shaped scaly ones, backs covered with mushroom-like projections and others that were a mass of thrashing hair-like tendrils. Some of the creatures had insect heads at every corner of their multi-angled selves, while others had the gaping mouths of amphibians or fish, or seething masses of oozing sticky tentacles that coiled and uncoiled endlessly, but what all of them shared in common was that they were sifting through the crumbly ground with their limbs and sucking mouths to chew and slurp and suck at fragments of food, absorbed in their feeding to the exclusion of everything else.

Sara edged forwards cautiously onto more level ground, and into the lower reaches of the silky mist and the feeding frenzy that it overshadowed. If the creatures were so hungry, perhaps they would see her as the best meal to come their way in ages. But even when she edged past them they seemed to be completely unaware of her and continued their frenzied munching and chomping.

Then one of the monstrosities stopped feeding and lifted one of its three burrowing heads from the soft detritus. It resembled a large flat circular crab with a warty maroon shell and dozens of legs that constantly undulated in waves like those of a millipede. As it revolved to face her, it extended a cluster of assorted hands and tendrils and pincers from beneath its shell to wipe clean the face that was rapidly extending towards her at the end of a long, flabby grey neck.

A surge of bile rose in her throat. It was the small round face of a human girl, barely out of infancy, with fat cheeks and brilliant blue eyes, and a corona of dirty golden curls. It licked its lips, then sniffed at Sara's feet with its button nose.

'Come and look at it,' it said in a glassy voice. 'It's like us. Has it come for the feeding, too?'

With this, the other necks neck emerged from the ground to reveal the tiny chomping mouths and round eyes of two more infantile faces, one with eyes of piercing amber, the other with a red stare.

This is reality. They're not a nightmare. They have to be real and I need to treat them as if they are. Every grain of sense within Sara rebelled against the possibility of what she was seeing, but she had come too far now to give in to the possibility that what she was experiencing might be an illusion.

The first head was stuffing the remains of a flabby, dark red morsel into its mouth with a sinuous limb that terminated in a writhing cluster of minute human hands. Fighting against the revulsion, Sara advanced a step, knelt down on the soft ground and faced it.

'I need to know where this place is. Can you tell me?'

The little mouth spat and retched and Sara felt a cold spray of spittle on her face. The creature's eyes opened even wider as it goggled at Sara, aghast. Immediately, the other two heads on their skinny necks swung towards her.

'You can't be here if you don't know where this *is*!' said the first head in a shocked whisper.

'You don't even exist if you don't know where you are,' said another, and then the third began to laugh hysterically, spitting black morsels from its mouth. The others joined in, spluttering and choking as the multi-limbed body revolved.

As it approached, Sara lunged for the vulturine neck of the first head and gripped it as tightly as she could. The crablike torso convulsed and the other heads screamed in agony as she dragged the astonished and terrified face towards her own.

'*Now* tell me that I don't exist,' she hissed. '*Where am I?*'

'Don't hurt us, don't! We were like you once. We never wanted to be like this. Don't hurt us!'

'Then tell me, *where am I*?'

'It won't change anything if you know,' squealed the head. Sara had not eased her grip. 'You will be the same as us. That's what happens - it takes you apart and you are never yourself again.'

Sara tightened her grip and the other heads screamed and lunged at her with their toothless mouths but she held steady.

'I will not be like you,' she replied in a low and steady voice. 'I am Sara Parkinson and you do not know what I have been through to get here. Nor what I am capable of.'

'*You came willingly?*' gasped the first head.

'Of course I did,' she said. 'We both did.' She was conscious that Karmel had finally caught up with her and was standing close by, in looming silence.

'Tell it, tell it now before it kills us,' screamed the other heads.

'I'm not an "it". I'm a woman, just like you would have been if this hadn't happened to you. Now tell me.'

'We don't know! If you want to find out, you'll have to ask the Horror.'

'If you're lying - '

'No! It's the truth! The Horror lives beyond the mist. Sometimes it comes here and we hide from it because it looks at us and it knows everything. You have to keep going up, then you'll find it.'

Sara pushed the head violently away. The creature flopped to the ground, sobbing and thrashing its dozens of legs in a frenzy of distress but she swiftly rose to her feet and began to head on and into the thickening mist, oblivious to its whimpers.

'Come on, Karmel,' she said brusquely without looking back.

He tried to hurry, and slowly caught up with her before she completely vanished into the thickening miasma.

'Did you have to do that?' he said. 'Whatever you think, that creature was at least partially human. It's not to blame for what happened to it.'

'We haven't got time for this,' she snapped, quickening her pace.

'You will stop. NOW!'

Karmel's words stalled her in mid stride. She had never heard him speak like this, not with such naked fury. She waited with her chest heaving, staring into the misty limbo, with a growing and shameful awareness of his presence and her neglect.

They had left the scavengers behind and were now completely immersed in the dense opalescent fog. If anything, the stifling closeness of their surroundings was even more disturbing than the mind-blowing vistas they had left behind.

'Do you know what this is?' said Karmel, trailing his fingers through the vapour and creating brief eddying whirlpools.

'I didn't mean to - '

'Do you know what this is?' he said again, louder and firmer. Sara shook her head.

'It's life. It's what remains of the vitality of every creature we saw on our way here, and countless millions more, except those poor reassembled monstrosities back there. Do you understand?'

'Please, do not patronize me, Karmel. Of course I understand. If those things back there are the residue of life and this stuff around us is the same, that's all the more reason for us to keep going. Time is running out!'

She walked on. 'And don't you doubt for one second that I knew exactly what that monster was. You said my time would come, and it has. Do you think that I didn't know how you felt when we saw that Kiklaydan child? Don't you think that I'm angry, too?'

'Sara, it was no monster. They... she was human.'

She kept walking. 'I know - and that's what terrifies me. I'm scared about what we are going to find on the other side of this and I'm even more scared by the possibility that we can't do anything about it when we get there. I'm no clearer about what I'm supposed to do than I was that afternoon when the car hit me. *Why don't I know what to do?*'

'Trust yourself and trust me. If nothing else, believe me when I say that we don't have far to go now.' He gave her a curious tranquil smile and walked on.

The fog thickened and darkened. Now that Sara understood the essence of their surroundings she sensed something akin to reverence. She was afraid that if she took a breath, she might be destroying a part of the tenuous living essence that lingered there, before she noticed how the mist separated as they walked through, then drifted back, intact behind them.

Without any warning, they had passed through to the other side. The fog rose in a vertical wall of silence at their backs, while overhead the sky was a uniform brown emptiness.

They had come to the edge of a twisted landscape of bare stone. It was channelled and folded into smooth ripples as though it had once been molten lava, but everywhere the ground was wrenched and chiselled into a dense forest of sharp spines and bulbous mounds that were so densely packed together that Sara could not see any way of getting through. If the Horror lived here, it would have to show itself to them.

Karmel, however, had suddenly tensed and was peering into the jumble of rock.

'Wait here,' he said, and began to walk tentatively at first then with faster and more confident strides. Now Sara could make out what he had seen, a glassy shimmer that was barely visible among the rocks. It looked almost like a diaphanous curtain of some gauzy substance, except that it was immobile.

Karmel spent a long time standing in front of it before he indicated for her to join him. As she approached, she saw that it was a translucent wall of clear material like rock crystal. The surface was mirror smooth and, inside, it was faintly luminous and alive with slowly shifting pulses of light. Then, as she attuned herself to its subtle glow, she saw that it stretched away on both sides for as far as she could see through the chaos of rocks and rose far above her to vanish into the brown sky. There was no doorway, no apparent way through and she was reluctant to touch it but she had the feeling that it was solid.

She could make no sense of it, but when she turned questioningly to Karmel, she saw that something remarkable was happening to him. His skin was more vibrant than she had ever seen it before, every tiny crystal was alight but, more than that, he was surrounded with waves of radiance like those within the transparent barrier.

Sara backed away. 'What's happening to you?'

'Don't be frightened,' he said, smiling radiantly. 'Remember I said we didn't have far to go? We are here.'

'But what is it?' she said, looking back at the glassy wall. 'Can we get through?'

'Go on and touch it,' he said. 'It won't hurt you.'

Sara ran her fingers over the surface. It was hard and cold - so cold, in fact, that it was like ice. Then she pressed her fingertips against it and found it to be completely unyielding.

'You could try for a thousand years to get through this and you'd never succeed,' he said. 'Every weapon in the universe would be useless here.'

'What are you telling me? That we have to go through? How can we if it's impossible?'

'*You* have to go through,' he said. 'I can't go any further.'

Sara shook her head in denial. 'No. How can you say that? We've come so far together!'

'Do you know what this is?' He turned to the barrier, his violet eyes reflected in the surface. Then he stretched his long arms out and put his hands on the surface and where they touched was like an incandescent furnace of white metal. 'It's the Five Gods.'

'The Gods of Kiklayda?' she said incredulously.

'Yes, that's right, but they aren't spirits or deities. They're crystals. This wall is made of the five crystalline structures that make me Kiklaydan but it's different and so am I.'

'Wait a moment. I need to think about this.' She walked away, until she was far enough back that the light of the crystal barrier no longer cast shadows on the ground and the brown sky and shadow-filled land encroached on her like an omen. In that moment, a barb of intuition touched her like a cold needle. It was the Mawdrik, and they knew exactly where she was.

She returned to Karmel. He had not moved and the white energy continued to flow between his hands and the barrier as if he was already a part of it.

'I've found what I've been looking for. It's the same as me, Sara, and it's alive!' He was exultant. 'This is why I'm here.'

'What does it mean, for us?'

'For us? It means that I can get you through to the other side. Only two can do it, me and the one you're looking for.'

Only now did he turn to her. 'Hold my hand.'

She did as he asked, feeling as though his touch was pure energy and had no material substance, and together they walked into the crystal barrier as easily as if it were made of air.

'Keep going!' he said, letting go of her. 'You mustn't stop!'

She stepped through and into a buffeting wind that whistled and moaned among the rocks and battered against the slab of glowing crystal. Karmel was still inside.

'Karmel!' she shouted. 'What are you doing?'

'I told you, I can't come with you,' he called, hardly audible above the noise of the wind. 'I have to stay here, or the door will close. You have to find Orla by yourself. It's you he wants, not me.'

'But I can't go on alone! Please, Karmel!'

'Don't be scared, Sara. It's the only way. If I leave now, you will be trapped inside this place forever. You have it in your heart to do whatever you have to. And I'll be here, waiting for you.' He sat down on the ground and arranged his robes about him.

Sara could feel tears in her eyes, but she fought to contain them. 'Are you sure this really is the only way?'

'Yes, my dear brave Sara. Go on, now. Do what has to be done.'

'And you'll be here, and we'll get out of this together?'

He smiled at her serenely. 'Go on. Don't look back.'

'I can't,' she whispered, the words almost lost in the battling wind. 'Not by myself.'

'You can,' he said, and she knew against all her fears that he was right.

4. The Realm of the Seven

Sara forced herself away from Karmel and took her first steps. She wanted to turn and run screaming back through the crystal barrier, from this place, from everything that had happened. She had lost François. Was she about to lose Karmel too? *Alone! I'm on my own.* She took a deep breath that was more a sob and then she wrapped her arms around her shivering body and walked into the jaws of the gale.

She had to lean into the powerful gusting wind to make headway, but at least the effort of doing so helped to take her mind away from the trauma of separation. The land was even more hostile on this side of the barrier and the endless wind had carved the rocks into saw-edged daggers and strange bulbous outcrops like giant mushrooms. Roiling brown clouds streamed overhead and squalls of bitter rain stung her face. After only a few hundred yards she had to search for shelter and crouched out of the wind while she hunted for her waterproof, then she pulled the cord of the hood tight and stepped back into the squall.

Sara began to pick her way slowly into the heart of the labyrinth, lowering herself down sudden drops into gullies and squeezing sideways through narrow crevices. Sometimes, she was forced to double back but as she made headway, the going slowly became easier and after less than half an hour's toil she broke free of the maze.

She was walking between the fluted walls of a narrow valley, the floor of which descended in shallow planes like wide steps into a heart of dense shadows. The reason for this was beyond her, until she saw that the edges of the valley were slowly arching over and closing in until eventually they joined overhead and she was entering the black maw of a tunnel. Not far in, it became so dark that she could barely see. Even worse, the wind had been forced into the narrow space and was now so powerful that Sara had to grope for the wall of the tunnel and flatten herself against it before she was able to edge her way onward, feeling with blind fingers in the dark and struggling every moment to stay upright.

Gradually, her eyes registered a faint grey shift in the tunnel ahead and she was fumbling onwards with a new spark of determination when she encountered nothingness and almost fell over. She had come upon a narrow passage leading off to the left and, in the mouth of this, the wind had deposited a thin layer of gritty material that Sara could feel crunching underfoot. And there, in the faint light, she could make out the faint but unmistakeable marks of bare feet.

She squatted down and studied them. They seemed to be those of a human being but they were twisted and emaciated, the left one with deep scuff marks as if whatever had made them was lopsided and deformed.

Sara had to master her fear and go on. If there was danger ahead, she would have to deal with it however best she could. The wind thumped and boomed and gusted through unseen passages above and below, and the dripping and trickle of water was all around her in the bald tunnel. She followed it steeply downwards then rounded a corner where it widened into a circular cavern with an uneven ceiling and a sloping floor. On the opposite side of this the tunnel continued sharply upwards, casting a faint oval of grey light across the floor of the cave. The far side of the chamber, where the crumbling ceiling dipped down and the floor dropped away, was in absolute darkness but in the dust on the edge of sight were more footprints.

Sara kept to the light as she tried to fathom out what might reside in the far reaches of the chamber, but she could see nothing.

'Hello?' The word died away on the chill air, but something shifted on the edge of vision and a damp waft blew over her from the shadows like a dying sigh.

'Hello.' There was a faint scuffling sound and a hint of movement, shadow against shadow. She spoke again and this time she was answered by a voice, cracked, fragile and seemingly as ancient as the rocks from where it came.

'What is it now? Have you come for more food? Well, you can go away! You've eaten all of them, all of my children…' It trailed off into an indecipherable mutter.

'Orla?' The muttering stopped.

'Do you know who I am?' She heard whispering then querulous mumbling as if the voice was arguing with itself.

'Orla, I'm Sara Parkinson. You told me to follow.'

'Follow you? Why would I want to follow you, whoever you are? No, no, that isn't right. It's not right, I say!' There was a silence before it continued, hesitant and questioning. ' You don't want to eat my children, then?'

'I don't know what you mean. You said my name, then you came to me in Granada. I'm here because of you.'

She listened to the lonely moan of the wind and the incessant drip of water as she waited for a response. Then came the uneven scuff of feet and a figure slowly emerged from the dark.

He was a shocking and pitiful sight, so distorted that Sara could barely piece together in her imagination what he might once have looked like. He would have been taller than her but his long white torso was twisted and bent and his horribly thin legs were bowed and malformed by old traumas. One arm was crushed into the hollow of his sunken chest, the palm of the hand permanently turned outwards, while the other trembled as it reached out to her, and had a hand that must once have been completely torn apart because the thumb and forefinger were now roughly fused to the wrist.

As he came towards her, step by painful step, his head was bowed almost to his chest, then he lifted his ravaged face to peer at her with dull small eyes. His left eye was completely displaced to his cheek, while his jaw slewed to the right and his mouth was a dark slit. What at first sight looked like a tracery of blue veins all over his body were the scars of old deep wounds, and Sara realized that her first suspicions were correct. He had been taken apart and remade in a travesty of whatever he had once been.

She felt neither revulsion nor shock; nothing but a profound pity.

'What happened to you? They destroyed you!'

Orla made an empty crackling noise. He was laughing.

'Clever *and* pretty. The universe has a grudge against me, do you understand?'

He wobbled towards her. 'Every time I leave my cosy sanctuary here it tries to take me apart again, and Orla becomes a little less than he was.' He wheezed and chuckled again. 'I can't say I blame it. I'd do the same.'

Orla reached out his functioning arm. 'Help me out of this hole. It's getting more difficult for me all the time.'

Sara didn't hesitate. She put one arm around his back and offered the other so he could lean on it. He felt like cold, dead flesh. His near eye flickered in what seemed to be an expression of gratitude, and he rested his slight weight on her. After a few paces, the short tunnel gave on to a small depression, open to the troubled sky but sheltered from all but the strongest gusts.

'Let me down, please - yes, over there, against that stone, out of the wind. We are old friends, this stone and me.'

She helped him sit awkwardly, feeling every creak of his emaciated body, then she sat down opposite him and leant back against the side of the hollow, pulling her thin waterproof tighter against the wracking cold.

Orla was completely naked and seemed oblivious to the bitter chill, but his mind was drifting.

'The wind likes to blow a little more of me away whenever it can. I talk to it and it helps me... me and my children, who are all in pieces. Yes, the wind likes to feed.'

He muttered and shook his deformed fist at the sky, then slumped down with his forehead on his bulbous knees. He seemed to have fallen asleep.

'Orla, can you hear me?'

'Of course I can hear you.' He twitched upright. 'I´m not deaf.'

'I didn't mean to offend you. I have some food. Would you like some?'

He focused his near eye on her again and Sara detected a suggestion of surprise and interest.

'Something to *eat*? Well, now. That's a revelation. I haven't eaten for... now then, let me see... ah, it must be a hundred years.'

She unwrapped a cereal bar for him. He held it clumsily between two fingers and started to nibble. Most of it fell to the ground but he kept chewing for a long time, licking the corners of his mouth with a colourless tongue.

'Wonderful. Completely exquisite. A feast fit for a - well, fit for me. I can't thank you enough.'

The food appeared to have restored some of his reason and focus.

'You haven't come from wherever you did to watch me drooling and spitting crumbs.' His sunken eye revolved and held her gaze. 'Have you?'

'You brought me here,' she said. 'You know what's happening out there, don't you. Maybe you can answer that question.'

'I only see glimpses.' He sounded infinitely sad. 'Every time I leave here I know the torment will be worse, but I have to go. To warn, but none of you listen! Idiots and imbeciles!' He flared into anger but like a short-lived flame, he was quickly spent. 'Except you, so it would seem. Pretty *and* clever.'

'That's what you were trying to do, all the time?'

'Hmm.' He looked away. 'Yes. To warn you… warn you about my interesting neighbours. They're cosmic collectors, you know. Have you seen their museum..? Dear me, they really should stay at home but they do like to go visiting. But somebody left the door open and there are so many unwelcome guests who want to come a-calling.'

'Do you mean the Mawdrik?'

Orla lifted himself on his good arm and contemplated her with his displaced eyes.

'The *Mawdrik*.' He said the word slowly, with an indecipherable but chilling emphasis. 'And who might they be?'

'Don't you know who the Mawdrik are?'

'*I* know who they are,' Orla retorted, 'of course I know. But do *you* know who they are?'

'Maybe I don't. You tell me, then.'

'They are my children, every one of them,' he said. 'I am the Mawdrik.'

Orla was the first to break the intervening silence. 'Are you revolted? Do you hate and loathe me, now that you know? Do you want to put your hands round my skinny neck and throttle the life out of me?'

'Why should I hate you?' she answered in a muted voice. 'I don't know anything about you, why you are here, what happened to make you like this.'

'But you *do* hate my children?' prompted Orla.

'Yes,' she had to admit. 'Yes, I hate them because they are destroying my world and they killed somebody very close to me. As for the rest, that's for you to explain. I am not going to assume anything.'

'You really are remarkable,' said Orla. 'Now that I have met you properly I can see that I wasn't wrong. I was afraid that we couldn't do what has to be done, but you have given me hope.' The breath hissed in his wattled throat as he exhaled. 'Hope. You truly cannot begin to understand what that simple word means to me.'

'I can't possibly know,' she agreed.

'Then you *do* have a chance. Unlike most of your kind, you have learned not to assume that you know what you don't or even worse… even worse, to invent a truth without imagining the consequences of such deceit.'

He was drawing breath as if to continue when he frowned, then looked troubled and began swaying his head from side to side as though he was trying to peer behind Sara.

'Where is the blue man? Didn't you bring him with you?'

'Do you mean Karmel? I had to leave him behind.'

'Oh. That's a pity.' Orla's ravaged face looked crestfallen. 'I would have liked to meet him. You see, we have something in common but you know that already, of course.'

He moved his creaking body and rested the side of his shattered head on the stone so that he was looking away from her, into the brown seethe of clouds. Now and then, when the wind dropped momentarily, Sara thought that she caught the trace of something, a low thunderous boom repeating itself over and over again. As she concentrated on filtering out the noise of the storm, she was more certain. She had heard it before, in a dream at the beginning of things and again, on Hyaquat.

'You can hear them, can't you?'

'What are they?'

'You'll see,' he said. 'I can tell you what you are here to do. That is the easy part. You have come to meet my neighbours, and to close the door after you leave. What you learn from them is another matter. But you should first understand why you are here and why I am to blame.

'You know my children. You have survived their excesses. I have to tell you that I am no different from them. In fact, you might say that everything they were and are and will be, they owe to me... and as you'll see, all that I am, I owe to them. I am the same as my beloved family in every respect except one. Do you know what that is?'

'You can travel to other worlds.'

'Clever and pretty, pretty and clever. Exactly so. You and I, alone in it all. And it is I who found the way here and brought my children, and I who opened the door for them, just like the blue man did for you. Why? Because we are hungry for knowledge and power but more than that, the Mawdrik are the most insecure and vulnerable of peoples and the unknown is the worst kind of terror for us.

'I opened the way and a thousand of my children came with me, to learn from me how they could make something greater of themselves than they already were. We are, after all, the Masters of the Universe, are we not? So isn't it our birth right to shine like the stars?'

'I know you don't believe that,' said Sara.

'Pretty *and* clever,' he said again, and this time the hint of a smile lifted the corners of his lipless mouth.

'And did you find what you were looking for?'

'Oh yes!' he said, bright eyed. 'I went on ahead and I found everything I'd hoped for and more, much more. It made me afraid. Imagine it. The father of the Mawdrik, *afraid*... but I had to go back and tell them.'

'What did you find?' she asked.

'You'll find out soon enough, for yourself. It will be far better that way but I have to warn you now, while I can. Do not forget that you will not have much time, and be careful what you ask. That was my great mistake. I was not careful.'

'Why?' she asked. A cold pang of anxiety clutched at her. *You will not have much time, and be careful what you ask.* 'What happened to you?'

'My children, my little ones.' Orla was labouring to breathe. 'They never knew what I found, because I couldn't tell them. I refused to tell them. You see, I also learned what they would become but they wouldn't listen... they never listen...'

And now, Sara understood. She reached over and touched his deathly cold arm.

'*They* did this to you.'

'Yes,' he said quietly without taking his eyes from the sky. 'They tore me apart in their rage. They scattered me like dust but it was already too late. I remade myself, to the best of my abilities, though it took many years and every moment of my existence since then has been an eternal agony.'

'What happened to the others who came with you?'

'They're still here. You'll see them soon enough, the poor ones. Oh, don't worry about it because they can't harm you. I told them to go but they didn't listen. They were so angry and it was too late. I had already opened the door. It was too late...'

Orla lowered his face and passed his arm in a rough motion across his eyes.

'And now something is loose that should never have been freed. Something precious has been broken, and it is my fault. You have already seen what it can do. It is running amok and what it takes it brings here and it will keep doing so until there is nothing left. But it has to be restored and its secret must be hidden with it. Do you understand? The door has to be closed behind you.'

Something is loose, but it must be restored. It made no sense whatsoever to her. But time was short too. That is what he'd said, hadn't he? She thought about everything he'd told her - Orla, the father of the Mawdrik, who had sat down with her and eaten a cereal bar.

'Why have you told me all of this? Why are you helping me?'

'You have every right to ask,' he said. 'Why trust the Mawdrik? You don't know that I cannot harm you. My children, now, they have every reason to be afraid of me because I could destroy them all in a moment, even now. I could do it with a thought but I love them still. I can see you looking at me and hating them even more because of what they did but please, don't pity me. Pity them, and hope that they can find a different path.'

'I will never pity them,' she said, 'but you… how can I explain this? It's not just that I don't have any choice but to trust you. I feel that there's good in you, whatever you did.'

This time, Orla really smiled, fighting against the handicap of his mutilated face.

'That's everything I needed to hear,' he said. 'I have waited a hundred years for this.' He began to struggle upright.

'It is time, Sara.'

She came forward to help him without a moment's hesitation. This time, she did not need to be asked.

'Where are we going?'

'Up. It isn't very far.'

The climb out of the hollow was fraught with difficulty. Orla could barely walk and the effort of raising one foot in front of the other to scale the difficult slope was almost more than he could endure, even with Sara's help. Worse was to come, because as soon as they raised their heads above the side of the hollow, they were struck by the direct force of the battering wind, and Sara almost lost her grip on his cold slippery body. But, by flattening her upper body against the ground she managed to drag him over the edge and into the lee of the nearest tumble of stones.

Orla seemed to be close to the limits of his endurance and was panting for breath, his sunken chest convulsing erratically as though his lungs no longer had the strength to pull in sufficient air to sustain him. Leaving him to rest, Sara lifted her head above the shelter and knew straight away where they were.

She had feared this moment, and now she knew that this return to the source of her nightmares was inevitable and always had been. A dismal grey hillside of scree and hunched boulders rose steeply from their shelter, into the driving rain and fog that rushed at her from the heights but nevertheless was not enough to conceal what waited for her at the top.

More potent still was the sound that even the strongest gale would not have been able to suppress, the long slow pound of seven thunderous beats, only this time she was hearing it straight from its beating heart.

'Go on,' said Orla. 'You'll have no problem in getting through. I didn't. Just keep walking and don't allow my children to distract you, whatever you might be tempted to do.'

He plucked weakly at her waterproof. 'Just one more thing. There is another, the one who took my place. My firstborn. Beware of him, of both of him. You won't forget, will you?'

'I'll not forget,' she said, 'but I'll come back for you.'

'I am sorry,' he said wearily. 'When you return I will not be here.'

'You're not staying here? You have a chance to escape!'

'Escape? But I am not trapped. Don't you understand? You have brought beauty into my life, and culmination.'

Orla's chest convulsed and heaved up, and when he subsided he appeared, in some way, less than he was before.

'We have been the Mawdrik for thousands of years. Before that we were the Violash and before that, the Strune. I gave us those names, but there was an eternity before then when we did not have a name, not even among ourselves. In all that time, I have never once fallen asleep… and I would so like to go to sleep. This is your time, not mine. I can let go now.'

'I won't let you stay here. It's inhuman!'

'As am I. Do you really think that there is anywhere for a creature like me? Besides, you already know what will happen if I leave here again. Finding you was my last time.'

'You're just going to stay here and die?'

Orla smiled again. 'Is that such a bad thing? I have lived down all the long ages of the universe, and now I am the first of my kind to accept that I have outlived my time, and believe me when I say that knowing it is pure joy. I can rest knowing that I did what I had to, to make amends, right at the end. Go on, Sara. You have little time left.'

She looked down at him, crumpled in the lee of the rocks, and knew that she could do nothing to persuade him otherwise, so she quickly knelt down and put a kiss on his cold forehead before he had time to realize what she was doing. Then she set herself to the wind and began trudging up the hillside with the rain driving into her squinting eyes.

Maybe it was the eeriness of the gale that moaned almost like a living thing in pain and misery, or the understanding that she was approaching that which she feared above everything else, that made the stark hillside seem so threatening to Sara. It could surely be no more than a mile to the base of the great wall but the ascent was steep and slippery with rain and every step was an effort.

In places the wind had scoured away the thin shale to expose planes of bedrock and she tried to walk on this more solid ground wherever possible. But the gale drove at her with the strength of pummelling fists and the unending sequence of seven reverberating booms was so overpowering that it might have been a physical entity setting itself against her. She advanced by slow stages of a dozen yards or less, wedging her foot at an angle in crevices every minute or so to prevent herself slipping as she tried to catch her breath.

She had climbed perhaps a third of the way and the boulder where she'd left Orla was hidden beyond the driving vapour when the movement of something caught her attention, a bleached and shapeless thing that shuddered and twitched in the lee of a boulder. Then she heard a terrible wail carrying on the wind, a noise so heartrending and desolate that she wanted to cover her ears and blot it out. She saw another of the grotesque shapes, partially buried in the soaking shale where it quivered in violent fits and starts, and then another. She tried not to look and to simply carry on climbing regardless, but it was inevitable that she would sooner or later pass right by one of them because there were more of them all the time.

And then she could not contain her horrified curiosity any longer. She had to know. Each one of them was tethered to the ground by a thick grey umbilical cord. Some of them had no trace of limbs and were nothing but worm-like torsos or the smudged vestige of an eye on a bulbous cranium, or had little remaining but a round, gasping hole for a mouth and a flapping piece of white flesh that scrabbled and coiled hopelessly on the ground. One reached out a fold of skin that could have been the remains of a hand, others curled up as she trudged by or mewled horribly as they strained away from her.

Now she knew what had happened to the Mawdrik. The something that she was about to encounter was feeding on what remained of those of Orla's children that had come here with him, a hundred years ago. A hundred years of the slowest, most deliberate annihilation imaginable, devouring their preternatural energy by excruciating degrees as though wreaking grim justice on the Mawdrik's own propensity for destruction. Sara realized with horror and pity that Orla had probably been the more fortunate. She would not wish such a macabre and lingering fate on anything, not even on the Mawdrik whom she hated.

And if she survived, would her fate be any less awful?

I can't think about it! I mustn't! At last she was approaching the wall. It was without end, just as she knew it would be. She remembered what Orla had told her and knew beyond doubt that to stop now would be a fatal error.

Sara kept walking. She was only a few yards away. If she was wrong, if she doubted herself for one second… and then she was inside.

We have been waiting for you.

She was immersed in warmth and complete darkness, and that was all. Whatever the nature of her whereabouts, it was completely lacking in other sensations. She thought that she was standing upright, but she could feel nothing underfoot and when she felt around, she encountered nothing. She wasn't even sure if she had really heard the words, or they had just been inside her head.

Sara remembered what Orla had told her. She did not have much time, but where and how should she begin if she was to finally understand?

'Who are you?'

You already know what we are, and it does not surprise you.

This time, she heard it. It was magnified and directionless, but it was her own voice.

'You are the voice of the Seven, aren't you?'

Yes.

Through all the traumas she had endured in getting here, she had scarcely given a thought about what she might find at the end. But now, she was aware that she'd known all along, even if knowing had not prepared her to ask the right questions. She had to do more than know. She had to *understand!*

'If you're what you say you are, why are you here? Why did I have to come to this place to find you?'

We are the voice of the Seven, and we are imprisoned within the Seventh.

'That doesn't make any sense.'

This was met with silence, but all around her something was becoming visible. It was a perfect circle of rainbow light and she was at the centre. She counted the colours from bottom to top - violet, indigo, blue, green, yellow, orange, red. Each band of colour pulsed bright in the same order, at precisely the same speed as the sound she now knew so well, and every time the band of crimson flared and dwindled, there was a pause before the cycle began over again.

'Why didn't you answer me?'

We answer questions. We do not pass comment on your subjectivity.

'What are you, then?'

We are knowledge.

'Okay, you're an oracle. What do you know?'

We know everything.

'There are different kinds of "everything". Be more specific. What do you know?'

We know everything.

This is not getting me anywhere. She had to approach matters from a different angle.

'You still aren't making any sense. Neither does the very first thing you said to me. You told me you had been expecting me but I hadn't yet asked you a question, had I?'

You asked the question in your mind, and you have already asked others which we have yet to answer.

'What? So you *have* been waiting for me?'

Yes.

She felt beguiled and confused, but then she remembered Orla's warning.

'How much time do I have here?'

You have thirty-nine minutes according to your understanding of time.

'Okay, okay.' That gave her thirty-nine minutes to solve the mystery that had turned her life inside out. 'And what happens after that?'

Your time here will be at an end.

It was too ambiguous a response but pursuing it would get her nowhere. 'What are you called?'

We have no names apart from those that others choose to bestow upon us.

'What would I know you as, then?'

According to the studies of the defunct person you know as William Grace, and based on the archaic belief systems of your world as explained to you by Maria Angustias Rodríguez Acosta, the names of Seven are Ru, Mah, Lei, Hiree, Dul, Horroth.

Sara was dumbfounded. *Six names, that was all.*

'Why haven't you told me all seven names? And if you're trapped here by the seventh, why don't you escape? I thought you were supposed to be some kind of mystic universal law that makes everything tick?'

We are knowledge. We are not power. We answer all questions.

'But not necessarily in my here and now, is that right?'

Yes.

'But how can you be this almighty Seven but be imprisoned here by part of yourself?'

We are a function of the Seven. Each has its place in the flux of the cosmos. Here and now, within the limitations of your understanding, is the time of the seventh.

Time was running out. Sara knew that she was not asking the right things, but she needed to know that she was not being deceived. Maybe they could show her evidence of something so unlikely that it could not be fabricated.

'Okay, we'll start again. I want you to show me something. Show me... I don't know... show me something from my own world, from the past. What about a dinosaur? Show me a tyrannosaur. Not a dead one, not a fossil. I want to see a living one. Can you do that or doesn't that count as a question?'

It does. We will show you.

Above the ring of colours, a dome of dazzling blue sky flourished into being. Sara was looking over a wide savannah dotted with giant ferns and trees that looked a little like conifers, while the coarse grassland was a dense short sward of horsetails and strange branching mosses. Dragonflies and other insects buzzed and swarmed everywhere.

Then an animal emerged cautiously from the dense cover. Considering its size, it moved with surprisingly light and agile footsteps before stopping to scratch its massive head with one tiny front limb. It was brilliantly marked with vertical red and blue stripes on a lustrous green hide, and it had a pale yellow belly with purple mottling, and mild dark brown eyes, and along its back and neck to the crown of its head, it sported a crest of olive green feathers. The creature was undoubtedly a tyrannosaur but as it glanced around with quick bird-like movements then lifted its head and gave a single loud musical call, all of Sara's notions of rampaging cinema monsters were forever laid to rest.

The image faded. If this was a true insight into Earth's distant past, what else could they show her? She needed to see more.

'What about the present and the future?' Silence. She had to think again.

'There are different versions of the present and the future, aren't there? Different dimensions?'

Yes.

'What about Endymion? What is Endymion? Tell me about it.' They couldn't know about Endymion from any source other than her and the few people she'd told.

Endymion is a world that exists parallel to your Earth. For many humans, Endymion epitomizes their idea of a peaceful and sustainable utopia.

'And Gul? I've visited a world called Gul. What's going to happen to it, in the future as it exists from the moment I escaped?'

As you know it, Gul is a dying world. Contamination, an unsustainable food chain and the collapse of its artificially maintained atmosphere will lead to the extinction of all human life. This will occur within seven generations of the epoch in which your visit there took place.

This surely had to be beyond question, but now Sara needed more to add fuel to the awesome awareness that was approaching her through the miasma of confusion.

'Can you choose what to show me?'

Within the criteria you set us, we are able to choose.

'Then show me something on the nearest planet in… that direction.' She pointed at random into the black void. The image that immediately appeared was an oscillating fragment that shimmered as it revolved like a shred of gold leaf.

'What is it?'

It is a single mote of dust. We have chosen this one for you, among all others on this world.

'Do you mean to say that you can show me *every* bit of dust, anywhere, in any universe?'

Yes.

'Show me more. I want to see this world.'

What followed was like a cinema sequence that panned out from microscopic scrutiny to a view of a peculiar, asymmetrical chamber. It was completely bare, with a yard-thick outer wall pierced by a rhomboidal window. A shaft of fierce red light angled across the floor and under a burning sky of fire and boiling clouds, massive boneless limbs writhed and churned all along the crimson horizon.

'That's enough!'

Oh my God. Is this *what the Mawdrik are searching for? The knowledge of everything, not as an abstract concept but in absolute reality?*

'Am I asking the right questions?'

No.

Something was not right. How could they be an impartial source of knowledge yet give her such a subjective reply?

'What is the right question?'

The right question is, 'what must I do?'

'Okay, then. What must I do?'

You must leave.

'What?' Sara was horrified. 'Is that it? Is that why I've risked my life to find you? Thousands of people have died, and for what?'

That is all you must do.

This was even more disturbing. This time, they had made no attempt to answer her directly.

'Why? Why must I leave?'

By leaving, you will accomplish your entire purpose in coming here, and you will leave with our final reply.

'I don't understand.'

We will give you the name of Seven.

'No!' Sara was drenched with cold terror. 'I don't want to know. Even Orla doesn't know what it is, does he? There's something very bad about this. You said it was the time of the Seventh - there's some kind of rhythm, isn't there? But something went wrong. *Didn't it?*'

There is imbalance. You will take the name and restore the Six.

'No! You can't make me!' And she was already running, out through the rainbow ring of light and trying to outrun the terrible destiny that was about to engulf her.

Now we will tell you the name.

'Never!' Sara lurched screaming out of the limbo and was immediately back on the rain-drenched slope where the remains of the Mawdrik army wailed and twitched among the rocks. *No, no, NO...* she tried to fight against the awful truth, but it was too late. Even if she'd been able to run faster than the gale, she could never escape from what was now a part of her.

Half way down the slope, Sara's headlong flight faltered when she skidded on the wet shale and stumbled to an uneasy halt. She knew that something had altered and she was at a loss to know what it was, until she became aware of the sound of her rasping breath, much too loud in the stillness. The beating heart of the Seven had stopped. She waited breathlessly for it to begin again, but nothing came. Even the gale had diminished to a fretful gusting wind that drove a fine drizzle slantwise across the hillside.

Then something fell from the clouds and struck the scoured rocks close by - a heavy splash of rain, or so she thought at first, but when another fell then more, she saw with a shudder of fear that the impact marks were jet black, like splashes of ink.

Within moments, the black rain became a downpour. There was a long roll of thunder that thumped and reverberated, and then a dark immensity spun away from the near face of the wall, a massive something that looked like nothing so much as an enormous shard of ebony glass. As it reeled into the clouds, two more fragments burst away in opposite directions like chips of rock being smashed from the wall, and came to an abrupt halt far overhead as if their trajectory had been interrupted by an invisible barrier.

She ran on, slipping and stumbling down the precipitous slope and past the empty shelter where she had last seen Orla, then over the rim of the hollow where they had sat and talked. The rain was falling ever more heavily and rivulets of black water spouted into the depression. Another thunder crack tore through the sky and more shattered pieces arced a dozen yards above her, each of them as big as a house.

Sara fled into the constricted passage, bumping and fumbling against the walls as she went, and reached the main tunnel in minutes, willing herself not to fall in the rushing torrent of freezing water that was creeping up around her ankles.

With the wind rising again she made it to the far end of the passage and into the brown storm light. During the time she had been underground, an ominous change had come over the sky. The angular black fragments were static far above her and more were accumulating all the time. She had already made the connection, that this entire place was sealed within a crystalline dome, the same within whose walls she had left Karmel. If the prison of the Seven was really breaking apart, as she suspected, whatever it had released would soon cover the entire interior of that dome and she would be trapped inside.

She was approaching the place where the forest of sharp stones closed in to thwart her escape. Every moment that passed, more of the brown sky was consumed by the unknown shadows, and the black rain sheared down so mercilessly that every gulley contained a gurgling torrent. She slipped and fell, cursing in pain when she caught her leg in a deep fissure, then in the effort of dragging herself free a knife-sharp spine of rock shattered and sliced into her palm and her blood splashed into the black water.

Karmel.

Then she caught a glimpse of the crystal wall through a cleft in the rocks, and with one last effort she dragged herself free of the maze, cradling her injured hand into her chest. Almost three quarters of the sky had been obliterated and the thunder was mounting to a continual roar that shook the ground and made the loose stones dance and skitter.

Sara was barely a dozen yards away from Karmel when she stopped running. He was still sitting on the ground inside the crystalline barrier with his arms folded in his lap. She could not tell whether or not he had seen her but there was a faint smile on his glowing face as though the mounting destruction behind her was nothing but a distant fantasy.

The rain pounded on her back as she hesitated, and then he saw her.

'Sara,' he called. 'Get inside, quickly.' His words were amplified by some effect of the transparent material that entombed him, as if he was already a part of something far bigger than himself.

'A wave is coming.'

She did not need to look back and see the roaring black tsunami that was rising over the rocky labyrinth. As she stepped through the barrier, the driving rain and thunder were shut off, completely and irrevocably. Inside, it was utterly calm.

Karmel unwound his legs and got up. He was waiting for her to speak.

'You're not coming with me, are you?'

He shook his head infinitely slowly as if he was profoundly weary. There was something of Orla in the gesture, and Sara felt right then that her heart might shatter.

'Please tell me I'm wrong.' Tears were rolling down her face.

'Don't cry, my sweet Sara. I've always known how it was going to be.'

'Why didn't you tell me?'

'Would it have made it any easier for you? Sara, I have to close the way. What's inside has to be preserved, but it must never be allowed to escape again. I am the only one who can do it. I have to stay.'

'Orla. He knew.' *The door has to be closed behind you*, he'd said, but he hadn't said who would be the one to seal it shut.

'Hold out your hand,' said Karmel gently. He dropped a small glassy object into her bleeding palm.

'Do you know what this is?'

'Yes.' She recognized it instantly. It was one of the floating spheres from the Volk's transition orb.

'I can't leave here without you. I won't.'

'You have to. You don't need me anymore,' he said. 'When we touched, I gave you more than just a memory of me, just as you have given something of yourself everywhere you've been. You have the strength to do this. Just focus on this and follow the left hand spiral, like we did together.'

'But… what are you going to do?'

'Oh, I'll sit here and think and dream, and listen to music. I have the banderil. Elgar and Beethoven will keep me company.'

'How long for? Karmel, tell me! How long?'

He merely smiled.

'Please don't do this, Karmel. I'll always need you.'

Karmel shook his head, then he looked into her frantic eyes with compassion.

'There's nothing that I can do, is there?' she said at last.

'Yes, there is,' he said. ' One last thing.'

'Anything.'

'Then hold me.'

She threw herself against Karmel and wrapped her arms tightly around him, crushing herself against his chest and sobbing into his shoulder, hoping against hope that she could take him with her, that there was another way. After too short a time, he seemed to read her thoughts and slowly pushed her away before saying, 'It's time to go. I will always love you, Sara Parkinson.'

Then she felt herself being drawn into the core of a twisting spiral of luminosity, the globe clutched tightly in her fist, and time and suffering vanished into the limbo, and then there was stillness.

5. Transition

Sara had been here before. As she gradually returned to full awareness, she felt again the unmistakeable aura of wellbeing and a sense of enveloping protection and when she opened her eyes, it was to see uncountable stars against the backdrops of deep space. A group of glassy spheres floated just over her head and when she opened her palm she found only a trace of sparkling dust from the one that Karmel had given her. The deep gash and the blood had completely disappeared, but under the healed skin she could see the dark trace of a tiny fragment of stone.

Everything was exactly the same as it had been the first time, except for one thing. She was not alone.

There was time to make ready. She could feel the weight of her wet hair and she smoothed it out with her fingers. Then she took off the waterproof, rolled it up and stashed it in the backpack. She was not going to need it again. When she was ready, she stood up and faced them.

Gathered outside the transparent globe in their hundreds were the Mawdrik.

Sara was not afraid, but even within the therapeutic confines of the globe she felt weary to her bones. She knew the Mawdrik would wait for as long as they needed to. Everything was now up to her.

'Listen to me,' she said. 'We have to end this.'

They were ranked in tiers, as they had been in the sky above Granada only there were twice as many here. One of them detached from the nearest level and came towards her, stopping just short of the outer globe.

'The Mawdrik do not end,' he said. 'This ending is for you alone.'

'Spoken like a true lumen,' she retorted. 'I've heard it before and I'm tired of it. Isn't it about time you started singing a different song? You must be pretty bored with this one.'

He smiled frostily. 'Do not waste the words that remain to you on futile attempts at mockery. You know why we are here and you know that you have no option but to give us what we require.'

'That's typical Mawdrik pretence, just like your father said. You can't hide your fear from me.'

Sara could sense the rage boiling inside him.

'You're almost scared to death, aren't you? You know where I've been. You know who I've spoken to.'

'That is irrelevant.'

'Do you know what's happening to your brothers and sisters? They're being slowly eaten alive. I almost felt sorry for them, even though they knew what would happen to them if they didn't listen.'

'You will *not* speak of this again.'

'Really?' she said with a short laugh. 'And I suppose you're going to stop me? As long as I'm here and you're out there, you've got no alternative *but* to listen to me. Isn't that hilarious? The mighty Mawdrik have run out of choices!'

'It is you who have no choice. You cannot escape, and we can wait. You are fragile. Within a short time you will begin to suffer the effects of dehydration. Soon you will become delirious and then you will accede to our requirements. We have no further need to discuss this with you. Negotiation is beneath us.'

His words were implacable, but Sara was able to see something that he couldn't. In the Mawdrik ranks behind him there was a quickly suppressed ripple of movement. Some of the lumen turned to each other as though sharing a silent communication, before order was restored to their shining legion.

'I've heard about your methods,' she said. 'You can't scare me with your threats. That is all you have, isn't it? Bullying and threats.' Sara began to pace around the perimeter of the globe so she could take in all of the Mawdrik. 'You haven't seen what I've seen. They were reaching out to me. They were begging me to help them. Don't you even care about your own kind?'

The lumen flinched.

'How dare you? You will not speak of this again.'

'I can see I've touched a raw nerve. What is it - guilt, shame, fear? I'm so glad. Well, I want you to know that I may not be showing it but I'm laughing at you, the way you laughed when you killed François. How does it feel when *you* are on the receiving end? You're pathetic.'

'Give us the name!' He was incandescent with fury.

'Oh, you want a name, do you? I can give you plenty of names but I don't think you'd like them very much.'

'*Give me the name!*'

'Give *you* the name? Whatever happened to *us*? Are you falling out with yourself?' She raised her voice. 'Listen to him carefully, all of you. Are you really sure he's fit to lead you?'

Once more, a quiver of movement passed among her besiegers.

'You will die here, Sara Parkinson.'

'If that's what has to happen, then bring it on, but I will never give you what you want.'

They faced each other silently through the impenetrable double wall of the sphere. Just then, the encircling Mawdrik drew back as one, and her interlocutor glanced up then threw his head back in shocked surprise. Two luminous forms were coalescing at a point above and beyond the gleaming white congregation.

'Good afternoon, Sara. We are pleased to see that you are in good health.'

Amini? Rishtini? The Volk floated side by side, undulating their opalescent mantles as they slowly revolved and descended over the upturned heads of the Mawdrik, throwing multi-coloured reflections across their white bodies.

The lumen had recovered from his initial shock and now he rose until he was on a level with them.

'You should not be here. You cannot come between us and our business.'

'When last we checked,' said Amini amicably, ' unimpeded travel throughout this galaxy was the right of all its inhabitants. You appear to be troubled, Kala. Can we be of help?'

'You - *dare* - our *name*?' He was named Kala, then, this first son of Orla who claimed the leadership of the Mawdrik.

'You have no power here. You cannot interfere with our will.'

'That is true,' said Amini. 'It is neither our right nor our intent to intrude on your purposes.'

Why are you here then? Sara wanted to scream at them. *Why don't you just leave them to watch me die?* But she said nothing because, all around the globe, blocking out the stars with their ardent fire, the Ships of the Volk were materializing by the score, their golden limbs tip to tip as they united to spangle the heavens with an awesome geometrical web.

'Do not seek to intimidate us with your machines,' said Kala threateningly.

'Ah, that is where you are mistaken,' said Amini. 'The Reem are not machines, you see. They are sentient beings, independently and, at times, impetuously minded. They are our friends and companions, not our servants. Did you not know this already? I must confess that I am surprised. After all, the Mawdrik know everything.'

One of the Ships detached itself from the formation and advanced on the globe, flexing its three limbs forwards so that it resembled the enormous clawed foot of a bird of prey. Another dozen followed it down and spread out to create a ring of golden fire that completely encircled the globe and with it, the Mawdrik army.

'If you allow Sara Parkinson to escape,' said Kala, 'we will hunt her down wherever she goes. We will never tire, we will never stop.'

'You will act according to your prerogative, of course,' said Amini. The nearest Ship was still stretching out its massive limbs. It was so vast that it could have entirely engulfed the globe. 'Others must act according to theirs.'

Suddenly, an orifice gaped wide on the underside of the Ship. Golden light flooded out and Kala was transfixed in the centre of it. At the same time, one of its limbs swept in and coiled tightly around the leader of the

Mawdrik. He struggled briefly then lay still in the gleaming coils, utterly helpless in their slowly constricting grasp. At the same time, the other Ships had extended multiple tendrils and were snatching dozens of the Mawdrik from their circle, while the others sped off in confusion and winked out of sight.

'We are the Volk,' said Amini. 'We do not violate our principles of non-intervention and benevolent cohabitation. However, the Reem have informed us that wherever you go, so will they. This is their decision, not ours.'

As one, the Ships released their captives, who vanished after their kindred into whatever unknown sanctuary they had fled to. Kala stayed long enough to cast a look of black and poisonous hatred at Sara.

'This is not the end,' he spat, mustering all of his venom to hurl this warning at her, and then he raised his arms and lifted away in a sweeping curve, gaining speed until, just before he disappeared, he etched a brief trail of flame across the stars like a falling meteorite.

'Are you unharmed, Sara?' As Amini and Rishtini drifted effortlessly through both walls of the globe to join her, the Ships remained where they were, shedding their light on the three of them so that they were immersed in a golden pool.

'I thought you were going to leave me to the Mawdrik.' The adrenaline had left her, and she felt as if she might collapse.

'We are bound by our nature,' said Amini. It extended one of its sub-dorsal vibrissae to Sara and touched her lightly on the shoulder. Instantly, she felt better.

'It is critical to who and what we are. Forceful action is completely unthinkable and abhorrent among the Volk.'

It paused. 'However, I believe that your race has a saying that is frequently applied to certain business negotiations and financial transactions: "Always read the small print first". Is that so?'

'Well, yes, but how…? Did you influence the Ships' decision?'

'We would never attempt to do so, and we express our opinions to them with great care. However, silence is sometimes the most eloquent form of communication.'

She thought about what the Volk had said. 'Okay. I think I understand, now.'

'I have to know,' she went on. 'Were you there, watching us? Karmel and me?'

'Whenever we were able to, until you passed beyond our knowledge and skill to follow you.'

'Do you know about Karmel? I've lost him. He had to stay.'

'The Volk grieve for him as never before. He will be remembered among us and he will be revered throughout the galaxy. We know that is of little comfort to you here and now, but we believe that he will live on in ways we have yet to understand.'

'There's something he said to me, before the end. He said he'd always known what was going to happen to him. Do you think that's true?'

'He always knew that he was destined to travel along a different path, but I do not know if he knew what that would ultimately demand from him. What do you think, Sara?'

'I think… yes, he knew. Now that I can look back on everything, there were so many signs. The strange thing … or maybe the wonderful thing … is that he found peace. Purpose. But I'm going to miss him. I'll miss him terribly.' She wiped the tears away with her sleeve. 'I think I knew too. It was always going to be me, wasn't it?'

Amini's kaleidoscopic colours were deepening.

'Your mother knew, and her mother before her. They were waiting for you to come of age but when the time came your mother was unable to protect and prepare you for the task that only you could perform.'

'My mother *knew*?' Sara was astonished. 'But she left me when I was a child.'

'It was necessary. The Mawdrik were tracking her. She believed that she could draw them away from you and in that, she was right.'

'Do you know what happened to her? If there's anything at all, please tell me.'

'She travelled to Hyaquat but from there we do not know what happened to her.'

Her mother had visited Hyaquat. *She knew!* So all her stories about desert spirits and strange worlds had been far more than bedtime tales. She had been trying to prepare Sara for her destiny all along.

'Let me tell you something about the universe,' Amini continued. 'Imagine it as an oscillating disk that revolves on an unmoving axis. It is both continuity and change. All of its functions - time, space, matter and energy - these exist in a continual state of flux, and when the oscillation is at its most pronounced, this is always counterbalanced by what your physicists would call an equal and opposite reaction. This has happened countless times before and whenever it does, order is restored and the universe continues within and outside of time as a self-perpetuating continuum.'

'Until this time,' said Sara. 'This time something went wrong, didn't it?'

'Something, as you say, went wrong,' Amini confirmed. 'The Seven have always functioned as a unity. Even though the balance has been restored, we believe that recent events herald a permanent change, the consequences of which we cannot begin to predict. Critical to this change has been your role.'

'I don't like the sound of that,' she said. 'Are you trying to tell me that it isn't over yet?'

'For the moment, yes. Now is a time for healing and restoration. The Mawdrik have been thwarted and we sense a divergence in their purpose. But you, Sara, you have been altered far more than any of us can begin to understand.'

'I know the name. The name of Seven. They gave it to me.'

The change that came over the Volk was short lived but frightening. Both of them simultaneously turned black.

'Do not speak the name. Do not speak it to us or to anybody. They gave it to you alone, for whatever purpose. Perhaps it is your calling to use this knowledge when the time is right, but here and now this is a secret that must not be revealed.'

'So what do I do now?'

Both Volk had resumed their kaleidoscopic appearance. 'Have you given any thought about where you are going?'

'Yes, but I don't know if it's even possible. If not I could go back to Earth, I suppose.' But there were too many painful memories back on Earth. François in the pouring rain of Granada, the life light fading from his beautiful eyes…

'Earth is becoming a very different place, Sara. Humanity now realizes that it is not alone, both in the world and in the universe, and that it can no longer depend on its old beliefs and institutions for security. The adjustment will be traumatic and your species will not easily accede to these truths. Furthermore, the Mawdrik have not yet relinquished their hold there and that which they unleashed may have retreated, but it will fester and grow again. We strongly advise against you returning.'

'I wish I knew how everybody was.'

'Thanks to the ingenuity of one Eileen Howkins who has kept us very well informed, we can tell you that the battle for Granada was won. The Mawdrik were forced to retreat there and Angustias and your friends are safe, although they have left the city for now and have gone to a remote place where they can rest and plan for the future. They have work to do.'

'I guess that Hyaquat isn't an option, either.'

'We have news about Hyaquat too. Although the devastation was considerable, the city of Yazoon survived. The colonies will rebuild, given time. We will help them.'

'No,' she said firmly, more to herself than to the Volk. 'I couldn't go back.' There was one nagging suspicion that would always trouble her about Hyaquat - that in the end, the seemingly random progress of the nameless Seventh had bent all its destructive force on her. And now, she knew its name.

Rishtini spoke for the first time. It flushed pink, and Sara had the strangest impression that it was laughing.

'Isn't there a third option?'

'Yes, but like I said I don't even know if I can.'

'You may be surprised to learn what you are capable of', said Amini.

'Well, okay then. Nothing ventured, nothing gained.' She opened her backpack and located the flower from Endymion. It was wrapped in crumpled tissue and when she uncovered it, she found that it was completely flattened and bent in on itself. But as she held it in her palm it spread wide and vibrated its translucent petals, as unblemished as when she'd been given it on that magical evening in another world.

'Do you really think I can do it?'

'You were able to travel here by yourself,' said Amini. 'I truly believe that you will always carry the legacy of Karmel with you.'

'At least I can try.' She cradled the flower in both hands. 'Will I ever see you again?'

'I'm sure you will, but do not think about that now. This is *your* time, Sara. Think of it as a time to heal and to live your life for yourself. Think about now and take joy in every moment.'

And, for the last time, Sara brought into her mind the image of the left hand spiral and focused all her hopes and desires on Endymion. She began walking, then passed right through the walls of the globe and on along the familiar inward path, until, when she looked back, the orb was just a white fleck of sparkling light dancing among the clouds in a brilliant blue sky.

She was waist deep in the silver-gold grass of a sun-drenched meadow. It was alive with orange and purple flowers dancing in the warm breeze, and fragrant with a medley of spicy aromas. The grasses were shedding their seeds and the air was filled with twirling motes like opalescent feathers. Brightly coloured creatures with gossamer wings flitted and chirruped everywhere and on the other side of the bridge across the shimmering river, she could see movement in the meadow that sloped up from the opposite bank. There were marquees and stalls and crowds of people, and Sara could hear lively music and laughter.

Then she heard the sound of a door closing and she turned eagerly towards the farmhouse on the hill, her heart leaping in anticipation. Somebody was walking down through the brimming garden to the gate that opened through the hedge at the bottom and gave on to the meadow. A tall man with dark hair, a man who she could hardly believe was real and *here*.

Sara called. He stopped and stared, and even from this distance she could make out his incredulous expression.

'Dream girl!'

They started running in the same moment and met in the long grass. He picked her up and spun her round and when he put her down again he crushed his mouth against hers.

'I knew you'd come back!' he said when they finally moved apart. 'Everyone said I was completely mad... you *are* real, aren´t you?'

She pulled his face down and kissed him again. 'That´s your proof of how real I am.'

'But what happened, that night? Where did you go?'

'I don´t think you'd ever believe me in a thousand years,' she said, laughing.

'Why don't you try me?' For a moment, he looked dubious. 'That is, if you're staying this time?'

'I am not going anywhere!' And she meant it with all her heart.

'What's your name?' he asked.

'Sara.'

'I´m Jedri. I was on my way to the Spring Fair. Will you come with me? So I can show them all that you really exist?'

'Of course I will. Come on!'

Then Sara took Jedri´s hand, and together they ran through the swaying grass of the meadow, across the bridge and into a bright afternoon that was filled with hope and newfound happiness.

6. Beyond

Hello? Are you still there? Oh, there you are. I thought you'd left me. It's so dark and still in here, I can't tell and sometimes you seem to fade away. I can't even feel my body any more… It's very odd, though. It doesn't hurt at all, but it's not right*. Do you understand?*

-

What did you say? Yes, yes, you told me before. I know who you are. No, I'm not afraid of you. Why should I be?

-

But you did what you could, or what you had to. We both did. Yes, I know what you said - that they deceived her, the Seven. Or rather, they did not tell her the whole truth. And now she has no idea of the danger she's in, her and the little one.

-

Maybe you're right, but I think that one day the Seventh will want its name back and when that happens, it's going to go looking for it. And Kala too - or should I say, both Kalas? That is what you said, isn't it - that there are two of him?

-

I wish we could do something, but we're both trapped here forever as I see it, and in any case you're dying, aren't you?

-

She left something behind? So there might just be a chance, then, if we can only find out how. And I have the banderil.

-

I didn't? Oh, I'm so sorry. I am forgetting my manners. My name?

My name is Karmel.